ALSO BY L.J. SHEN

BAD BISHOP

L.J. SHEN

Bloom *books*

Published by Bloom Books, an imprint of Sourcebooks
1935 Brookdale RD, Naperville, IL 60563-2773
(630) 961-3900
sourcebooks.com

Cataloging-in-Publication data is on file with the Library of Congress.

Printed and bound in the United States of America.
KP 10 9 8 7 6 5 4 3 2

AUTHOR'S NOTE

This work of fiction includes portions of American Sign Language. Though I tried to remain as true to the language as possible, I took some artistic liberties.

This book is filled with gory descriptions and violent deaths. It is unapologetically dark. If you find morally gray characters hard to stomach, please know that no number of Tums will be able to help you digest this book.

For a full list of the content warnings, visit here: shor.by/kMi5

SOCIETY OF VILLAINS TREE

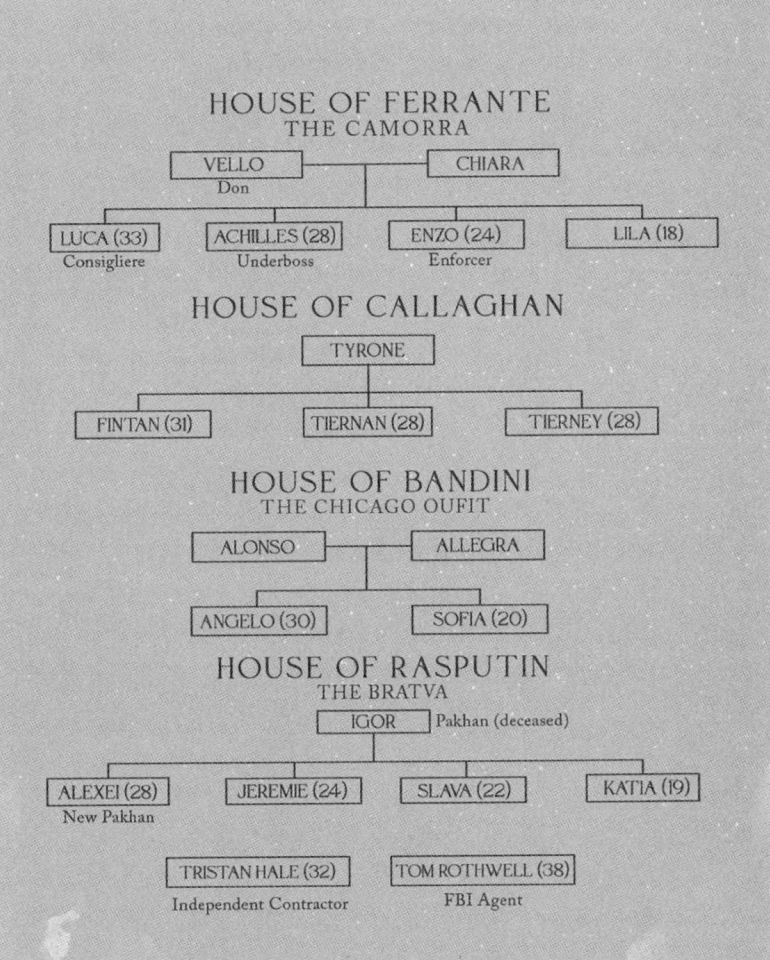

HOUSE OF FERRANTE
THE CAMORRA

VELLO — *Don* — CHIARA

LUCA (33) — *Consigliere*
ACHILLES (28) — *Underboss*
ENZO (24) — *Enforcer*
LILA (18)

HOUSE OF CALLAGHAN

TYRONE

FINTAN (31)
TIERNAN (28)
TIERNEY (28)

HOUSE OF BANDINI
THE CHICAGO OUFIT

ALONSO — ALLEGRA

ANGELO (30)
SOFIA (20)

HOUSE OF RASPUTIN
THE BRATVA

IGOR — Pakhan (deceased)

ALEXEI (28) — New Pakhan
JEREMIE (24)
SLAVA (22)
KATIA (19)

TRISTAN HALE (32) — Independent Contractor
TOM ROTHWELL (38) — FBI Agent

To all the readers who complain that my heroes are always irredeemable jerks...

I'm afraid I have terrible news.

Here I opened wide the door;—
Darkness there, and nothing more.

—Edgar Allan Poe

May the flowers remind us why
the rain was so necessary.

—Xan Oku

term: BAD BISHOP

In chess, a bad bishop is a bishop
that is blocked by its own pawns,
making its scope and the number of
squares it can control very limited.

A bad bishop is considered irredeemable.

PLAYLIST

(Best enjoyed when listening in this order)

"NAnthem Vol 1"—A.M., Shaone & Pepp J One

"SuperVillain Origin Story"—whatyoudid.

"Aria"—Lucariello feat. Raiz

"In A Grave"—notefly, HVLO & IOVA

"Don't Talk"—Cheska Moore

"Won't Run Away"—Kaphy & DEIIN

"Animal Instinct"—The Cranberries

"Clubbed to Death"—Skeler & Devilish Trio

"Sugar"—Apollo On The Run & Georgina Black

"Pink Venom"—BLACKPINK

"Seven Nation Army"—The White Stripes

"Shout"—Tears for Fears

"No.1 Party Anthem"—Arctic Monkeys

"As the World Caves In"—Matt Maltese

"Forever Young"—Alphaville

"9 Crimes"—Damien Rice

"Only When I Sleep"—The Corrs

AFTERWORD

Don Machiavelli "Vello" Ferrante was dying.

It was the worst-kept secret in the Mafia.

His diagnosis was a mystery, his decline rapid; death scratched its pointy claws on his door.

Penetrated the paper-thin, yellowing leather of his skin.

Drip-drip-dripped from his dim, dry eyes.

It was pathetic—*unacceptable*, even—that he reeked of it.

The stench of dysfunctional liver and kidneys exuding from his shriveling body.

The putrid breath.

The unraveling of his mortal existence.

Vello hated games, with the exception of chess.

He was a master chess player.

Chess was good. Smart. Strategic.

Chess was *war*.

You conquered and divided. Captured and ruined.

Most importantly, chess was fair.

All of it wouldn't have mattered, if Don Vello wasn't important.

As it happened, he was the big boss. The ruler of New York.

Being the head of the Ferrante Camorra clan meant he was free to choose whoever he saw the most fit to be his successor.

There was Luca, his oldest son and natural heir. Part aristocrat, part horseman. Calculated and quiet. Smooth and cold as marble.

Achilles, his middle son. Feared by all and loved by none. A Greek warrior. A monster that contorted itself into the form of a human, always one moment away from bursting at the seams.

And Enzo, his youngest son. With the warm, whiskey eyes and pliant nature. Far too handsome than any man had the right to be. The charmer. The *persuader*.

Now there was his son-in-law, too, thanks to Lila's marriage. Though he seemed too unhinged to reign over anything that wasn't hell.

And then there was his favorite. His secret son. His golden boy. *Essere il Beniamino.*

Not a high-born Ferrante, but capable nonetheless.

He'd come into play. But not now. Not *yet*.

He had a rook and a knight, a bishop and a king. A few pawns, and a queen.

Vello stared at the Battle of Waterloo chess set in his office, stroking his chin with the little energy he had left.

He could live like this for months. Maybe even years. But he knew when he wanted to die, and how. All he needed was to appoint his successor.

One of them was going to take his place. To lay claim to his blood-soaked territory.

From the entire East Coast to Naples, Italy.

Become the don of the Camorra. The indisputable ruler of the underworld.

But *who*?

Luca
Achilles
Enzo
~~Tiernan~~
Essere il beniamino

CHAPTER ONE
TIERNAN

362 DAYS TO SELF-DESTRUCTION

Pain.

It was one of my favorite delicacies.

I savored the hot lick of a sharp knife, the icy kiss of metal shackles, the explosive heat of bones crushing beneath knuckles. Really, there was nothing better than getting a little fucked up to remind me I was alive.

Apparently though, even I had my limits.

I found them in the basement of the Ferrante crime family. Zip-tied onto a wooden chair that reeked of shit, piss, and dried blood. My face was swollen from being beaten to a pulp for the last forty minutes.

The first twenty were enjoyable enough. Fuck, I even got a little stiffy when Achilles took out the brass knuckles. Now, however, I'd overindulged. This was overkill, even for a pain connoisseur like me.

The actual violence wasn't the problem; death was always an option in my line of work.

I just hadn't realized the cause of mine would be boredom.

I was half tempted to finish their job and slit my own throat.

It was better than listening to them droning on about my little... what shall I call it? *Art project.*

"My, my." Achilles drove his fist into my face, sending me careening across the floor. An inferno of blood exploded from my nostrils. "I see why the Rasputins call you Deathless. You refuse to fucking die."

A metallic grunt skulked up my hollowed chest. I shifted my body so as not to crush my wrists under my weight, darting my tongue to catch the river of blood snaking along my cheek. "Maybe you're just bad at killing people."

A forceful blow found my ribs. This time it was Enzo Ferrante, the baby brother. Felt like he ruptured my liver. As if the poor organ didn't have its hands full as it was. "Zip it before I skin you scrotum to face, Callaghan," he warned, his voice cheery and cordial.

When were we getting to the good part? Time was money, and unlike the Ferrantes, I had to earn my keep every night.

Enzo spat on an open wound in my face, his saliva irritating my raw flesh.

In return, I spat a ball of phlegm and blood on his shoe.

"Christ, these Louboutins are hand sprayed by Banksy," he muttered. "Have you no shame? And to think I send you Christmas cards every year."

He did. Though I never opened the fucking letters.

The Ferrantes ruled 90 percent of New York. Personally, I wouldn't put them in charge of an automatic door. I reigned over the remaining 10 percent, and with a deadlier fist. I was the future. They were the past. And they knew it.

Some people collected stamps. Others coins. I collected my enemies' craniums. It was an economical hobby, if not a little messy. It also sent an accurate message—I wasn't someone you wanted to fuck with, over, or in general.

Consequently, there was a human skull discarded between us. My little weekend splurge. The skull belonged to Igor Rasputin, the head of the Bratva. Well, *ex*-head now, evidently. This was what got the Ferrantes' panties in a wad.

"Mind Igor's cranium," I said dryly. "I plan to use it as a penholder."

"Gonna be hard to pen letters without hands, Alexander Hamilton," Luca tutted.

A flicker of irritation passed over my face. A rare flash of humanity. Luca noticed. He pressed on. "What'd you think was gonna happen when we called you here? You killed the West Coast's pakhan in our territory."

"And you're welcome."

"Excuse me?"

"If you took better care of said territory, he wouldn't be coming here, fucking your whores, sampling your drugs, poaching your soldiers."

Achilles moseyed over to me. His fingers fastened around my neck, his thumbs hiking my Adam's apple up my throat. Choking me to death on my own cartilage? Creative. I despised all things mundane, and that included artless murder. Achilles Ferrante was a cold-blooded monster. But hey, at least he wasn't mediocre.

His brothers pulled him back before he cut off my air supply, slamming him against the wall. The three broke into an argument in Neapolitan, their lips moving a mile a minute.

Waiting for them to stop bickering, I examined my surroundings in boredom.

As far as torture chambers went, this one was adequate. Stone walls bracketed the room. It was dark, cold, and packed with medieval torturing devices. The iron maiden, the rack, the pear of anguish. There was also a generic knife rack, a chainsaw, and a wall of artillery. It was Disney World for psychopaths. And I wasn't allowed to test any of the rides.

The door at the top of the steep stairway was padded with noise-canceling foam. No one was coming to save me.

Not that there was anything to save.

No soul.

No heart.

No conscience.

I was an animated corpse. Bones, muscles, flesh, and menace. Vengeance was my fuel, and it was enough to keep me moving, just about.

At last, Luca broke out of their human circle. He grabbed me by the collar and pulled me back into a sitting position. He popped a cigarette into my mouth, flicking his Zippo to torch the tip.

So we got into the good cop/bad cop portion of the night. Yay fucking me.

"You killed the head of Bratva," he surmised, voice shredded by cigarettes. "We have good business with them. Drugs, weapons, recycling routes. You're costing me money, Callaghan. And I *like* money. You know what I don't like?"

"A clean pair of fucking lungs?" My gaze halted on the cigarette in his hand.

"People who stand in the way to my money. I always find creative ways to get rid of them."

"Send me the bill," I drawled.

"It's not just monetary." Luca kicked the pakhan's skull sideways. "New York belongs to us. When you go around killing people in our zip code, it makes us look like we don't have a grip on our own ground."

"Where's the lie?" My voice was distant and disinterested. "What the fuck was a Bratva boss doing deep in Camorra territory?"

"Family function," Enzo ground out. "His nephew's graduation. Igor asked for permission, which I personally granted. You made me look like an idiot."

He didn't need me to look like an idiot. He was doing a fine job by himself.

"I found him exiting your club," I reminded him.

"It was a very emotional ceremony, okay?" Enzo said earnestly. "He took the nephew to have his first drink there. Adorable, if you ask me."

"My beef with the Rasputins extends beyond geography and politics. I won't stop until I kill the entire family." I spoke around the cigarette. I didn't smoke. Not very often, anyway. Here and there, and mostly weed. I was far too committed to my other vices—violence and greed—to pick up a third one. "And if they dare set foot in this city, I sure as fuck am going to take advantage."

"Let's hope your beef with them extends into the afterlife, too." Achilles slapped my back, nearly making me cough out a lung. "Because next time you take liberties in Camorra territory, I'll smoke your ass like a pork's butt."

"Considering they've been eyeing New York for years now, you'd be a fool to intervene." Talking sense into the Ferrantes was the equivalent of fucking a roadkill into resurrection, but just like a wayward squirrel, something compelled me to try.

"New York's ours," Luca snarled.

"Is it?" I marveled. "I own the Bronx, and the Russians have been buying Manhattan land for years now. What you have with them isn't business, it's a hostile takeover." I spat out the cigarette. "You've been losing prestige for a solid decade. Once you lose the Upper East Side, the empire falls. It's already decomposing. Why do you think your father hasn't picked any of your sorry asses to replace him yet? You reek of weakness." I managed to keep my irritation out of my tone. *Just.* "Give me a blank check to finish the Russians off."

"You want us to think you have our best interests in mind?" Luca took a drag of his cigarette, wafting the smoke sideways. "After all this time?"

I'd known these fuckers since I was fourteen. They aged like a fine corpse.

"I'm killing them because of my own personal vendetta." I cracked my neck. "Our interests happen to align, that's all."

"What business do you have with them?" Luca propped his winged boot on Igor's skull.

A locked jaw and a jaded stare were my official response.

"You'll have to kill a shit ton of soldiers before you get to Alex Rasputin." Enzo tapped his lips.

Igor's son. Bratva's second-highest rank. The next pakhan.

"Don't threaten me with a good time."

"That's a big-ass operation you got there." Achilles scrubbed his knuckles over his cheekbone. "Even if we let you go on your deranged quest, you don't have the manpower."

"I could use a helping hand." I arched a meaningful eyebrow.

"No way are we getting ourselves into a full-blown Mafia war." Luca shook his head. "Not my circus, not my monkeys."

"Fine. Stay out of my way, then."

Achilles mulled my words over, the menacing glint in his eyes sharpening. "My problem with your proposition is twofold."

I stared at him impassively, knowing another fucking TED Talk was about to ensue. Goddamn Italians and their love for words.

Achilles didn't disappoint.

"One, we're the ones who'll get the brunt of it when Alex gets fished out of the Hudson River," he said.

That was an easy fix. I could kill him anywhere on the map. "And the second?"

Achilles pushed off the wall, stalking over to me and crouching down so our faces were an inch apart. He was one gruesome motherfucker, with a face even a blind mother couldn't love. Rumor had it every inch of his flesh was scarred, burned, or both; every part of his body from the chin below was covered in elaborate ink.

"I still haven't punished you for killing Filippo," he rasped.

Not this shit again.

Ten months ago, I offed one of the Ferrante soldiers when I kidnapped a woman he was watching over. Pure collateral damage. Nothing personal.

"I already told you. I thought he was cannon fodder, not the family pet."

"Would that have changed things?"

Not really. But people—even sociopaths—liked to play the what-if game. To ponder the alternatives for the path their lives had taken.

"I'd have aimed for the heart, so his face wouldn't look like Irish stew."

The Camorra loved open-casket funerals. Seemed a bit ambitious considering their occupation if you asked me, but no one fucking did.

"Che palle." Achilles slapped me with the side of his gun, sending my face flying sideways. My boredom morphed into impatience. I really needed to go check on my businesses.

"You've been a thorn in our side for far too long, Callaghan." Luca produced his own gun from his holster. Cocked it.

Who was he kidding? If he wanted me dead, I wouldn't be here, listening to their lecture. Death was a luxury they didn't offer me. Instead, I had to watch their meltdowns on loop.

"Nah, man. I say if the Irish and Russians want to off one another, we should let them," Enzo suggested gleefully. *"Muoia Sansone con tutti i Filistei."*

"Enough with the chitchat," I growled. "Just do what you have to."

"Enzo. Knife," Achilles ordered. Enzo glided toward us, disposing of his knife in Achilles's open palm. The latter grabbed a fistful of my hair, tilting my face upward. Our eyes met.

"You know." Achilles pressed the blade to the center of my neck. The tip traveled upward, toward my chin. "The bullet you put in Filippo's head came out of his eye socket. We never found his eyeball."

Eyeball it was, then.

Not a terrible loss. I'd seen enough of this world and hated it and everyone in it.

"Filippo was close to me as well." Luca jammed his fists into his pockets. The blade of Achilles's knife trekked north, sailing across my cheek and toward my left eye. "But you'll be no use to me completely blind. I'll take my favor some other time."

"Your sainthood's in the mail," I drawled, never breaking Achilles's stare.

"Right or left?" Achilles asked.

"Your pick." I hitched a shoulder up. "But do it in the next five minutes. I have underground casinos to run."

"Your next stop is the ER, shitbag."

If I had a sense of humor, I'd laugh. Getting my eye plucked out without anesthesia wouldn't even rank as the fiftieth worst thing that happened to me in my twenty-eight years on this planet.

"Losing an eye will have its perks."

"Is that so?" Achilles took the bait.

"For one thing, I'll no longer have a 20/20 vision of your Freddy Krueger face."

Achilles's nostrils flared, rage rolling off him like lava. "*Occhio per occhio, dente per dente.* Open wide, motherfucker."

I didn't flinch. Not when the edge of the knife poked the side of my eye, forcing its way into the socket. Not when it pried my eyeball from the depth of my skull. And not when I felt it sliding out of the hollow space. I remained still, muscles lax, posture languid, shoulders rolled back. The picture of calm and tranquil.

That was the thing about me.

I never flinched.

I. Never. Fucking. Flinch.

They called me Deathless for a reason. I enjoyed defying my own demise.

My eyeball was now sliding completely out of my body.

The room was lethally quiet, save for my labored breaths. Achilles held my eyeball between his fingers and cut the six muscles that connected it to my brain, then the sheath of optic nerve attaching it to my brain. He stepped back.

Hot, thick liquid decanted down my eye socket to my cheek. I licked it with an easy smile. Tremors ghosted my spine and arms, my body's reaction to the shocking invasion, but I welcomed the discomfort, making it a part of me.

I was very good at enduring pain. Very good at distributing it, too. I was going to get Achilles in the next round. Touch something of his and destroy it so thoroughly he wouldn't be able to recognize it for what it once was.

I had the patience, will, and time. The only thing I lacked was morals.

"*Damn.*" Enzo gave a low whistle. "Glass half full, Callaghan— you're never gonna have a problem dressing up for Halloween."

"He was too pretty for his own good, anyway," Luca spat on the floor. "We did him a favor."

"I believe this is yours." Achilles tossed my eyeball into my lap, turning around and disposing of the knife in Enzo's hand. I could only see shadows through my right eye, probably due to the excessive adrenaline. Nothing a couple pints and a good blowie couldn't fix.

"We done here?" My tone was cool, neutral.

"Make sure you get rid of the Rasputins' bodies out of the city limits. No paper trail, Callaghan, and *no* fucking feds." Achilles picked up his whiskey tumbler from a table midstride, his back to me. "Enzo, cauterize his veins so he doesn't bleed all over Mama's new carpets."

Enzo patched up my eye and cut the zip ties on my wrists from behind.

"Hey, nothing personal, right, Callaghan?" He clapped my shoulder, winking. "We're still on for that poker night next week?"

"Sure." I curled my index and middle fingers into Igor's eye sockets, as though his skull was a bowling ball, tucking it under my armpit. A spider crawled up from one of the sockets, hurrying up my arm, searching for an escape. "Nothing personal."

Eyeball in pocket, I leisurely stopped to admire their different torture devices on my way out.

CHAPTER TWO
LILA

The ground shook beneath my bare feet.

A flash of a shadowed figure zipped past me from the corner of my eye.

I snapped my gaze up from the sketchbook in my lap, on high alert. I was sitting on the stone fountain in the courtyard, pouring the shape of the Amalfi Coast from memory onto the page.

I wore my pink satin nightgown and my hair was in a loose, long braid. It was pitch black, save for the amber light spilling from the windows.

My vision had always been good. Compensation for what wasn't, Mama told me.

I spotted a figure prowling from our entrance door toward a gunmetal Mercedes-Benz G 63 that blocked one of our three garages. An uncommonly tall male, pale as a vampire and equally as frightening, stalked outside. He wore a dark coat and moved like a serpent, gliding through the night with the unnerving slickness of someone who belonged to it.

Look away now, quick, before he sees you, Mama's voice reproached in my head. *You're not to make eye contact with people, Lila!*

But what was the harm?

It was too dark for him to notice me.

I'd always watched people secretly. It was the morsel of normalcy

I was still allowed. My loneliness was so intimate, so familiar to me, it became a friend in itself. It was my only companion other than Mama and Imma.

I kept staring, hoping it was Tate Blackthorn. The man who gave me the most wonderful present I'd ever been gifted—a dance. A moment of feeling like a woman.

Not a child, not a disabled person, a *woman*.

It happened a year ago at my brother Luca's engagement party, and I'd been playing it in my head every night since. My most monumental moment in my eighteen years on this planet was with a complete stranger who used me as a tool to make his wife jealous.

And the sad part was…I'd let him do it all over again. This was how badly I craved human connection.

My eyes drank in his silhouette—obstinate jaw, chiseled cheekbones, features as smooth and icy as winter frost.

Could he be Tate? Could he give me another dance? Could I be so foolish as to ask for one?

He weaved through the shadows dancing across the pebbled front yard. Stopped. Tipped his head up to the moon. The moon stared back, like they were sharing a secret.

The light from one of the windows caught his hair, tangling into the strands. It burned burgundy. Rusty, like medieval copper. Not the gleaming stygian of Tate Blackthorn.

My solar plexus tightened.

It wasn't him.

This man looked like he was sprung from fire. His hair tousled like dancing flames. And still… He appeared unbearably cold. I had the feeling I'd get frostbite if I touched him.

The pencil slipped between my fingers.

Hit the cobbled ground with a *clink* I couldn't hear.

The man stopped abruptly. Froze.

Shit, shit, shit.

He heard.

I wasn't supposed to be outside. Alone in the dark.

My legs clayed into stone. I couldn't run even if I wanted to.

His head twisted in my direction. Slowly. Leisurely. Almost tauntingly.

Our gazes clashed in the moon-frosted courtyard. Two animals—a predator and prey—standing on opposite sides of a riverbank.

His shadowed face twisted. He was contemplating something.

Assessing. Scheming.

A rakish half smile pulled at the corner of his lips.

A decision had been made. My belly coiled into knots.

He advanced toward me. I scooted back, my butt dragging along the fountain's edge until I felt the water skimming the back of my thighs. It was ice cold. Running would be futile. He'd chase me, then catch me, then punish me.

I knew that, even though I didn't know *him*.

As he got closer, I saw he was missing an eye. The entire left side of his face was scarlet red. His nose was broken. A human skull was pinned under his arm.

And yet…he was beautiful. Beneath the blood, drainage, and fluid coming from his eyeball, and bruises, and gore.

Beautiful like violent art.

His entire demeanor was abrasive, even without all the blood. Like his existence was an attack on mine. And yet, I couldn't look away.

My heart felt like something foreign I accidentally swallowed. I wanted to vomit it out of my body. I'd never been so scared in my life.

His mouth moved, and my eyes clung to it.

"Well, well, well. What have we here?" He examined me through his one good eye, lethally amused. "If it isn't the Ferrantes' innocent little princess."

Even though I read his lips and couldn't hear him, his voice somehow still rolled against my skin, gripping the back of my neck, forcing me to look up and meet his gaze.

He raised his free arm, tracing his knuckles along my cheek. My eyes flared, and a scream stranded in my throat. His still-warm blood painted my cheek.

"What should I do with you? Fuck you, kidnap you, or simply kill you?" he mused aloud.

I had every reason to believe he'd do all three.

My brothers weren't nice people, and his meeting with them obviously didn't go as planned, judging by his face. This was retaliation. I was his payback.

His hand ascended my cheek, fingertips gliding across the shell of my ear. He paused. I thought he'd rip it clean off my head. Instead, he seized the ribbon keeping my fair hair in the braid, pulling it slowly, rubbing it between his fingers with rapt fascination. My hair tumbled down my back.

He licked the corner of his lips, his stare invasive, detonating all of my walls at once.

I forced myself to meet his stare. My whole body trembled with fear, but I didn't scream, didn't try to run away, didn't do anything stupid.

I lived with psychopaths. I knew the surest way to become prey was to act like it.

"You're the simple one." He assessed me through his hooded, cold eye.

I didn't answer, but his words stung.

That's what people said behind my back.

To my face, too.

That I was simple. Dumb. Disposable. A punishment the Ferrantes were saddled with for their grave sins. Hell, even my father called me his pretty little burden.

Vello Ferrante had made it clear he had no use for a daughter beyond marrying her off to someone whose alliance he sought. And so my entire life had been carefully constructed to ensure he thought me unable to be married.

The only way to escape marriage to a mobster was to be unable to be married. More specifically—to pretend I had a developmental disability.

My mother came up with the scheme when I was a child, and I went along with it, trusting she knew best. While a pretty, ditzy woman was a mobster's wet dream—a person with actual struggles, in need of assistance and care, wasn't something men in this line of work considered.

It had nothing to do with morals and everything to do with them being the scum of the earth.

He let go of my hair, seizing the front of my neck punishingly. His gaze lingered on my face.

Slowly, he lowered my head into the gushing fountain. He was going to drown me. The realization kicked my heart into high gear. I fought the urge to wrap my fingers around his arm, to try to untangle it from my throat. There was no point.

Instead, I closed my eyes as my hair sank into the water first. Ice-cold liquid engulfed my skull.

I love you, Mama.

I love you, Luca, Enzo, and Achilles.

I love you, Imma.

I even love you, Papa, despite everything.

I'll watch over you from heaven.

Suddenly, I was jerked back up. My eyes flew open.

I'd think he had a change of heart, but I knew he possessed no such organ. He pulled a pocketknife from his peacoat, flipping it open and pressing it to the corner of my eye. Yup. Just as I feared. He just figured he could make more mess chopping me.

I held my spine straight and my chin high, forcing myself not to swallow hard.

If I must die, I'd die like a Ferrante.

We weren't good people, but we were warriors.

And warriors didn't cower.

I stared at him with fierce defiance. The darkness around us held its breath.

The knife kissed my skin, poking, tightening, reminding me what was at stake. It was dull. I knew he'd choose a dull knife. Sadists often did.

The knife began traveling along the edge of my left eye. I choked on a pool of saliva in my throat. Still, I pressed my lips shut.

He tilted my chin with the edge of his knife, forcing me to stare more closely at his grotesque face. "Beauty is such a fragile thing, Raffaella. I can tarnish your face with one stroke of a knife."

The stranger raised his knife-wielding hand, gathering momentum, and swung it toward my face. I squeezed my eyes shut and stopped breathing, my muscles tightening as I waited for the punishing explosion of pain.

A pain that didn't come.

Shakily, I pried my eyelids open, pulse hammering. My body was slick with sweat.

A gleam of mirth flickered along his lifeless eye.

The man tucked his knife back into his coat, businesslike. He was playing with my life, screwing with my head, and swallowing every ounce of my fear, all while looking dry as a bone.

I stared at him, slack-jawed, waiting for his next move.

He grabbed something from his pocket, uncurling my fingers between us, putting it there and making me close my fist over it. It was small and slippery. Round. A shell-less snail?

I uncoiled my fingers, staring down. My heart sledgehammered its way past my rib cage.

An eye.

A human one.

His eye.

I wanted to drop it but I knew better than to defy him.

He leaned forward, until our noses almost touched. He smelled of blood, gunpowder, and dark, haunted woods. It was an oddly pleasant, sinister scent, and it seeped into my system, touching a corner inside me I didn't even know existed.

"Tell your brothers that next time they fuck with me, enter my territory, or otherwise disturb my business, I'm going to hunt you down, fuck every hole in your body, slash that pretty throat, then dump you at their doorstep to bleed out. Understand?"

I was going to do no such thing.

For one thing, my brothers weren't supposed to know I understood their language, let alone spoke. For another, I wasn't his errand bitch.

I stared at him defiantly, saying nothing. I had a feeling he knew I understood him.

"Good." He straightened, releasing my throat from his hold. "Now run, *Gealach*. Because when I catch? I kill."

I sprang to my feet and sprinted back inside barefoot, leaving my canvas and pencils outside, as fast as I could before he changed his mind. Panicked breaths tore at my lungs.

Halfway through the journey to my front door, I realize he ripped the spaghetti straps of my nightgown. My breasts were exposed. Every inch of my upper body was smeared with his blood.

I felt the ghost of his hands slithering up and down my flesh. Warm and callused and alive.

Weeks after, I'd ask myself if he was a figment of my imagination.

A nightmare. An omen.

But no, he had to be real.

I knew.

Because I kept his eye.

CHAPTER THREE
LILA

TWO WEEKS LATER

"*Madonna Santa*, Chiara, your daughter is such a beauty. What a shame she'll never marry!" Tammy, Mama's friend, raked her gaze along my frame, clucking her tongue.

I wore a pink chiffon dress with off the shoulder pleats and a tight corset. My long pale hair tumbled in waves down to my waist, haloed by a tiara of snow-white roses. They were real roses, twisted into one another. The tiny thorns dug into my skull, but Mama always said that beauty was pain.

Mama picked the tiara and outfit.

She dictated my wardrobe. My activities. My future.

I felt a little ridiculous in the white satin gloves and high heels. Like I was playing teatime with my dolls, something I did publicly sometimes to make people believe I was mentally delayed. I *hated* the teatime routine and always thought it was overkill. But as Mama said—in our world, one can never be too pretty or too cautious.

Besides, it wasn't every day my eldest brother was getting married. And to a princess from the Outfit, no less.

Sofia's family was well known in Chicago. So influential were the Bandinis that the wedding attracted none other than the president of the United States, Wolfe Keaton, and First Lady Francesca Rossi-Keaton.

Luca and Sofia stood in the far corner of the room, careful not to touch or look at one another as they politely mingled with their guests. My brother was tempered in movement and thinking. Eerily still and cold as a fish. He looked like he was attending his own funeral, not his wedding.

Sofia seemed to share his desolation. Misery was stamped on her lovely, tan face like the angry welts of a belt.

"Yes, well, in our world, marriage is overrated." Mama huffed. "I'm relieved Raffaella won't be subjected to a marriage with a cruel man who would cheat and disappear on her for days on end. I gave Vello three boys, and he shaped them into merciless killing machines. Lila is my reward for fulfilling my end of the bargain. Mine to keep and protect."

Tammy and the rest of the women in the circle nodded.

"Speaking of awful husbands…" Mina, another friend of Mama's, flashed a sly smile. "I saw Tony's Alyssa in the shops the other day. She had a black eye. Swore up and down it was due to undereye fillers gone wrong. Just three months ago, her arm was in a cast. Does she think we're all stupid? She's barely even twenty-seven. And with three kids already." Mina tsked. "I always told my Pietro to keep away from that man. He's a hot-tempered one, Tony."

"And what about Maggio?" Tammy clucked her tongue. "Cheatin' on his wife left and right. Three bastards out of wedlock, all on child support, and he still sees the mothers regularly. One of them even works for him. The *baldracca*."

"They're all as awful as each other." Mama's mouth twisted in disgust. "Cheating, beating their wives, bringing trouble to our doorsteps. Men are terrible creatures. The world would be a better place if women ruled it."

"What, and miss our weekly gel manicure and hair appointments?" Tammy snorted, sparking a chorus of giggles. "No, thank you. They can do the hard work while we pamper ourselves. We earned it."

"It's not all bad." Mina gestured a manicured hand to the ballroom in our mansion. It was dazzling. With gilded pillars, marble arches, and frescoed ceilings so high you could barely see the medieval paintings on them. The room glowed golden by candlelight and chandeliers, its deceiving warmth masquerading the awful people inside it.

I craned my neck past the sea of puffy hairdos, searching for Tate Blackthorn.

"Are you going to Ischia for the summer?" Rita asked Mama, her lips curving around her words in the corner of my eye. They were all sipping on champagne while I was holding a pink lemonade.

Everything about me was pink. My wardrobe. My room. My ruddy cheeks.

"Of course." My mother's face immediately relaxed at the mention of our summer house. "Lila and I enjoy the sun, the food, the culture. Ischia is our home."

Mama and I spend two months out of the year on the Italian island to get away from the men in our family. I liked going there. I was able to live more freely. I read in public, played sports, and did cartwheels on the beach. I had a Latin tutor and a math teacher. My mother took me to the movies to watch old Italian films, and I never had to play with dolls or school my face to a blank mask of nothing.

At home, I needed to hide these abilities. My intelligence.

"You should come," Mama told the three women, but I knew she didn't mean it. She loathed her friends. Loathed everyone and everything connected to the Camorra.

"What a marvelous idea," Rita cooed. "I'll speak to Antonio, see if we have any plans."

I wondered why they did that. Made plans they weren't going to execute. Feigned excitement about things they didn't care about.

My heart skidded to a halt when I finally found the subject of my interest.

Tatum Blackthorn.

He stood across the room, next to Luca, Sofia, Enzo, and Achilles. Half man, half god. A timeless marble statue towering over mere mortals. Slung on his arm was his beautiful wife, Gia. Draped in a red satin gown, she exhibited her pregnant belly. I wondered what it felt like to be loved like her. To have someone accept and adore your every flaw, your every win, your every breath.

Mama and her friends quarreled in the background, but I didn't watch what they were saying. I was laser-focused on the Blackthorn couple.

Lila, this is unbecoming. You can't keep staring at someone else's husband, Mama's voice scoffed in my head. I knew she was right, even though my interest in Blackthorn wasn't romantic at all. All I wanted was another dance.

My eyes followed Tate's lips as they shaped around his words.

"If you so much as look in her direction, I will scoop the other one out. And unlike the Ferrantes, I won't stop the blood loss."

A sharp elbow found my ribs—Mama's way to tell me to stop staring—and my gaze quickly scurried to the person Tate spoke to.

A tall, agile man in a sharp suit, just like 80 percent of the room. And yet, I immediately recognized him, and bile hit the back of my throat.

The coppery hair.

The black eye patch.

The languid, fuck-you stance of a hunter quietly surveying the room for his next target.

His taciturn indifference to it all.

The man who nearly drowned me and then handed me his eyeball.

I wrenched my gaze away from him before he noticed me.

Next to him was another man who was unmistakably his brother, maybe even his twin.

"Oh, the music started." Rita clapped excitedly. "Let's gather around the newlyweds for their first dance."

My feet shifted heavily toward the human ring forming around Luca and Sofia. The couple assumed their place robotically, with Luca taking the lead and moving to what I assumed was a waltz. Their faces were grim, their eyes dim with apathy.

Papa wedged himself between Mama and me, slinging his arms over our shoulders with a cunning grin. He appeared gaunt and yellow, but happy for a change.

"D'you see who's here, Lila?" He turned to look at me. "The president of the United States, no less. And he brought his wife, too. This marriage puts us in a different league. The Ferrantes are going to be the new Kennedys. Mark my words."

I blinked at him, pretending not to understand what he was saying.

"Eh, *che Dio ti benedica*. Your head just keeps your ears apart." He patted the top of my head, laughing rancidly. "God really was cruel to you, *cara mia*. Giving you so much beauty and nothing to do with it."

Ignoring the urge to smash his head against a sharp object, I returned my attention to Luca and Sofia. The waltz ended, and when another one began, a stream of couples flooded the floor. Everyone paired up like magnets, drawing toward one another in perfect harmony. Couples swirled and fluttered. Laughed, hugged, and twirled. I watched Tate Blackthorn holding his wife close, whispering in her ear, paying no heed to the tempo everyone else in the room was shackled to.

Enzo dipped a famous model to the floor, his lips a breath away from hers.

Achilles had a shoulder pressed against the wall, surveilling the room with his dead eyes, hands in his pockets. He didn't dance, and I wondered if it was out of choice, or because no woman was brave enough to touch him.

"Roger, please." My mother tapped a waiter on the shoulder. A middle-aged man spun around in his uniform, holding a silver tray filled to the brim with champagne. "Get Lila more pink lemonade," my mother prompted. "Two ice cubes. Plastic cup."

No sharp objects for me. My mother said I had severe mental impairment, which put me at age six or below on the scale.

A handsome, fair-haired man approached us from the center of the room. I recognized him instantly. Angelo Bandini was in his early thirties, impeccably mannered and dressed, and prominent in his family business. Sofia's older brother.

He kissed Mama's and Papa's cheeks, then turned to me with a hopeful smile.

My heart fluttered against my rib cage like a butterfly testing its new wings. I forced myself not to smile back.

"Might I ask the youngest Ferrante for a dance?" I watched his lips move. He opened his hand, offering it to me.

My fingers twitched in anticipation beside my body.

"My daughter doesn't dance," Mama said.

Angelo chuckled good-naturedly. "Surely, just once? With her new brother-in-law. I'll be a perfect gentleman."

Mama stepped forward, cementing herself between us. I couldn't see what she was saying, but Angelo's beam morphed into a scowl. The sharp movements of her arms told me she was yelling. The blood drained from my face.

Mama had always been overprotective of me. Most of the time I was grateful, but this time...this time something dark and resentful unfurled behind my rib cage.

"Oh, I wouldn't count on this, Lady Chiara," Angelo's mouth moved smoothly as he stepped back. A sheet of brutality draped over his expression. "I could count the things I wanted and never got on one hand and intend to keep it that way." His gaze flitted to President Keaton across the room and the woman he held possessively in a waltz. His wife, Francesca.

"Forgive my wife." Papa inclined his liver-spotted head. "The wedding preparations have left her exhausted and distraught. She means no disrespect, Bandini. My daughter..." Papa pinched my cheek, then kissed his fingers. "She's simple, you see."

What a prick. Mama told him to stop using this derogatory word, but he never listened.

"No hard feelings, Don Vello." Angelo's lips expanded into an insincere smile, which my father returned. He then yanked Mama by the elbow, dragging her reluctant figure to the dance floor to save face. Angelo strode away, but not before giving me one last derisive look.

I stood alone, surrounded by couples.

Jealousy clogged my throat. I normally didn't mind being left alone—preferred it, actually—but right now, I hated it.

I turned around and stormed away, shouldering past catering staff and uniformed waiters. The main entrance was swarming with soldiers and security, so I slipped through the wine cellar's door.

I was immediately clasped in a womb of darkness.

Crimson Key was an island tucked between Florida and the Bahamas. An independent jurisdiction that belonged to my family. *The Devil's Playground*, as the rich called it.

It consisted of our mansion, a few hotels of award-winning grandeur, golf courses, and casinos. Trusted friends of the family had snowbird properties here, but it was Ferrante turf through and through.

Tropic humidity licked at my skin. I felt suffocated—by the heat, my dress, and most of all, my family.

I glared behind my shoulder at the arched windows of the ballroom. Usually, when music started playing, I retired to an adjoining empty room, laid on the floor, and closed my eyes. The bass reverberating against my spine mimicked the tempo of the music. It was the closest I could get to listening to it. Right now, though, I didn't want to lie still.

Wrenching my heels off, I stomped barefoot past the Roman balustraded pool and the densely planted cypresses framing the estate, farther down, toward the thick woods enveloping the back of the property. I kicked the dirt with a huff as I left the pickleball court and pool house behind me, putting more space between the wedding and me. At the end of the vast expanse of tropical trees was a strip of pearly-white sand kissing the Atlantic Ocean. It was my secret spot. A place I often visited on the island when no one was paying attention.

I didn't care that I was soiling my dress with dirt and mud. Didn't care that Papa was going to be furious. That Mama was going to be worried. I wanted to lick my wounds privately.

Ten minutes later, I reached the end of the woods. I fell down to my knees, the cold grains of sand digging into my fine bones, and stared at the blackened ocean, biting my lower lip. I grabbed a handful of smooth rocks, tossing them out to the ocean.

Never would I hear the sound of waves crashing on the shore.

Skip. Skip. Skip.

Never would I waltz to live band music.

Skip. Skip. Skip.

Never would I sing along to a familiar tune.

Skip. Skip. Skip.

Never would I kiss a stranger's mouth, warm and soft and alive, feel their pulse beneath my palm, or whisper secrets into a lover's ear.

The last rock sank into the water without skipping.

An angry roar ripped from my throat. Broken, desperate, yet I couldn't even hear it.

Behind my back, there was a castle, and dancing, and lights, and *life*.

There were plans, hopes, and dreams.

There were people with agency over their own decisions.

Suddenly, a hand clasped my mouth from behind. I gasped, my eyes flaring in horror. An arm wrapped around my throat forcefully, dragging me backward. It was so unexpected, it took me a second before I dug my toes into the sand, bucking, fighting the intrusion.

Somebody followed me here.

And that person knew we were far enough not to be seen or heard.

Panic flooded my system and kicked my instincts into high gear. Whoever held me was male, strong and in a frenzy.

I bit the hand that clasped my mouth, sinking my teeth into his flesh until the metallic taste of blood detonated in my mouth. My attacker jerked, tumbling down to the sand and taking me with him. I fell against his torso, his forearm still pressing hard against my throat. Pressure filled my ears. I fought and kicked and clawed, thrashing and roaring, a wild thing; his fists came down on my face, my neck, blow after blow, making my ears ring. My fingernails punctured his skin, digging so deep they broke and splintered. Something long and thick swelled against my butt. It promised pain and punishment and made the blood freeze inside my veins.

No. No way. I won't let it happen.

I writhed like a reptile, twisted sharply. I managed to bite his arm, sinking my teeth into his skin until it split, and managed to break free.

Air. I was finally able to welcome it into my searing lungs. I took a greedy gulp of it.

Looking back was a luxury my time constraint couldn't afford. Instead, I army crawled across the sand, desperately blinking away the stinging blood from my eyes. My crown of roses fell to the sand. In the dark, I could see that the flowers weren't white anymore. They were dark red. Drenched in my own blood.

My breath rattled in my lungs like a coin in an empty tin.

Breathe.

Breathe.

Breathe.

He snatched my ankle, yanking me back with force. Flipped me to my back roughly, then used a knife to slash the front of my dress, leaving a trail of hot, searing pain across my skin. I arched, crying out in horror. I kicked and punched him, too panicked to take in his features in the dark. It felt like trying to fight my way out of a fishing net. He was everywhere, all at once, too heavy, too much.

Sharp, frenzy eyes flared in the dark, taking in my bare breasts, my nipples, my stomach.

I recognized those eyes. Had seen them before. Two barrels of a gun, staring back at me.

I cataloged him into memory. Filed every plane of his face, each individual hair in his eyebrows.

I'm going to draw you.

And then I'm going to find you.

And then I'm going to kill you.

If you are stupid enough to let me live after this.

As he pushed my panties down my thighs, a peculiar calm washed over me.

In order for him not to kill me, I had to pretend I didn't know what was happening to me. If he thought he could get away with it, he'd spare me.

I stopped fighting, letting my muscles lax, forcing my mind to drift elsewhere.

Ischia sunsets. Boat trips. Busy markets. Books. Imma's grilled prosciutto and mozzarella sandwich.

He pushed a chemical-soaked rag to my face, one hand pressing against my mouth. I held my breath while he slapped my right breast, laughing as his hand skated down to the space between my thighs.

Men are filthy. Mama's words rang in my head. *They make you suffer when they have their hands on you. Never let them.*

A lifetime passed. And then another. I became dizzy with lack of oxygen. The rag pressed harder against my mouth and nose. Finally, my traitorous body took a sharp inhale of breath. The chemicals rushed into my system. My eyelids grew heavy, my body slacked. I became a rag doll.

Boneless. Weightless. Defenseless.

My body melted into the sand, my mind drifting to the clouds. I was far away now, somewhere he couldn't hurt me, no matter how hard he tried.

The last thought to cross my mind was that this *stronzo* could still kill me.

My last hope was that he would.

CHAPTER FOUR
LILA

EIGHT WEEKS LATER

For the first few hours every day, everything was blurry.

A fuzzy world devoured at the edges, like I was staring at my reality through a frost-coated window.

This morning was no different.

I pressed my clammy forehead to the cool toilet seat, waiting for the nausea to propel me into another round of projectile vomiting.

The only thing to come out at this point were acidic fluids. I barely ate, and whatever I did consume I ended up retching soon after.

A small, cold hand pressed against my back, twisting away damp ringlets of hair that had stuck to my skin. I stared up at my mother miserably.

"*Get that demon out of me,*" I signed in ASL. "*I can't take it anymore, Mama.*"

"Still don't remember his face?" she asked, ignoring my demand.

I shook my head. "*It was dark, and he drugged me.*"

She placed a gentle kiss over the crown of my head. "Don't you worry, *bambina mia*. Mama will fix this for you. I always do."

My body jerked forward. My mouth opened on its own accord, and another wave of puke tsunamied through me.

The devil put its seed inside me. That's what Mama said when she thought I couldn't read her lips. Her precious daughter was ruined forever.

I felt dirty. Used. Like my entire existence shrank into those few minutes when it happened. It defined me. Consumed me.

There wasn't enough water in the world, not enough soap in the universe to make me feel clean again.

The bruises were gone, but the scars lingered. The phantom wounds tore open at night, gushing memories I couldn't escape.

I hadn't stopped bleeding for eight weeks, even though I missed my last period.

Defeated, I glided from the toilet to the floor, curling into a fetal position, closing my eyes and wishing, begging, *praying* to wake up someone else.

I came to half an hour later, still trapped inside myself.

Stretching my legs shakily, I slung my elbow over the toilet seat, pulling myself up. I treaded out of my bathroom and into the hallway.

I was about to go down the stairway and look for Imma, when I noticed Papa's office doors were ajar. I stopped.

My parents were inside, standing in front of a grand, gold-plated mirror. This allowed me to read their lips. My mother was crying, her coiffed hair ruffled in disarray.

What did he do now? Take another mistress? Kill another one of her friends' husbands?

I pressed myself against the wooden door, curling my fingers around its edge and watching them through the mirror.

"Let me take her to Italy. I know a doctor in Capodimonte who can deal with this discreetly. She'll recuperate there."

He gave her a cold, unnerving stare.

"*Chiara*," he said. Even without hearing his tone, I knew this was a warning.

"Please. We need to get her an abortion." My mother dabbed a handkerchief to her swollen eyes. "Before it's too late."

"*Stai zitta*! Out of the question." Papa pushed his fingers into his receding white hair, yanking it about his scalp. "This is God's will. I won't defy Him."

"She was *raped*, Vello. *Fuck* your God."

He advanced toward her, slapping her hard with the back of his hand. My mother's face flew sideways. The ring on his pinky left a stamp-sized mark. I pressed my palm to my mouth, muffling a gasp.

It wasn't the first time my father hit my mother.

But it was the first time he did it in front of his sons.

Achilles, Luca, and Enzo stormed into my line of vision. This appeared to be a family meeting about my future. One I wasn't invited to, as usual.

"*Basta! Basta!*" Enzo broke my parents off, giving Papa a violent shove. "My upbringing is fucked up enough without adding domestic violence into the mix."

"The hell you think you're doing, Dad?" Luca thrust my father behind his desk, using it as a buffer between him and Mama. "Next time you raise a finger to my mother, you'll have no hands to wipe your ass with. Am I clear?"

"Watch your mouth." Papa heaved in his seat, catching his ragged breath. "I'm your father and your don."

"I don't care if you're the fucking pope. You touch my mother—you pay."

My father poured himself a drink with trembling hands. A conversation ping-ponged between him, Luca, and Achilles. Since Luca took a recliner across the room and Papa had his back to me, Achilles was the only person I could clearly see and whose lips I could read.

I was going to have a baby I didn't want. A baby by a man who raped me. How could I love it? How could I take care of it? Would they even let me keep it? Would I *want* to? Both options were frightening and overwhelming.

My father and brothers thought I had intellectual disabilities. Only Mama knew the truth.

"He owes Luca a favor." Achilles lit himself a cigarette. A heavy ball of lead settled in the pit of my stomach. "He'll do."

Him? Him who? What will he do?

Did they know who did it? Were they going to force me to marry him?

I'd long come to the conclusion true love was a myth. Like Santa Claus, or the Tooth Fairy. I'd yet to find one happy couple in the entire Camorra. But I never thought I'd be paired with the man who did this to me. Surely, not even my family was this cruel.

Luca said something that made Achilles scowl and mutter, "Right, because we have plenty of accountants and nice, respectable dentists to fucking choose from, don't we?"

I blinked, registering the unfathomable.

They were marrying me off.

Not to the beast who raped me, but rather, to the first willing man who'd accept such a foul deal.

"His character aside, he's the only motherfucker who can protect her as well as the Camorra. The king of disorganized crime."

Character aside? That sounded hardly promising.

Achilles took a drag of his cigarette, releasing two wrathful streams of smoke through his nostrils. "And say what you will about the Irish, but they take care of their own as much as we do."

Luca must have stood his ground because Achilles added, "He's the only man deranged enough to entertain this fuckery. Of course I'm protecting Lila."

"Have you lost your goddamn mind? You can't marry our sister off to that dipshit." Enzo bulldozed into my vision, tossing a hand toward Achilles. "He's a psychopath. I've seen him cut a man's tongue and feed it to his wife for snitching. Lila is pure and innocent and—"

"Pregnant." Papa slammed his palm on his mahogany desk, rattling the entire floor with its force. "She's pregnant and can't give birth out of wedlock. We can't marry her off to anyone in the Camorra because word would get out. They'll know someone dared rape her, and we'd be a laughingstock."

"She'll give birth here at home. It'll be our secret," Mama said decisively. "Then we'll give the baby awa—"

"No. Too many people coming and going." Papa shook his head. "Too much staff. It'll leak."

"We'll go to Ischia—" she started again.

"And have an abortion," he finished for her, mouth twisting crookedly into a sneer. "I'm not dumb, *Amore mio*. You're not going anywhere with that girl."

That girl.

This was what I was reduced to. A problem. An embarrassment. An issue to sweep under the rug. Anger bloomed in my chest. For the millionth time, I wondered if I did the right thing by deceiving the entire world about my so-called condition.

I could've been a debutante. Suitors and made men would've jumped through hoops to impress my family. I could've bargained a better position for myself to enter a marriage. Now I was leftovers. Scraps. A hot potato my family wanted to toss into someone else's hands.

"All you care about is prestige!" Mama grabbed a Deruta vase from the mantel midstride and threw it at my father. She nicked his temple before the antique shattered on the floor. Plucking a fire poker next, she swung it in his direction, this time aiming for his chest. "*Madonna Santa!* Who cares what people say? You're not handing her off to a murderer. She is mine."

Luca pried the poker from Mama's hand before she managed to land another strike on Papa, but it didn't stop her kicking the air in protest. I'd never seen Mama this way. Not even when Papa got one of his mistresses pregnant.

"This is all your fault." Papa stubbed his finger in my brothers' direction. "You've been soft. Soft on the Russians, on the Irish, on the Chicago Outfit. There's someone out there who thinks he can walk all over us." He pointed at the window. "What happened to your sister sits squarely on your shoulders. Now look who we have to give her to."

"Vello, no." Mama switched from fighting to pleading, dropping to her knees, folding over. "Please. Don't do this. She's everything to me."

"He's right. She must be wedded," Achilles said dryly, ignoring Papa's accusations.

I knew Luca and Enzo loved me. They always showed it in small brotherly ways. But Achilles took after my father. His heart was an iron fist clenched tight, always ready to deliver pain. It beat for power, money, and corruption. He had no more soul than the chess pieces sprawled on my father's board.

"This needs to happen immediately. We can't have people question the timeline," Achilles added.

"And the baby?" Enzo flipped his pocketknife, cut-cut-cutting shallowly across his thumb to take the edge off.

"Sofia and I will take it." Luca ran his knuckles over his jawline. "Or it can stay with Lila and some nannies. We can send Imma to live with her."

Immacolata was the nanny who'd raised my brothers and me. She still lived and worked on our estate.

"But I'm not excited about the idea of Callaghan." Luca stroked his angular jaw. "Enzo's right. He's a menace."

"A menace who rules South Bronx and sits on a mountain of his enemies' skulls. The man has no fear or morals. He's a liability. A wild seed. We need to strike an alliance with the Irish." Papa's words were swift and final. "He's my biggest headache right now. I need to nip it in the bud. This will tie our businesses with his. We'll throw him some incentives, give him territory, and kill two birds with one stone."

"*Sei un coglione*," Mama snarled, rising to her feet. "He gave your daughter his eye."

My life drained from my body.

This was who they wanted me to marry?

The awful man without the eye who threatened to drown, chop, rape, and kill me?

"The shit are you talking about, Mama?" Achilles swung his entire body in her direction, scowling.

"It's true." She tilted her chin up, straightening her spine. "She was doing her little doodles on the fountain outside the night you brought that godawful creature into my house. He found her and gave her his eyeball. She was covered in his blood, her hair all wet from the water when I found her. This is how depraved the man is. Taunting this poor, innocent girl."

"Uhm, and you didn't think of—let's see—*telling us?*" Enzo stared at her incredulously.

She hitched a shoulder up. "I didn't think we'd have to see him again, and I didn't want to trigger Lila. You know how delicate she is."

Luca squinted. "And he didn't rape her?"

"Well, no, but—"

"And he didn't *kill* her?" Achilles frowned.

They made it sound like him sparing my life was a heroic act. I wanted to scream until my lungs caught fire.

Luca curved an eyebrow, contemplating. "Maybe he spared her because of her disabilities?"

Achilles and Enzo shot him disbelieving glares.

"Riiiight." Enzo chuckled sarcastically. "Because he's just that kind of stand-up guy."

"He's not the catch-and-release type." Achilles scratched his jaw. "And he is not prone to mistakes. Something's fishy."

"Probably your breath," Enzo suggested sunnily. "Have you been with any more of my exes recently?"

Sometimes my brothers said crude things I did not understand. This was one of those times.

"Maybe he decided to finish his business at Luca's wedding," Dad marveled.

"And this is fine with you?" Mama went red. "Marry her off to her rapist?"

"Tiernan Callaghan has grand aspirations. I'd rather work with him than against him. Lila will give birth as a married woman, and we'll be able to put that *pazzo* on a leash."

"And if he abuses her?" Luca leaned a shoulder against the wall, a godly sculpture, arms crossed around his middle.

My father huffed. "How much does she understand, really?"

A lot, Papa. More than you'd ever know. The only thing I can't do is hear, and that is entirely not my fault.

"Set up a meeting," my father concluded. "Tomorrow, at the latest. I want the entire Irish clan here."

"No, no, no!" My mother fell to her knees again, pounding the carpeted floor with her fists. "I won't let you take her. I won't. You can't do this to me. She's all I have left."

But there was no point.

I knew as well as she did, once my father made up his mind, there was no changing it.

My mother's plan to keep me safe and unwed failed in spectacular fashion. Everything we'd worked for was in vain.

I was pregnant and getting married to Tiernan Callaghan.

And I had no say about it.

CHAPTER FIVE
TIERNAN

291 DAYS TO SELF-DESTRUCTION

There was only one thing I hated more than a Ferrante brother.

And that was *two* Ferrante brothers interrupting me while I was splitting the G. The heavenly act of taking the first, large sip of a freshly poured Guinness.

I was sitting in Fermanagh's, going over the books, when Enzo and Achilles showed up at my door.

I drew my weapon and aimed it at Achilles's head. Let's be honest, a bullet would only do his face good.

"That's a weird way of saying hello." Enzo flashed me a friendly smile.

"I don't acknowledge lesser life-forms."

"*Ouch.* That is so uncalled for." Enzo almost pouted. "If it wasn't for me stitching your ass, I'd be visiting a cemetery right now, not a lively pub."

I forgot how chatty the Ferrantes were. Already, I wanted my fucking time back.

"What brings you down to my humble kingdom?" I asked.

"Maybe we just missed you." Enzo tossed his knife in the air with a shrug, catching it by the hilt.

I cataloged the Italian jokester. A preppy black peacoat and black hoodie combo, slim fit chinos, and a three-hundred-buck haircut. He looked about as scary as a moldy piece of marshmallow.

"Have your fill, lover boy. You just entered my territory unannounced, and I have every reason to make lasagna out of your brain. Frisk them." I jerked my chin toward the Camorristi men.

Three of my soldiers stood up, stomping over to the brothers and patting them down. They raised their arms sideways with a disgruntled look. I grabbed my phone and took a picture of the humiliating moment.

Astonishingly, they were both unarmed.

"What do you want?" I grumbled.

"Come with us, and we'll tell you." Enzo tilted his head to the Humvee parked outside.

"Tell me here. I don't serve at the pleasure of your crown."

"We have an offer for you." Achilles's tone suggested his offer was to drink cyanide straight from the source.

I used the muzzle of my gun to scratch my jaw. "What do you want in return?"

"Not enough," Achilles grumbled. "And the offer is time-sensitive, so hurl your ass this way now."

"Bold of you to barge in here looking for a favor and put me on a deadline."

"Look, either you're coming or we'll move down our list to another asshole who'd take this deal."

"I'm coming armed." I re-holstered. The brothers exchanged looks. Achilles jerked his head in a nod.

They led me to their Humvee, glancing at me every now and then to ensure I didn't put a bullet in their heads. I had no plans to do that. *Yet.* Anger made you stupid, and stupid got you killed. Whatever they needed from me, they were desperate enough to ask for it nicely.

Achilles, Enzo, and Luca—who waited in the driver's seat— bickered in Neapolitan the entire way to their Long Island mansion.

They sounded pissed, though it beat me as to why. All the Russians I'd killed after our little reunion had been dumped far beyond the city limits. I even attended Luca's wedding. He and his new wife had the sizzling chemistry of a toothpick and a bucket of piss.

We arrived at their manor. Last time I was here, I lost an eye. Now, I was losing my bleeding patience.

We spilled into the foyer. Two curved, grand staircases stared back at me. Intricate columns in ivory and gold. Vaulted high ceilings, rich Persian carpets, baroque paintings, and so much gold my healthy eye nearly bled itself into blindness. The design was a mix of expensive, tacky, and over-the-top.

Servants rushed to take my coat and offer me refreshments. A wry chuckle escaped me. Last time I was here, I was a prisoner. Now, I was royalty. Oh, how the tables had turned.

"Not one word, Callaghan." Achilles got in my face, his finger an inch from my good eye. "In fact, try not to breathe. Your goddamn existence chaps my ass."

Ignoring him, I stalked inside.

"By the way, love the pirate look." Enzo slapped my back from behind, catching my step. "Really suits you."

"I don't swing that way."

"Don't mistake my hate boner for a proposition," he said smoothly, but the tips of his ears reddened. "Neither do I."

"Sure, buddy."

Eager to finish the conversation with a man so dumb he probably dropped out of the University of Life, I stepped forward, deeper into the house.

Luca and I ascended the curved stairway. Enzo and Achilles trailed behind. I considered all theories during the ride here and still hadn't figured out their angle for this meeting. They gave me the okay to kill Alex and his siblings as long as I made their bodies disappear, which I hadn't even done yet. Other than that, I had no outstanding beef with the Italians.

We marched through the corridor and into the first set of double doors leading to Vello's office. Luca opened the doors, and Achilles shoved me through them.

Sitting behind his desk was Don Vello himself, wearing a paisley cravat and a three-piece. He looked like a sphinx cat in a suit. Pale, mostly hairless, wrinkly, and too frail for his scowl to be taken seriously.

The rumors were true, then.

He was dying.

To his right, on an upholstered velvet settee, were his wife and daughter.

Lady Chiara was bawling her eyes out into what, at some point, was a tissue. She stared at me like I pissed in her grits this morning. I didn't take it personally. That tended to happen with women who knew what I did for a living.

The vast room was paneled with mahogany and filled with pictures from Camorra events—weddings, funerals, and baptisms. There was an elaborate, gold-gilded chess set on the desk in front of Vello.

In one of the two seats in front of him was my da, wearing his Sunday best and a placid expression. Next to him was my older brother, Fintan, and my twin sister, Tierney.

My irritation turned to apprehension. What the fuck was my entire family doing here?

"Callaghan. Thank you for coming." Vello gestured to the chair in front of him.

I glanced around. "What's the story? We throwing a party? Enzo's balls finally dropped?"

Vello signaled to the chair again. "Have a seat."

I sauntered painfully slowly just to piss everyone off before sprawling on the recliner opposite him.

"Do you enjoy making people wanna bash their heads against the wall?" Achilles seethed.

"Of course," I answered matter-of-factly. That he'd even ask was disconcerting.

"Let me start by saying nothing we'll discuss here will ever leave this room." Don Vello stood up, limping toward a drink cart with his cane. "If I hear you as much as breathed about it to anyone else, I'll make sure to kill your entire family in front of you before slaughtering you. That includes your father and siblings, who kindly grace us with their presence today."

His words, calm and deadly, brushed right past me. He plucked two small glasses and a bottle of Amaro del Capo from a mini freezer, returning to his seat and setting the glasses in front of us. His knees gave out, buckling him back into the seat. His fingers trembled against the bottle of liquor. I wasn't about to offer him help. I wouldn't piss on a Ferrante if one was on fire. It was a matter of principle.

Vello filled the glasses halfway. I snapped my fingers and motioned upward.

"Keep going. I've a feeling I'm going to need it."

He filled my cup until the liquid sloshed over. I picked it up and downed it in one gulp, slamming it against the table. "Why am I here?"

"Lila is pregnant," he announced, reaching for an engraved box. He produced a Cuban cigar, ran it under his nose, and bit off the tip with a scowl.

"I see." I ran my tongue across my teeth, considering the information. "Who the fuck is Lila?"

Whoever she was, I hadn't done the impregnating. I'd sampled my fair share of Camorra princesses, but never in the traditional, baby-making ways.

"Raffaella. Lila. My *daughter*." Vello's molars ground into dust.

Ah. Raffaella. The youngest. Mentally three, the lads at the poker tables whispered. Which still put her a few dozen IQ points above Enzo.

"Congratulations?" I yawned.

"*Che idiota*." Achilles scrubbed his face with his hand.

"That's a bit harsh." I tsked. "She's your sister, after all."

The taunt made Achilles bulldoze in my direction. Fintan lunged to his feet, blocking his way to me.

"Another move toward my brother and you'll be God's problem."

"Sit your ass down, Fintan. You're not even a made man." Luca's voice dripped in disdain.

I toyed with the ring on my pinky, still annoyed I left a perfectly poured pint of Guinness for this shit.

"Lila was raped during Luca's wedding," Vello provided.

Everyone in the room shifted uncomfortably. Mrs. Ferrante let out a strangled sob. Fuck's sake. Was there a bottom line to all of this?

And then Vello stared at me in a way that indicated the bottom line might be that *I* did the raping.

"Don't look at me. I've very few red lines, but raping children is one of them." I tapped my pinky ring. "Besides, I only do blowies and anal. Less chance of giving the woman an orgasm."

Vello screwed his fingers into his eye sockets. Luca stared at the ceiling. Enzo looked like he was about to hurl his knife straight between my eyes.

"I pray for your soul," Chiara muttered.

"Don't have one, but cheers."

"Actually, the fact most people in the underworld would believe you're a child rapist is exactly why you're here," Achilles said.

"I already told you; you've got the wrong guy."

"You're not being blamed for anything, son," Da clarified.

"Doesn't sound like it." I thunked my glass Vello's way, signaling for him to top me up. "Happy to do a paternity test."

Vello pushed another glassful of alcohol toward me, staring at me shrewdly. "That won't be necessary."

"Do you guys think it's a Camorrista?" my twin sister asked curiously. "A turncoat?"

Luca dragged a hand over his face. "We're still connecting the dots."

"And you need someone discreet to find the rapist?" Tierney guessed. "Is that why you called us here?"

It made sense they wouldn't task one of their own with the job. This was a PR catastrophe for a crime family who made a living being feared.

"I can hunt him down," I offered. "But I charge up front, and I ain't cheap."

Vello chuckled, staring me down like I offered him a hearty bowl of vomit. "If I wanted an assassin, I'd hire Tristan Hale. I only work with the best."

Hale did make an art of killing people, but I wouldn't say he was better. We had different execution styles. Mine was more eccentric. I liked to put forth my imaginative nature. Besides, Hale was a masked man. No one knew what he looked like. Technically, I *could* be him.

"So." I twirled the liquor in my small glass, staring down at it with boredom. "You gonna tell me why I'm here, or beat around the bush for another hour?"

"We want you to marry Lila," Vello said.

I ceased the twirling. Stared him down. I knew he was losing the battle to whatever the fuck was killing him. Didn't realize he also lost his faculties.

"Marry my daughter, Callaghan. Claim the baby as your heir."

"No," I said simply.

"Wait!" Tierney lurched forward in her seat. "W—wait. Hear him out."

I shot a glare at my family. My father shrugged.

"People will believe you're ruthless enough to take someone like...*Miss Ferrante.*" He cleared his throat. "You thrive off your merciless reputation. This'll serve you well. We'll have Ferrante business, connections, resources. They'll open up the port for us. We'll be able to get shipments from Europe. Unchecked."

The PANYNJ was riding our ass six ways from Sunday, confiscating my drug shipments on a regular basis. The Ferrantes had no such problem. They owned the port, organization, and workers' union.

"And I'll be able to break my deal with Achilles." Tierney tried snatching my gaze, her voice reeking of desperation.

The deal.

Achilles Ferrante's greatest sin in my book wasn't even clawing out my eye.

About a year ago, when I kidnapped billionaire Tate Blackthorn's wife, just minding my own business, as a part of work, Achilles held Tierney hostage for a few hours. We'd ended up striking a deal where she'd agreed he'd choose her future husband, and in return, he released her.

"Nice try." Achilles afforded her a smile. "Your ass is mine, sweetheart."

"What do you even care about my love life?" Tierney threw her hands in the air. "You're gay."

"That's a rumor you started," Achilles said laconically. "Good to see you know how to spread something that isn't your legs, though."

"We both know I'm spreading nothing. You assigned me a chaperone."

"*Enough.*" Vello's palm came crashing down onto the table. "You two aren't the subject. Although, now that we veered off-topic— Achilles, you cannot marry the mouthy Irish girl. She's impure."

"Toxic as all hell." My sister kicked back, crossing her legs with a grin. She wore black Chanel logo stockings and a black dress that wanted to be a handkerchief. "I'm no Eve. More like Lilith."

My sister was a sight. Men desired her. Women detested her. It made her an extremely lonely creature, even though she had hundreds of fake friends.

"Your behavior is shameful." Vello's lips curled.

"I suggest you keep your opinions about my sister to yourself," I warned Vello. "It'd be incredibly rude of me to kill a man in his own office."

"Oh, let him vent." Tierney rolled her eyes, examining her dark nail polish with a pout. "The only time I'm interested in what a man has to say is when my personal shopper calls to tell me the new Balmain collection just dropped."

"So." Vello returned his attention to me. "Back to our negotiation."

"Fuck your negotiation." Fintan pointed a shaky finger at Vello. "She's damaged goods. Why should my brother receive someone else's scraps when he can marry a Mafia princess like Francesca Rossi?"

"Did you just compare your brother to the sitting *president*?" Achilles tilted his head, his dark eyes dancing with wicked amusement. "My fucking God, I knew you were an alcoholic, but I didn't know you were a tweaker, too."

"Damaged goods, huh?" Luca ran his tongue over his teeth.

"You heard it right." Fintan's flat tone held no hesitation. "My brother deserves a debutante, not a teenager with a bastard in her womb. He's the rising king of the underworld."

Luca shook his head, jerking his chin toward Fintan. Enzo nodded, waltzing over to my brother, grabbing him by the collar, and dragging him down to the basement of terror.

I was pleased Fintan was going to get a rib or two cracked. It'd keep him away from the gambling rooms for a while.

"Why me?" I asked Vello.

"You have a last name and are above killing women."

"Glowing endorsement, but I killed three."

Chiara gasped. I never said they didn't deserve it. Sue me for being an equal opportunity feminist.

"You're single, powerful, and discreet." Vello ignored my confession. "And we'd rather fight with you, not against you."

Prying the truth out of a Ferrante was like milking a cockroach.

"Why isn't she getting an abortion?" I asked. "Seems easier than pawning her off."

"Surely, as a fellow Catholic, you understand why." Vello scowled.

"As a man who has committed every sin in the Bible and invented new ones in the process, I don't consider myself a son of God." I reached to grab one of his cigars, running it under my nose. "Truth be told, we're not even second cousins. Besides, she's a fucking fetus."

"She turned eighteen two months ago."

"Tiernan will take good care of Lila," Da said earnestly. I didn't know where he got this idea from. I wouldn't trust myself with a bleeding houseplant. Not even a succulent, and those apparently didn't need much water. "He won't harm her. And this'll squash all territorial and trust issues between the Irish and the Camorra."

"Doesn't she have severe intellectual disabilities?" I asked. "I'm not here to wipe someone's ass, no matter how beneficial to me."

"The fuck is wrong with you?" Achilles bared his teeth. "Don't use that derogatory language."

I couldn't help but toss my head back and laugh. Achilles being inclusive was the height of comedy. I'd seen this man rip a person's asshole with construction tools as a form of interrogation.

My best-kept secret was that I was not, in fact, a bigot. But in my line of work, not being an ignorant bag of shit was hardly a flex. I had a reputation to uphold. I was the man God didn't want in hell from fear he'd corrupt its residents.

"Lila is self-sufficient." Chiara straightened her spine, her urge to defend her daughter overriding her disdain for me. She had dark circles under her eyes. "She doesn't require any assistance to fulfill basic tasks such as eating a meal and tidying after herself, as well as using the bathroom and showering independently. Besides, she'll be with me all day, every day. She has activities to attend to. Occupational therapy. Swimming. Horseback riding. She'll barely be at your..." She twisted her upturned nose in revulsion. "*Place.*"

"I'm not marrying her," I drawled, so we could start bargaining. I would marry a fucking crack pipe if it brought me closer to my end goal. I had no scruples to speak of. But I wasn't doing it for free.

"Rethink your answer, Callaghan," Luca demanded. "You owe me. Filippo, remember?"

"Kill one of my soldiers to even the score." I kicked my feet onto Vello's desk, tossing the unlit cigar back to the floor. "I'm not giving your sister my ring and my name to get in your good books."

"Look at her." Vello gestured to the helpless creature on the couch. "Would it be so terrible to claim this fine woman as your own?"

"*Vello*," Chiara warned. "You're taking advantage of her mental disabilities."

"I'd have done this regardless, considering the circumstances," Vello said. "You know that."

I had to tilt my entire body to look at the Ferrante girl, thanks to her brother plucking one of my eyeballs out. She sat primly on the edge of the settee, hands in her lap, staring down at her feet.

I didn't need to look. I already knew she was fucking gorgeous.

It was why I spared her meaningless life the night Achilles took my eye.

Tarnishing her soft skin with my blood, putting fear in those sapphire blues, had been enough to get my dick hard.

She was fawn-like in features. A tiny little thing. Utterly angelic. Her pale gold hair flowed in succulent waves down to her ass. Her frame was narrow and slim, and the swell of her tits was magnificent under her lilac buttoned-down dress. Her face was the pinnacle of perfection. Hand-drawn high cheekbones, elfin nose, cerulean eyes, and pouty, pink lips. The elegant arch of her eyebrows was delectable. Even her nostrils were flawless. She held zero resemblance to her brothers, with their Roman noses, square jaws, and amber tans. Not to mention Vello, who had the underbite of a French bulldog.

If this creature was a pure-blooded Ferrante, I was Peter the Apostle.

Tragic was the fact such beauty was wasted on a woman who could never use it as a weapon. Although, judging by the way she stared back at me now, she looked like she wanted to spear me into the nearest rusty fence. Very Ferrante of her.

It occurred to me Vello just sacrificed his only daughter for me to do to her as I pleased. Snap those shapely legs like twigs. Make her pay for every single thing her brothers did to me. She wouldn't breathe a word. Even if she could, it'd be too late. She'd be mine.

To own.

To control.

To abuse.

Every single person in the room knew this fact. Yet, it was a price they were willing to pay. All of them, with the exception of her mother, who hardly had a say.

I turned back to the don. "She's a corker, I'll give you that, but a pretty cunt is just that—a cunt. It feels the same as any other in the dark. Sweeten the deal for me. Offer me something I cannot refuse."

"*Tiernan*," Da growled.

Vello held his hand up. "It's his right to consummate this marriage if he takes her as a wife. As long as he doesn't damage her, I'll allow it."

Chiara completely lost it. She flung from the couch, throwing herself onto Vello, her fingers wrapping around his neck. She started yelling in Italian.

Luca and Achilles didn't intervene.

"*A santa Chiara dopp'arrubbato mettettero 'e porte 'e fierro*," [1]Vello spat out, not bothering to spare her a look. He hit the panic button under his desk with a yawn. Two Camorrista soldiers stepped into the room.

"Gentle with her," Luca said coolly. The two men pried the hysterical woman from her husband, escorting her out of the room.

---

[1]   "You're trying to protect something after the loss has already occurred"; "too little, too late".

"You're a bad bishop, Tiernan." Vello dragged a bishop piece across his chessboard. "You have all these ambitions—eliminating the Bratva, taking over swaths of New York, getting into politics, but none of the manpower and only half the funds. You're blocked whichever way you go. Camorra here, Russians here, feds there. Can't move left, right, backward, or forward. You're stuck." He knocked a pawn on the chessboard with the bishop. "I can help you with that. I can unlock all these doors you've been craving to open. *Tiernan*," he raised his voice, his eyes searching mine, "I have the key."

"I'll claim the bastard by giving it my name only. I'll not be involved with your daughter or the child. She can live under my roof, and I'll fuck her occasionally, but nothing more."

"Continue." Vello pressed his fingers together. He was an old wolf. But an old wolf was still a wolf. He wasn't going to hand over half his kingdom.

"In exchange, you're gonna help me finish off the Rasputins."

The room fell quiet.

Achilles was the first to bite. "Fuck it." Smoke engulfed his words. "They want New York. We'll have to deal with them sooner or later. It'll send the right message to our enemies, too."

"What's the message?" Luca asked.

"That we always notice and never fucking miss."

Vello turned to look at Luca.

He jerked his chin. "It's been a long time coming."

Vello inclined his head. "My soldiers are at your disposal."

"Your sons, too."

He needed to have real skin in the game. Plus, I didn't rule out getting Achilles killed for what he did to me.

"Our hands have been clean for far too long." Achilles's voice cut through the silence like scissors. "Blood. Power. War. We crave it. Our soldiers, too. It's time."

Vello contemplated this for a moment before nodding.

Well, shit. If this was his opening gambit, he really needed this reunion.

"And I want Harlem. North. South. All of it," I pressed on.

"Keep dreaming, pretty boy." Achilles flicked his cigarette out the window.

I stood up, knowing I wouldn't make it past the threshold. They were desperate to clean their hands of the girl. I turned around and headed for the door. Vello's words stopped me midstride.

"I'll give you Harlem on one condition," Vello's death-drenched voice croaked. "You find Lila's rapist and take revenge. Discreetly. Show your loyalty to us, prove that this union between the Ferrantes and Callaghans is more than business. If you do this for me, if you find the man and kill him, I will give you Harlem. Not before."

Expanding the Callaghan territory and dragging the Ferrantes into my war was too sweet a deal to turn down. I wanted to conquer New York, so I could leave Tierney and Fintan something behind. Means to live comfortably after I was gone.

Plus, I never shied away from wet work.

Pivoting, I reached over to his chessboard, using a bishop to knock down every piece around it. "Send me all CCTV footage from the wedding weekend."

I stalked out of the office without sparing my new bride a glimpse. Chiara was in the hallway, wrestling with the soldiers on the carpet. I sidestepped her. Behind my back, I heard the sound of the glass shattering in Vello's fist, Achilles ranting in Italian, and Luca barking at his soldiers to unhand his mother.

Only Lila stayed silent.

Not for long. I smirked.

I was very good at making people scream.

CHAPTER SIX
LILA

The next time I saw my fiancé was at our wedding. By then, I had fully digested what was happening, and I was ready for a fight.

It was just my luck the Valium my mother crushed and slipped into my pink lemonade wore off when the priest informed my now-husband he may kiss the bride.

I pressed my lips into a firm line, holding my breath. There were eight hundred guests at our wedding. Not one of them raised concerns about the bride being allegedly not of sound mind, and no one objected to this farce.

I hated the Camorra. The Irish. The *world*.

My husband's eye—shamrock green, with golden speckles swimming inside it—twinkled with malice, reminding me its twin had been excised by my brother, and it was now time to take revenge. Through *me*. The black eye patch made his face ruggedly handsome. He looked like a well-scrubbed pirate. One who wouldn't mind tossing me off the ship.

A possessive hand snatched my waist, and he leaned in, tilting me down to the cheers and claps of our audience. Any hope his disastrous reputation was exaggerated snuffed like a brittle candle-wick in the wind. His lips crushed against mine, spreading into a spiteful smile.

"*So fucking sweet.*" His mouth moved over my own. Even though

I couldn't see it, I could *feel* his words digging into my skin like the tip of a knife. "*I can't wait to corrupt you.*"

A whisper of heat teased my stomach. Something I'd never felt before. It felt like someone spilled syrup inside me.

The guests went wild. Whistling, clapping, and cheering.

My father had insisted the wedding take place on Crimson Key. He wanted to show everyone it was business as usual. Signal nothing bad had happened here. But the fact our wedding took place only two weeks after the emergency meeting with the Callaghans spoke volumes. It was enough to raise suspicion among his soldiers. They were obedient, not stupid.

My father swore up and down Tiernan Callaghan had insisted. How he swore to fight the Camorra's wars for a chance to make me happy. Lies dipped in folly.

Everything about the manor made my skin crawl now. Every inch of it was soaked with the memory of my brothers carrying me back at dawn, muddied and bloodied, a torn rag doll.

Was my rapist in the crowd tonight? Was he watching? Basking in my misfortune? Laughing at the turn of events? Did he put two and two together? After all, this wedding was me paying for the consequences of his actions.

I couldn't remember his face. Only the evil glint in his eyes. But I wanted to. Oh, I wanted to remember, to tell my brothers, to give him the painful death he deserved.

What I *did* remember was the once-white tiara of roses. How the petals turned red when he'd split my lip, cheek, and forehead. I couldn't stomach seeing roses from that day forward. My wedding was decorated with lilacs only.

Tiernan released me from his hold. I nearly collapsed on my ass but managed to grab onto the wedding arch. When I looked up to see if my husband noticed, I saw his broad back striding into the enthusiastic crowd, like a titan rising from the ocean.

After the official ceremony, Mama and Imma rushed me

upstairs, away from prying eyes. They gave me water and dry crackers. Imma knew the secret of my pregnancy. She was like my second mama. An ample, tanned woman with silver hair, kind eyes, and drab gray dresses.

I placed my hands on the marbled banisters of the second floor, the ballroom stretching below me like a naked woman on canvas. White colosseum columns arched upward, onto a round ceiling painted with Raphael's *Transfiguration*. Clouds of pink and purple lilacs sailed from every corner of the room, and the golden glow of a thousand candles licked the muraled walls.

It was different from Luca's wedding, where everybody mingled and danced together. The Irish and Italians didn't mix. They sat at different tables on different sides of the room, drinking different liquor, eating different dishes.

"You should let her watch the wedding, Lady Chiara. It's hers, after all." Imma pushed away flaxen locks from my eyes, dabbing my face with powder. "And make sure one of the boys warns Callaghan to be gentle with her."

I put my hand to my lips. They still stung where Tiernan's mouth touched, the ghost of that ravenous, greedy kiss that took but didn't give.

I turned to Mama so I could see her answer.

"Luca assured me it's taken care of." She popped another pill and tossed it down her throat without water, refusing eye contact with me. Her third Valium today.

Apparently, Luca squeezed some kind of promise from Tiernan not to touch me on our wedding night. That should put me at ease, but I oversaw Luca telling Enzo how Tiernan's promises were worth less than a three-dollar bill. He wasn't a Camorrista. He didn't abide by the Omertà. The code of silence and honor.

"*He gave Blackthorn his word he wouldn't kidnap his wife, and ten days later, the woman was tied inside his van, tranquilized to her fucking eyeballs, roughened by his soldiers,*" Enzo had spat out.

"He's hurting her before he even laid a finger on her." Imma's eyes tapered. "He's disrespecting her in public." Her gaze traveled down below, and I followed it.

My husband's copper-haired head, rising at least three inches above the heads of everyone else in the room, sliced through the parting crowd of well-wishers. He had an aura, a pull about him that made people clear the way, stop, and stare.

A brunette bombshell was at his heel. Big, puffy hair, scarlet lips, and generous cleavage. They weren't walking side by side, but she was chasing him around in a tiny beige cocktail dress and red-soled heels, touching his wrist, her smile triumphant.

"*Che baldracca*," Mama hissed, white knuckling the banisters. "Send Enzo up. Now."

My brother showed up immediately, flush-faced and clearly drunk. "Mama?"

"Who's the *stronzo* parading around at his own wedding?"

"A Dallas Cowboys cheerleader." He ran his knuckles over his jawline. "Don't worry. It's all a part of the plan."

"Is the plan to make us look like weaklings?" she sneered. "Because it's working."

"The plan is he comes to his wedding suite well sated and... *satisfied*." Enzo cleared his throat.

My mother's face relaxed somewhat. "Make sure the whore gets fired."

"Yes, Mama."

The women who raised me had a very specific idea for what constituted a good woman.

A good woman dressed modestly, spoke quietly, and didn't hold a job. Much less a job that required showing off her body.

"Also, she's wearing white head to toe. Bad luck for the couple. Tear that dress and put her in something drab."

"On it."

Leave it to my mother to be angry at the woman for breaking the dress code, rather than sleeping with the groom.

But Enzo was onto something. Maybe the cheerleader was going to satisfy my husband's needs for tonight. I sure as hell wasn't going to let him touch me.

Who said he'll ask for your permission?

I was going to fight. Consequences be damned. I didn't care that I wasn't supposed to understand what was happening. The jig was up. I had nothing left to pretend for.

Tiernan and his companion disappeared from view. Mild relief and acidic irritation swirled in my gut.

It was common practice for a man to take a mistress or two in our world. But it was courtesy to conceal her from view. If not from your associates, then at least from your wife.

About an hour later, a Camorra soldier gingerly knocked on the door of the honeymoon suite, where Mama and her friends gathered around me. Little girls in bridesmaid dresses jumped up and down on the bed. Italian tradition, to invite fertility to the newlyweds' bed.

The married ladies, Mama included, sat on chairs. It was custom that only virgins were allowed on these sheets. It didn't stop my mama from letting me sit on the edge of the bed.

"Lady Ferrante." He bowed his head. "Raffaella is being called for the speeches. They're wheeling in the cake."

"Oh, Fabio, she's too tired." She waved him off. "Leave us. But do send over some food and a hamper of tea."

He didn't move.

Her eyes narrowed. "Yes?"

"Her husband wants her there."

Silence. Dark, ominous energy poisoned the air.

"Speeches?" Mama huffed sarcastically, keeping her poise. "They don't even know each other. What is there to say? Besides, I do not take orders from peasants, and neither does my daughter."

"The don asked to relay the message." The soldier bowed his head lower, switching from Italian to Neapolitan. "He thinks it shows strength through unity. I'm sorry." His throat bobbed. "She needs to come."

And come, I did. I was ushered back downstairs, where my mother reluctantly disposed of me next to my new husband. He was surrounded by his father, brother, sister, and Irish soldiers, and spared me no look.

I noticed all three of the siblings had the same, impossibly rare hair. Blood-red burgundy, rich and dark like aged wine. Their father had ordinary, dark brown hair. They must have taken after their mother.

Was she here? If so, how come I hadn't met her?

I knew nothing about my groom.

Only that he was wild and exquisitely violent.

That the men in my family found him incontrollable and infuriating because he didn't fear them.

A few minutes later, Tiernan's brother stood up and clinked a fork to his champagne flute. He made a speech I couldn't lip-read, since his back was to me. He looked remarkably like my husband, and yet nothing like him at all. The same ruby hair and green eyes, athletic build, and aristocratic strong features.

But this was where the similarities ended. Whereas Tiernan dripped power and cruelty, his brother looked like a well-groomed accountant, one of the many you could find on Wall Street. He lacked that devil-may-care air, the easygoing charisma.

Since I couldn't read Fintan's lips, I turned to look at my family's table. My mother's face was gray and lifeless. My father and brothers' masks of indifference were on, but I could see through their cracks. The throbbing vein in Luca's forehead. The strain in Papa's neck. Enzo's slight scowl. Achilles's insatiable thirst for revenge and gore.

Then it was my husband's turn to deliver his words. He stood, grabbing me by the waist and yanking me up with him. I gasped at the sudden invasion. He wrapped his arm around my neck, tucking me under his armpit like I was his captive.

The crowd shifted uncomfortably.

He studied the room, his silence somehow louder than everyone else's.

His lips moved, and my eyes clung to them.

"Look at her." He snatched my jaw, tilting my face upward, exhibiting his trophy. "So clean. So pure. So *innocent*," he taunted.

He smelled...warm. *Alive...* Like sex and violence and something else, not entirely terrible, but nevertheless catastrophic.

"The most beautiful woman on the continent. No close seconds. They call her a vision, a masterpiece, a myth. From now on, she only has one name—*mine*," he growled, twisting my face by my chin to look him in the eye. A sadistic smirk touched his lips. "I cannot wait to devour my little forbidden fruit tonight. Touch the untouchable. Sully the pristine. Turn the elegant Ferrante princess into a Callaghan delinquent."

The raucous laughter quaked the walls and settled in my stomach. My father choked on his glass of brandy, nostrils flaring. Luca's hand settled on his gun in his holster, flicking his gaze to my father for the okay to start a war.

But it was my mother who threw me into a state of pure panic. She stood up and stalked outside, a veil of Camorra wives trailing behind to comfort her.

Crying wasn't an option. I wasn't going to give the bastard the satisfaction of seeing me break.

Mama and I had carefully made sure I didn't show emotions, but our plan had backfired. Being allegedly a person with intellectual disabilities didn't matter anymore. I was pregnant and wed. My walls of protection had shattered one after the other. I was unraveling like a loose thread in a sweater. I knew Tiernan would pull and tug until I was completely bare.

My husband dropped my chin. "Consider this your first and last warning." He spoke to the room, but stared only at me. "Raffaella Callaghan is mine. Nobody is to look at my wife, speak about my wife, or breathe in her direction. She's under my protection now. The first to cross the line will be the last. They'll be made an example." His gaze dragged across the room, which collectively held its breath. "There will be no body to bury, no ashes to spread, no memory to spare if you're stupid enough to disrespect her. *Us.* Understood?"

They all did, judging by the horrified looks in their faces. Tiernan's attention halted on Angelo Bandini, and a chill chased across my spine. The dread that slowly dripped into my gut all day turned into a tidal wave.

Why did Angelo unsettle me so much?

Why was the sight of my brother-in-law so distressing to me?

"You know, I never was a fan of Italian weddings." Tiernan dragged his thumb across my lower lip, parting it to reveal my white teeth. "Too much pathos for my liking. Now, blood? Big fan of that. I think it's time I shed some tonight."

There'd be no blood on the sheets, as he very well knew.

Unless he draws it some other way.

The men in the room stood up. Cheered, clapped, whistled.

It was time.

"Move," Tiernan ordered. One word. Yet, my entire universe shriveled into it.

When I didn't, he gave my back a push.

I stumbled forward, and my legs did the rest, automatically carrying me toward the foyer. He glided behind me, his gaze searing the back of my neck. I tried to go as slow as humanly possible to prolong the inevitable.

When I wasn't fast enough for the *stronzo*'s liking, he bypassed me and tossed me across his shoulder.

The crowd followed us up the curved stairway, hooting and throwing rice at us.

Tiernan took the curved hallway to the honeymoon suite. The one Luca and Sofia had stayed in weeks ago. And my cousins before them. Achilles and Enzo would too, once it was their time to wed.

The last thing I saw before he kicked the door shut behind us was my mother's face peering from beyond the crowd.

Her hands moved quickly as she signaled me in ASL.

One word.

"*Fight.*"

CHAPTER SEVEN
LILA

As soon as the door clicked shut, Tiernan tossed me across the room on the four-poster bed like I was an old suitcase and slithered toward the writing desk. His movements reminded me of a viper seconds before striking its target. Languid, controlled, discreet.

The windows were open, allowing the briny summer breeze to drift into the room. The curtains danced playfully across the walls. I watched fixedly as he removed enough weapons from his body to start a medium-sized New York gang.

He unholstered two guns, a silencer, and a couple of knives, lining them up neatly next to an ancient flower vase, a charcuterie board, and chilled champagne with two glasses. He removed his tuxedo jacket and tie—cut, as per Italian tradition—rolling his dress shirt up inked arms corded with muscles and veins. My heart twisted into a painful knot when he turned to me. Our eyes locked.

My new husband never blinked. It made the hairs on my arms stand on end. It was like he decided to compensate for the loss of his other eye by never closing his good one.

I wanted to beg for mercy. The only thing stopping me was the knowledge that he got off on fear. I saw it the night at the fountain.

Weakness would only encourage more cruelty.

His eye landed on a painting of a crucified Jesus above the headboard.

"Your parents sure know how to set the mood." He plucked a fig from the charcuterie board, tossing it into his mouth on his way to the en-suite bathroom. "Wait here, and don't do anything stupid."

"*Don't damage her.*" Papa's words haunted me.

He could leave me unmarred from the shoulders up. No one would ever know.

Everything else was fair game.

I didn't waste time. Scrambling to my feet, I rushed to the desk, grabbed one of his guns—heavier than I'd imagined—and aimed it at the open bathroom door with shaky fingers. He reemerged a few moments later, zipping himself.

A gun was aimed at his head. Yet, all he did was stare at me with leisured amusement, like I was a lab rat trying to work out a Rubik's Cube.

I was used to being underestimated. Still, for some reason, I couldn't bear that this man thought I was so toothless.

"Put that down, *Gealach*. That is a grown-up toy. I'll have your mother send your crayons and coloring books over tomorrow." Tiernan fished out his phone, frowning at a text message. I knew the basic mechanics of guns from watching the men in my family handling them.

I flicked the safety with my thumb.

The sound made Tiernan's gaze flit back to me.

He sighed. "Fuck's sake." He flew toward me, grabbed the gun by the mouth, seized the silencer from the vanity table, and screwed it on. "It's one in the morning. Show some decorum." He handed the gun back to me, staring at me with a glint in his eye, daring me to hurt him. He pushed his chest against the gun, his dark gaze penetrating my soul, squeezing it with his ice-cold fist.

His heart thudded against the silencer.

Slow. Steady. Calm.

Not one muscle in his face moved.

He was calling my bluff.

He was not only calling my bluff, but suffocating my soul, touching me without permission, and pushing me to my limits like no man had ever done before. My rage, my fear, all gathered in the pit of my stomach, like a storm building momentum and speed, an anger that sat dormant for years...

I pulled the trigger.

The force of the blow tilted the gun upward. The recoil made me stagger back, and I hit the wall, falling to the floor.

The bullet grazed his shoulder. Crimson spread across his pristine white shirt.

I shot my husband.

The most vicious, bloodthirsty man in America.

Terror gripped me, and I crawled on my hands and knees toward the door.

Tiernan unbuttoned his dress shirt unhurriedly. His face gave away nothing.

He let his shirt slide down his arms, using the tip of his shoe to press the door shut to stop me from fleeing. I forced my gaze to travel up to him.

"You know, if you were a real Callaghan, I'd have taken you to the shooting range to work on your aim. We have a reputation to uphold."

He had a sculpted body with a prominent six-pack, defined pectoral muscles, and a tattoo running from the side of his ear along his right shoulder.

Oderint Dum Metuant.

Let them hate as long as they fear.

He leaned down and reached for me. I forced myself not to flinch. I thought he'd hit me, but all he did was pry the gun from between my fingers. "Open your mouth."

Even though he looked calm, something in his eye told me that if I wouldn't, he'd put a bullet in my head. And unlike me, he wouldn't miss.

Slowly, I let my jaw slack. He pushed the pistol's muzzle between my lips. Slowly, almost sensually. It was still hot, the gunpowder sour against my tongue.

"Wrap those pretty lips around it," he instructed coolly.

My eyes stung with tears, and I followed the instructions I wasn't supposed to understand. I acted on pure instinct. I didn't want to die. I didn't want to live, either. But I didn't want to leave this earth before I killed my rapist and at least plucked this bastard's other eye out.

My husband looked bored out of his mind. Like shoving guns down people's throats was a daily occurrence for him.

"Next time you try to shoot me, you better not fucking miss, because this'll be my cock. It's thicker than the gun. I'll watch you choke on my cum as punishment. Understood?"

I didn't answer. Screw him.

I stared up at him, shaking with rage, and spat the gun out of my mouth.

He shook his head in response. "Get your ass in the bathroom and get ready for bed while I clean myself up."

I staggered to the bathroom, locking the door behind me. I clutched the edges of the sink, stared into the mirror, and swallowed air to draw in some oxygen. I wished I had a phone. Mama wouldn't let me have one. She said phones created zombies, and everything I needed from life could be found in our library.

My eyes drifted to a condom in a foil packet on the vanity. I recognized it from an anatomy encyclopedia I read a few years ago.

So he was planning to rape me after all.

Not as long as I have breath in me, stronzo.

Searching my surroundings frantically, I found a glass vase next to the clawed bathtub. I tossed the fresh roses in the trash—couldn't look at them, anyway—and drained the water down the sink. I rolled the vase inside the skirts of my wedding dress and crouched down to the floor.

The door rattled behind my back. He didn't trust me. Or maybe he just got tired of waiting to claim what was now his. Either way, I had no time.

I smashed the vase against the floor, hoping the layers of fabric silenced the thud, and picked the sharpest shard of glass from it. I scurried up to my feet, ripping the door open. Tiernan stood on the other side of it.

He arched a brow. "Done with your hissy fit, fetus?"

I launched the shard at him, stabbing him just above the elbow. I was going for his veins, but he was tall, and my vision was blurred by adrenaline. He dodged me quickly, moving like a striking serpent. I tried again, blindly lashing at him, but before I knew what was happening, he wrapped himself around me from behind, yanking the shard from my hand.

"Note to self." He dragged me to the bed, shoved me against one of its posts, and efficiently tied me to it using his own belt. "She's not very good with taking orders."

Not from assholes who cheat on me five minutes into the marriage, I wanted to bite back.

He disposed of all of the broken glass in the bathroom and hid all of the weapons in the room.

When he was finally done cleaning up after me, he untied and sat me down on the edge of the bed and crouched before me. "You have to stop trying to kill me, Lila. It's giving me a massive hard-on, and I've never been good with delayed gratification."

I glared at him skeptically. I wasn't even sure what he meant by that.

"I'm not going to fuck you," he explained plainly. "Not tonight, anyway."

My eyes darted to the condom on the vanity in the open bathroom, my throat bobbing with a swallow. He followed my line of vision.

"Bold of you to assume you're worth my time." A smile tilted the corners of his lips. It was mocking and humorless, but the first I'd seen from him. "The condom isn't meant for you. I was supposed to fuck someone else. Unfortunately, I wasn't in the mood for a brunette."

My shaking subsided little by little. Nobody had ever used these words with me. In truth, people hardly spoke to me at all. When they did, they treated me like a small child.

Tiernan slanted his head. "How much do you understand?"

I didn't answer him. I still hadn't decided what'd be the best course of action to protect myself in this marriage.

"You gonna stop trying to kill me?"

I shrugged noncommittally.

"Very quixotic." He rubbed his thumb across his lower lip. "How about a six-hour ceasefire until morning?"

This time I nodded. I was exhausted. Hungry, thirsty, and overwhelmed with my own existence.

"Same bed?" he offered.

My eyebrows slammed together.

He grinned in response. "Have fun on the floor, then."

I assumed the tiny square of bathroom carpet as my bed, curled into a shrimp-shaped figure, crying myself to sleep. Tiernan didn't suggest I take the bed, nor did he check on his whimpering, hiccuping wife.

The marble beneath me was cold, the pins in my hair too tight, the corset too suffocating, but I was safe.

Locked away from the big, bad monster.

At least until dawn.

CHAPTER EIGHT
TIERNAN

A loud bang on the door woke me up.

"Wakey wakey, Sir Kills-a-Lot," Enzo's voice sing-songed from the other side. Of course, the cheerful bastard was a morning person. "Time to fulfill your end of the bargain."

My end of the barg—?

Bollocks. I forgot the stupid blood-on-the-sheets tradition. Vello needed it to prove his knocked-up daughter was a virgin. I wasn't normally in the habit of following directions, but in this case, we needed to keep a united front. It'd be bad for business if people knew I married a knocked-up woman.

I grabbed my phone, sifting through my last messages.

> Luca: Don't you dare touch her.
> Achilles: Not even a peck on the cheek, asshole.
> Tiernan: Stop blowing up my phone.
> Enzo: Touch a hair on her head, and your phone won't be the only thing exploding.

Seeing as my wife stabbed and shot me last night, I had at least two semi-open wounds to tarnish the expensive sheets with. Funny, the don didn't mention she was violent. Probably because he knew it'd turn me on.

"Ten minutes." I stretched across the bed. I could practically feel Enzo hovering on the other side of the door like a floating piece of shit in a public restroom.

"Is Lila okay?"

I threw a glance at the locked door of the en suite, from which annoying whimpers had drifted until four in the morning. "Grand."

Silence seeped through the door crack.

"Did you…" He paused, clearing his throat. "Honor our deal?"

Barely, I thought sardonically. *That second time she tried to stab me, I leaked enough precum to glaze a Cinnabon.*

"I did." I slung an arm over the mountain of silken pillows behind me. "Despite her constant begging. She was really asking for it."

I was supposed to get my dick wet after the ceremony to ensure I was sated by the time I got to the suite. The Ferrante brothers had offered to pay me 50K for every month I didn't touch their sister. All in cash. Unfortunately, the cheerleader spoke too much and sucked too little, so I cut her loose before I even unzipped. Not that it mattered. Even a good fuck wouldn't be enough to calm down the fire Lila ignited in me whenever she tried to kill me.

Which was pretty bleeding often considering we hadn't known each other for more than eight hours.

Smashing a vase inside her dress was a nice touch. I wasn't sure about her cognitive abilities, but I deduced she knew exactly what happened to her and wasn't keen on a repeat.

Rubbing the sleepiness from my eyes, I stood up and banged on the bathroom door.

"Up." I cupped my morning wood, dying for a piss. "We need to hit the road."

The Ferrantes' private jet was due to leave at noon, and I still had to present the sheets, have breakfast with a bunch of Italian dimwits, and meet with the Camorra to strategize the attack on the Bratva.

The door slid open, and Lila reappeared. Even with smudged makeup and a wrinkled dress, she was still fucking gorgeous. Her looks were a problem. I made a mental note to chop that pretty hair and maybe add a scar or two to her face.

"Breakfast's in ten. Get dressed." I shouldered past her, tugging my sweatpants down and taking a piss.

She went about her business quietly, and other than a few death glares, didn't show great enthusiasm to kill me this morning.

Once I was done brushing my teeth, she slipped into the bathroom and returned with her hair in a loose French braid, a fresh clean face and a pink ruffled dress. She needed to stop dressing like a toddler. Shy of her wedding dress, everything I'd seen her in looked like it was plucked straight off a Baby Gap hanger.

Avoiding my gaze, she padded toward the door quickly.

"Stop," I ordered.

She did.

"Sit." I pointed at the unchristened bed.

She followed my instructions, defiant anger rolling off her stiff shoulders.

I had all the good intentions and warmth of a reptile, but I still recognized she needed to know what the fuck she was doing with a knife if she planned to wave one around frequently.

I dug a Swiss knife from my pocket. Her eyes flared as I crouched in front of her.

"Quick lesson in anatomy and stabbing people, since it's less work than teaching you how to use a gun." I flicked the blade open on a sigh. "When you attack someone, you want to be lethal and strategic. Don't just wave it around like you're trying to swat a fly." I had no idea how much of this shit actually registered. Since I wasn't in the habit of repeating myself, she better fucking pay attention. "You go for the main blood carriers. The faster they bleed out, the slower they are to chase you. Radial and ulnar arteries." I pointed at my wrists with the knife, making a horizontal slit motion less than an inch away. She blinked. "Jugular veins." I pointed at my own neck. "Cubital fossa." I poked the blade inside my elbows. "The chest seems like an appealing option, but due to the thick layers of muscle and bone, it's hard to penetrate without proper force."

She stared at me silently, taking it all in. She was either the stupidest creature I'd ever met or the smartest. It was also possible she was a spy. A way for the Ferrantes to harvest intel. I filed that in the back of my head.

"Now, if you want to inflict superficial wounds, go for the shoulders. Forearms. Palms." I handed her the knife. She took it, uncertainty swimming in those Nordic eyes.

I extended my palm in her direction. "We need to sully those sheets in the next minute. Go vertical to avoid hitting the nerves. This way." I dragged my finger along my palm.

This was a twofold exercise. One, I wanted to check her cognitive abilities by giving her a complex instruction. Two, I wanted to flush the hunger for my blood out of her system. My guess was she bottled up a healthy dose of feminine rage these past eighteen years. She had a scratch to itch.

She didn't make a move.

"You've been wanting to do this since we got here." I held her gaze. "This is your one and only chance. Next time, I'll retaliate."

Her nostrils flared, a flash of the Ferrante wrath flickering in her pupils. She leaned in, aiming the blade at my throat. She smelled decadent. A heady combination I'd yet to detect on human skin. Like flowers and summer and innocence and *mine*.

It was time to start looking for a fair-haired, dainty mistress I could pretend was her from behind.

"There you are," I drawled, my gaze never wavering from hers as she pushed the blade against the throbbing vein in my neck. "Now be a good girl and finish the job."

She grabbed my wrist, opened my palm, and slashed the inside of it. It was a straight, vertical line from my thumb to wrist with the precision of a pathologist.

Intellectually challenged, my ass. She understands complicated assignments.

This was an unfortunate turn of events for my new wife. Because if I found out she was a mole—which I now suspected—I was going to punish her. Severely.

I raised my palm between us. Blood snaked down my forearm, twisting like ivy. We both watched. Her in fascination, me with dry amusement.

"First time drawing blood?"

She licked her lips quietly.

"Here. Have a taste." I pushed my bloodied hand in her face. "One of the many perks of marrying a psychopathic murderer is I'm in no position to judge you."

I was fucking with her. Testing her limits. Stretching and pushing them to make them burst so I could unveil what lurked beyond that porcelain doll facade.

Her eyes hooded, and her breathing labored. She snatched my wrist with those dainty fingers of hers and jerked it to her cherry-blossom lips.

She forked my fingers with her hot, wet tongue, tasting my blood, ravaging it like a hungry, feral thing. She growled, high on her own newfound ferocity, and I saw it then. Who she was.

A monster, like the rest of her family.

A pretty monster, but one who was capable of killing just like any other.

It was a thing of beauty, watching her feast on my blood. Submitting to her brutal nature. The way her eyelids fluttered shut, the shallow panting that made her tits bounce in this odd, erratic rhythm. Her sweet tongue moved in and out between my fingers, catching every drop.

I hoped she was a spy, because then, I'd have a very good excuse to punish her. And punishing a Ferrante was something I'd always had an appetite for.

Sucking in a breath, I stood up and fisted the unspoiled snowy sheets, tainting them pink.

A knock on the door reminded me there was a world outside of this suite, and that it was time for me to conquer it. I glanced at my wife, who had a postorgasmic, dopey look in her eyes and swollen lips. She didn't seem so innocent and compliant under the morning light.

I turned my back on her.

"Limp your way to breakfast."

I disposed of Lila at the women's breakfast table on the patio along with Fintan, Tierney, and two of my soldiers before meeting with the Ferrante men. I didn't trust the Camorra with her safety. They fucked up once, and though she couldn't get pregnant again, I didn't like people touching my shit. My siblings were trustworthy. Chaotic and extremely messed up, but reliable.

"Where'd the blood on the sheets come from?" Luca's business-like tone gave nothing away as he and his brothers escorted me to Vello's office.

I uncurled my fist and showed him his sister's handiwork.

Luca nodded. "I'll send someone with the cash tomorrow."

"Next month I'm bumping it up from fifty K to eighty."

"The fuck?" Enzo protested. "Why?"

"I got a preview when she changed this morning. You're lowballing me. That pussy's worth a lot."

All three brothers trained their faces to a hard mask, but their flared nostrils gave their rage away. I never understood Italian conservatism. Tierney could get railed by every man on this island for all I cared as long as she consented to it.

"Don't parade your whores in front of my sister ever again," Achilles finally clipped out. "It's disrespectful to the family."

I followed them down a curved hallway with black and white checked marble and headless Roman sculptures. "Consider yourself lucky I haven't raped her."

I doubted I ever would, but I did like keeping people on their toes. Money could keep me sated for only so long. I was promised a docile little maiden and ended up with a venomous demoness. All bets were off now.

We arrived at the tall double doors leading to Vello's Crimson Key lair.

"If I find out you touched her, I am going to snap your windpipe like a wishbone," Luca said in a conversational tone.

"Your sister tried to kill me three times before breakfast," I notified the worried brothers.

Achilles and Luca exchanged perplexed looks, both raising their brows.

"She doesn't like it when you change her routine," Enzo explained. "Think about it, man. She can't control shit. Predictability is the only power she has."

"And surely, you weren't shocked by this turn of events." Luca's canine smirk made me want to bash those white teeth down his throat. "You bring out the violent murderer in people, Tiernan. Like Enzo plays with knives, and Achilles performs autopsies on his victims for shits and giggles. That's your *thing*."

"What's your thing?" I marveled. "Moping around like a teenage girl who's just been dumped?"

"Cleaning up after everyone's mess." He paused, giving it some thought. "Always doing the right thing."

"Morality is mediocrity's dry-cunted sister."

I burst through the French doors of Vello's office, tossing the sullied sheets on his desk. He was in the midst of what looked like a dialysis treatment, two uniformed nurses fussing over him behind his desk.

He examined the bloodstained sheets with furrowed white brows. "Did everyone else see it?"

I nodded, helping myself to a drink at his liquor cart, making myself right at home.

"Drinking at eight thirty in the morning has a name," Enzo pointed out behind my back.

"Yes. It's called fun." I poured three fingers of whiskey from the decanter, slinging the amber liquid down my throat.

"I don't remember offering you a drink, son," Vello said.

"I don't remember asking."

"Good. Now that unpleasantries were exchanged, let's talk shop." Luca lit the cigarette dangling from his mouth. The three brothers took their seats around Vello's desk, which left no room for me. Just as well, as I didn't plan to stay long.

"What's your strategy?" Vello asked me.

"We wait for the perfect timing." I swung my gaze between them, pouring myself another drink. "Then, we ambush them when they least expect it."

"Ambush them? In their own territory?" Enzo's eyes narrowed. "That's a war declaration."

"Wars have the tendency to end you if you don't end them first," I said curtly. "If we wait around twiddling our thumbs for the Russians to strike, we'll lose. Better to throw our big dicks on the table and get it over with."

"You can't just barge in and go on a rampage," Vello coughed out. A dying horse on his way to the glue factory. No wonder the Ferrantes hid him from plain sight.

"What a preposterous thing to say. Of course I can," I countered. "You've been playing too much chess, Vello. Once you start moving knights and bishops, sacrificing pawns, you alert your enemy he is on a battlefield. Better to let him find out when there's a sword wedged between his ribs."

"Fine. Let's say we ambush them," Achilles said. "Then what?"

"We leave a void in the West Coast." Luca took a drag of

his cigarette, smoke skulking out of his nostrils. "Vegas, LA, San Francisco, Bakersfield, and the border."

"We'll divide them between us and take over." I prowled over to them, plucking a U.S. map from my back pocket and splaying it on Vello's table. "Appoint our own people, open our own charters. The Russians run a basic operation. Weapons. Human trafficking. Cartel. Igor never struck alliances with American governmental bodies. Mayors, senators, feds. Waltzing in and taking over will be a piece of cake."

"And if his soldiers come for us in retaliation?" Enzo arched his brow.

I shrugged. "We kill their families and make them watch. Once we go through the first and second ranks, the rest will slink away."

Vello rubbed his chin, tugging at the dialysis cords hooked to his arm. "And when do you suggest we strike?"

"A few months, when the dust settles." Now that Igor was dead, the Bratva was in disarray. "His son Alex is a capable man, but he's in Russia now, tangled up in cleaning up the mess his father left behind."

"When's he coming back?" Luca asked.

"Not soon, is my guess. Igor spent the last four decades cozying up to politically connected oligarchs who are now being persecuted by the new Russian government. He needs to rebuild connections there. Start from scratch."

And find a wife. Now that Igor was dead, his sons needed heirs, fast. Like the Camorra, the Bratva liked to keep things in the family.

"What about the other brothers?" Achilles said.

"Jeremie and Slava are in the United States," I said. "So is the baby sister, Katya. I hear she wants to go to college on the East Coast, so Alex might contact you to ask for permission to send her to Camorra territory."

"You moonlighting as a college adviser?" Enzo snorted. "How the fuck do you know where she wants to go to school?"

Because I make it a point to know every time a Rasputin shits, eats, or breathes.

"Sam Brennan's been keeping tabs for me. The siblings are holding down the fort in Vegas." I shrugged. "Push comes to shove, I can always fly to *Moskva* and finish Alex off myself. Throw the system into chaos, then take down the rest of the Rasputins here."

"*Moskva?*" Vello's mouth tugged at one corner.

"Moscow," I corrected. *Fuck.*

"That's not what you said," Luca pointed out.

"That's what I fucking meant."

But it was too late. A chink had chipped in my armor. They detected it. The disease festering underneath my ragged exterior. My secret.

"So, we wait for your word to strike?" Achilles finally spoke.

"Yes."

"Timeframe?"

"Six to seven months."

They looked between them. My jaw flexed. "They won't make the first move. They're recuperating from the pakhan's death and waiting for Alex."

"It's not that." Luca shook his head.

"Am I missing something? Do you have some big plans for that period?"

"No, *stronzo*, you do," Enzo spluttered. "You're welcoming a baby."

I was welcoming bleeding nothing. I wasn't going to stick around for their sister nor for the bastard in her womb. I had other plans. Ones that didn't include a family.

"I can multitask." I plucked a pen from Vello's desk and circled my desired Bratva territories. "Be on standby. I'll send word when I have an update."

Making my way to the double doors, I stopped at the sound

of Vello hissing my name. His voice was as frail as his diminishing body.

I glanced over my shoulder. "Yes?"

"Have you started looking for Lila's attacker?"

No. It was the last thing on my mind. But I guessed the sooner I was done with this, the sooner I could have Harlem and expand my territory.

"Don't worry. You'll have his skull on your desk before the bastard's born."

CHAPTER NINE
LILA

The sun slinked beneath thick gray clouds as Tiernan's Mercedes weaved in and out of lanes on our way to Hunts Point. He was talking on the phone, and I was relieved not to be the center of his attention. His undivided focus was a very dangerous place to be. I didn't plan to visit it often.

And there was something else.

Every time he looked at me, I had a feeling he was seeing past the charade. My lies. The pink puffy gowns and vacant stares.

The only edge I had over other people were my secrets. And his cold, assessing eyes told me he could pry every last one of them out of me without lifting a finger.

We hadn't communicated since the morning in the honeymoon suite. I didn't know whether our silence was a good or a bad thing. I just knew I didn't regret devouring his blood. I wanted him to know I was no pushover, and I wanted proof he was mortal, after all.

He was. His blood was warm and thick and rich. It lingered in my mouth like warm toffee.

Despite my family owning most of the city, I'd only been to New York City a handful of times. Even then, I only ventured into the upscale parts of Manhattan. The Bronx was different. I crushed my nose to the window like a kid, watching the dense urban landscape flash by through a cloud of my own condensation. The buildings, streets, and people deteriorated in shape and condition the farther we drove into the neighborhood, until all I could see were littered sidewalks, dilapidated buildings, and drug addicts.

The Mercedes stopped at a red light, and a woman slammed herself against my window, making me jerk back with a gasp. I snapped my head to Tiernan. He rolled down the automatic window, not sparing me a glance.

I looked back at the woman.

"Callaghan, tell McGee to hook me up. You know I'm good for it." She slung a scabby arm along the windowsill. Her skin was heavily punctuated by purple marks.

I turned back to my husband, who sprawled his arm over my headrest, his forearm almost grazing my ear.

"You haven't been *good for it* in two months, Stella. I'm not fucking JPMorgan. I don't offer an overdraft plan."

My gaze fluctuated between them.

"Who's the princess?" She jerked her chin to me.

He didn't answer. Just stared at her. Was he ashamed of me?

She puckered her lips in a whistle. "Looks classy."

He threw me a detached look, like he forgot I was even there. His lips were flattened into a grim line. "Anything else?"

"Look, I'll take shifts at The Pink Kitty again." She bristled.

Tiernan smirked darkly. "Nobody wants to fuck you in your state."

"There's always a client for a warm pussy."

"I only employ clean whores. Ones who pee into cups every week. That's why the police let me run this neighborhood."

"Then what do you suggest I do?" she sputtered.

"Drop dead," he said crisply. "It's the humane option."

"Give me something to overdose on, and I will."

"Flattered you'd think I have a shred of humanity." He rolled the window back up. I didn't understand their conversation. I pinned him with a questioning glare.

"A prostitute," he explained.

My jaw slacked. I'd never met one before.

One of the most astonishing things about my husband was that he didn't treat me like I was an idiot. An inconvenience, yes. A pain in the ass, certainly. But he looked me in the eye when he spoke to me and explained things unfiltered.

"She has sex with people for money," he clarified. "Sometimes for drugs."

I swallowed down a bitter lump of sympathy, turning my head back to the window. I felt his body quaking beside me with a quiet laugh.

We stopped in front of a tavern called Fermanagh's. An ancient castle spurted between decayed ruins, almost comically beautiful against the bleakness it was surrounded with. It was obviously a cathedral turned into a pub. Boasting French Gothic architecture, rib vaults, and stained-glass windows. My heart picked up speed. This was where I'd live? The upstairs of a pub?

Though Fermanagh's sparkled like a diamond in a pile of mud, everything around it still looked like it came from a horror film. Chain-link fences plagued with trash, graffiti everywhere, and faded shop signs.

Tiernan's bone-chilling gaze met mine. "Not in Kansas anymore, are you, Dorothy?"

This was a far cry from the green pastures, country clubs, and mega-mansions I was used to.

I followed him out to the entrance of the pub, where two massive Irish soldiers stood on guard. They bowed their heads at my husband, clearing the way for us. A couple of errand boys jogged to the car to fetch our suitcases. Mama had sent most of my stuff to the apartment before the wedding, so I didn't pack a lot.

We stepped into the pub, which was warm and candlelit. A huge Irish flag covered the domed ceiling. The place was packed, the stench of alcohol, piss, and sweat assaulting my nostrils. I swallowed back bile, clutching my belly. Tiernan advanced to the bar, leaving me behind. His brother manned the bar, wearing a suit and barking orders at the staff. They exchanged a few words, after which Tiernan clapped his brother's back and motioned for me to follow him.

We went up a side stairway near the kitchen, where two more soldiers waited. The place seemed as guarded as my Long Island home. Somehow, it did nothing to ease the knot doubling and tripling in the pit of my stomach. I watched my husband's muscular back, clad in a black dress shirt and charcoal slacks, as he took the stairs two at a time. We arrived at a corridor with two doors facing one another.

He slid a key into the left-hand keyhole, pointing at the opposite door. Since he had his back to me, I couldn't see what he was saying. I bit my lower lip and followed him inside. A thousand questions swam inside my head.

The apartment was scarcely refurnished, clean, and as cold as a freezer. I guess that's what Mama meant when she used the term bachelor's pad. Blacks and grays, modern fixtures, and a kitchen more virginal than Mother Mary. His errand boys disposed of our suitcases and scurried away without a word. Tiernan filed into the hallway, and I trailed behind him hesitantly, drinking in my new reality.

It was a short, stuffy corridor, with only two doors. The first one led to my room. He pushed the door open and stepped aside, expecting me to enter my new cage.

I peered inside. Mama's servants must've prepared it beforehand. It had my pink duvets, huge dollhouse, wood-carved chairs and table with my tea and china set which I loathed. Her silent way of reminding me I needed to keep the charade alive. I wondered if she sent me any books. My Kindle. My sketchpad. My pencils. The things I loved and what kept my sanity intact.

My back was to Tiernan. When I turned to look at him, a

scathing scowl was stamped on his face. He shook his head. He must've been talking to me, and I completely ignored him.

Oh, well. He better get used to it. That was my strategy for our entire sham of a marriage.

The more he believed he couldn't communicate with me, the better the chances he'd leave me alone. I needed a way out of this place and back to my parents' house. I had to speak to Mama.

Offering him an empty stare, I drifted to the dollhouse at the foot of my bed, crouched to my knees, and plucked two Barbies from their pink lounge chairs by the fake pool. I picked a smiling wax figure, taking a small brush and running the comb through her synthetic hair.

A few moments later, I threw a glance behind my shoulder.

Tiernan was gone.

But the knots in my stomach remained.

CHAPTER TEN

TWENTY-FIVE YEARS AGO
OYMYAKON, RUSSIA

The little worm was finally going to die.

It only took three years.

And, well…yes, fine, *slipping poison into his formula bottle and, later, food every now and again.*

Igor couldn't put a bullet in his head. Killing a baby in cold blood felt like shedding the last layer of civilization separating him from being a demon.

It was a mistake to take the twins. This fact he willingly admitted, but only to himself.

He should've let them die in the bitch's womb.

But the temptation had been too strong, the sorrow too raw, the pain too fresh.

Tyrone Callaghan had taken the one thing Igor couldn't replace—his heart.

"You should come see him, sir." Olga nudged her swinelike face between his office door and its frame. "His fever hasn't broken in five days. The closest hospital is a two days' journey away. I doubt he'll make it."

Igor set his pen down and plucked his shuba from the back of his chair.

The turndown fur collar tickled at his whiskers as he trudged out of the wooden cabin. He picked up his rifle on his way out. Mercy killing, *he told himself.* Luba would not be mad at me for that.

A thick sheet of white covered the roofs and what few vehicles were parked outside the encampment.

Barren roads encircled the former gulag camp Igor had purchased from the Politburo shortly before the union had collapsed. He turned it into a training camp for his future Bratva soldiers and a prison for his adversaries.

He made good use of the work camp facilities. The barbwire gates kept his prisoners from escaping. The punishment cell block was the classroom in which valuable lessons were learned. He forged warriors, not little pansies.

They trudged the length from his firelit office cabin to the living quarters, snow crunching under their boots.

Olga—heavy, short, unbearably pink—pulled the door open, fighting the force of the swirling winds. The stench of sickness and rotten teeth hung in the crisp air. The children slept in their coats and working boots on long planks of wood stretched on either side of the wooden cabin. They were too exhausted to wake up to the sound of Igor stomping across the rotting floorboards, his hand lantern rocking from side to side like a ship caught in a storm.

Igor stopped at the foot of the plank.

Tiernan—ridiculous name, he marveled for the millionth time—was sandwiched between his sister and Alexei Rasputin. Igor's own son hugged his friend close to his chest, his shuba flung across the little worm. A rare mink sable worth a fortune. And he put it on that Irish scum.

Igor wanted to welt Alex from head all the way down to his little toes, but knew Luba—had she been alive—would disapprove of it.

He'd already found himself another wife, Natalia. Twice as young and thrice as pretty. She was pregnant now. But she was no Luba. Nobody was his Luba. And so, he did not strike the boy, though he richly deserved it.

Tyrone said he killed Luba by accident. Igor didn't believe him.

At any rate, his Alex, his Lyosha, was the only piece of her he had left. And he intended to keep him unsullied.

Igor toed his son's hand from Tiernan and pointed his rifle at the sick boy.

"Oh, but look, Igor." Olga sent a pudgy hand to the worm's forehead, running her fingers over the damp bloodred locks. "His fever is finally breaking. He was convulsing so horribly earlier, I thought he would die. His sister and little Lyosha kept him warm. Forced milk into his mouth. Looks like he'll pull through, after all."

Igor curled his mouth in dissatisfaction and lowered the rifle slowly.

"What was he doing when he fell ill?"

"Just peeling potatoes, Mr. Igor. He is only three. Too young for lumber work. I let the young ones peel potatoes out in the cold. It is good for them to get used to the temperature. But I can allow him to work inside until he gets stronger."

"No," Igor said decisively. "Keep him outside, and make sure he works tomorrow. Full day. He needs to earn his keep."

Igor wanted to tell Olga to keep Alex and Tiernan far away from each other, but it was futile.

The only way to keep his son from the little worm was to pull him out of the camp and let him live with him and Natalia.

And he was far too selfish to let a toddler interfere with all the joys the young, reckless woman brought to his bed every night.

CHAPTER ELEVEN
LILA

An entire week ticked by.

I managed to avoid my husband with encouraging success.

We slipped into somewhat of a routine.

Tiernan was not an early riser, but I was, so I usually tiptoed out of my room at around seven in the morning and made myself avocado toast and some coffee for breakfast. I cleaned and washed the dishes after myself, dressed up for the day, and slipped into the kitchen of Fermanagh's.

The kitchen was empty at that hour, which allowed me some privacy until my mother arrived armed with three bodyguards and took me with her to Long Island. There, I went about my normal day—drawing, reading, horseback riding, studying musical theory. I attended speech therapy, honing my phonological skills, and read thick old books that smelled like musty inns and coal fire. My mother still let me ride horses, and I had a feeling she was secretly hoping for an accident that'd relieve me of both my pregnancy and tyrant husband.

Mama brought me back to Tiernan's apartment at six or seven every evening. My husband was never home before three or four in the morning. This suited me well. But even though I managed to evade the bloodthirsty villain my father and brothers handed me over to, I still couldn't find any sense of peace or relief.

I was terrified of the pregnancy, which everyone had been ignoring thus far, waiting for an invisible clock to turn until enough time passed between the wedding night and conception.

Would my family let me keep the baby after birth? Did I even want to?

I also knew I'd have to face Tiernan at some point. Considering last time we stayed in the same room together I tried to kill him, and he fed me his blood, I wasn't looking forward to that.

A silly part of me hoped if enough time passed, Tiernan would eventually forget about my existence. That quietly, I would slink back into my old life. Back in my parents' house. To those summers in Ischia. To the universe my mother so carefully crafted around me to protect me from the underworld.

"*Has he touched you? Has he tried to take liberties with you?*" Mama demanded to know now, in the back of the Cadillac that took us from Long Island back to Hunts Point. She signed the question in ASL, so that our driver and bodyguards wouldn't notice.

"*No,*" I signed back, my mind drifting to my wedding night. To the reckless, fleeting pleasure I found in devouring his blood. "*I never even see him.*"

"*Thank goodness. We need to get you out of there before he strikes.*" Mama moved her hands with the same precision she did her hair and makeup and chose her frocks. She was a beautiful, well-kept woman. But I looked nothing like her or my father. "*The man is a ticking time bomb.*"

"*How do you plan to do that?*"

"*I'm talking Luca into finding a way to break the arrangement. He was never fully on board with this union in the first place.*"

"*Do you think he can do it?*" Despite sinning on an hourly basis, my father considered himself a devout Catholic. He would never let me birth a child out of wedlock.

"*If not, I'll try something else. I'll save you, bambina mia. No matter what.*"

The car turned the corner into my neighborhood. I gnawed on my lower lip, tempted to tell Mama how I was really doing. I hadn't been sleeping—not since Luca's wedding, really—living off two or three hours of interrupted naps every day. I wasn't eating well, either. Only a piece of avocado toast in the morning to push down the nausea. But it seemed as though she was sick with worry as it was. I didn't want to make her anxiety even worse.

"*I pray that Luca succeeds,*" I signed.

"*He will. In the meantime, I want you to take this.*" She rummaged through the Birkin bag in her lap, pulling out a shiny, top-of-the-line cell phone. My heart stuttered to a stop. I had never owned a phone before. Mama was vehemently against it. She didn't even give me our Wi-Fi password for my Kindle. If I wanted to download a book, I had to go through her first.

She placed the phone in my hands. "*Promise me you won't go on the internet, Lila. It's awful there. Full of terrible things that will ruin your innocence.*"

How much more was there to ruin, I wondered? The worst had already happened to me. I was raped and got pregnant. I couldn't even remember my rapist's face, so I wouldn't get justice or closure, either. Were there other reasons my mother was so adamant I stay away from the elusive internet? Not that it mattered. She was my only ally in this world. I didn't want to upset her.

"*I promise.*"

"*Good. I put my contact number there, as well as Imma's and your brothers'. Also 911. You can text me when you get lonely. But remember, only contact the others in case of an emergency. They're not supposed to know you're literate.*"

My brows knit into a frown, and I asked the question that had been sitting on the forefront of my mind all week. "*Why does it matter? I'm already married. Our plan didn't work.*"

She stared at me for a beat, anger flushing her face ruby.

Leaning forward, she gripped my arms almost painfully. "*You think you have nothing more to lose? Your pain hasn't even started. There is still so much more to suffer through in a marriage to a mobster. If Tiernan finds out you are not a person with intellectual disabilities, he will demand to consummate the marriage. You will be raped not once, Lila, but every single night. Sometimes multiple times a day. He will put another baby in you, and then another one. He will continue seeing his mistresses, which I am sure you are not dumb enough to think he doesn't have. He'll parade them around, just like he did on your wedding day. Their perfume will be on your sheets. The scent of their desire on your husband. He will not wash himself before he enters you. He'll want you to smell them. To know you are nothing but a tool for him. And when your beauty fades, he will replace you with someone younger and stop touching you altogether. But by then, you will feel different about him. Sex forms attachment, Lila. You will want him to be yours like you are his. You'll fight back, and he'll beat you. This is what Mafia men do. They break your heart first, and then they break your spirit, and finally, they break your body. We might still be able to get you out of this marriage if people think you are not sentient. You have to keep the secret alive, Lila. You must."*

Tears made her bottomless onyx eyes glitter. I hadn't seen her this upset since my family found me on the shore, battered and bruised, a man's semen dripping down my inner thigh.

I knew she was speaking from experience. From a place of deep, all-encompassing pain. I also knew I had an older brother somewhere in the universe, the fruit of an affair my father had with someone else, and that this brother—whoever he was—was Papa's favorite child. He still saw him often. Showered him with gifts, attention, and guidance. His identity was securely wrapped up in mystery, a privilege no Ferrante sibling was ever afforded. We weren't given a choice about who we were. We were born into the world of blood and violence, of unspeakable sins, our paths carved by the bloodied hands of my father.

The idea of going through another rape shook me to the core

and grounded me back in reality. No way was I going to let that happen.

"*I'll make sure he doesn't know,*" I promised, ignoring the knot forming in the pit of my stomach. "*Don't worry, Mama.*"

She pulled me into a hug, her tears soaking the front of my lavender chiffon dress.

CHAPTER TWELVE
LILA

Another week passed.

I still couldn't eat or sleep and was plagued with thoughts and fears about my faceless, nameless assailant. He was always there, prowling in the periphery of my existence, ready to pounce.

He was a free man. Living among the Camorra and Irish. After all—he was at Luca's wedding on a secluded, invitation-only island. If he did it once, what stopped him from doing it again?

Tiernan had warned people off from touching me, but so did my family the minute I was born. If the monster who put a baby inside me didn't fear Don Machiavelli, what guarantee did I have he'd fear my husband?

I was deathly afraid of meeting him again. Not just in reality, but also in a dream.

Because in my dreams, there were no Irish soldiers and security detail. No formidable, skull-collecting husband who broke the fingers of people who dared to touch his things. There were no gatekeepers. My rapist could saunter right in. Take me against my will again.

My brain swam with these thoughts all night, every night, but especially tonight, as I stared at the ceiling in my room, clutching my stomach in a death grip.

Snap out of it, Lila. You still need to find a way to escape this marriage and figure out your pregnancy. This is no time for a meltdown.

I thought back to what used to work when I was a small child and couldn't fall asleep. Imma would make me warm milk with a spoonful of honey. Looking back, it very well could've been a placebo, but it always worked like a charm. Suddenly, I craved the strange drink, consumed by the thirst for it. Was this my first pregnancy craving?

Glancing at my new phone, I saw the hour was half past midnight. Still plenty of time before my husband returned home from his wicked biddings. I slid my feet into my fluffy slippers, cracked the door open, and crept down the hallway.

Rounding the corner where the hall kissed the living room and open-plan kitchen, I stopped dead in my tracks. The lights were off, save for the amethyst backsplash of the kitchen. The marble shone in soft purple, offering a clear view of the scene.

My husband, and the person he was with.

A woman with blond hair the same length and shade as mine was pinned to the kitchen island beneath him.

They were both fully dressed, but he was doing something mean to her from behind, holding the same position my horse, Silver Lady, took when the breeder brought a stallion to her.

He was *mating* her.

My mouth fell open, my throat parched with panic and horror. To make matters worse, the idiot wasn't even entering the right hole.

The cell phone in my hand dropped to the floor. Both their gazes snapped to me at the sound. I stood there, in my stupid, *stupid* pink pajamas with the yellow and blue butterflies, and stared back in shock.

Even though I didn't think things could get worse, somehow, they still did.

Tiernan picked up his pace, his good eye boring into mine. Cold. Hard. Dark as my most illicit, awful nightmares.

He was taunting me.

A moan of fury parked in the back of my throat. I didn't let it loose.

He coiled his long, lithe fingers around the front of the woman's neck, like she was an animal he was taming, not breaking his stare from mine. That was when I noticed she was wearing a pink, knee-length dress. A LoveShackFancy staple.

I recognized it, because it was *mine*.

He touched my clothes? *Stole* them? Gave them to his mistresses?

My heart pounded furiously. Mama was right. Men were the work of the devil. I was never going to let him touch me.

"Jesus Christ, Callaghan." The woman snapped her head back from the kitchen island, her eyes flaring at the sight of me. Her forehead had a red mark from being pressed against the hard surface. She looked nothing like me, despite the general characteristics. Her eyes were dark and a little too far apart, her mouth thin and wide, and her nose slightly crooked. "Your wife's awake!"

Tiernan grabbed her by the hair, pinning her cheek back to the kitchen island so that she faced me. He closed his eye, looking tortured. "Shut up."

"She's watching."

He thrust harder, deeper into her.

"She's not firing on all cylinders," he muttered.

Oh my God, my mind screamed. *What do I do?*

I could run back into my room and lock the door. Every cell in my brain commanded me to do that. But that would be the logical, perceptive thing to do. Tiernan was not supposed to know I understood societal situations. Especially after I messed it up our first night together, tried to kill him twice, then cut him up the way he'd asked.

I decided not to cower, run, or hide. That would be the natural response of a sentient person.

Instead, I plastered on my usual blank expression and casually made my way to the fridge. I watched their heads in my periphery following my footsteps. They seemed puzzled by this turn of events, as they should be.

He was still riding the woman's rectum when I nonchalantly tossed open the fridge, letting bright light flood directly into their faces. The woman cringed and squinted.

I extracted a carton of milk and gave it a sniff. Beneath my pajamas, my knees trembled, knocking into one another. But on the outside, I calmly set the milk carton on the counter, reached up on my toes, and opened the cabinet, extracting a clear glass.

I didn't look at their faces. I wasn't supposed to behave like anything was amiss. I poured myself some milk, scooped a spoonful of honey, and shoved it in the microwave for a minute. With my back to them, I watched the seconds slip on the microwave clock, then took my drink out.

I was maybe six feet away from my husband, who was currently screwing somebody else, and it was time to face him again.

I took a deep breath.

Spun around.

My eyes met Tiernan's.

And I couldn't help it.

My need to defy him overrode my self-preservation.

I gave him an airy smile, tipping my glass up slightly in a salute before taking a long sip. It was a small gesture. Barely detectable in the dark. Just to keep him guessing.

The taunt didn't go unnoticed. My husband ripped himself out of his whore, grabbed her by the hair, and spun her around, shoving her to her knees. She opened her mouth wide and flattened her tongue. He tore the condom off his penis and dumped it on the floor. My pulse roared between my ears. Confusion, mixed with morbid curiosity, churned inside me, and something weird happened to my body. I felt warm butter melting in the pit of my stomach. I set the glass down shakily on the counter. I didn't want to drop it.

"Ain't gonna suck itself, Becky."

She hurriedly took his penis into her mouth. I stood there, dumbfounded. *Madonna mia*, these morons were trying every hole possible other than the one babies came out of. And his thing was just in her rectum. This couldn't be sanitary.

One thing was for sure—sex was a form of punishment wives were expected to endure in order to bear children. No wonder Mama did her best to shield me from it.

I snatched my glass of milk and advanced toward the bedroom. I left the carton on the counter. He could put it back himself.

Casually, I kicked Becky's *real* clothes on the floor—a cheap neon red minidress and fishnet stockings—under the TV credenza. Who knows? Maybe she'd have to go back home naked.

I locked my room behind me.

CHAPTER THIRTEEN
TIERNAN

What the *fuck* was her problem?

More importantly—what was mine?

I couldn't finish. No matter how hard I tried. Every time I came close, a vision of my wife with her cerulean eyes and haughty, pert nose scrunching in distaste floated into my vision. She was strangely indomitable.

And Becky just kept fucking *existing*, the daft cow.

The nuisance moaned in her cigarette-soaked voice, which could not have been Lila's. She didn't smell anything like her, either. The amount of perfume she spritzed herself with could probably drown a rhino. The dress looked wrong on her, too. Lila's waist was slenderer, her tits perkier and fuller. And their skin was different. In texture. In color. Beneath the tips of my fingers. Lila's was slightly bronzed, sun-kissed from Italian vacations and smooth as velvet. Becky's told the story of too many dicks, too little sun, and a rough life.

It was the equivalent of craving fine, aged whiskey and settling for stale piss. I had no one but myself to blame. Becky was nothing like my wife. The only thing they had in common was their hair color, and even that felt like a cheap knockoff. Becky's came from a bottle. I threw her out so fast, she stumbled down the stairs with her knickers bunched around her knees.

Also—did my wife really want milk that bleeding bad?

Lila did not seem to care one iota about my cheating on her openly and provocatively. It shouldn't bother me. Fuck knew nothing else ever did. Yet, somehow, I found myself...dissatisfied. The *audacity* of that woman.

On paper, she wasn't supposed to understand what she just saw. In reality though, that woman drew a perfectly shallow, straight cut in my palm, bypassing every important organ.

Lila exhibited zero signs of developmental delays, and when my tech guy broke into her therapist's files, her diagnosis was vague at best.

I paced the living room, raking my fingers through my hair.

What ticked me off the most—there was a list, and it was fucking long—was that she didn't seem at all appreciative of the gallant gesture I put forth.

I could've taken her four times a day. It was my marital right. *Duty*, even. Christian burden, some would say.

Nice newfound Catholicism you've got there, buddy. Goes well with all the murder and torture.

My main problem with this marriage—apart from its existence—was that I suspected my wife was faking her condition.

On our wedding night, she acted like a frightened young woman who very much knew she was about to spend the rest of her life with a man who collected his enemies' skulls as souvenirs.

In the past two weeks, she barely left her room other than to go to her parents'. She was strategic. Cunning. I fucking hated liars. They reminded me too much of myself.

But there were other things that didn't add up.

She didn't register half the shit that left my mouth. The other half was met with blank, empty stares. The day she moved in, a car lost control and slammed straight into Fermanagh's, breaking all the street-facing windows. The sound alone rattled the walls. Yet when I looked at her, expecting her to jump in fear, she was staring at the lighting fixtures on her bedroom ceiling disapprovingly, oblivious to the noise.

Against my better judgment, I stalked toward her room, rapping on the door. It was half past midnight, but she'd live. It wasn't like she had important shit to tend to tomorrow morning.

There was no answer. I banged harder. "Open."

I knew a load of bullshit when I smelled one. And my wife? She reeked of insincerity. One moment she couldn't hear an atomic explosion, the other she carved my hand like she was performing a carpal tunnel surgery.

Yeah. No. *Fuck. That.*

She opened the door just before I kicked it down. Barefoot, blank-faced, still not looking directly at me. I supposed beautiful things didn't want to be reminded of the ugliness in the world.

Tough luck, darlin'.

"What's two plus two?"

She blinked innocently, laying it on extra thick just to piss me off, I suspected.

"How many fingers am I holding up?" I held up three fingers in the air.

Her gaze was stubbornly glued to my chest.

Perhaps an incentive was in order. "How about a new dollhouse if you use that pretty head of yours for more than just gawking and give me an answer?"

She actually arched a sarcastic eyebrow; good to know I wasn't the only cynical asshole around here. I stepped into her personal space, eating the space between us, clasping that little pointy chin of hers that was more enticing than Becky's entire bleeding body.

"Listen carefully, Lila. I'm a bad man who does terrible things, and I do them exceptionally well. Stay out of my way, and you'll live."

She gave me a slow, provocative, *are-you-done* blink.

As it happened, I wasn't.

"But if you're a mole, if you were sent here to spy, I'm going to kill you." I rubbed her velvety chin with my thumb, back and forth.

"Probably fuck you to death. I like to press people's trigger buttons. What happened with Becky tonight won't even be the appetizer, *Gealach*."

Her unbothered response came in the form of peeking over my shoulder to see if Becky was still here.

"She's gone," I said.

Lila yawned into the back of her hand, waiting for me to do the same. She had a point. Nothing was keeping me here. It was the middle of the night, and she hadn't done anything to warrant my unwelcome visit. If anything, I was the one who screwed another woman on the surface where she ate her avocado toast every morning.

We'd had a routine where we avoided each other efficiently, and there was no reason to disrupt the arrangement. Complete separation was what we'd both wanted.

People thought I was an impulsive *sonovobitch*, when really, being this level of psychopath required a good deal of strategy. I didn't just *do* shit. I thought it through. And I couldn't think of one good reason why I was standing here in front of her instead of tending to my million and one pressing businesses.

Still, something in me refused to let it go.

Whatever that something was, it wasn't logical.

"Next time you see me preoccupied, you'll walk away or join the fun." I dropped my fingers from her chin.

Another vacant stare.

"While we're at it—don't open the door if I seek you out at night. Only let the devil in if you're prepared to let him drag you into hell."

She slammed the door in my face.

Locked the door from the inside.

Then I heard a dead bolt.

A dead bolt? I didn't install a bleeding dead bolt inside the rooms.

I stared at the door and grinned.

I forgot to mention one thing.
Once the devil wanted something?
He didn't take no for an answer.

CHAPTER FOURTEEN
LILA

I was wilting.

Like those white pretty roses I wore as a tiara at Luca's wedding. The ones that were tainted by my own blood.

I couldn't chase away the hazy memories of the night I was attacked. No matter how hard I tried to outrun them, they always caught up.

The pain. The humiliation. The faceless man grunting, leering, *taking*.

And it wasn't just that. The time was approaching when my pregnancy would be announced. Doctor appointments would be booked. It would become real, and I wasn't ready to be a mother. I wasn't even ready to be a wife.

Not that my husband was interested in one.

Then there was my sleep deprivation. I was exhausted and agitated, prone to making mistakes. I should've never smiled at Tiernan spitefully. That opened a Pandora's box. Now he suspected I was spying for my family. And he told me exactly what punishment I'd receive if he deemed his suspicion to be true.

Mama was in Chicago. There had been some issues with Luca and his wife. Sofia left the house, and Papa sent Mama to Sofia's parents to try to calm her down. Mama wanted to bring me along, but apparently my *stronzo* of a husband denied the request.

Now I was stuck in the Gothic cathedral-turned-tavern, all alone and with nothing to do.

I didn't have my Kindle nor any physical books. Mama said it was too much of a risk, in case Tiernan found them. I was running out of pages in my sketchpad.

I had a little money. Cash. But I couldn't leave the apartment. Guards were swarming all over the place. A part of me wanted to knock on the door opposite ours. But ultimately, I was too scared to find out who awaited behind it.

What if it was Becky? Or another mistress?

In lieu of entertainment, I started toying with my phone. I familiarized myself with the settings. With the different icons that seemed to yield to my command each time I touched them. There were a lot of options to choose from. Books to read, games to play, articles to explore. It appeared that the entire, whole wide world was sitting in my palm, just waiting for me to discover it. The same message kept popping up, though, infuriating me to no end.

No internet connection.

No internet connection.

No internet connection.

A frustrated growl tore out of my mouth. I shook my head, tossing the phone onto my bed beside me. A tremor shot up my spine. A sign of the entrance door slamming shut. I froze.

It was only four in the afternoon. Tiernan should be at work, probably checking on his gambling joints and whorehouses.

Who the hell just walked in?

Maybe one of his guards decided to take a spin on the helpless girl.

I jerked open my nightstand drawer and pulled out a butcher knife. Tiernan had forgotten to hide it when I first moved in. Rookie mistake. He had cleared out the apartment of everything else lethal. I tucked the phone into the waistband of my sweatpants and advanced toward the hallway.

My heart dropped at the silhouette of a long-legged woman in knee-high Louboutin boots and a black faux fur coat. Huge Miu Miu sunglasses covered her face.

Lovely. Another one of my husband's sex workers, I thought before she spun toward me, her marvelous bloodred hair flinging in slow motion across her shoulders.

Tierney.

"Oh, good. You're still alive." She tore the sunglasses from her face, tossing them onto the kitchen island along with her Chanel bag. She strutted to the fridge. "Tiernan asked me to check on you."

He did? Why? He was perfectly happy to let me rot here alone for two weeks.

"Is that a butcher knife in your hand?" Her face popped from the fridge, which she closed with a kick of her stiletto, hugging fresh eggs and a jar of olives to her chest. "Can't blame you, girl. I want to kill my brother at least five times a day." She rolled her sparkling emerald eyes. "The only thing stopping me at this point is selfishness. What if I ever need a kidney donor, you know?"

I placed the knife on the counter, watching her in fascination. I'd never met a woman who was so unapologetically herself. Every Camorra woman I knew tried to fit into the mold the men in her life created for her.

"*Jaysus*, it's boiling in here. He lets you put the thermostat on seventy-six?" She peeled off her coat, revealing a burgundy evening dress, almost the color of her hair. "He has it bad for you, girl. In the twenty-eight years we've spent together, he hasn't once let me close a window to fight the chill."

I did change the thermostat on my third day here. It was originally set to forty-two. Even two pairs of socks and a puffy sweater couldn't ward off the cold. My guess was he hadn't noticed. He was barely home, anyway.

Also…twenty-eight? That was his age? I was only eighteen. He already had an unfair advantage over me without adding life experience into the mix.

Placing my elbows against the kitchen island, I studied her, waiting for an explanation for why she was here. Tierney arranged the food items on the other side of the island, extracting tiny ciabatta buns from a paper bag I hadn't noticed before.

"Tiernan said you're losing a bunch of weight. He wants the deal with the Camorra to be fruitful, so he asked that I make sure you eat. Don't worry. I won't force you." She flashed me a smart-ass smile. "You'll *want* to eat my Tunisian fricassee. It's decadent."

I noticed she had a tattoo running from the side of her neck to her shoulder.

Oderint Dum Metuant.

It looked faded, blue, and uneven. The kind of tattoo you'd get from an amateur in prison.

Tiernan had the exact same one, I realized. They probably got it together.

"My God, look at you." She reached across the island, snatching my jaw between her black almond nails, angling my head left and right. "You're breathtaking. You look like a younger Doutzen Kroes."

I had no idea what she just said. Maybe I misread her lips. The sleep deprivation was really taking its toll on me.

Tierney continued chatting away, not letting the fact that I didn't respond to her stop her or even slow her down.

"My secret ingredient is this." She drummed her fingernails over a small glass jar with a red paste inside it. "Pilpelchuma instead of harissa. It's a chili garlic paste. I think your Italian palate will appreciate it." She winked, then went on to drain a tuna can and dump a few eggs and potatoes into boiling water. "Tiernan and I spent a few months in North Africa hiding from…oh, let's call them *eager friends*." She chopped parsley and red onion thinly. "We were in hiding, fourteen, and school wasn't on the menu, so I had a lot of spare time to learn how to cook, ride, drive, survive." She hitched a shoulder up. "We've become *very* good at surviving, by the way. In case you want to kill him."

My brain screeched to a halt. Something didn't add up. Before our nuptials, I oversaw Enzo and Luca discussing Tiernan. They said he lived in Ireland until he was fourteen, which was when his father moved him and his siblings to New York. No one mentioned anything about North Africa.

I knew next to nothing about my husband's background. Shame Tierney couldn't be trusted. I'd love to pick her brain.

"But enough about my glamorous life. What's going on with you? How are you settling in?" Tierney licked the sharp knife in her hand, tongue lolling across the green-leafed edge. She slapped a generous amount of the red paste onto the now deep-fried bread. She then filled the bread with soft-boiled potatoes, tuna, sliced boiled egg, parsley, and prune-like black olives dripping oil. The sandwich overflowed.

She turned to face me, sighing at my stubborn silence. "You can trust me. I have no loyalty to T. Not since he let your cunt of a brother dictate my love life. Do you know Achilles makes me walk around with a chaperone to keep me from screwing people?"

I didn't, but it sounded exactly like something Achilles would do. It did surprise me that he bothered in the first place. Unlike Luca and Enzo, Achilles never took an interest in another human seriously enough to make an effort.

I winced sympathetically. She caught the gesture, her pouty lips quirking to one corner slyly. "My day shift bodyguard is waiting outside the apartment right now. A Camorra soldier. Do you happen to know how to get rid of those?"

I almost shook my head. *Almost.* I'd never gotten rid of a bodyguard before. Never tried.

"So far, I've only managed to make their time with me miserable but not shake them off completely. I drag them for days-long shopping sprees and gossip sessions with the most boring socialites

I know." She plucked a spatula from a cabinet, pointing it at me. "I used to strip in front of them and make them watch. Drove them nuts. The entire exercise was to keep me from having sex with other men. So I blue-balled Achilles's staff. I'm sure they told him, because they're no longer permitted to enter my bedroom." She stopped, beaming conspiratorially. "Or apartment, for that matter."

She pressed the spatula to the top of the sandwich, locking all the juices and ingredients in. I rounded the island so I could stand next to her and see what she said.

"My brother is more toxic than a king cobra. Unfortunately, you can't choose your family and metabolism, so this is what I have to work with. But I'm only loyal to myself. If you want to be friends, we can be friends. I'll keep any secrets you have. And if you help me get rid of Achilles…" She trailed off. "We could help each other, you know? We women have to stick together. Especially in the chauvinistic underground world."

Her offer was tempting. Almost as much as the mouthwatering sandwich she slid onto a plate and dragged in my direction. She also made me a smoothie from frozen mango, banana, strawberries, and Greek yogurt with a dash of date syrup. Maybe it was because I finally had company, or maybe it was because I hadn't eaten properly in weeks, but I ravaged the food and smoothie in four minutes flat. She stared at me like I was a forest animal making up for lost time after months of hibernation.

I sat back on the chair at the dining table, filled with gratitude. I wished I could thank her, but I didn't trust her enough. She sat opposite me, watching me intently. I liked her a lot, despite her affiliation with my husband. And I was horrified by what my brother was putting her through.

"Hey. Let me program my number into your phone." She reached for the cell phone Mama gave me, which sat at the table between us. "What's your passcode?"

Shit. Shit. Shit.

The phone was supposed to be a secret. I wasn't supposed to know how to have one, let alone know how to operate it. I charged it in my walk-in closet, under layers of clothes, and only brought it outside because I thought Tierney was an attacker who broke inside.

There was no point denying I could operate it at this point. The lie would only be more glaring, since I obviously walked around with it. I pried it from her shiny nails, punching the four digits and handing it back to her. She frowned as she programmed in her number.

"Why are you not connected to the internet? Did Tiernan not give you the Wi-Fi?" She laughed, swinging her gaze to me.

Her smile dropped when she saw my face. The mixture of desperation and hope that shone through it. She licked her lips.

"Want me to give it to you? I steal his Wi-Fi on the daily. Eat the rich, right?"

I knew what she was doing. She was trying to lure me into showing her I understood her. I shouldn't play along. It was dangerous. And yet...

Digging my fingernails into the skin of my palms, I nodded slowly.

She sucked in a breath and quickly clicked a few things on my phone, giving it back to me.

"Done."

I smiled a thank-you, hoping I wasn't going to regret putting my trust in her. I'd never had a friend before. But if I could have one...I wanted it to be her.

"I better head out." She peered around. "I'm going to an Emilia Spencer art exhibition."

My face lit up at the mention of the artist. I loved her work. Mama even bought me a cherry-blossom painting of hers for my seventeenth birthday. It fit my old room nicely with all the pink.

"What, you like her?" Tierney drummed her nails on the table. "She's supposed to be good. Honestly? I know jack shit about art.

But her husband's a bigwig, and I promised Frankie I'd try to get him to endorse Wolfe for a second term."

Frankie, as in Francesca Keaton. Wife of President Keaton. Papa always went on about how unfair it was that the Irish were good friends with the president, even though his wife was Italian American.

"Hey, you wanna come?" Tierney frowned. "I can introduce you to Emilia. Super sweet lady. Can't say the same about her husband."

I hesitated before shaking my head in response. If I came with her, it'd be an admission of what I was—and what I *wasn't*. I wasn't ready for that.

Tierney sighed, stood up, then leaned to squeeze my shoulder. "I'll come again soon. *Eat.*"

She departed, leaving me with working internet and a lot of free time.

Three hours later, I was sitting with my back pressed against the wall of my walk-in closet, my phone plugged into its charger, reeling.

I could barely breathe.

The internet was full of things. Helpful things. Terrifying things. So many inventions I didn't know existed.

Smart gloves that help hearing-impaired people speak.

Vibration bracelets to alert you to different sounds around you.

Robotic translators.

Transcription apps for phone calls.

Even a cinema app that tells you about films playing in your area with subtitles and audio descriptions.

I was floored. The options were infinite, and all of them could help me in my journey as a hearing-impaired person. I wondered if Mama knew about all these things. If so, why didn't she say anything?

The only constant in my life, the sole thing keeping me

grounded, was the knowledge that Mama would always do the right thing for me.

Now, I wasn't so sure anymore.

A quick search showed me so many options and shortcuts to make my life more enjoyable. And yet, I was never made aware of them. Moreover, Mama actively forbade me from using the internet. *Why?*

It only further fed the flame of my rising anger.

Funny, how I used to think I was content. Safe in my little bubble of security.

The last eighteen years felt like a lie, a sham.

A cage my own mother shoved me into, then locked the door, and threw the key into the ocean.

The bubble had burst, the bars melted, and I could now see clearly into the future.

Either I showed people who I was and demanded to be treated with respect.

Or I'd end up exactly like my mother.

Invisible, inconsequential, and bitter.

CHAPTER FIFTEEN
TIERNAN

Tierney: She ate everything. You need to pay her some attention. It's not her fault her parents are assholes and her husband is psychotic.

I stared at the text message my sister sent me.

I never cared what women put in their mouths unless it was my cock, and my wife was no exception. Until now.

Lila had been losing weight. A lot of it.

Now, I wasn't an expert, but I was pretty sure she was supposed to gain, not lose, weight in her condition. Infuriatingly enough, her beauty didn't diminish along with the rest of her frame. She remained too delectable for her own good.

Her beauty wasn't here nor there for me. What I needed was to make sure this woman didn't drop dead from malnutrition. The Ferrantes' army was crucial for my plans against the Rasputins.

If I wanted my siblings safe, I needed to finish them off.

I knew the solution to my predicament. Namely, to stop vying for every World's Worst Husband Guinness record. I could do that. In theory, anyway. My chief problem was that her absolute dryshite of a mother refused to send over any of her staff to keep my wife company.

I didn't have time to play house with little girls. Figured the best course of action was to assign her someone she knew and trusted.

I'd called Luca and asked him which of the staff Lila would like with her. He said she'd want Imma.

When I called Chiara to ask her for the woman, she flat-out refused.

"You didn't let me take her with me to Chicago, and now you want a babysitter for her?" she'd barked. "Fat chance, *stronzo*."

"She's not going anywhere without proper Irish security, and I can't send my soldiers to Chicago because the Outfit would decapitate them before the sun's up," I'd explained stoically. "Punishing her through me is the height of idiocy. Surely, you're not that fucking daft. The family eejit is Enzo."

Enzo wasn't really stupid, but he was both perky and agreeable, which was almost worse.

"My daughter shouldn't be living with you for another minute, Callaghan."

"Bitching about the situation won't fix it," I'd volleyed. "Your daughter looks like a corpse. She isn't eating or sleeping. She is under my care, and we both know I don't give two shites. Either you send someone over to put her back together or watch her slow and painful death," I'd threatened. "Happy to send pictures."

I'd thought this would make her put the damn maid in one of their executive cars and send her my way.

To my surprise, the witch stood her ground.

"Let her die, then. See how that works out for you. My husband might not care much, but my sons?" She tutted. "They'd kill anyone with an Irish last name in your zip code."

My fingers flew over the screen now.

> Tiernan: Cancel all your engagements for the next few
> months. Your new job is to feed her and make sure
> she sleeps.

> Tierney: She's not a Tamagotchi, Tiernan.
>
> Tiernan: Tell me about it. She costs more than twenty bucks. So act accordingly.

My sister replied with a middle finger emoji, forever the picture of eloquence and grace.

I thrust my phone into my back pocket, then proceeded to unlock my apartment door. It was eerily quiet, the only audible sound coming from the industrial fridge in the kitchen.

Spending time with my wife was at the bottom of my to-do list, but bigger sacrifices had been made throughout history to achieve one's objective.

Who knew? Maybe she'd try to kill me again and things would actually get interesting.

I raised my fist to knock on Lila's bedroom door, realizing it was slightly ajar.

A rare oversight. Lila was an expert at locking herself away from me.

Taking her error as an invitation, I stepped inside, finding the room empty. The adjoined en-suite bathroom was also vacant, which meant she was probably in her walk-in closet. I stopped at the night-stand next to her bed. Her leather-bound sketchbook sat there, a pencil tucked between the pages. I made no effort to be silent or discreet. I figured if she was naked, it'd give her time to get dressed before she greeted me.

I flipped the sketchbook open, my brow furrowing. I didn't know what I expected. Maybe finger painting or stick figures of people with lines for bodies and circles for heads. But it wasn't *this*.

This was…

Fuck me, it was *spectacular*.

A pencil drawing, realistic and shaded to its finest detail, like an old black and white picture.

The portrait of a man was vivid, alive, and…familiar. Very familiar.

Hold. The. Fuck. Up.

Tate Blackthorn.

My wife drew Tate Blackthorn's entire dick-ass face. From *memory*. Smoking a cigarette, staring into an invisible camera, his cocky half-smirk on full display.

The urge to burn down the sketchbook along with the entire street slammed into me, but I suppressed it. Of course, my wife, who was knocked up with someone else's baby, was also obsessed with my archenemy.

Of. Fucking. Course.

Perhaps she wasn't raped, after all? Tate was at Luca's wedding. She obviously adored the motherfucker. Yes, he was married, but he wouldn't be the first filthy rich mogul to cheat on his wife when a young, pretty thing dangled herself in front of him.

What if she opened those creamy legs of hers for him?

I tipped my head back, taking a deep, greedy breath. My list of people to murder kept growing. The saying was accurate—there really was no rest for the wicked. But, I mean, a fucking afternoon off wouldn't hurt.

Tate lived in the UK. I didn't have time to start expanding my business into Europe.

Her drawing subject aside, my wife was either a savant or a genius. For her sake, I hoped she was the former. I'd hate to kill her and the unborn baby in her belly.

No.

That wasn't true.

The truth was, killing them would solve many of my problems. It'd just create a thousand new ones in the process.

Feeling much less inclined to honor her privacy now, I dropped the sketchbook on her nightstand, proceeding into her walk-in closet.

She was, indeed, dressed.

She also had her head buried in a cell phone she wasn't supposed to own, sitting cross-legged on the floor, eyes glued to the screen. Her pupils moved from side to side.

Left. Right. Left. Right.

She can read.

Venom spread inside my veins.

Can you read?

What else can you do?

Are you here to spy?

Is Blackthorn your baby daddy?

Are you texting him now?

I wanted to pick her up, pin her to her bed, and fuck every single answer out of her.

Or, I marveled, maybe she was watching something. Her mother mentioned she let her watch classical concerts. After all, this wasn't the response of someone who was just caught doing something they shouldn't. She completely ignored my presence.

I rapped on the wall, crossing my arms and leaning against the doorframe.

She didn't look up.

Little shit.

I stepped inside, entering her line of vision. Her head jolted up, and her mouth dropped open.

Recognition and horror filled her pretty eyes.

"Hello, *wifey.*"

She scrambled to her feet, shoving the phone into her pocket and jutting her chin up defiantly. The facade of an insentient child was slipping almost as fast as my patience for this marriage.

I knew asking outright wouldn't get me anywhere. Lila was a Ferrante through and through. If not by blood, then by nature. I couldn't break her through torture.

But hey, it'd still be fun trying.

"Do you like fucking married men, *Gealach?*" I pushed off the doorframe, entering her domain. After that sketchbook, she couldn't convince me she was intellectually challenged if her life depended on it. In a way, it did.

She stared at me steadily, refusing to balk.

"Do you like spreading your legs for older men?" I strolled leisurely in her direction. Blackthorn was twice her age. She had no business sucking the old man's cock.

"Do you call him Daddy?" I taunted.

She answered with a slow, bored blink. She wasn't going to fall down on her knees and beg for forgiveness. My young wife had pride, and fire in her eyes.

I stopped when my abs were flush against her chest. She was tiny. Finishing her would be easier than killing a fly.

"You know he'd never leave his wife for you." I arched an eyebrow, smirking. "He's crazy about her. Was fully prepared to give me the keys to his kingdom when I kidnapped her. You were just a quick fuck."

Her cheeks flushed, and finally, *finally*, the mask slipped and her emotions showed.

"Did you fuck him?" I palmed her face, tilting it up, forcing her to stare at the grotesque husband of hers. Without the eye. Without the *soul*.

Her nostrils flared. She said nothing.

"Answer." I clutched her jaw tightly.

She spat in my face in response. Her saliva hit my left cheek.

"Grave mistake, sweetheart."

It was time to terrorize an answer out of her.

I reared my fist backward.

Lila whipped her head sideways, bracing herself for the hit, but didn't close her eyes. Her jaw locked, her eyes blazed with anger. My knuckles landed square against the wall above her shoulder, denting it. The crack looked like spiderwebs.

A soft gasp escaped her. The first time she made a sound. It was so fucking soft I second-guessed I really heard it.

Shit. What was I doing, unraveling over a child bride?

It was time to try another tactic.

Threatening her with rape, murder, and the decimation of her already destroyed life didn't work. Maybe I'd get more bees with honey.

"There's an Italian deli down the street." I stepped back. "Make yourself presentable. Wear something that isn't fucking pink." I grabbed my jaw, working it from side to side. "You could use some fresh air." She hadn't left the apartment since her mother left for Chicago.

As expected, she didn't answer. But her teeth captured her lower lip contemplatively.

She didn't hate the idea of leaving the house.

A weakness. I can work with that.

I pressed on.

"They have homemade gelato."

Her throat bobbed with a swallow. She was conflicted. Confused. Torn between loathing me and longing to escape the cage I shoved her into.

She needed to eat, get better, and not stand in my way of dismantling the Bratva. The rest could be figured out later.

For instance, with what method did I plan on executing Tatum Blackthorn?

My current preference was dousing him in gasoline and making a nice campfire out of him. Roast some s'mores with the fire of his flesh and make her eat it.

I'd make her watch, too.

"Move it, Barbie." I stepped sideways to clear the path for her. "Hurry up, and you just might make it to see the famous Hunts Point sunset."

We walked in silence side by side on the littered street. Logic dictated I lived where I ruled, so Hunts Point it was.

Fintan lived with Da in the suburbs. They didn't care for rough neighborhoods. Tierney and I, however, showed our strength by making it our stronghold.

It made little difference that my da wasn't around. Tyrone never truly was. Technically, he was alive. But for all intents and purposes, he was good as dead. Murdered the night they killed Mam. He was a ghost. Living. Breathing. Attending meetings. Pretending to be alive. I'd been managing the family business since I was a wee lad. Tierney and Fintan helped.

Lila was bundled in a pink faux fur coat covering a pink flowery dress. A silent fuck you to my order that she wear something less childish. Other than hurling a whole-ass flamingo on herself, she did everything to let me know she intended to do the exact opposite of anything I asked.

She drew hungry, curious gazes that were promptly snuffed out by my lethal, intimidating glares.

I sowed terror everywhere I went, but especially in the South Bronx, where my word was gospel.

The orange sun dipped under the decrepit buildings, swallowed by urban decay. Lila took everything in with wide, alert eyes.

We entered Maggiano's, where I picked up a basket and jerked my chin to signal her to start loading it. The food in my apartment left a lot to be desired. I preferred nourishing, dense in protein nutriments. Shchi soups, caviar, cold meats, pickled eggs, fermented dairy, and black breads.

Life had taught me that anything that could entice you could weaken you. I ate like a beggar and fought like a king. And I never loved anything that could die, other than my siblings.

My wife didn't realize it, strolling through the narrow aisles of the minimart, but everybody was staring at her. A shelf stocker fell off his ladder following her with his eyes, a woman with a baby and drab clothes sucked in a breath when she passed her, and a group of pimpled teenagers froze in their spot, practically drooling.

Lila tossed various dry pastas into her basket, along with white truffle butter, cherry jam, and biscotti. When she reached for a top shelf on her toes to grab a lemon panettone, I stepped behind her and put it in the basket myself. The top of her head didn't even reach my chin. And when I looked down and saw her tiny figure engulfed between my large feet, a visual of her getting brutally raped on Crimson Key by some asshole assaulted my mind, making my fist involuntarily clench.

She ducked her head under my arm, hurrying toward the deli and plucking a number from a ticket dispenser. She paused, realizing I could see that she possessed the forethought to do that.

I nonchalantly strolled to the front of the long line of people and motioned for her to join me. She winced, clearly unhappy about cutting the line, but pointed at what she wanted quickly, not making a scene.

Olives. Glazed artichokes. Focaccia. Tuna-stuffed red chili peppers.

When we headed to the register, her eyes halted on a gelato display.

She needed to gain weight, or her brothers would take her away and my entire operation would flush down the shitters. I snatched her arm and marched her to the gelato. Her eyes flared at the sight of the pastel-colored ice cream. She swallowed hard, but didn't make a move.

I led by example, ordering three scoops. She did the same, pointing at the colors. When we got to the register to pay for everything, the owner's son—a guy in his mid-twenties with a mushroom haircut and juiced-up muscles—couldn't rip his gaze from her long enough to scan our groceries.

That he had two fucking working eyes to admire her with pissed me off to begin with. On top of that, he looked exactly like the dashing Italian guy she'd probably end up with if she didn't lie about her condition. It was the cherry on the shit cake. He grinned at her, and she gave him a shy smile. The chances of him living to see next year significantly dropped.

"Did you find everything you were looking for?" he cooed.

"She found a husband who owns the entire neighborhood," I answered on her behalf. His gaze jerked to me. Recognition flashed in his eyes, and his face drained of color.

"Y—yes, sir. Of course. I was just trying to be polite." Gulping, he pushed our shit faster into grocery bags, forgetting to scan half the items.

"Being too polite to my wife might be hazardous to your health."

"I—I'm sorry. I didn't realize…"

"Stupidity is not an excuse. This is your first and final warning."

Once he got everything packed, I sent one of my errand boys to unload the groceries in my apartment and took Lila to the waterline. The direct view was of Rikers Island—not exactly the lights of Paris—and left a lot to be desired. Then again, I never romanced anyone in my life and wasn't going to make exceptions for my wife.

All the benches overlooking the water were taken, but one wrathful gaze toward an elderly couple occupying the closest bench sent them tumbling to the other end of the street.

Lila settled on the bench; her brows crumpled in disapproval.

We watched the water. I sifted through my gray matter for an olive branch to extend to her. It wasn't in my nature to appease, or even to negotiate, but Tierney was right. I needed this girl alive.

"You can be happy here," I lied, holding my gelato without eating it.

She gave me a questioning look, her delicate frown deepening.

Progress. Her isolation from her mother took its toll.

"As long as you don't cross me and play by my rules, I'll let you thrive. You can come and go as you please. Hire your own staff. I can buy you a place next to your parents." *One I would never set fucking foot in.* "You can pursue your artistic ambitions. Study." Her face lit up before she was able to conceal it.

I continued, knowing I had her full attention now, and not for the wrong reason for a change.

"Luca told me you go to Ischia every summer. You can still do that. Not this year, but the next one." I wasn't going to stick around for next year. What did I care, throwing empty promises in the air?

She had the audacity to scowl at me. The little shit might have let Tate Blackthorn touch her. *Impregnate* her. It wasn't particularly significant in any way, other than the carnage-fueling thought that he touched something that was mine.

She squinted at the horizon, popping the little spoon into her mouth, suckling it. The motion sent a throbbing ache straight to my cock. Sweet and merciful Jesus. I did not believe in karma, God, or anything else not backed by science, but it appeared I was paying for my sins by marrying the most enticing creature on planet Earth, knowing damn well I couldn't have her.

The ice cream was melting in my hand, and I tossed it into the trash can next to the bench, irritated that I now had a sticky hand on top of a raging hard-on with nowhere to sink it into.

One of those problems could be mitigated by a quick hand wash. The other was here to stay.

Lila finished her gelato and the waffle cone that came with it. Quietly, she picked up my ice cream-covered hand and uncurled my fingers. She twisted her head, holding my fingers open as she stared at my palm.

She wanted to check the injury she inflicted on me. Unfortunately, it was covered in green gelato.

She studied the gelato stain, frowned, then brought my hand to her mouth, flattening her hot, wet tongue over it and licking it off me.

I growled, my blood roaring in my veins. Euphoric desire flooded me. This felt better than sodomizing any professional escort I'd ever laid hands on.

She was dangerous.

For my plans.

For my goals.

For that useless thing inside my chest.

The mark resurfaced. The wound had healed, leaving only a pale, pink scar. She rubbed her tiny thumb over it, and that simple move threatened to change my entire brain chemistry. I yanked my hand back and stood up.

"Enough." I buttoned my coat with one hand. "You're not a fucking dog, Lila. Stop licking everything you encounter."

I spent the walk back to the apartment silently contemplating why the fuck I didn't kill her at that fountain and save myself this headache. I'd never shown mercy to anyone before.

And the one thing I saved just might end up killing me.

CHAPTER SIXTEEN
TIERNAN

"Fuck."

Pressing my hand to a four-inch gash in my torso to stop the bleeding, I collapsed into the passenger seat next to my brother in his nickel-gray Porsche.

Fintan floored it before the cops arrived to scrape off the body I left three streets down from Fermanagh's. An Albanian aspiring mobster had tried dealing meth on my turf and had the audacity to stab me when I informed him he was trespassing.

Sighing, I tossed the two bullet cases I collected from the crime scene into the central console for my brother to get rid of.

I hated amateurs. People should have to pass a bar to get into the field of organized crime. I swear my line of work attracted the stupidest people on planet Earth.

"Do you have to bleed all over my 993 Turbo, Tierney boy?" Fin flicked his green eyes to me. I knew he was only half joking. He loved that bleeding car.

"Drop me off and I'll walk home."

"Home!" he roared. "I'm taking you straight to the hospital, little brother." His breath reeked of whiskey.

"I'll wrap it up when I get back." I removed my hand from the stab wound, peering at it through my black dress shirt. Blood gushed out in a thick river. I groaned, pushing the base of my palm back onto it.

"You sure?" Fintan had one arm slung against the open window.

"Positive. I'm not going to Barnabas at two in the morning unless I need my head stitched back to my body. Even then, I'd probably cab it to Presbyterian."

"Why not?" Fintan pushed, scowling at the road ahead. "Natalie works there. She's always happy to see you."

"I bet she is. I put her through med school."

Natalie was a poor girl from the neighborhood who needed a leg up. She also happened to prefer anal, so we'd had an agreement of sorts, where I paid for her school and, in return, she was my fuck buddy. I hadn't seen her in almost a year, though. Not since she started her residency.

"Drop me at Fermanagh's," I said. "And for shit's sake, go over the books again and tell Da to send someone to pick up the supplies in the port."

"Whatever you say, lad."

"You've enough alcohol in your system to drown a mermaid."

"I only had a couple pints," he mumbled defensively. "I can hold a drink, ya know."

"The problem is you usually hold eight or nine. Per night."

He sulked. "I said it's under control."

"Tell that to your 200K debt in your own bleeding casino." I rarely broached this subject, but I rode a criminal high whenever I was in pain. It got my dick hard and I tended to look either for a fight or a fuck. And since fucking wasn't in my near future, I chose a fight.

"I've made progress, mate. I did." His fingers danced around the steering wheel, knuckles paling in anger. "I'm going to therapy now. Putting in the work."

"How long since you hit the blackjack table?"

"Over three weeks. I swear on my life."

I narrowed my good eye at him.

He laughed nervously. "I mean it! Ask my therapist."

There was no need. I had eyes in every underground casino the Callaghans and Ferrantes owned.

I nodded. "Keep that shit up, Fin. Once we go after the Bratva, all of us become targets. You need to stay sharp."

"I am, brother. *Mionnaím ar uaigh ár máthar.*"

My jaw clenched. Tierney and I knew very little Gaeilge. Not for lack of desire on our part.

I'd never set foot in my own motherland. Neither did she.

Everything I was—the accent, the tradition, the pride, the flag—was a sham. Da was an Irishman. So was Fintan. Not us. Tierney and I had always been a separate unit from them. Only difference was, I loved Tyrone and Fintan ferociously, never held what happened to us against them. Tierney never forgot and never forgave.

"How's Maggie doing?" I changed the subject.

"Riding my ass about proposing, now that my wee brother is married. Gave me a deadline until Christmas. And Becky?"

"Why would you ask me about a slag I see every other month when I have a wife?"

"She isn't much of a wife, though, is she?" He parked the Porsche in front of Fermanagh's, cutting the ignition. "I don't like what this is doing to your reputation, brother. Being accused of sleeping with this girl-child. I still think it was a mistake."

"It's done now." I popped the door open, swinging my leg to the sidewalk.

Dizzy. So dizzy. *Fuck.*

Before I got out, I glanced behind my shoulder, pausing.

"Did you forget something?" Fintan blinked.

"Yeah," I said. "Drink on the job one more time, and I'll kill you."

I staggered into my dark apartment, clutching at my chest.

Perhaps skipping the hospital was a mistake, after all. I based the change of heart on the three liters of blood I smeared across the staircase like a human fucking slug.

With a hiss, I dragged myself along the hallway to the master bedroom, crashing against the wall, marring it in red. Once in my bathroom, I flicked the light on and unbuttoned my dress shirt.

I was no pussy, but this was a serious knife injury. He went deep. I was surprised there wasn't an exit point.

Sensing my need for privacy, my wife, who had never shown interest in spending time with me, appeared at my bathroom door. Now she wanted my company. She wore her pale hair in a messy bun, and a white satin babydoll that really brought out every delectable curve in her body.

"Now's not a good time." I popped the first aid kit open, lining up Betadine, tape, and gauze on the bathroom counter.

Through the mirror, I saw her examining the trail of blood I left behind, slack-jawed. Eh, so this was why she ventured here. Probably hoped to find me dead.

"Either use that open mouth to suck my cock or walk out of here and let me stitch myself in peace." I kept applying pressure to my wound while unscrewing the Betadine spray with my teeth.

She loitered at the threshold, likely emboldened by the fact that I was too preoccupied to follow up on my threat. Blood slinked from between my fingers. I needed to call one of my soldiers on-site to assist me.

My wife continued to stare, nibbling on the dead skin around her thumbnail.

"Jesus fuck, Lila." I swiveled toward her. "Get out. Don't worry about the blood. I'll send someone to clean that shit up."

She grabbed my wrist, her sharp blue eyes dancing like cold fire.

She tugged me out of the bathroom. I didn't have time for this nonsense, but something compelled me to humor her.

That something was more than likely my moronic dick.

She led me to my bed, where she put a gentle hand on my

shoulder and eased me down, fluffing my pillows and laying me across the mattress.

Lila put her palm up, signaling me to wait, then ambled back to the bathroom. I heard the water in the sink running. She returned to the bed and flicked on my bedside lamp. I grunted as light flooded the room. My wife parked her pert little ass on the edge next to me, peeling my hand off the open wound.

Clutching my shoulder to keep me still, she used a wet, warm towel to wipe off the blood, then sprayed the shit out of the wound with Betadine. My nostrils flared, the burn eating away at my flesh like acid. "Bollocks."

She gave me a disapproving glare to let me know she didn't appreciate my language, then pressed clean gauze to it.

"Get more gauze and tape," I bit out. "I'll wrap it up."

Her gaze dropped to my lips, like it always did. If she wanted a kiss, all she had to do was ask.

She shook her head adamantly, glaring at me as she motioned with her hands. At first, it looked like she was holding invisible cutlery. Then, I realized, she was mimicking suturing.

Something clicked in my brain.

She put me down for elevation, disinfected the wound, and was now draining it before…

Stitching me up?

What was she, a bleeding nurse now?

"If you don't know how to stitch, knock on Tierney's door down the hall. She'll call for help." Doubtful I had enough time, but I wasn't in the mood to be poked a bunch of times.

Her eyebrows slammed together. She looked pissed off I doubted her abilities.

"Fine. There's a suturing kit in the cabinet in the bathroom," I groaned. "Don't bother bringing the analgesic spray. I thrive on pain."

She moseyed back into the en-suite bathroom. I followed

her with my eyes, wondering how she was going to get out of this one.

She just revealed her entire hand to me. Not only did she not have any intellectual issues, she also knew how to treat potentially fatal wounds. Did she tend to her brothers like this? The thought of her touching other men—even her kin—made my skin crawl.

Lila returned. She removed the gauze and resprayed the wound to disinfect it, then used the needle driver to grab the needle. Her hands were steady, her breathing calm. Pushing the needle in a ninety-degree angle at the edge of my wound, she began stitching me up.

I stared at her face. She looked like an angel. One I'd very much like to stick my cock into. She sewed with stoic practicality. It was her eyes that gave her intelligence. They saw everything, and I wondered if they also noticed how out of my fucking depth I was where she was concerned.

She was everything I couldn't control, and it drove me wild.

"How long are we going to do this song and dance for, Lila?" My gaze drifted down her satin babydoll, to those full, perky breasts and tight nipples. Down her flat stomach, to the junction where her panties were hidden by sun-kissed, slender thighs. "Where you pretend to be incapable and I pretend to buy it?"

Her throat bobbed with a swallow.

"They call me Deathless, you know," I hissed, my voice groggy. "I survived six assassination attempts and fuck knows how many more gunfights. Wouldn't it be ironic if what takes me out is a sloppy stab in the chest by a fucking nobody?"

Lila's face remained impassive. Her hands on my bare flesh were sweet torture. Her fingers tingled and teased, like little flames licking at my skin.

I wondered what other talents she was hiding.

And if Tate Blackthorn knew about them.

"You should let me bleed out," I mused, watching her unwavering expression. "You know you want to."

Not a muscle in that perfect face of hers twitched. She wasn't going to break. Not even crack. For a reason beyond my understanding, Lila decided to spare my life, but didn't deem me trustworthy enough for her confessions. For her words.

I focused on the delicate contours of her face, wondering when I last saw something quite as superb. Never, was the definite answer.

"I'm not letting you go, you know." My voice was calm, final, before I let my eye flutter shut. "You're mine. Only fucking mine. Till my last breath."

She pricked my skin with her needle, extra hard.

And I smirked, knowing she heard me.

CHAPTER SEVENTEEN
LILA

Stupid, stupid, stupid.

Why did I help him? Why didn't I look the other way and let karma finish the job?

I'd been awake as usual, staring at the ceiling, when I felt the sharp bang of the entrance door reverberating through my spine. When I walked out of my room, I noticed the carnage.

I wanted to let him die…

But something inside me refused to be as ruthless as the men in my life. And while Tiernan was a terrible human, he never crossed my red lines. He didn't force himself upon me, made sure I always ate, and even took me to see the sunset.

I knew, from watching old Mama-approved movies, that allowing your wife to stab and shoot you didn't qualify as romance. However, in our world, it made for a damn decent husband.

Besides, I never missed a chance to suture.

It was my first time stitching a human. Not that he needed to know that. All my other experience was with pig bellies and chickens. Imma was a nurse back in Naples before she joined our family. She'd taught me some useful skills to help me pass the time, since I didn't go to school.

But the most dangerous thing of all wasn't Tiernan finding out, beyond any reasonable doubt, that I wasn't intellectually impaired. It wasn't even the fact that he frightened me with his even pulse and dead, abrasive stare the entire time I worked on his wound, unmoved by the pain.

No. It was the complete and utter chaos that swirled in my body at our briefest touch.

On our wedding night, I thought I needed to hurt him to feel the gooey, warm honey in the pit of my stomach. Now, I realized, I simply needed to *touch* him.

His body felt good. All lithe, sculpted muscles. Inked with tattoos I wanted to trace, and study, and maybe even kiss. Warm. Alive. *Safe.* The latter was stupid, I knew. The man promised he'd force himself on me if he found out I was a spy.

But he had so many chances.

So many opportunities to take what our world deemed was his. Yet he didn't.

The hatred I wanted so badly to cling onto was slipping between my fingers like quicksand. Maybe it was Stockholm syndrome. Or maybe I realized my ire should be directed at my father and my rapist.

Either way, Tiernan "the Deathless" Callaghan was no longer the man I hated the most.

Worse still, he no longer felt like the enemy.

CHAPTER EIGHTEEN
TIERNAN

Three days later I sat in Fermanagh's back office, surrounded by Luca, Achilles, Fintan, and Sam Brennan.

The latter was Boston's most formidable ex-mobster. Now retired in Switzerland with his doctor wife and their frankly demented number of kids.

I pulled him out of retirement because he could find a grain of salt in a pile of shit. Figured I could use reinforcements in my search for my wife's attacker since I had my own plate full.

He cost a pretty penny, but I considered every dime well spent.

"I cropped the raw CCTV footage into the twenty minutes during and after Lila took off from the ballroom." Sam swiveled his laptop toward me, flicking his finger to the screen. My wife appeared in grainy resolution, hurrying toward the exit. "My IT guy did a body count of the room and all the other wired locations on the premises. All eight hundred guests and staff were accounted for. All, aside from fifteen men that disappeared within that timeframe. I compiled them into a list."

"And you caught them leaving through the main entrance?"

Sam shook his head. "She slipped through a side exit, probably the secret passage in the wine cellar. The attacker followed her. That part's not wired."

"Show me the list."

Luca dragged it across the executive desk in my direction. I stared at the names. Two in particular popped out to me.

Tatum Blackthorn.

Angelo Bandini.

"There's also a murky shot of a man trailing behind Lila, twenty yards away." Brennan leaned in from behind me, fingers dancing on the keyboard. He fast-forwarded forty seconds after Lila left, zooming in and clearing up the resolution.

"That's a good start," my brother said.

Fintan didn't smell like the floor of a seedy nightclub this morning. A step in the right direction.

"Did we ID him?" I asked.

Sam tsked. "He never gave us a good angle. Makes you wonder if he scoped out the place in advance."

"Who from this list had been to the manor prior to the wedding?" I tapped the piece of paper, handing it back to the Ferrantes. Achilles snatched it, scowling.

"Tate and Angelo. All the rest are strangers. Most are acquaintances from the bride's side. And I'm pretty sure we can cross off the seventy-six-year-old with the oxygen tank." He pointed at some Italian man's name. "Doubt he has the stamina for the offense."

I ran a hand over my dress shirt. My wound was healing nicely. The stitches were neatly applied, dabbed with antibiotic and covered in adhesive bandages. The morning after Lila put me together, she left a note with a list of medical supplies I needed to replenish. Her silent way of admitting she was literate.

"Forget about the exit point they took," Sam said. "You need to look into every name on the list. *Every. Single. One,*" he enunciated.

I understood exactly what he meant.

"Don't cross anyone off until I say so," I ordered. The CCTV footage continued rolling on the screen, people leaving and entering through the main entrance. A movement caught my eye, and I sat up straighter.

"Brennan, roll it back."

He did, backtracking it thirty seconds.

"Stop."

I swatted him away and rolled my index along the mouse pad, moving between the twelve cameras in search of a better angle. When I found what I wanted, I zoomed in. "See that?"

"See what?"

"Our suspect. It's from a different angle. He's smirking."

It was grainy as shit, and everyone had to squint at the monitor, but they saw it, too. His upper face was hidden by one of the many marble arches in the room, but it looked like he was grinning straight into the camera.

"He's tall." Luca ran his knuckles through his stubble. "Six two, maybe six three. Look at the height difference between him and Pasqualino."

"And Caucasian," Sam added. "Wears a fine suit. But we can't make out much else."

"*Yet*," I said.

I was going to track this human cum stain down if it was the last thing I did on this overrated planet. "Run all your programs on that tape until you get a match. In the meantime," I picked up the suspect list, "I want every man of interest on this list in surveillance. PI on their tail around the clock, tap their lines, hack their phones, write a dissertation about their lives, and bring it back to me by the end of the month."

"Everyone?" Fintan repeated.

"Everyone."

"On it." My brother collected the paperwork.

"What's the sudden rush?" Luca arched a brow. "You've been perfectly content sitting on this task for weeks with no movement. Vello told us we needed to put fire under your feet to make sure you haven't forgotten."

"I haven't forgotten," I clipped out.

I had, in fact, forgotten.

But then Vello's daughter saved my life, and I felt the need to repay her somehow.

Slaughtering the man who hurt her would even the score. And the Callaghan clan would be seizing full control of Harlem as a bonus.

"Any word on Alex?" I asked Sam.

"Still in Russia, off the grid." He shook his head. "No movement in his bank accounts, either."

I jerked my chin in a nod. He'd resurface. Most of his business was in Vegas. And I needed the time to scope out his mansion, warehouses, and anywhere else I might corner him.

"You and the Ferrante girl…" Sam clicked his laptop shut, sliding it into his leather courier bag. "Is this a love match or a strategic alliance?"

"Strategic," Luca supplied.

Sam gave me a once-over, lifting a mocking brow. "Coulda sworn Callaghan has skin in the game."

I said nothing. Entertaining idiots wasn't a part of my job description.

"This is how it starts." Sam slid on his biker jacket, zipping it up.

"She's just business."

"So was Aisling, my wife." He checked his Rolex, screwing a ballcap on. "Six kids later, and it's safe to say my business turned into pleasure."

I watched him retreat, feeling sorry for him.

Just because he got attached to a pussy didn't mean it'd happen to me.

CHAPTER NINETEEN

TWENTY YEARS AGO

"Psst. Tiernan. Tierney. Over here."

Lyosha whispered from behind a batch of shaved logs. Tiernan knew better than to humor him.

He was eight now.

Old enough to climb trees and chop them into logs.

Old enough to tear a rabbit's fur from its body clean.

To crawl into darkened mining holes.

Old enough to fight, to shoot, to kill, to survive in the Siberian wilderness.

Tiernan drove his axe into a log, chopping it in half. He stood up and wiped his brow, glancing at his twin sister. Tierney was bundled in her coat, stacking the logs neatly, a silver curl of frost escaping her pink lips. Snow gathered on the tip of her lashes.

"Don't be tempted," he warned.

She shook her head, continuing with her work.

"C'mon, we can play marbles," Lyosha coaxed, his face popping from between the logs, grinning widely. His eyes were icy blue, as pale as the landscape around them, and his hair was rusty gold, the color of a king's crown. He was the pakhan's son, and that fact didn't go unnoticed; he received more food, more milk, warmer clothes, and was

allowed to skip chores. Instead of working, he was taught physics and math, classical music and literature. Knowledge he eagerly passed on to the twins.

Alex always disappeared from camp around Novy God. Igor took him to Moscow to watch ballet and fill his belly with the finest food.

"Marbles?" Tierney paused, her interest piqued. Snow caked her hair and eyebrows. Months before, she'd lost a toe to the frost. Her brother had pacified her by promising her all the pretty shoes money could buy to hide the loss when they grew up.

"Well, not marbles as such. But I found some bullet cases in the forest." Alex uncurled princely fingers, extending his hand in her direction. "We can use them instead. It's almost the same."

The twins knew they weren't allowed to play. The punishment for such an egregious offense was a bullet to the head, and neither of them wanted to die, though they weren't quite sure why.

By now, they knew how they were brought here. Knew Igor killed their mother, carved her stomach, and pulled them out. Knew they were Irish, that they had a father and a brother somewhere far away. Igor took pleasure in tossing pieces of the puzzle that was their lives in their direction, watching them scramble to put things together.

"Can't," Tiernan told Alex. "It's against the rules."

"Oh, fuck the rules." Alex snorted. "Live a little."

"If I live a little, I'll die a lot."

Alex laughed, juggling the bullet cases like a circus clown with balls.

"Suit yourself." He popped a shoulder, swiveled, and sauntered into the open mouth of the white forest.

Tierney paused once more and stared down at her palms. Every inch of them was covered in blisters and calluses. So rough was her skin that she could run a burning flame through it and still not feel a thing. She looked up longingly toward the woods.

"Not worth it," Tiernan said shortly, raising his axe and slicing another log in two.

Tierney was quiet.

All the other kids around them worked diligently. Olga weaved between them, inspecting their handiwork.

"What's the point of staying alive if we aren't living?" Tierney wondered aloud. "Look at us. They cut our tendons so we cannot run. Starve us so we cannot fight. I have never played a game. Never felt the sun on my skin. Never been loved by someone who isn't you."

"Our father loves us," Tiernan reminded her fiercely. "Our brother, too."

"Yes, well, they aren't here, are they? For all we know, they forgot about us."

A tear rolled down Tierney's cheek. It froze before it could land on the ground.

Guilt gnawed at Tiernan's gut. He hated seeing his sister unhappy. She was the only thing he had. The only thing he knew how to love.

"Thirty minutes till lunchtime," Olga announced, briskly making her way up the stairs to the main cabin to oversee the meal preparation. Girls Tierney's age prepared lunch—hot tea, black bread, a slab of butter, and if they were lucky, sardines. But Tierney was never allowed the luxury of kitchen duty. Igor said she needed to be a warrior, so one day he could send her and Tiernan to kill their father.

Tiernan knew they had thirty minutes before Olga would check on them again.

"Fine," he bit out, already regretting it. "But we'll make it quick."

They ran, following Alex's footprints in the snow.

They found him in no time, bullet cases splayed on a stump. They joined him. Alex elbowed Tiernan's rib. "Hey, don't worry. If we get caught, I'll take the fall."

He believed him.

Lyosha always shared his food, his milk, his clothes, and his warmth with him.

Time betrayed them in the same way it betrayed all kids caught up in a game. When they realized it, they ran so fast the snow seemed to melt under the ferocity of their terror.

Tiernan was the first to make it back to camp. He collided headfirst into Igor's frame.

The pakhan was standing at the door to the dining hall, blocking the entrance.

The breath was caught in Tiernan's throat.

Igor was holding his gun. He pointed at the twins with it. "You two. Come out back with me."

"Father, no!" Alex threw himself on Igor.

The man shook him off like he was a rabid animal, huffing. "They broke the rules."

"So did I." Alex straightened his spine. "I asked them to come. It was my idea."

Damn his stupid son, and damn his lack of animal instinct. The Callaghan twins were the enemy. If Alex couldn't see that, he was never going to make a good pakhan. Luckily, Natalia had given him two more sons—Jeremie and Slava. Jeremie already lived here in camp. Slava would join his brothers shortly.

Jeremie and Slava were a good mix of their parents—cold, jaded, unfeeling. Alex was tainted by Luba's DNA. Kind, caring, and abundantly generous.

"Alex, shut up," Igor barked.

"If you kill them, you'll have to kill me, too."

"Fine. I will give them a chance to survive. We'll play Russian roulette." Igor smiled. "And you, Alex, will do the honor of shooting."

Tiernan's heart stuttered to a stop. He and Tierney exchanged looks. Igor motioned for the three of them to follow him back where they came from. Alex was silent and rigid. When they arrived at the stump in the woods, Igor handed his son the gun.

"The revolver can hold six bullets. Put in three."

Alex did as he was told. He was good with guns. A great aim. A small comfort for Igor.

Lyosha aimed at Tierney first. Her chin wobbled; her eyes begged. He pulled the trigger.

Click.

It was empty. She fell down to her knees, heaving, sobbing, wetting herself. The hot liquid of her urine momentarily stole the numbness from her cold legs.

Alex turned the gun to Tiernan. Flinched.

He loved him, that was the truth of it. More than he loved his father, and his brothers, and maybe even himself.

Because Tiernan taught him how to be brave. No matter his circumstances, he refused to be a victim.

Tiernan didn't shake. His eyes didn't beg. He stared at him head-on.

"Shoot!" Igor roared.

Alex pulled the trigger, howling in pain.

Click.

Empty.

Tiernan didn't flinch. Didn't even sigh in relief. Just stood there, cold and resilient and more alive than all of them combined.

Alex dropped to one knee, vomiting onto his own lap.

"Koshchei," Igor spat out dejectedly. It was the eleventh time in eight years the little worm escaped death. So many illnesses. Accidents. Stray bullets. Rat poison his body seemed to resignedly accept. Igor was always on the verge of killing the Callaghans with his bare hands. The only thing stopping him was the knowledge that his late wife wouldn't have wanted that. Kids, no matter how sullied and evil, were precious in her eyes.

"That boy is utterly deathless. He is going to kill all of us one day."

CHAPTER TWENTY
TIERNAN

I flipped through Lila's sketchbook again while she was taking a shower.

My wife drew what she remembered, and if she by chance remembered her attacker's face, that mattered.

I didn't find any new portraits, but I did find music sheets. Dozens and dozens of them. Since Alex had taught me solfège when we were kids, I recognized some as Mozart and Beethoven. That, in itself, did not impress me. Any monkey could copy and paste music sheets from the internet. What piqued my interest were the ones I was not familiar with. And were not, in fact, classics at all.

I downloaded a piano app on my phone and played them out. They were completely original pieces. Fucking fantastic, too. Expressive, dramatic, elegant, and Gothic.

They could be someone else's. Just because Lila wrote them didn't mean she composed them.

They could.

But somehow, I knew, with stark clarity, that it was my wife who came up with them.

CHAPTER TWENTY-ONE
LILA

Mama was back from Chicago, but the relief I expected to feel never arrived.

I was clocking in eight hours of phone time a day. Researching gadgets for the impaired of hearing. There was a list sitting in the bottom of my nightstand drawer of things I wanted to purchase and try out. I needed to figure out how to order them from the internet without asking for Tiernan's help. It didn't look like the vendors accepted cash.

Unfortunately, Tiernan became even more insufferable after I saved his life. He now insisted we have dinner together every evening. He brought delicacies from the Italian deli and spent the entire length of the meal watching me through his emerald eye, chipping at the walls I built around me with his ruthlessly cold exterior without speaking one word.

He let me come and go as I pleased, as long as I was escorted by four bodyguards. Since I was terrified of men, he sent Tierney with me whenever I visited Mama. I was so upset with the latter for hiding the internet from me, I ended up spending most of my time with Tierney, anyway.

I wasn't sure why my sister-in-law had agreed to spend all this time with me. It neither fit her personality nor her busy social calendar. Yet she seemed happy to be with me. Always babbling away, showing me funny memes on her phone, asking me to show her the stables, the gardens, the pieces I left behind.

Today, I decided to take a break from Long Island. I sat at the living room window, watching the grimy street with my back to the door, when something soft tickled the space between my ear and neck. I squirmed, swatting it away, swinging my gaze up. My husband stood before me. He was clad in a smart peacoat, a loose gray scarf, and designer wingtips, shiny enough to display one's reflection.

He was impeccably dressed. Not as lavishly as Camorrista—he had no jewelry, no diamond earrings, expensive watches, and silky shirts—but rather, like a *man*.

That fickle heart of mine missed a beat at the sight of him.

I had even warmed up to his eye patch.

He twirled a feather between his long fingers, his brow arched in wry amusement. "Head in the clouds, *Gealach*?"

The subtext stunned me into near-tears. He called my name, got no response, realized I couldn't hear him, so instead of touching me to alert me of his presence, he used a barrier, a buffer between us to signal he was here.

Now that I thought about it, my husband kept a healthy distance from me unless we were having one of his one-sided arguments.

Something melted inside me, and I offered him a small smile, which he didn't return. He put the feather back inside a decorative bowl on the credenza. "You have an OB-GYN appointment in thirty minutes. Get dressed."

My mood soured, giving way to the metallic, cold blade of fear. It was becoming real. The pregnancy. The baby. The *marriage*. I stilled, refusing to budge.

My mother promised she'd be the one to take me to the appointment. I forgot all about it.

Suppressed it from my memory, most likely.

Why wasn't *she* here?

Tiernan waltzed over to the kitchen to grab himself a protein shake and returned, his frosty exterior impenetrable. "Move it. I have a five o'clock appointment downtown."

I peered around uncertainly. Not communicating with him was painful at this point. I wanted to ask about my mama.

Reading my mind for the millionth time, he sighed. "Your mother asked me to take you. Said she's under the weather."

I crossed my arms over my chest. I was waiting to see if he'd touch me. *Hurt* me. A messed-up part of me hoped he would. This way, I'd be able to stop the temptation of confiding in him. My traitorous heart would cease cartwheeling every time he entered the room.

"Very well." He moseyed over to my room, returning a moment later holding my phone. My eyes flared in panic. He couldn't take away my phone. It was the only thing keeping me afloat.

How on earth did he even find it? I'd been hiding it underneath a loose floorboard ever since he caught me using it.

"Two options. One, you give me trouble, and I break this thing into five pieces." His fist tightened around the device. "Two, you get dressed and play the obedient wife for an hour, and I link my PayPal to your phone and let you buy all the shit on your little supermarket list at the bottom of your drawer."

My jaw slacked. When did he see it? Probably during one of my visits to Mama. He'd been snooping around my room. I'd be upset about it if I hadn't returned the favor. At this point I could give guided tours in his master bedroom.

"Nice handwriting, by the way." His smile stretched further. "Very neat."

My cheeks flushed.

I was starting to see there was no fooling my husband. He knew where I kept my things. What I was thinking. What I was doing. What made me tick. Knew I wasn't intellectually impaired. That I understood everything he said and did.

And he knew his coldness repulsed and fascinated me in the same breath.

Also, what was PayPal? Probably a type of credit card.

I licked my lips, considering his proposition. Why did he care that I visit the doctor?

Reading my mind once again, he said, "Your family won't fulfill their end of the bargain unless you're taken care of."

Of course *he* didn't care. I had no illusions about that.

…so why did I feel a pang of disappointment nicking the spot just beneath my breastbone?

"Take the mask off, Lila. I know you can read. I know you surf the internet. I know you can write, and stitch together a wounded motherfucker, and probably split atoms. You're coming with or without the confession. Be a smart girl and take the deal."

I stood up and stomped my way to my room, where I changed into something hideously pink to piss him off. We left the house with a flock of guards split into two vehicles. My husband was on a phone call the entire way.

The Mercedes stopped in front of a preppy Manhattan building. Tiernan got out first, followed by two of his soldiers, before he gestured for me to follow. The second set of guards trailed behind us.

We broke off from security when we entered the elevator in the sleek lobby. By now, I was so nauseous I was surprised I didn't vomit my heart onto the floor. My palms were clammy, and my limbs felt like overcooked noodles.

My stomach was still flat, and the morning sickness was now almost completely gone, so I allowed myself to pretend I wasn't pregnant most days. Now someone was going to touch me. Show me the baby. The child of my rapist. Make me face the reality I'd been ignoring for three months.

I was barely eighteen. I'd never even had a proper kiss. The kiss during the wedding ceremony didn't count. And I knew nothing about babies.

When we got to the reception, my panic flared into sheer terror.

"Dr. Driscoll is unfortunately indisposed." A flirty receptionist batted her fake lashes at my husband. She looked like one of my brothers' mistresses. Big hair, boobs, and a small brain to match. "But her husband, Dr. Maguire, stepped in to cover her appointments for the rest of the afternoon."

A *man* was going to touch me?

A *man* was going to put his hands on my most private parts?

Jerkily, I looped my fingers around Tiernan's forearm, digging my nails into his hard muscles.

"That won't do," Tiernan said calmly, dismissively. "I specifically requested a female doctor."

He did?

"Totally, yeah, I understand." The bubbly receptionist flipped her hair with a smile. "And Dr. Driscoll will take over moving forward. It's just this specific appointment—"

She stopped. Tiernan didn't even say anything. His stony glare told her it was nonnegotiable. What was his voice like? Raspy, I'd imagined. Rough around the edges, just like the man himself.

"I see you're not happy," she said.

A thin, humorless smile. "Smart girl."

The receptionist swallowed. "Let me see if Dr. Lockerby is available…"

"Is Dr. Lockerby a woman?"

"Hmm, yes. Her name is Meredith."

"You do that, while I help my wife settle in the examining room. Remember—if she's uncomfortable, I'm uncomfortable. And if I'm uncomfortable…" He trailed off, casually leaning a shoulder against the wall and exposing the gun in the holster beneath his tailored peacoat. "Everyone gets *real* uncomfortable."

We huddled down the corridor and slipped into room number seven. A faded blue hospital gown waited on the edge of the examination table, folded neatly into a square.

I turned to Tiernan to tell him to look the other way and caught the sight of the door clicking shut. He left, the scent of expensive leather and musk lingering in the air like the swollen pulse of a kiss.

It was the first time I was alone somewhere new since the assault.

Was he coming back?

Was I going to face the doctor alone?

My anxiety won over. I picked up my phone and texted Mama. It was the first time I had initiated a conversation with her since she came back from Chicago.

> Lila: Why didn't you come to my OB-GYN appointment?
> Chiara: I'm sorry, honey. I have a terrible headache. It shouldn't be too bad. Just do as the doctor asks.

Bullshit. She knew how triggering this was for me. Knew how this pregnancy came about.

Trembling, I reached for the zipper in the back of my dress. It took me three attempts to remove it. I picked up the hospital gown and examined it. It was missing a part. Front or back, I couldn't tell. But one side was purely made out of strings.

Which way was the right one?

Tears collected on my lower eyelids. Since they were going to check my belly, I guessed I needed to wear the gown with my front exposed. I quickly tied the strings beneath my breasts and around my stomach. What a stupid design for a hospital gown! What was even the point of it?

I laid on the examination table, realizing to my chagrin there were stirrups on either side of it. I pressed my thighs together tightly. I didn't want to be touched. To be seen. To be prodded like an animal.

It was the absence of Tiernan that made me realize I trusted him more than I cared to admit. Not with my heart, or with my happiness, but with my body. It was more than I could say about any man other than my brothers.

The door opened and Tiernan stepped back inside. I quickly

swathed an arm over my breasts and pressed a hand to my groin to hide myself. Despite my mortification, I was relieved to have him back. He closed the door and swiveled my way, his gaze landing on my exposed skin.

The ice in his pupil snuffed, replaced with something else. Heated and urgent. It was the first time he looked...*bothered.* By something. By someone.

"What's this?" His lips moved around a tight jaw. His gaze was trained hard on my face, refusing to travel lower.

I tossed him an incredulous glare that said, *What does it look like? I'm waiting for my examination.*

He pressed his lips together, and I had a horrible, devastating feeling he was suppressing a laugh. The door opened a crack again, and he turned around, slamming it shut.

What was happening?

Panicked, I scooted to the edge of the table, watching as he ate the space between us with one step. His palms were splayed where I could see them, lifted in surrender.

"Not gonna touch you without permission."

Why would he need to touch me at *all*?

Oh, *God.* The gown was the other way around, wasn't it? My face flamed cherry-red, down to the tips of my ears.

"Help?" he offered.

I nodded. My ears were on fire.

"I'll have to touch you."

My heart nearly raced out of my chest. I jerked my chin in a second nod.

He grabbed me by the waist and lowered me to the floor with gentleness that made me question if he touched me at all.

Shame swirled in my stomach. I was humiliated and mortified.

"Close your eyes if it's too much."

He reached for the tied strings at my front, tugging them free without touching my skin. The heat of his body, of the masculinity he radiated in electric pulses, made my nipples pucker. They stood on end, pink, sharp, and needy. So needy. It felt like his body spoke to mine in a language only they understood. I fought the urge to press against him, to lean my body against his.

I worried if he touched me somewhere, *anywhere*, I'd combust. It felt like I was on the verge of experiencing something big and foreign and exciting.

His expression remained inscrutable as he slid the sleeves off my shoulders.

The soft caress of the air between us made my stomach dip and my nipples harden even more.

They now grazed the expensive fabric of his dress shirt.

Gasping, I covered them with my hands. I stared at my feet to hide my blush.

What was wrong with me? Why was my body doing this?

My husband clasped my chin, tilting my head up so I could see him.

"It's normal." His neck strained with veins I hadn't seen there before. "Your nipples will go down in a sec."

I stood completely naked before him. The air buzzed and sizzled with an energy that bound us together, vining us in invisible ropes.

I didn't know what was happening to me, because suddenly, I wanted him to hug me. To *kiss* me. Show me how to order things from the internet. Take me to see sunsets.

There seemed to be an increasing number of reasons why I should reveal my secret to Tiernan, and none at all why I should keep hiding.

And if he'd want to have sex with me? Maybe it wouldn't be so awful. If sex really was terrible, wouldn't mankind be extinct? It seemed to run contradictory to the foundations of civilization.

Tiernan twisted the gown to the other side and covered my chest and stomach. He turned me around and secured the strings tightly around my back. Paused. Took one, deep, enormous breath

I could feel in my own lungs, like he was gathering every atom of self-control in his body.

Then I felt him step away.

I scurried back to the examination table, and he opened the door, gesturing for the doctor to enter. It was a woman. She had gray short hair, thick glasses, and a stern face. She asked me if I approved of my husband being present during the examination.

I nodded.

Tiernan sat beside me, readjusting his slacks. He kept folding his legs and changing positions in his seat, like he had ants in his pants. He refused to look at me.

My anxiety notched up another level when the doctor looked over the chart my husband filled out on my behalf. I ping-ponged my gaze from her to him when they spoke.

"I understand Mrs. Callaghan is nonverbal?" she asked.

"Mm."

Was helping me really putting him in such a sour mood he couldn't even *speak*?

"Will you be communicating on her behalf?"

"Uh-huh."

Well, hardly, seeing as he refused to even *speak*. My God, was touching me really so appalling to him?

The look on the doctor's face suggested she was appalled by the idea he had impregnated me, and she made no effort to conceal it.

"You indicated in the form that her last menstrual cycle ended six weeks ago." She raised her fist to her mouth, probably clearing her throat.

"Eight days before our wedding."

That wasn't true. It had been at least thirteen weeks. But my father and Tiernan must've figured out a timeline to coincide with our wedding.

The obstetrician placed the clipboard on a counter, removing her reading glasses and cleaning the lenses with the edge of her white robe. "In that case, I recommend a vaginal ultrasound. It's unlikely we'll see anything substantial through an abdominal ultrasound, and I'd like to check for a heartbeat and get your estimated due date."

"She'll get an abdominal check," he replied, unblinking.

"That's not advisable at this stage of the pregnancy. Besides, she'll have to endure those further into the pregnancy, when we check her cervix for dilate—"

"Should I go ask for a doctor who speaks English?" Tiernan threw his thumb toward the door. "I said nobody fucking gives her a vaginal check."

Feeling my cheeks heating, I put a hand on his arm. His gaze jolted, meeting mine. I offered him a brief nod.

She was right. I *was* going to have to endure this sooner or later.

His jaw was so tense I was afraid his teeth were about to snap, and if I didn't know any better, I'd think he was as uncomfortable with the situation as I was.

"Fine," he bit out, still staring me down. "But you operate under the assumption she's a virgin."

The doctor offered him a withering look. "Do you take me for an idiot?"

"Absolutely. Case in point, you're arguing with me." He shook my touch off him. "I'm watching you, *Doc*."

Tiernan didn't care about me. I had to constantly remind myself of that. But ever since I stitched him up, I seemed to have gained his respect. There was an unspoken agreement between us, that we'd look after each other, at least physically.

After a few more questions, Dr. Lockerby took out something that looked like a curling iron and put a huge condom on it. She slathered it with a clear gel. Her lips moved, but I was too flustered to follow them. I pressed my knees together harder, scooting up the examination table.

No.

No. No. No. No. No.

"We need five minutes," my husband announced.

The doctor stood up and shuffled out of the room, looking none too pleased about the delay.

I cast my tear-filled gaze at his face. My heart was pounding so hard it thrummed between my ears.

"You don't have to do this."

I shook my head. It needed to be done.

"No one can hurt you anymore, *Gealach*. Remember that."

Taking a deep breath, I stretched my open palm in his direction. He hesitated before lacing our fingers together, giving me a firm squeeze. His skin was rough and coarse, *hot*. Still staring at me, he opened his mouth to call the doctor back.

Dr. Lockerby returned. I allowed her to slip my feet into the stirrups and buried my face in Tiernan's neck. He smelled so good, I felt heady and drunk. The doctor's device poked at my entrance, cold and foreign, and I gulped down my hiccups, determined not to cry.

The device slowly slipped inside me, penetrating my sensitive flesh. It was met with resistance. My muscles clamped around it, pushing it back, refusing to surrender.

It burned so badly I stopped breathing altogether.

After a few seconds, Tiernan nudged me from his neck and pinched my chin with his fingers, looking me in the eye. "Hey. The doctor asked that you try to relax."

Easier said than done, but I nodded, my eyes clinging to his face desperately.

I sucked in a breath, feeling full and stretched and uncomfortable. Pressing my lips together to suppress a scream, I focused on the hard planes of my husband's face, trying to picture him doing this to me with his penis. From the glimpse I'd caught the night he was with Becky, his thing was the size of a Dyson Airwrap.

"Release those muscles for me, Lila." His thumb stroked my cheek. Soft, soft, *soft*.

For me.

My muscles uncurled of their own accord, accepting the device. Dr. Lockerby slipped in a few more inches.

He held my stare, and when I remembered he always seemed to read my mind, I blushed from the crown of my head to my little toes, because I imagined him there instead of the device.

And…I wasn't repulsed by it. Not at all.

Tiernan scrubbed his thumb back and forth along my knuckles, using his other hand to smooth away flyaways from my forehead. "That's it. Good girl," he fussed. "I knew you could take it. You're doing so good. I'm proud of you."

He gave me more words in a span of two minutes than he did the entire duration of our marriage. And I basked in them like a flower in the sun. Something behind my breastbone fluttered. A combination of desire, warmth, and pride. I swallowed down a small moan of pleasure.

My body squeezed back at the device, but no longer because it didn't want it there.

I noticed the doctor swiveling on her round chair toward a small screen and reluctantly ripped my gaze from Tiernan to see what she was saying.

"Well, Mr. and Mrs. Callaghan, there is certainly a heartbeat, and a healthy one." She pointed at a white dot on the screen that kept flicking on and off.

A pulse. My baby has a pulse.

The revelation was unsurprising and earth-shattering all at once. My secret, my burden, my shame. My eyes zeroed in on the small white dot.

Thud. Thud. Thud. Thud. Thud.

Its little heart beat like a rabbit caught between canine teeth. Cornered and forced into existence.

It wasn't the baby's fault that its father raped me. It didn't ask to be conceived. It was blameless, just like me.

"It appears that your wife is thirteen weeks along, not six."

He shrugged.

"Mr. Callaghan?" The doctor arched a brow, demanding his words. She looked rather disgusted with the entire ordeal.

"What can I say? My sperm is an overachiever."

Something dark passed between the two of them. It made the small hairs on the back of my neck stand on end. She was the first to break their stare-off, clearing her throat.

"Good news is you'll have a Christmas baby. I'm setting the due date for December twenty-fifth."

"February thirteenth," Tiernan corrected.

She licked her lips, eyes darting around the room, searching for help that wouldn't come. "Mr. Callaghan, I cannot—"

"If the baby arrives prematurely—say, late December—we'll call it a happy surprise." He used the tip of his shiny wingtip to roll her chair from the monitor and let go of my hand. Leaning over, he seized control of the keyboard and fixed the due date on her computer. His demeanor changed completely.

This was why he set up the OB-GYN appointment. To fix the timeline of our tragedy. Now it all made sense.

"W-would you like to take a prenatal blood test to find out the gender?" Though I couldn't hear her, I knew she was stammering by the way her lips quivered.

"Unnecessary." Tiernan glanced at his watch before I was able to nod.

"Perhaps your wife doesn't feel the same way."

"In that case, she's welcome to voice her preference."

"Can she?" The doctor cast her terrorized gaze upon me.

"Oh, she can." He sat back. Gone was the man who cooed and fussed me into loosening my muscles. Who held my hand and brushed my knuckles so gently I could cry. "She chooses not to. Right, Lila?"

How dare he dictate whether I found out the gender or not? He was strong-arming me into communicating with him by taking away my agency. Already, freedom was a precious extravagance I could only dream of.

The doctor rolled her chair back to her computer, typing on her keyboard. "Do you know where you'd like to give birth?"

"Home," Tiernan announced, again disregarding my preferences. "She'll have a home birth."

Her fingers halted over the keyboard. "I'm not a fan of home births."

"What a coincidence. I don't give a fuck."

"Deep breath now, Mrs. Callaghan." The doctor flattened her palm over my abdomen and slowly slipped the device from between my legs. She tossed away the condom and latex gloves and stood up to wash her hands.

She spoke directly to Tiernan about appointments and schedules, then left the room.

Keeping my chin locked to keep it from wobbling, I slid off the table and waddled to the corner chair where my folded dress awaited. When I turned back around, Tiernan stood toe-to-toe with me. My blood was boiling with anger.

He plucked the dress from my hands and started helping me put it on, but I shoved him out of my way and tramped over to retrieve my shoes, ignoring the sticky coldness between my thighs.

I caught him speaking to me through the mirror, but didn't bother reading his lips. I thought we'd reached some kind of ceasefire. Then he went and made decisions that weren't his to make. The frustration of not being able to communicate this to him, to explain what angered me, made a rash break out across my neck. Great. I was becoming *allergic* to not talking to him.

I got dressed quickly and waited behind him at the reception desk while the flirty receptionist set us up with another appointment. When she gave him the clinic's card with the date written down, she also slipped him her number. He pocketed it coolly, turned toward me, and strode outside.

Now, I wasn't just fuming.

I was *murderous.*

I never should've stitched the bastard up. When the elevator slid open and we poured into the lobby, he pressed his hand to the small of my back. I slapped his touch away, even though his four soldiers were standing there, staring at us in disbelief.

Ignoring their bewildered expressions, he clasped my wrist and guided me to an alcove behind the elevator bank. My back pressed against a silvered building directory. He bared his teeth, getting in my face.

"Got something to *say* to me, wifey?"

I offered my middle finger and an angelic smile.

He tipped his head back and laughed humorlessly.

"How much of a pushover can you be, Lila? I make your decisions for you, I take away your will, your words, your bleeding freedom. I took that whore's number." He pointed upstairs. "I'll keep pushing your buttons until you break, because I refuse to play dumb like the rest of your family. Your brother took out my eye but make no mistake—I can still see through your bullshit."

He had a point. Still, I wasn't going to reward his bullying with my trust.

Anyway, why did he care about my words so much?

"Everyone underestimates you. You're smart, cunning, and have skill," he explained. "You can be an asset to me. One of my many lethal weapons."

Of course he wanted to use me. Men like him only cared about expanding their empires.

Tiernan tilted my chin up. "One last chance to speak before I pry the words out of you. You won't like my method, *Gealach*, so you better start talking."

Was he *threatening* me?

He made me crazy. Feral with rage and desire. I took a deep breath and nodded. His features relaxed.

"Good. Now wha—"

I spat in his face, a taunting smile pulling at my lips.

Gone was his wry amusement. His expression promised retribution and pain.

I believed him. My husband wasn't one for empty threats.

All the same, he needed to remember who I was.

Yes, a girl.

But also a Ferrante.

That night, I stared at my flat stomach in front of my bathroom mirror.

Turning sideways, I sucked it in all the way, ribs poking, to find the silhouette of my womb curving into a hillside.

There's a baby in there.

I allowed myself a moment of joy. I'd always wanted to be a mother and never thought it could be possible due to my lie. I might be stuck with a husband who made Satan look like a kitten, but I'd always have my child.

I would love them.

Cherish them. Raise them with all the warmth and affection their father—both biological and by marriage—would never offer.

I'd never had anything of my own. Now? Now I was going to have the most precious thing of all.

An ally.

A legacy.

Something worth fighting for.

Someone worth *living* for.

CHAPTER TWENTY-TWO
LILA

The next day, I visited Mama in Long Island. I decided to skip my daily dinner with Tiernan. Punish him for his behavior. For that reason, I didn't bring Tierney along. She'd adhere to her brother's rules and drag me home kicking and screaming before seven. Not because she wasn't loyal to me, but because he was the head of the Callaghan clan. His word was gospel.

I went alone, braving the proximity to Tiernan's men. They appeared too fearful to look in my direction, let alone touch me. My husband's mere existence was an invisible cloak I wore at all times that made the few people I came in contact with petrified.

I'd never punished anyone in my life. Never spat at anyone. Never flipped them the bird. I tried to figure out why I felt comfortable doing it to someone so violent and bloodthirsty. I came to the conclusion that I felt confident taunting my husband because no matter how awful things were between us, he never physically hurt me.

He was supposed to kill me that night on the fountain. Rape me the night of our wedding. Or any other night thereafter.

Yet, he never did.

His careful, indomitable control meant I was always safe from his wrath. He kept himself on a leash.

When I made the journey back home at ten at night, Mama joined me to help me feel safe.

I'd been trying to patch things up between us, but my anger and disappointment still lingered.

"*How come you didn't come to my appointment?*" I signed to her. "*I know it wasn't migraines. You always have them and never cancel your engagements.*"

"*You know how difficult your pregnancy has been for me.*" Her lips curled petulantly. "*I'm still coming to terms with it.*"

Fury boiled inside me. I was pretty sure my husband also wasn't a fan of the situation, yet he showed up and walked me through it.

"*Anyway. I think I'm getting closer to convincing Luca to sabotage your marriage.*" She patted her silver updo. "*He promised he'd talk to Tiernan. See if we can negotiate a way out.*"

"*Papa would never let me have the child out of wedlock.*"

"*You wouldn't be unwed.*" A sly glint lit her pupils. "*When I was in Chicago, I spoke to Angelo. He said he's willing to step in and marry you. Good man, Angelo. He impressed me with his business and character. He'll be better for you.*"

A bone-chilling shiver rolled down my spine.

"*Papa wouldn't let me divorce. It's against his faith.*"

"*He might not have a choice. Luca and Achilles are taking over, and they have other ideas on how to run things.*"

As much as my current husband drove me to the brink of madness, my instincts told me Angelo would be a trillion times worse. I had nothing to back up this notion with. It was a pure, primal gut feeling. One I knew better than to ignore.

"*I'm not sure it's a good idea,*" I admitted. "*Tiernan is a jackass, but better the devil you know.*"

Yesterday, I disrespected my husband in front of his soldiers, spat in his face, and he still fed me an Italian dinner and sent my clothes to be drycleaned along with his own batch.

"*Don't tell me you're warming up to him.*" My mother's hands flew about wildly. "*You belong with me at the estate, not with this stronzo. Angelo said he's willing to lend his last name and that you can live with me most of the year. He wants nothing to do with you. It will be wonderful!"*

Was this plan about my well-being and my baby's, or about her? I couldn't tell anymore.

"I don't want to marry Angelo, Mama."

Her face hardened. *"Are you letting that dirty man touch you, Lila?"*

I shook my head, so disappointed I could hardly breathe.

"Why did you never buy me any of the life-altering devices for the hard of hearing?" I changed the subject.

"What?" Her eyes flared.

"Why did you keep me from the internet?"

"What is this man filling your head with?" She scowled. *"I did it for your own good. And you will marry Angelo if I can make it happen, because I still know what's good for you better than anyone else."*

When the vehicle stopped in front of Fermanagh's, I itched to warn her not to make any plans before discussing them with me, but knew there wasn't any point.

My mother could move mountains and tear the moon from its place, and still, she wouldn't be able to release me from Tiernan Callaghan's clutches.

He didn't let anyone touch what was his.

Even if he didn't care for it one bit.

Four soldiers escorted me into the pub and up the stairway to the apartment. When I reached my door, they stayed in the corridor. I recognized a Camorra soldier outside of Tierney's apartment, Marco, surveilling her on Achilles's command. I sent him a dirty look, fed up with anyone and anything with a penis.

I pushed the door open, tugging my jacket off and hanging it on the hanger. The place was dark. It was approaching eleven, and even though I was the one who didn't show up to dinner, the fact Tiernan had left gnawed at the corners of my stomach.

I pushed the door to my room open, stepped inside, and stumbled back in shock.

The world blurred at the edges, and a red mist of fury tainted my vision.

On my bed, with the pink satin covers and fluffy pillows, was my husband, sitting next to the gynecologist's receptionist, holding her by the hair.

They were both fully clothed, and she was stomach-down on my mattress, staring dumbly up at him. He held her at an arm's length, far enough that they didn't touch, close enough that I still wanted to kill him.

My sketch of Tate Blackthorn was on the floor, ripped into minuscule pieces, his piercing eyes staring back at the chaos unfolding.

Something tangible snapped inside me. I felt it crack my chest open, and all the anger rushed out like pus.

I'd had enough.

"Go ahead. Fuck her." I shaped my lips around the words, knowing they were understandable enough, after years of clandestine speech therapy. "I'll go find myself a plaything, too."

Swiveling on my heel, I stalked toward the door.

Tears flew from my cheeks, hot and angry and utterly unstoppable.

He wanted to break me, and he did.

I spoke.

I spoke.

I practiced with my speech therapist, but not enough that it felt natural. It still felt like I was trying to chomp rocks between my teeth, and I never attempted to do it with anyone else. Not even Mama.

He'd taken it too far and broke the fragile trust between us. This absolute hussy of a woman, on my bed, on my *sheets*.

He'd smirked when he saw me. Like he wanted to get caught. But, of course he did. He did it in my room.

Yanking the door open, I shouldered past the wall of Tiernan's soldiers and took the steps down. The men were so stunned, they just stood there and watched. I didn't make it four steps before my husband scooped me up by the back of my dress, boxing me against the wall between his huge arms.

He still smelled of her. A mixture of cloying, flowery perfume and a Victoria's Secret body mist.

"She speaks." He looked like the least surprised man on planet Earth, grinning devilishly. "What a fucking miracle."

I slapped him hard, glad his soldiers witnessed it. Maybe he'd finally hit me back.

I hoped he'd hit me, and I'd be able to tell my brothers, and they'd kill him.

His face didn't budge a millimeter, his good eye didn't flinch. He was immune to pain, to emotions, to *humanity*.

"I figured out what it is," he said conversationally, scooping up a tear on my cheek with his index finger and popping it into his mouth.

I stared at him with faux boredom, my heart nearly racing out of my chest. Every muscle in my body screamed at me to hurt him back.

Tiernan leaned forward, his lips moving slowly. "You're deaf."

All the air left my lungs.

No one knew this. No one but Mama and Imma. How did he figure it out?

"Your speech was the final nail in the coffin," he explained, watching me watch his lips. "Though I had my inkling for some time now. You never seemed to acknowledge me unless I was right in front of you, where you could read my lips. I tried dropping shit whenever we were in the same room—mugs, hardcovers, small furniture—waiting for a reaction that never came."

I gulped. I always found his clumsiness to be out of character whenever I found a shattered glass in the kitchen.

Did he find my speech funny? Weird? I wished it didn't matter. It *shouldn't* matter to me. Yet it did. Because, as much as I hated it, I cared what he thought about me.

"I speak ASL," he said after a beat. "Tierney, too."

I reared my head back, surprised.

What were the odds? And why on earth did the twins learn ASL? I was starting to suspect they weren't with their father and older brother the entire length of their childhood.

He snapped his fingers once. His soldiers evacuated the hallway. The Camorrista hesitated for a moment, deliberating, before Tiernan shot him a glance that sent him stumbling downstairs.

We were alone.

Tiernan signed to me, "*Tell me something. Anything. Now.*"

His movements were smooth. Confident. It was the last nail in my lie's coffin. The temptation to speak with someone who wasn't my mother was too great.

I raised my quaking hands to answer him. "*Go to hell.*"

"*Grew up there. Never going back. Let's try again.*"

"*I hate you.*"

"*I tolerate you.*" The admission seemed to slip from him without permission, because his jaw locked in annoyance. "*And I don't tolerate people very often. Third time's a charm. Say something.*"

"*Get rid of your whore.*"

It was the first time I saw him smiling with mirth, not sarcasm. All the other times, his smirk was tainted with darkness. Still, he didn't blink. I wondered if he closed his eye when he slept.

"*That's better, Gealach.*"

He marched back into the apartment. I followed him. The receptionist was standing outside my room, reapplying her lip gloss, using her smartphone as a mirror.

I wasn't a violent person, but she knew he was married with a *baby* on the way. I was pretty sure I could kill her and get acquitted by the jury.

"Brandy?"

"What's up?" She clicked her small mirror shut, batting her lashes at him.

"Get the fuck out. You've served your purpose."

Her jaw hung open in shock. "Are you serious right now?"

"I'm always serious."

"You didn't even…we didn't even…wait." She held a finger up. "What was my purpose?"

"Making my wife yell at me." He tugged his wallet out of his breast pocket, pulling a wad of rolled cash and patting her cheek with it. "Here. Use it to buy some self-respect."

"I thought you said you aren't together."

At this point, I lost my patience. With a huff, I wrenched out Tiernan's gun from his holster and pointed it at her.

She shrieked, stumbling backward and hitting the wall. For the first time in my life, I was glad I couldn't hear.

"Stop this nonsense, Lila. The paperwork would be insane." Tiernan touched my shoulder.

I gave him a shut-the-hell-up look.

He sighed. "If you want to kill her this much, at least let me drive us somewhere secluded."

I swiveled toward him, pointing the gun at his face.

"Care for a rerun of our wedding night?" I spoke out the words.

He arched a sardonic eyebrow, posture as languid and laid-back as a big cat. "Don't mind if I do. I'm not picky with the way you touch me, as long as you do."

When I turned back to Brandy, she wasn't there anymore. Probably ran off while I was contemplating blowing my husband's head off.

"My gun?" He opened his palm for me to dispose of the weapon.

"No." I tucked it into the waistband of my pink ensemble. I

raised my hand to sign to him. "*Next time you bring your whores to my apartment, I'll just assume I walked into a suicide pact.*"

He studied me with an approving sparkle in his eye, a wolfish grin on his face. He almost looked…proud.

"*I mean it, Tiernan. No more sluts.*"

"How about you sit your ass down and answer all my questions? If I find them sufficient, I might grant you your wish. If not, get ready to see me fucking the entire Northeast population."

Even though he deserved his other eye plucked out for this answer, I did acknowledge he was entitled to some explanation. Deceiving your lawfully wedded husband wasn't an ethical thing to do. Even if he was a bloodthirsty murderer.

I walked over to the couch and perched myself on its edge. He joined me on the opposite recliner.

"How do you compose music if you're deaf?"

His question surprised me. First, because there were so many bigger questions to ask. Second, because he wasn't supposed to know that.

"*You're going through my things?*" I scowled.

"At least once a day," he said easily.

"*Why?*"

"You fascinate me."

I contemplated arguing with him, but that'd be hypocritical of me. I did the same thing. Came with the territory of living with a complete stranger.

"*How did Beethoven?*" I signed. "*He was deaf, too.*"

"He lost his hearing gradually. Did you?"

I shook my head. "*No. But the principle is the same. You study the patterns, follow the cues, and come up with sequences that seem in sync. Writing music is analytical, more than anything else.*"

"Do your brothers know you're wicked smart?"

He thought I was smart?

I licked my lips, ignoring the heat spreading behind my rib cage. "*Only Mama and Imma know the truth.*"

"Why?"

"It's better this way. I've been deaf since birth. When I was two, they started running some tests to eliminate issues. I didn't respond to my own name and didn't speak a word. Their initial diagnosis was that I was on the spectrum. It was extreme medical malpractice and completely changed the course of my life."

Opening up felt like stepping out to the sun and feeling its rays on my skin for the very first time. Oxygen hit the bottom of my lungs. There was freedom in claiming who you were.

"Mama and Imma loved me all the same. Mama took me to classes and therapists. She dedicated her whole life to taking care of me. Imma taught me how to cook, how to knit, how to bake, how to suture."

Our eyes met, and something behind his mossy pupil softened.

"I was six when they found out I had been misdiagnosed. By then, I had taught myself to read, write, do a three-hundred-piece puzzle; Mama kept it all hush-hush. She and Imma were livid with the injustice and initially wanted to sue. But by then, people started noticing me. Powerful men in the underworld came knocking on Papa's door, looking for an arranged marriage when I turned eighteen. The Cosa Nostra. The Bratva. La Eme. Mama realized my fate would be as bleak as hers if I went that route—a cheating criminal husband with blood on his hands. Someone who would bring me nothing but trouble and heartache. She decided to spare me the woes of matrimony, so we kept my abilities a secret."

Tiernan's face remained unreadable. He continued staring at me silently, fingers laced together.

"Because my brothers compete over the don's throne, Mama said they couldn't be trusted with my secret. She worried they'd sell me out to our father to win points with him. At some point during my adolescence, the lack of intellectual stimulation became too much for me. That's when Mama started taking me to Ischia. It was close to our home base of Naples, but still far enough from Camorristi eyes for me to do the things I couldn't do at home. I learned Latin and math and physics every summer. Attended

soccer games and played tennis. Ischia holds my only good memories," I admitted. "*I want to go back. Maybe with the baby. I wouldn't mind living with security, if that's your requirement. And we wouldn't have to put up with each other. I just want to be free.*"

He flicked invisible lint from his charcoal slacks, ignoring my words completely.

"Your mother wanted to spare you marriage with a mobster. That ship has sailed. Why did you keep pretending?"

I pressed my lips together, wondering if I should be completely honest with him.

Yes. I was so tired of keeping everything inside.

"*She said if you found out that I'm sentient, you would insist on consummating our marriage. And that you'd try to extract Camorra secrets from me. I don't know any, by the way.*"

Tiernan stroked his chin.

"*Will you?*" I asked.

He didn't answer. A born strategist, and he still hadn't made up his mind.

"Are you in love with Tate Blackthorn?" he asked out of the blue.

"*No, but I'm fond of him.*"

"Why?"

"*He gave me a dance. My first taste of normalcy. My dream is to listen and dance to music. And he made a part of it come true. Whether he knew how much it meant to me or not, I'll never forget his kindness.*"

"That's your dream?" he asked. "To hear music, and dance to it?"

I nodded. Surprisingly, I wasn't shy or embarrassed about it. Even though it felt like stripping my soul naked, for him to know something intimate about me.

"And your art?"

Another rush of heat spread across my chest.

No one had ever referred to my sketches as art. Mama called them my little doodles.

"*I sketch because it passes the time. But I'm no artist.*"

"To define is to limit."

Tiernan stood up and strolled to the alcohol cart, flipping two tumblers and pouring brandy into them. There was a real bullet in the decanter. He returned to our seats and handed me a drink.

"*I'm not twenty-one,*" I signed, which seemed ridiculous, seeing as giving an underage person alcohol was the least of my husband's lawbreaking history.

"But you're eighteen."

"*Yes.*"

"Legal in Italy. You're Italian. I see no flaw in this logic."

"*I'm pregnant.*" I stared at him in disbelief.

"You don't have to be." He took a sip of his brandy, studying me hawkishly. "I won't stop you from getting an abortion. We can tell your father it was a miscarriage. It will free you from the burden of motherhood. From doting over your rapist's bastard. The only thing you need to be aware of is that you'd still be bound to me by marriage. I won't let you go. Too much is riding on my Bratva operation to give up the Camorra's alliance."

I swallowed hard as I considered his proposition. There *was* room for deliberation. The baby belonged to a violent rapist. I was too young…

"If you keep it, I'll never love it. Never regard it as my own." His lips moved, piercing through my thoughts. I swallowed hard.

"*I want to keep it.*" I placed the brandy on the coffee table between us. "*I've always wanted a child of my own.*"

He shrugged, tossing his drink back in one gulp and staring at the bottom of his empty glass.

He seemed lost in thought for a moment, and I wanted to draw him back to me. As much as his attention unsettled me, it also reminded me I was alive in some strange, amorphic way.

"*How am I supposed to sleep in my bed after you screwed someone inside it?*"

Tiernan threw me a distant glance. "I didn't fuck her. Didn't even touch her. She was an interrogation device, and it worked. As for your question—as a matter of fact, you shouldn't sleep there at all. Your place is in my bed."

"*You cheat on me and you want me to sleep in your bed?*"

"You cannot cheat on someone who isn't yours."

"*Do you want me to be yours?*" I blinked in disbelief.

"Not particularly." His words dripped pragmatism. "We're not sexually compatible."

"*Why?*"

"You require tenderness and warmth. I only fuck women in the ass and, if I'm feeling benevolent, let them blow me instead."

"*Does this mean I can take a lover, too?*"

"Sure." He motioned with his hand to the door. "Knock yourself out."

I scowled, realizing his game.

"*No one would touch me because I'm your wife.*"

"I wouldn't count on it. The world has no shortage of idiots." He stood up, unbuttoning his shirt. "But you should know that there's a bounty on the head of anyone stupid enough to look in your direction, your own bodyguards included. Six million dollars, to be exact. Now, I suggest you move your shit to my bedroom if you want to sleep anywhere untouched by other women. I never let my hookups into my bed. Or." He peered around us. "You can sleep on the bathroom floor again. Avoid the sofa, though. Some heinous things happened on it."

"Aw." I stood up quickly, scrunching my nose in disgust.

With that, the bastard sailed toward the hallway. He stopped before disappearing inside the corridor, snapping his fingers as he glanced at me over his shoulder.

"Oh, two more things. One—you're never to miss dinner again without a good reason. This is a sacred time between us."

Sacred, my ass. We spend the entire duration of it every night trying to kill each other with hate glares.

"And the second thing?"

"Don't feel so sorry for yourself. Tragedies are excellent teachers, Lila. Learn, absorb, and conquer."

CHAPTER TWENTY-THREE
TIERNAN

243 DAYS TO SELF-DESTRUCTION

Deaf.

Not intellectually impaired.

Not developmentally delayed.

Deaf.

Sharp. Intelligent. Cunning. Talented. Slightly unhinged, which—let's admit it—only added to her allure.

Beautiful beyond words, art, and cultural standards.

A mixture between sweet, naive, and goodhearted, yet blood-thirsty enough to put a bullet in someone who crossed her.

Thank fuck I had no heart, or we'd have one hell of a problem.

I fell into a recliner in my bedroom, rolling my tongue over my upper teeth. I already had another stiff drink in hand, but there wasn't enough alcohol on this continent to numb the fuckery that was going on in my head.

The last forty-eight hours were a disaster. First, there was the OB-GYN appointment. She was so small the doctor wrestled to push the ultrasound wand inside her. Beads had actually formed across the old hag's forehead, and I was ready to tear the doctor's head off her neck.

When Lila placed those baby blues on my face and held my

hand, all the sadist in me could think about was plowing my massive cock inside that sweet little cunt.

She squirmed and moaned with discomfort, but it was me who had to adjust myself seven times sitting next to her so my cock wouldn't rip a hole through my trousers.

The doctor noticed, too. I was pretty sure I'd be banned from the establishment if it wasn't for my notoriety.

And her body. *Jaysus.* That body would be the death of any straight man. She straddled the seam between willowy and youthfully plump. With a trim waist, long legs, and dainty arms, all sun-kissed to perfection. Her tits were heavy and full, the curve of her arse round and bold.

The reception bimbo was a cheap plot device on my end. I'd recognized her as a former exotic dancer who worked for one of my establishments a few years back. She'd recognized me as the man who once left her a five-hundred-buck gratuity after doing unholy things to her.

I knew she'd be the tipping point for my wife. I'd studied Lila in recent weeks. She was a hotheaded Italian under all those pink frocks and innocent stares.

For the first time in my life, my thoughts were scattered in a dozen different directions. I usually prided myself on my ability to dissect the micro from the macro, the important from the neglectable.

Until now.

There were too many moving parts.

First—the baby.

Lila wanted to have it. Didn't surprise me. She was incapable of hurting anything innocent, even an unborn fetus the size of a fucking grape.

Second—what the fuck was Chiara playing at, making her daughter pretend to have no intellectual abilities, denying her pleasures and opportunities?

And why didn't she supply her with means to make her life better? A hearing aid? Apps and gadgets?

My wife had been robbed not only of her freedom and choices, which was standard for women in the underworld, but also from education, music, culture, arts, sports. Deaf people lived full, satisfying lives. They became doctors and scientists. Climbed mountains and broke glass ceilings.

I had no expectations of Vello. Fucker was the level of narcissist who barely noticed there was a world around him. But how could Lila's con gig fly under Luca, Achilles, and Enzo's radar? They grew up with her, for fuck's sake.

They were natural-born killers. Their jobs were to observe, learn, plan, and execute. My distaste for them aside, they were capable men. Was Lila that excellent an actress, or were they simply that self-absorbed?

The answer didn't matter. What mattered was they had failed her. Every single one of the Ferrantes. And the bad news was, I was hardly any better. Chiara was right. As soon as her daughter opened her mouth and I listened to her talk, the first thing that sprang to my mind was that I could fuck her now.

She was fair game.

Fuck Achilles's duffel bags of cash.

I saw her at the doctor's. The way her body reacted to mine. Those sweet, rosy-pink nipples were calling for me. It was the first time I wanted to put my mouth on a tit. The first time I wondered what it'd feel like to fuck a pussy.

Funnily enough, I, too, was inexperienced between the sheets. In a different, more depraved way, but nonetheless a virgin by some technical standard.

Lila was my first kiss—if you could call it that—and if I were to ever screw her, I'd need to do it the right way. I wasn't ready for that. Maybe not even capable of it.

She drove me mad. I wanted to throttle, kiss, and fuck her, all in the same breath. Not wanting someone to be scared of me went against my own brain chemistry. Fear was my most trusted weapon. I wielded it over everyone, other than Tierney and Fintan.

But if I truly wanted Lila's pussy—which, I was beginning to suspect was the case—I had to tone it down.

And maybe no more hookers.

Fine, *definitely* no more hookers.

Sex was neither here nor there for me. I could take it or leave it, depending on my schedule, workload, and its availability. Going without wouldn't be a first, or particularly difficult.

But this was a headache I didn't anticipate. A complication that wasn't a part of the arrangement.

I'd deal with that later, though.

I knocked my drink back.

I'd handle it.

I always handled it.

CHAPTER TWENTY-FOUR
TIERNAN

The next morning, I found my useless brothers-in-law and their cuntbag of a father on the golf course adjoined to their olive orchard.

After dropping Lila off at the main house, I borrowed one of their vintage golf carts from the stables and made my way to them, making it a point to run over all the flowerbeds and knocking down any Mother Mary and Jesus garden gnomes I suspected were pricey.

The golf course stretched across five acres, boasting manicured lawns, grooves, valleys, and dips. The seaside cliff offered natural ravines along the coastline. The Ferrante men were on the driving range next to a bucket of balls, shooting the shit and hitting balls directly into the mouth of the ocean. I came to a screech, blocking their carts' path, and hopped out.

Vello was the first to notice me. He straightened his posture from crouching over his walking cane, muttering something in Neapolitan. A heartfelt greeting, no doubt.

I casually plucked one of the golf clubs from the leathered stand bag midstride. A vintage piece that looked expensive as shit.

"What's up, man?" Enzo raised his head from his ball, and I used the opportunity to swing the club and break it over the side of his arm.

"*Stu puorc e merd!*" He dropped to his knees with a rough cough, clutching his arm. "The fuck was that for?"

"What the—" Luca began, before I grabbed another golf club, breaking it in half over my knee and slicing his shoulder with it. It was less than a stab, but more than a poke. Enough to draw blood but not warrant stitches.

Having realized I wasn't playing, Achilles sprang into his golf cart, tossing his half-dead father behind him on the passenger seat.

"Think carefully about your next move, Callaghan," Achilles warned dryly. "My sister is too young to become a widow."

I picked a third golf club, spinning its base across my index as I paced toward them, my blood bubbling in my veins like champagne.

"Don't pretend you give a shit about her."

"Callaghan," Vello barked out. "Whatever you're angry about, I'm sure we can—"

"She's not intellectually impaired, you oversized used condoms." I raised the club, slamming it against the vintage golf cart. Judging by Enzo's wince, it cost a pretty penny. "She's *deaf*. Smarter than everyone in this family combined."

"What?" Luca threw a look of disbelief to his father.

"Did I fucking stutter?"

Enzo shook his head. "You're saying she has no learning disabil—"

"She sutures like a surgeon and draws like Da Vinci."

Luca's mouth pressed into a hard line, his eyes darkening as he took that in.

Achilles said nothing. He simply stared, his sooty eyes as unsettling as a shallow grave.

"I mean, it's not far-fetched." Enzo rubbed at his arm, looking between his brothers. "When you think about it...she follows directions, holds eye contact with Mama and Imma. And he's right. She's pretty rad with the pencil. You've seen her shit. It's *good*."

"Still doesn't explain why she'd want people to believe she's incapable." Luca locked his jaw.

"To throw the suiters off her scent," Achilles said solemnly. "She wanted to avoid getting married to a Mafia prick. Didn't work." He leveled his eyes on me, turning his sharp gaze to his father. "Your response?"

Vello looked spaced out. My guess was his pain meds kicked in and slowed his mind. He shook his head. "This is the first time I'm hearing about this."

"You think Mama kept a secret from you?" Luca looked skeptical.

"Wouldn't be the first time," Vello murmured bitterly. "And she never wanted Lila to marry someone from the trade." He was quiet for a moment. "We could've formed an alliance with the Bratva through her. Their son was interested."

The thought of Lila being touched by Alex Rasputin was enough to make me hurl each and every one of these assholes into the ocean.

I tsked. "You're stuck with me, I'm afraid."

"I can't believe Mama kept this from us." Enzo ran his knuckles over his jaw. "Lila, too."

"Lila was persuaded by your genius mother it was for the greater good," I drawled.

"How come?" Enzo frowned.

"Because most mobsters look like wet farts and possess the same amount of charm," Achilles guessed. "And she knew where this was headed."

"We need to talk to Mama," Luca said.

"Good idea." I grabbed a fresh club and swung it over my shoulder, advancing toward my cart.

"Came to fetch you first before I go meet her."

"Why?" Luca asked.

"Because you're the only people who might stop me from killing her."

The Ferrantes arrived at their manor before me, probably realizing

I was pissed enough to follow through with my threat to shoot the matriarch of the family. By the time I parked the golf cart and walked inside, they were all sitting at the table in the kitchen, breads, soups, and salads spread before them. There was a soccer game playing on a gilded framed TV, and a blue *forza Napoli* scarf draped over the dining chairs. The men were barking orders at the soccer players on TV like they could hear them.

I finally met the elusive Imma. She was sitting with Lila, feeding my wife a hearty Italian wedding soup, cooing at her. Chiara was there, too. Everyone was already eating, but I didn't mind. We weren't really family, and thank fuck for that.

"Chiara. A word." I planted myself between her and my wife.

"It's *Lady* Chiara," she enunciated through pursed lips. "And I do not appreciate your tone."

"You can say whatever you wanna say to her right here," Achilles informed me, sprawling on a seat and lighting himself a cigarette.

I reached across the table and yanked the cigarette from his mouth, flicking it into his drink. "Not in front of my wife. This applies both to your cigarette and the conversation."

"You just threatened to *kill* her, bro," Enzo pointed at me with his spoon.

"If we reach an understanding, she'll probably get to live."

"You'll be six feet under if you threaten my wife again," Vello drawled, staring bitterly at the bowl of food he probably couldn't stomach. "Your audacity is starting to grate on my nerves, son."

"Should've thought of that before you invited me into your family."

A tug on my wrist made me look down at my wife.

"*You get more bees with honey,*" she signed.

"Fine." I shook her off. "If your mother's pathetic life means something to you, I guess she can keep it."

Chiara put a hand to her diamond-decked neck, staring at her daughter with anger and betrayal.

"You speak to him now?"

"She does," I supplied. "As she should. I'm her husband."

"*Mama, please.*" Lila's eyes were begging.

Chiara looked the other way. Something happened in my body. Something that didn't even happen when I watched my sister almost get shot to death in a game of Russian roulette when we were kids.

Rage. Potent and red and inescapable.

"Mama, you told us Lila can't understand us." Luca kneaded his temples. "You said she is mentally four years old."

"I said what needed to be said to keep her safe." Chiara straightened her back primly.

"All this time… We could've talked to her." Enzo's lower lip curled.

"You dodged a bullet." Achilles turned to Lila. He didn't seem any more rocked by this revelation than he was by tomorrow's weather forecast. "Asshole would've talked your ear off."

"*Achilles,*" Chiara chided.

"He started it," Achilles said gravely.

"Look at me. I'm the picture of a good brother." Enzo gestured to his baby face. "How did I start it?"

"You were born," Achilles deadpanned.

"Does this mean we'll all have to learn ASL now?" Enzo swirled his tongue over a spoonful of soup.

"Yeah," Luca growled. "All of us. Nonnegotiable."

"Ugh, I suck at languages."

"You suck at everything," Achilles comforted him.

Luca turned to Lila, his scowl softening. "I'll take ASL up immediately. In the meantime, if you need anything, you text us."

Lila nodded, offering him a warm smile.

"This is madness." Vello glared at his wife. "You cost me a good business deal. We'll have words later."

"Hold up." Enzo raised his palm, turning to me. "How do *you* know ASL?"

"Grew up in a military school. They only let us speak one hour a day, and we were chatty bastards." This skimmed the truth without really revealing it.

Vello motioned to his daughter, who turned to look at him. "Lila. Come here."

She tore herself from her soup and gingerly shuffled in his direction. My eyes never wavered from them. I didn't trust anyone who was willing to hand his daughter off to me.

He put a hand on her cheek. My fingers curled against the back of her empty chair, squeezing. "*Bambina mia.*" He tilted his head. "You sneaky little shit. I always knew you weren't an idiot. No child of mine can be stupid."

My nostrils flared. My wife's face drained of color.

"Lila," I clipped out. "That's enough. Come finish your food."

But my wife seemed to have enough of people bossing her around. Giving me the middle finger, she stomped out of the kitchen. Enzo stood up and followed her, muttering, "Nice going, *stronzi.*"

"She'd have never done this a month ago." Achilles pointed at me with an unlit cigarette, deducing he could smoke, now that she was gone. "You're spoiling her, Callaghan."

I wasn't doing jack shit other than not standing in her way to figure out who she truly was. She'd been kept on such a short leash here, her family naturally assumed she was a docile little thing.

"Mama." Luca turned to Chiara. "What you did to her was inexcusable. Did you really think you could get away with it?"

Chiara opened her mouth to talk, but at this stage, I was past my Ferrante family quota for the year and wanted to get out of there. I turned to her again. "Either we have words or I'll just assume you want me to break the happy news about my wife's incredible wits on a Times Square billboard." I withdrew my phone, making a show of it. "If I move quickly, I might be able to get Post Malone to make an announcement at his Madison Square Garden show tonight."

Life seeped out of her face in real time as she considered my ultimatum. She knew I'd follow through. I'd done a lot worse for a lot less.

Chiara tipped her head up, a gesture that reminded me of her daughter, rising to her feet. "Follow me."

We entered the second family room, tackily decorated and full of gold-framed paintings and shiny fabrics.

"Should I call for Imma to make coffee?" she asked, about to take a seat on an upholstered sofa.

"No need. I intend to make it quick."

"Very well." She stood up and waltzed over to me, keeping her features schooled.

"You robbed Lila of living a normal life, which is the bare fucking minimum. You made the entire world think she isn't capable, when in fact, she's the only child of yours I would let use heavy machinery."

"I gave her everything she ever needed," she countered. "My only sin was trying to protect her from men like *you*."

"Men like *me* are unavoidable." I straightened my cuffs.

"And what would she have done? Go to school? Find a boyfriend?" Chiara huffed. "Why dangle a normal life in her face if she could never truly have it? She'd have been miserable."

"Her life *was* miserable. You've cut her off from everyone but yourself."

"She had Imma, too," she said defensively, hugging herself. "And many tutors. Summers full of culture and fun on Ischia—"

"Nothing to prepare her for married life," I cut her off.

"If my plan had worked, it wouldn't have been necessary." Her hands balled into angry fists. "She wasn't supposed to marry a psychopathic monster."

"Yet, here we are."

"Not for long." A smile stretched across her lips. "This marriage won't last."

"Glad you brought up this subject." I stepped forward, getting into her personal space. "Because next time you try to conspire to take her away from me, we'll be doing less talking and more shoveling dirt over your body."

We stood toe-to-toe. She was small but fierce, like her daughter. Under the coiffed mane, designer dress, and delicate features was a beautiful demon Vello was too much of a coward to unleash. His loss. I wanted to drink from Lila's darkness in big gulps.

"You want me to believe you'll hit a woman?" She tipped her chin up in fake bravado.

My mouth twisted with a lazy smirk. "To keep my wife, Chiara, I wouldn't *only* hit a woman, I'd chase God himself with a fucking baseball bat."

"You told Vello you wouldn't kill me."

"I lied."

"You'll spark a war."

"This is an incentive, not a deterrent." I stared deep into her eyes. "Anything else?"

"Stop pretending you care for her." She pushed at my chest in frustration. I didn't budge.

"Why? Sore spot?" I tilted my head sideways. She was clearly nothing but an expensive uterus for the don.

She ran a shaky hand over her hair. "Hard to believe Jesus died for your sins."

"No one asked him."

"You walked into this family two minutes ago and you already think you know what's best for her? Tell me, do you have her best interest in mind, now that you're planning a full-fledged war with the Bratva?"

She had a point. Lila wasn't my top priority. But she pushed her way somewhere to the middle of the list. Before getting my dick wet, but after taking out the Bratva.

"Don't pretend you have her best interest in mind." She pressed on. "She means nothing to you."

"You're wrong. She does mean something to me. She's my best

business deal by a long mile, and I intend to keep my end of the bargain."

"It's the same business deal Vello made with me, and we all saw how it turned out." Tears rimmed her eyes. "She deserves someone who loves her."

"She'll settle for someone who protects her. Oh, and I'm taking Imma today if I have to pry her from your cold, dead fingers. *Imma.*" I snapped my fingers loudly. Imma appeared from the hallway, sticking her head through the doorframe. I knew she was eavesdropping, because her face kept poking through the crack in the door when she thought no one was looking.

"Somebody called my name?" Imma asked in faux innocence and a strong Italian accent.

"Pack a bag," I ordered, not breaking my stare-off with Chiara. "You're coming with us."

"Where are you going to house her?" My mother-in-law feigned amusement. "Your shoebox apartment can't fit a mouse."

"She'll take Lila's room."

"Right." Chiara snorted. "And where would Lila sleep?"

"With me."

"What makes you think my daughter would stoop this low?"

"The fact that she already *has.*"

Lila tossed, turned, and didn't sleep all night, but she never left my bed yesterday.

Chiara's jaw swung open. I reached with one finger, closing it for her.

"*Game. Set. Match.*"

CHAPTER TWENTY-FIVE
LILA

I'd really done it this time.

Mama wouldn't even *look* at me.

Didn't acknowledge my existence the remainder of the evening. What did Tiernan say to her?

It made my stomach churn with panic, guilt, and something else, something I didn't think I was capable of—hate.

I hated that she crumbled like a sandcastle when the going got tough. That she took a step back from me because I did the most natural thing in the world—communicated with my husband and opened up to him.

That night I slipped into my husband's bed again. I didn't hate it as much as Mama told me I would. I actually kind of liked having a firm, hot body next to mine. It made me feel secure.

And now I had Imma in the next room. She would keep me company, fill all those daytime hours I'd used surfing the internet. I found myself choking up with an unfamiliar emotion toward my husband. Somewhere between lust and affection, with a heavy dose of frustration thrown in.

I tossed and turned, as usual, until sometime around three o'clock, Tiernan turned me around to face him. He looked wide awake. He was still wearing his eye patch, even though I suspected he normally took it off at night. It seemed uncomfortable, and he often adjusted it, revealing the imprint of the string that held it together.

"What's wrong?" he demanded.

"*Nothing,*" I said. "*I don't sleep much at night.*"

"Always, or since the rape?"

"*Since the rape,*" I admitted. "*I'm afraid he'll come for me again.*"

"Wish for it, *Gealach*. Because if he does, I'd find a way to kill him a hundred times over."

I gave him a slight smile. He was still insufferable, but, as bizarre as it was, he felt safe. I hadn't realized I was waking him up, though.

"*If you want me to move back to my bedroo—*"

He caught my wrists, stopping me from completing the sentence. "Forget about the other room. This is your new bed now."

"*Okay.*"

"Anything I can do to make you less fucking jittery?"

"*Well…*"

I realized the only reason I could read his lips in near-complete darkness was because I found them the most fascinating thing on planet Earth. I wanted to draw them a thousand times over and ink them into my memory. To touch them. To…kiss them, even. Sometimes.

He was beautiful. And I had a feeling he found me attractive, too. I even found sick pleasure in realizing he dressed up Becky in my clothes to pretend she was me.

Tiernan gave me a quizzical look, still waiting for my words.

"*I don't know anything about you. Maybe if I did, it'd make sleeping in your bed not as weird.*"

"What do you wanna know?" He turned to his nightstand, flicking the soft light on.

"*Favorite food?*"

"Beef jerky."

"*Favorite color?*"

"Don't have one."

"*You must have one,*" I insisted. "*Everyone has one.*"

He studied my eyes in the dark for a beat, then finally said, "Blue."

"*When did you arrive in the United States?*"

"Fourteen."

"*Have you been with anyone else since Becky?*"

He curved an eyebrow, scanning me.

"Does it matter?"

"*It does to me.*"

"Why?"

"*Because if you're not true to me, I won't be true to you. And it doesn't matter if you kill him after. I spent my entire life being overlooked and disrespected by my family. I won't repeat the same mistake with you.*"

"No." A muscle jumped in his jaw. "There's been no one else."

Relief flooded me.

"*When did you lose your virginity?*"

"Twelve," he answered matter-of-factly.

"*What?*" I asked, smiling awkwardly. Surely, I misread his lips.

"*Twelve,*" he signed with his hands. "Although, it was hardly sex in its traditional form. I was forced to sodomize someone at gunpoint."

I sat up straight with my back against the headboard, staring at him in shock.

"They wouldn't let me stop until I came. Whoever came last had to drink the content of everyone's condoms. I was so repulsed by the idea, I forced myself to do it. She bled all over my cock. But I managed." He flashed me a cordial smile. "Still wanna know things about me, *Gealach?*"

I did, actually. More than ever before.

"*Who did this to you?*"

He gave me a wry look. "Next question."

"*Is this why you prefer anal sex?*" I had time to Google what he did to Becky. Apparently, it was intentional.

"It's the only thing I know."

My eyebrows shot to my hairline. "*Do you enjoy it?*"

He contemplated the question. "I taught myself to disconnect

my body from my mind when I do it. It's a low-stake sexual inter-
action. For pleasure only. Plus, it's a fuck you from me to the people
who forced me to do it. I now do it because I choose to, not because
I have a gun to my head." He was silent for a moment. "It reminds
me of who I am."

"*And who are you?*"

"A filthy beast concealed under impeccable clothes."

I considered his words, offering him a confession of mine in
exchange. "*I don't remember much of the rape, but I do remember it hurt
a lot. Not just the blows to my head and the punches to my body. The part
where he entered me. It felt like he was ripping me to shreds.*"

"Rape and sex are not the same thing, Lila. Sex can be great."

"*How do you know? You've never had that kind of sex.*"

"I have my sources."

I was starting to suspect he was telling the truth, but since he
didn't offer to have sex with me, I did not volunteer myself. I did file
it in the back of my head that Mama was wrong about sharing a bed
with a man. She said Papa stank of sweat and his slutty mistresses,
and that he snored. But Tiernan only smelled of Tiernan—leather,
musk, danger, dark woods—and even if he snored, I couldn't hear it.

"*What's the nickname you call me?*"

"Gealach."

"*Yes. What language is it in?*"

"Irish Gaelic."

"*What does it mean?*"

"Wiseass."

"*That's not very nice.*"

"I'm not very nice, *Gealach*."

"*What if the Bratva kill you?*" I readjusted on the bed, not-so-
accidentally brushing my arm against his warm skin. "*Who will
protect me then?*"

"My brother, sister, and the Camorra." He reached to tuck a lock
of hair behind my ear, staring at the golden strand with a faraway

look on his face. "You'll never be without protection. Your father won't send all three of your brothers with me because he still needs a new don. And." He grabbed another tendril, this time rubbing it between his fingers. "If I die, you'll be a widower. Your pregnancy will still be legitimate. You'll give birth, and down the line, can marry someone else without any stigma or prejudice."

Though this scenario should appeal to me, I found myself sick with the prospect. I didn't want anyone else. I wanted him to want me. Even if I wasn't sure if I was ready for what it meant.

"*This conversation is silly, because you won't die.*"

His gaze rode up to meet mine, and instead of his usual shark-like, dead stare, there was a boyish expression, almost...*hopeful.*

"Why? Would that sadden you?"

"*Why wouldn't it sadden me? You are a person. A life lost is always a tragedy.*"

Whatever flicker of hope shone in his eyes died a quick and violent death.

"That's a very nice thought to have about a man who contemplated raping you on your wedding night."

He pulled back from me. Mockery dripped from his expression. I didn't believe him. But it still stung. I turned around sharply, fluffed my pillows, and slammed my head against them.

I felt his bare, muscular chest rumble against my back as he scooped me from behind, his body engulfing mine to keep me anchored and stop me from tossing about.

He waited for my muscles to unclench, for my body to relax against his and accept his touch. His breath skittered over the back of my neck. A heady mix of mint and whiskey. It was the latter that made me wonder if surrendering to affection, to the basic need to be held by another human, was not only difficult to stomach for me.

It took twenty minutes before I was able to regulate my breath and stop feeling like I wanted to jump out of my skin. By then, I thought he was asleep again.

"Lila." His lips shaped my name over my ear, slowly, sensually. "*Lee-lah.*" My stomach bottomed out, heat spreading inside it, traveling to my groin. "I'm an excellent marksman and a terrible enemy. Go to sleep, sweetheart. Nothing can hurt you now that I've laid claim on you."

CHAPTER TWENTY-SIX
TIERNAN

What I needed to do right now was read the file Sam Brennan sent me on Lyosha's adventures in Moscow, then try to gauge his next move.

What I did in practice, however, was streamline the entire night of Luca's wedding to figure out which guest had followed her—Angelo or Tate.

Tate's motive was flimsy at best. He was happily married, his wife had just given birth to their son, and, judging by the fact he had almost set the entire city on fire when I kidnapped her, it seemed unlikely he'd jeopardize his relationship for a quick shag. Then again, Angelo was a member of the Chicago Outfit. Touching the Camorra princess was a war declaration. One the New York–based Mafia would win by a landslide.

I was hitting one dead end after the other. The crime scene was contaminated now, and my suspects were high-profile enough to refrain from conducting themselves sloppily. Their phones and computer records all came back spotless.

"It's not Angelo who did this," Achilles said.

"He's my best bet." I cracked my knuckles.

"Let me spell it out for you, in case I wasn't clear enough." Achilles stacked his feet on my desk at Fermanagh's, sitting back leisurely. "I'll be fucked and damned if I let you drag an Outfit and family member into my dungeon and watch you shred off his skin with a kebab slicer to interrogate him based off your hunch."

"It's not a hunch," Fintan said heatedly. "He disappeared right after she did for an entire hour before he came back. He's also the single, childless one between the suspects, so fewer strings attached."

"So did the fourteen other men," Achilles pointed out.

"Thirteen, seeing as we crossed off oxygen tank fella." Tierney was keeping score.

"Shut up, *piccola fiamma*. The grownups are speaking now."

"*Piccola fiamma?*" I arched an eyebrow.

"Little flame." Tierney rolled her eyes coquettishly. "He has a slight obsession problem. I tried to gift him an autograph and a pair of used underwear, but he's relentless."

I scowled at Achilles. I didn't appreciate him shutting my sister up. I appreciated even less that he seemed to haunt her no matter where she went.

"Oh, and no one's asking for your permission to talk." Tierney skewered him with a glare. "Mr. They-Haven't-Built-a-Condom-Big-Enough."

"I've good news, sweetheart. The condom's been built. Wanna give it a try?"

"I could do without watching my sister and brother-in-law engaging in verbal foreplay while we work." I returned my attention to the suspect list in front of me. "Let's stick to the subject."

"Luca's in Chicago, so I'm speaking here on his behalf," Achilles said. "And I'm telling you he won't be game to interrogate his wife's brother unless you come to him with a concrete piece of evidence."

"Okay, can I play devil's advocate here?" Tierney paced along the small office.

"Doing the devil's PR is actually the perfect job for you, if you weren't too lazy to hold one," Achilles mused. Tierney shot him a deadly glare but continued.

"Angelo is basically family to the Ferrantes. He's going to be seeing Lila socially for decades to come. Why would he run the risk Lila would snitch?"

"How the bleeding hell can she snitch?" Fintan frowned. "She's nonverbal."

Achilles shook his head. "It was a misdiagnosis. She is hard of hearing, but intellectually astute."

"*What?*" Fintan's eyes nearly bugged out of their sockets, and he turned to look at me. "You knew about this?"

I nodded.

"When did you find out?"

"Pretty much on our wedding night, when she tried to kill me several times," I said dryly. "She confessed a few days ago."

"She speaks?"

"ASL, yes. It was obvious from the get-go intelligence wasn't the issue." Tierney stopped at the open-space kitchenette, pouring herself a three-hour-old coffee. "Jury's still out on her brother, though."

"I'll have some of that coffee." Achilles pointed at Tierney with the hand that held his cigarette. Everyone in the room, including the coffeepot, knew the order wouldn't fly.

Astonishingly, Tierney poured another cup. She strutted her way to Achilles's side of the desk, raised her arm, and poured the dark liquid over his head. He snatched the paper cup quickly—no more than a few droplets of coffee grazing his attire—and flicked it on Tierney's dress. She sucked in a breath, staring at him in rage. Her miscalculation surprised me. He was, among other things, an assassin. Killer instincts were what kept him alive.

"You asshole!" she growled.

"Tierney, get out," I ordered.

"What? Why me?"

"Because you'll end up hitting him, and something tells me he'll hit you back, and then I'll have to kill him, which will derail all my plans."

"He should be the one to go!"

"I need to negotiate Angelo with him."

"You know what? Screw all of you." She stomped away, slamming the door so hard the walls rattled.

She'd get him next time. My twin shared my uncanny ability to turn rage into power.

Achilles flaked drops of coffee from his Tom Ford shirt, turning to me. "As I said, Angelo's motive doesn't add up."

"Neither does Tate's," I responded.

"Why isn't Lila solving this predicament?" Fintan frowned, gathering the documents in front of us into a stack. "Surely, she could point the attacker out for you if you showed her pictures of all the men in question."

"That's the problem." I tapped a pen to my desk rhythmically. "She remembers what happened, and has vague flashbacks, but she doesn't remember his face at all. Probably blocked it as some sort of a coping mechanism. And since Achilles cares more about saving face than about his sister…" I trailed off.

"Bring me a shred of proof he did it, and I'll help you gut him alive," Achilles said. "You've got the wrong guy, Callaghan. If I didn't know any better, I'd think those pesky things called feelings are clouding your judgment."

"I'd be lying if I said I don't want to kill the bastard myself," I conceded. But it had nothing to do with feelings. I needed to bury the secret with him.

"Stand in line, fuckface." Achilles tossed his phone between his fingers. "I don't think I'll even be able to get a few kicks in, with the way Enzo and Luca are consumed by it. You still keeping your filthy hands off my baby sis?"

He was talking about the nice duffel bag full of cash he disposed of at Fermanagh's every first of the month.

Not for long.

"For now," I said noncommittally.

"Mama said you sleep in the same bed. Is that right?"

"Yeah." I ran a hand over my hair. "Your sister has trouble sleeping. It's better with someone around."

"And you don't mind spooning?" Achilles snorted.

I said nothing. It was none of his goddamn business what Lila and I were doing at night. Suddenly, I had less need for that duffel bag full of cash.

Fintan stood up, knocking his coffee cup over the documents I had printed out.

"Shite," he hissed.

Achilles rolled his eyes. "How do you let him work with you? He's a useless drunk."

"And Enzo is a fuckboy who likes making coats out of his victims." I hitched one shoulder up. "You don't choose family."

But if I could, I'd choose Fin all over again for the way he walked through fire for me.

"I'm not drunk," Fintan mumbled, gathering the damp papers and taking them to the nearest trash can. "Just tired."

"Anyway." I jerked my chin toward Achilles. "All the other suspects are low on my list after reading Brennan's report. Tate and Angelo are at the top. I suggest we start with bringing Tate in and take it from there."

"Might require a little legwork. He's in England now, fawning over his newborn." Achilles collected his wallet and cigarette pack from my desk, standing up.

"Guess we'll have to lure him back in the good, old-fashioned way."

CHAPTER TWENTY-SEVEN
LILA

I sat crisscrossed on Tiernan's bed, examining my treasure.

As promised, he bought me everything I wanted from the internet and opened an Amazon account for me, where he taught me how to order things. It was a fairly simple process, which infuriated me even more, because why did Mama cut me off from such a great invention?

There was a mouthwatering number of books about arts and music in front of me, a new Kindle—connected to the internet this time—a vibrating alarm clock, a bed shaker, sound field speakers, and a Bluetooth microphone. I also splurged on new sketchbooks and pencils.

I picked up my phone and checked if Mama answered my last message.

> Lila: Are you really cutting all ties with me because I speak to my husband? Do you understand how utterly deranged that is?

The message was read, but there was no reply. It had been a week since her showdown with Tiernan, so I gathered she made her decision. I was dead to her.

With a sigh, I opened a new message bubble and texted Enzo.

> Lila: How's Mama doing?

> Enzo: Still butthurt. Fuck her, though. It's for her to work out with herself. You did nothing wrong.
> Lila: It's a huge change for her.
> Enzo: Nah. It's a huge change for YOU. If she can't be there for you, she deserves to stew in it until she comes to her senses.

Even though I knew he was right, talking about it made tears sting my eyes.

> Lila: And how's your arm?
> Enzo: Better. Even managed to rub one out yesterday.
> Lila: Rub what out?
> Enzo: Oops. Nothing. Is Tiernan treating you well?

I googled the meaning of *rub one out*. Gagged. Reopened our text window.

> Lila: No complaints here.

I was downplaying it, of course. The truth was, I liked my husband. I liked our dinners. I liked his dry sense of humor and sardonic smirks and that he spooned me from behind at night just to make me practice being touched. I still couldn't sleep at all, but at least I could be in the same vicinity with an intimidating, muscular male without recoiling.

> Enzo: I still can't believe you can talk. The amount of gossip sessions we could've had about our messed up family ☹.
> Lila: We can always play catch up.
> Enzo: Don't worry. I have a feeling we're about to get some fresh material soon, between Luca and Achilles.

I smiled, shaking my head. My phone vibrated, alerting me through a special app that the front door had opened. It was one of the many gadgets Tiernan had installed for me.

A moment later, my husband appeared at our bedroom door, parking his shoulder on the doorframe. For a moment, he just stared at me.

"Hi." I smiled. He didn't.

"Have you slept any tonight?"

"*I'm fine.*"

But I wasn't.

I knew he was disgusted with the baby growing inside me, and I had a feeling he was going to find a creative way to get rid of both of us once I gave birth.

He avoided touching my belly completely when he held me at night, sticking to my shoulders, my rib cage, my waist. As if my midriff was radioactive.

My husband pushed off the doorframe, advancing toward me. "Get dressed. We're leaving in fifteen minutes."

"*News to me.*"

His penetrating gaze told me he did not appreciate me lipping back.

I sighed. "*Where are we going?*"

It couldn't be the OB-GYN, because I switched to someone else and booked my own appointment online, so I knew exactly when it was. The prospect of seeing Brandy again gave me the hives. And I didn't trust myself not to bash her head against the reception desk.

"The shooting range. I'm going to teach you how to use a gun, since not knowing how to use one doesn't stop you."

My spine straightened. His words from our wedding night tumbled back into the forefront of my mind.

"*If you were a real Callaghan, I'd have taken you to the shooting range to work on that aim. We have a reputation to uphold.*"

Did that mean I was a real Callaghan now?

I decided to get dressed and do what I was told for once. I made my way to the walk-in closet in my old bedroom, and Tiernan followed me. We both stopped in front of my messy shelves. When I gave him an annoyed look, he explained, "Can't wear any frilly pink dresses or tutu skirts. Go for comfy jeans and a tee."

"*Got it. Would you like to watch me put them on?*" I asked sarcastically, since he wouldn't budge.

It was so liberating. Being sassy and daring and...*me*. Being me. I spent my entire life wondering who I truly was under the facade my mother made me put on. Being the girl she wanted me to be. And Tiernan let me find out who I truly was. As it turned out, I had a bit of a temper.

"Yes." Simple. Unapologetic. Cold.

Nibbling on the corner of my lower lip, I considered it. He'd already seen me naked at the doctor's office, and his gaze felt so good on my skin that just thinking about it made me want to moan.

"It'll be good practice for you. If you ever want to try sex." He slipped his hands into his front pockets.

"*With you?*" Butterflies exploded in the pit of my stomach.

"I'm your only option."

"*But I don't want to do it the way you do.*"

"I know."

His answer was loaded. My heart beat in an uneven staccato.

"*So you are saying you are going to take me the way you take other women?*"

"No." He tore his gaze from mine, suddenly exhibiting acute interest in the ceiling. "I'm saying you're not the only one who's growing up here."

I chose a pair of skinny jeans and a tight riding shirt and put them aside as I slowly stepped out of my pajamas. Tiernan stood at the doorway and drank in my every movement. A few weeks ago, I'd have a panic attack from the prospect of him being so close to my naked figure. Now, I resented him for not walking over to me and kissing me like in the movies.

Stepping out of my pajamas, I stood before him in nothing but my white cotton underwear. I had a little baby bump. It was small and hard. When his eye moved over me, head to toe, he took his time touching and caressing every inch of my body with his gaze. But when it reached my lower abdomen, his eye skated over it quickly.

I gulped, putting my clothes on. Bitter disappointment exploded on my tongue.

When we slipped into his car, I noticed there weren't any soldiers with us. I found it peculiar, but not unwelcome.

"Whatever happened to only teaching your real wife how to shoot a gun?"

"Gotta renew my own permit." He adjusted the rearview mirror. "Figured you could use a class or two."

He infuriated and confused me. One moment he offered me sex, the other he looked disgusted with my belly. His behavior gave me whiplash. And the worst part was, I couldn't discuss it with anyone, because Mama disowned me and Tierney's loyalty was with my husband.

We arrived at the shooting range twenty minutes later. Tiernan got out of the car and rounded it, opening the door for me.

It was a massive black building that looked like a gym from the outside. The first floor was a weapon shop. Tiernan placed his hand on the small of my back and steered me to the second floor through the stairs. The upper floor was the actual range. There was a lobby manned by a guy with a backward baseball cap and a black Henley, firearms and earmuffs on display behind him. There were also stalls, divided by black walls. A few people were practicing, and the scent of gunpowder and hot metal slipped into my nostrils.

Tiernan and the guy at the lobby exchanged bro-hugs.

"Callaghan, my good man. How's it been?"

"Jace. Is my wife's gun ready?" Tiernan parked an elbow on the counter.

My *what?*

Jace nodded, reaching under his counter and taking out something that looked like a luxury brand shoebox. He dragged it across the counter toward me. My eyes darted to my husband.

He jerked his chin. "Open it."

I popped the lid hesitantly, my mouth breaking into an involuntary beam.

It was a hot-pink gun, studded with diamonds around the muzzle. The trigger was covered in pure white silk. It was ridiculous, over-the-top, and completely me. It was also the first gift Tiernan ever gave me.

"Wilson Combat SFX9." Tiernan's lips moved in my periphery. "Custom made."

Before I could stop myself, I flung my arms over his shoulders and pulled him into a grateful hug. He froze between my arms, his arms at his sides.

It reminded me that Tiernan had his own issues with intimacy and maybe embracing me from behind was all he could offer me right now. He touched people only on his terms.

Still, I didn't step back. On the contrary, I hugged him even tighter, wanting to suck in all of his trauma.

Eventually, he defrosted, his posture relaxing against me. He didn't hug me back, but he didn't push me away, either. I took that as a small win. After a few moments, he pulled back gently. He cupped my jawline, peering into my face. "You like it?"

"*I love it.*"

"Good, because you'll be carrying it at all times starting today. Here. I'll show you how to load and case it."

I spent the next twenty minutes with Tiernan, who familiarized me with the mechanics of the gun. Most of it I recognized from seeing my brothers practicing their shots as teenagers in the backyard. After Tiernan was certain I knew the ins and outs of handling and operating my firearm, we picked the farthest booth in the range. He put eye protection and earmuffs on me.

He placed himself right behind me in front of the shooting target—a printout of a faceless man—and engulfed my hands from behind, lacing my fingers into the gun to put me in position.

My heart kicked into high gear at his proximity. He was so much taller than me, he had to crouch when he tugged one of my earmuffs behind my ear and placed his lips close so I could feel the shape of his words on the shell of it.

"First things first, you always treat your gun like it's loaded. You never shoot until you're sure of your target and everything beyond it. Nod if you understand."

I nodded. I did understand. But I was too busy with the sensation of his body pressing against mine to actually *comprehend*.

"We all have a dominant eye. Mine was taken by Achilles. Yours is your right eye. Its pupil moves first when you read lips. This is the eye you'll always keep open. Nod."

Another jerk of my chin. I felt his erection digging into the curve of my lower back. He made no attempt to shift away, but also didn't draw any closer.

Would it really be so bad if we had sex the way he preferred? It wasn't like I had anything else to compare it to. And something in me wanted to please my husband.

"Your goal is to form small groups at the same point to check your accuracy. Choose a spot on the target."

"The center of his chest," I answered verbally. He nodded, his stubble brushing against the side of my neck.

His scent. His touch. His very existence made me drunk.

"Pay attention to your wrist. Here." He adjusted my hands. "This'll help you avoid jams. Watch your stance, baby." He kicked my legs apart, and the movement was so confident and erotic that something inside me clenched and heated.

Baby.

"The wider your legs are, the firmer your core. Now I want you to show me a good, steady grip. Yeah, just like that. You're ready."

Evidently, I wasn't.

My first shot hit the target's head. My second—his shoulder. The third one got his throat, and the fourth finally got the center of his chest, through sheer luck rather than technique. Tiernan walked me through my many mistakes. He had good input. Too bad I couldn't concentrate on anything when his body was glued to mine, his hands encasing my own, his scent wrapping an invisible hand around my throat, squeezing erotically.

Desire.

Just like that, I understood perfectly all the Roman legends and Greek mythology stories about empires falling and heroes sinning for lust.

The session lasted for another hour before Jace knocked on the side of our booth.

"Callaghan. You're up."

Tiernan nodded and motioned with his hand. A clean target sheet was placed in front of us. This one was rolled all the way to the back, twice as far as the length I trained with.

Tiernan unloaded my gun, emptied my chamber, and handed it back to me. He nudged me aside, the loss of his body against mine leaving goose bumps across my arms. I stood back and watched as his target started moving, jerking from side to side on its cord. Tiernan raised one steady hand, and in two-second increments, shot the target in the head eighteen rounds with chilling accuracy.

By the time they rolled the target toward us, there were only two bullet holes in the center of the forehead and nowhere else. He basically rammed through the exact same spot over and over again.

"Legend." Jace slumped against the wall, a postorgasmic look on his face. "Fucking legend."

Tiernan turned toward him, tossing our earmuffs into his hands. "Out."

Jace floored it out of our booth.

"What's wrong?" Tiernan swiveled to scowl at me.

"*Why do you think something is wrong?*"

"You've been staring."

Blush crept up my cheeks. I was completely taken with a man who did no more than tolerate my presence in his life so my family could help him.

He didn't choose me. He was forced into this union.

"*I'm just annoyed with myself for doing so poorly,*" I lied.

Explaining I was daydreaming about him kissing me silly was out of the question.

"Seen worse." Tiernan unloaded his pistol. "Your brother Enzo couldn't shoot an elephant if it sat right on top of him."

I gave him a chiding look.

"*You're lying.*"

His stone-cold expression remained stoic. "Why do you think he prefers knives?"

"*You're jealous because he's good with his hands.*"

"And I'm not?"

"*I wouldn't know. You haven't touched me much.*"

His smirk was mocking, amused. "Are you flirting with me, wifey?"

I pushed at his chest, my face unbearably hot. "*Hardly.*"

"Looks to me like you are." He cocked an eyebrow. "Don't worry. It's working."

"*Maybe guns aren't for me.*"

"Guns are for everyone." He threw me an incredulous look. "Especially the wife of a man who just killed the Russian pakhan."

"*Is that why I have so many bodyguards?*" I asked. "*Because of the dead pakhan?*"

"Why the fuck else?"

"*Because of what happened to me.*"

"That won't ever happen again. You're mine now, Lila."

"*But the Russians can still hurt me,*" I pointed out. "*Maybe the answer is not to be married anymore.*"

I gave him my back, stomping out of the booth. I wanted to escape this feeling. This urgency. The need to touch him. To conquer something inside him I wasn't even sure existed.

Tiernan clasped me by the wrist, yanking me back to him. My body slammed against his, my full, tender breasts colliding with his abs. He glowered at me, a hint of disgust pulling the corner of his lips down.

"You want me to kiss you." He stared at me abhorrently, like I was deranged.

I barked out a laugh, snatching my wrists back so I could answer. "*You're delusional.*"

"You're more fucked up than I suspected."

How could he read me so well? It drove me to madness.

"*I just might kill you,*" I warned.

"I just might let you," he deadpanned. "Why?"

"*Why what?*"

"Why do you want us to kiss?"

"*Because…*" I spluttered, dying of embarrassment. "*Well, forget about it!*"

I spun again, but he tugged me back to his body, grabbing my jaw and tilting my head up.

"I may not be good."

I huffed, wanting to strangle him. This absolute *idiota*.

"*I think we can handle one bad kiss.*" My hands moved clumsily. "*We both survived far worse.*"

"Whiskey in a teacup," he muttered to himself, staring at me in fascination. "Unassuming to the naked eye. But so sharp. And oh, that bite."

I didn't have time to ask him what he meant.

His lips fastened over mine.

We both stilled, holding our breaths. Tiernan was the first to put his hand on my face, snaking his other one around my waist, drawing me in.

It was cautious and exploratory. Like treading into a foreign body of water. At first, it was so soft, I second-guessed its own existence. A tentative brush of the lips. A breath that passed between us, where I couldn't tell who inhaled and who exhaled.

But then he applied more pressure against my mouth, and the decorum and elegance my mother taught me all flew out the window as I pressed all of me against all of him and opened my mouth, darting my tongue to trace his lower lip.

It was plump and warm. My toes curled inside my shoes.

His deep groan of surrender echoed inside my body. His mouth opened over mine, his hand sliding into my hair. He tugged on the elastic holding my hair in a ponytail, letting the yellow tendrils fall across my face, deepening our kiss.

It felt like slowly drifting into a sweet dream while slightly drunk on the finest wine. Our tongues touched for the first time, and fireworks exploded in the pit of my stomach. All my blood rushed between my legs. I clawed at his chest, rising on my tiptoes, demanding more.

His mouth became frenzied, greedy, nipping and biting and kissing and tonguing. We kissed for a few minutes before he ripped his mouth off mine, staring at me feverishly, a stunned glint in his eye. We were both panting hard.

"Shit." He wiped his mouth with the back of his arm. "*Fuck.*"

My heart bottomed out. Did I do something wrong?

But then he grabbed my face roughly and kissed me again, even more wildly. I locked my arms around his neck, moaning into his mouth. He hoisted me up to wrap my legs around his waist, pressing me against the cubicle wall. I could feel the thuds of gunshots popping against my spine each time someone took a shot in the range, and the vibration seemed to hum in a tiny, secret place in my core. Wild and fast like my heartbeat. My husband tasted so good. Like coffee and mint and absolution. His cock was nestled in my opening through our clothes, pulsating against it.

I pulled my mouth from his, gulping a quick breath, and released my hands from around his neck to sign, *"Do you think we're doing it correctly?"*

"Don't fucking care." His teeth caught my bottom lip, sucking it into his mouth. "I want more of it."

We kissed again. This time our tongues danced together, and I dished it as good as he served it. I was putty in his hands. Hands that knew how to shoot the same target down to the millimeter. Hands that killed, tortured, and destroyed many lives.

Hands I knew would never hurt me.

My husband. My protector. My macabre fantasy.

Rubbing my breasts over his torso, enjoying the friction against my nipples, I traced the tip of my tongue along his lips, and then kissed him more deeply. He groaned against my mouth, sucking my tongue ardently.

The fabric of my shirt teased my skin, begging to be ripped.

It took everything in me to tear my lips from his, and I only did that because it felt like I was wetting myself. My underwear was damp, even though I didn't feel like peeing.

I pressed my palms to his chest, and he immediately set me down, releasing me from his hold. But whereas I was panting like a rabid animal fleeing a predator, he appeared to be unaffected, save for his swollen, pink lips and the erection in his slacks.

"Okay?" he asked.

I nodded.

"You look terrified."

My cheeks flamed with heat. *"Something happened."*

"Yeah. No shit."

"Not that…"

He wiped his lower lip with his thumb, searching my face.

"I think I had an accident."

God, this was excruciating to admit. But what if that meant something was wrong with the baby? I knew nothing about childbearing.

"You think it was an *accident?*" he repeated dispassionately. I felt him retreating back to his usual sullen mood. "Well, we don't have to do that again."

"*No. Not the kissing part. I…I think I wet myself.*" I felt my eyes glass over with unshed tears. How humiliating. How utterly unbearable that this was how my first kiss had ended. "*I hope it's not blood. My panties are all wet. I need to check.*"

He stared at me. In disbelief at first, then with something else altogether. Hunger, delight, and amusement.

I had a feeling he wanted to laugh again, and that made me furious. Even if he didn't want this baby, that didn't mean he needed to be happy about it. I pushed off his chest, scowling.

"*This is serious. Where's the restroom?*"

"*Gealach.*" He scooped me up by the waist, spinning me once as though I was a child, in a moment of heartbreaking gentleness. "Nothing's wrong with you. We got a little carried away and your body—your smart, healthy, *functioning* body—got itself ready in case we were going to have sex."

"*What do you mean?*" I glowered. He put me down.

"Nothing is wrong with the baby or with you. Your body self-lubricates when it gets turned on, because your brain tells it you're about to have sex. It's natural."

"*Oh, thank God.*" I collapsed against the wall, crossing myself. "*I thought something was seriously wrong with me.*"

"Get used to it, *Gealach.*" He pushed forward, leaning down to capture my mouth with another kiss. He held my face up, so I could see his lips when he spoke. "You're going to be very wet for me, very often, and you're going to love every fucking minute of it."

A few minutes later, we were in the lobby with Jace, who was hunched over a pile of paperwork.

Tiernan watched as Jace stamped his concealed-carry permit. Then my husband quietly slid my ID across the counter to Jace and jerked his chin toward it. "Process this one, too."

Jace froze on the other end of the counter. His eyes landed on my birthdate, and his throat bobbed with a swallow.

"She's, uhm…" He coughed into his fist nervously. "Not twenty-one yet."

"You saying I can't math, lad?" Tiernan raised a perfect eyebrow.

Jace rubbed at the back of his neck.

"Wh-what? No, man. Not at all. My bad. I'll get that permit handled straight away."

When we got into the car, I decided to needle him again. It was my favorite new pastime.

"*Why wiseass?*"

"Mm?" He twisted his Rolex on his wrist.

"*My nickname. Why did you call me wiseass the first time we met, on the fountain?*"

The night you almost killed me; I didn't complete the sentence.

"Because," he said slowly, "calling you hot ass didn't seem appropriate at the time."

I grinned as I stared out the window, watching the scenery wilting as we left the pretty parts of New York and entered Hunts Point.

CHAPTER TWENTY-EIGHT

FIFTEEN YEARS AGO

The last time Tiernan had seen the sun was ninety-six days, three hours, and fourteen minutes ago.

Just as well, as he'd always preferred the moon.

The moon was a constant. It appeared every night, be it winter or summer, providing him with the kind of stability the pesky sun never could.

And it was beautiful. Pale and glowing in the ocean of darkness.

The moon was his friend. His assurance that no matter what, something bright waited in the gloominess.

He was lying in his cot next to his sister. Tierney was fast asleep, wrapped in both their blankets. He always gave her his.

"Does it ever get any warmer?" a heavily accented voice asked to his right.

Tiernan slowly turned his head to detect its source. A man in his late sixties, pale and malnourished, shivering under his quilt. He wasn't going to make it to the end of the month. Tiernan had seen people like him come and go. He was usually the one tasked with scraping them onto a gurney and dumping them in an unmarked grave.

"Niet," Tiernan said simply.

And then, because he was curious—because he'd always been

curious about the outsiders who came there—he asked, "How did you get here?"

"Prisoner of war, you could say." The stranger sat straighter in his cot, his back flat against the wall. "I am an American. I was dumb enough to steal Igor's shipment. Name's Michael."

"Tiernan."

"Doesn't sound too Russian." Michael crumpled his rather ugly face.

"It's not."

"Do you speak English?"

"Niet."

Silence. Somebody moaned at them to shut up. Tiernan ignored the plea. Alex was away for Novy God, probably eating caviar in front of a crackling fire.

"Do you want to?" Michael asked.

Tiernan considered his question. It would be good to know English so he could communicate with his family when he and Tierney escaped. He had every intention of doing that. But English would be useless short-term.

"Igor speaks English," Tiernan said after a while. "I wouldn't be able to communicate under his nose."

"If it's communicating under the radar you're after, you should learn the American Sign Language," Michael said. "I can teach you. My wife is deaf. She taught me to speak it. Always drove my friends nuts when they came over and couldn't understand what we were saying."

Tiernan liked that idea. He liked it a lot.

"You don't have more than two weeks in you," Tiernan said tonelessly, nonetheless.

"I know," he allowed. "But two weeks are enough if you make the most of them."

Tiernan was a fast learner. So was Tierney.

"All right. What do you want in return?"

They bartered everything in the camp. Food. Drink. Clothes. Medicine. The older kids bartered sex, too. But Tiernan refused to let Tierney do anything stupid for a bowl of porridge.

"*Your clothes. Blankets. Coats. Anything to fight this cold.*" The man shivered, coughing into his fist. Splatters of blood flaked his blue skin.

Tiernan ran his finger over the burn marks on his knees. Igor had tortured him with fire before he went to Moscow for the holidays. The abuse he had taken was becoming too dangerous. He didn't have time to waste. He needed to get out of here.

"*That's too much for a few language lessons,*" Tiernan said.

"*If you give me your food and clothes until I die, I will help you escape here.*"

Tiernan cocked his head.

"*It's too late for me,*" Michael acknowledged. "*But you still can. If you ever find your way out of these gates, you take the road of bones to Yakutsk. That's a twenty-hour drive, so you better have a car. Once you're there, go to Lenin Square. Every day, at exactly noon, a man named Dima will wait beneath the statue. He is my ride out of Russia. My wife pays him well. He'll take you out of here. Tell him Michael sent you.*"

"*What if he doesn't come there anymore?*"

"*Impossible. My wife said she'll pay him to do it until the day she dies.*"

That sounded like a risky plan and a load of bullshit. Then again, Tiernan had no other choice. He'd never set foot beyond these gates. Hadn't known a place other than this work camp.

He could drive well enough. He transported logs back and forth using vehicles. But he and Tierney would need a car and some food. A map of the Sakha. And, of course, the code to the main gates.

"*You need to escape or die trying, Tiernan. This is no way to live,*" Michael said. His lips were so chapped they hardly moved.

Tiernan shed his jacket and handed it to him. Not because he cared, but because he needed Michael alive to teach him sign language and everything there was to know about the outside world before he expired.

Michael burrowed into the fox's fur. "*Thank you.*"

"*Least I could do.*"

CHAPTER TWENTY-NINE
TIERNAN

228 DAYS TO SELF-DESTRUCTION

"Callaghan, you dumb fuck."

Tate Blackthorn rubbed at his eyes tiredly, hooked to lie detector wires in the Ferrantes' dungeon.

Sam was sitting on the other end of the screen, monitoring his answers. He arched a smart-ass eyebrow. "No lies detected."

"Ouch." Enzo smiled ruefully, playing with his knife in the seat next to Brennan. "Blackthorn decided to club Tiernan with a truth stick. Someone get the first aid kit."

"You're just here to answer questions," Luca informed Tate laconically, lighting up a cigarette.

"Nothing more. *For now.*"

Tate turned to face him, somehow looking both calm as fuck and angry as hell. "This is bullshit. Your brother-in-law just gave me two black eyes and a split lip."

Guilty as charged. As soon as I saw his sorry face, I was reminded of Lila's sketch and something compelled me to make his features just a little less symmetrical. It wasn't like he was shopping for a wife. He already had one.

"We pulled him from you in time," Luca reasoned. "He didn't break your nose."

"Night's still young," I pointed out. If Tate was Lila's rapist, his nose was going to be the least of his problems. I was going to hang his balls on a meat hook from the ceiling and kill him over weeks, if not months.

I didn't usually indulge in long, torturous killings—I lacked the time and patience. But something made me especially rabid for the rapist's blood.

It was that stupid kiss at the shooting range last week. It undid my goddamn existence.

My whole life derailed from that moment forward. My entire days were currently planned and arranged around kissing and dry-humping my wife like a bleeding teenager. We spent every night practicing in bed. She didn't realize it, but she was making loud, porn-worthy sounds. I didn't want to alert her, because she was self-conscious as it was about her lack of hearing, but it made for very awkward breakfasts with Imma.

My new maid thought I was screwing the little girl she had raised.

Only Lila was no longer a little girl. She was shaping up to be a woman. One that no longer found it scary or distressing when her panties got soaked.

We were working our way up to second base. Slowly. Not only did I not want to scare her off, but I had my own hang-ups to sort through. Giving up the way I sought pleasure meant giving up my armor.

"I didn't rape your sister," Tate snarled at Luca, pulling me out of my own thoughts.

Sam readjusted his tall frame in his seat, keystroking some commands on the polygraph.

"How about you shut the fuck up and wait for me to ask you questions?" he suggested pleasantly.

"You're messing with my baseline diagram."

Tate shot him a death glare.

"Don't be so butthurt," Enzo tutted. "If you did it, you deserve to die. You knew it could happen. Men in our line of work... We die while we're still alive. Young and strong."

"He's not that young," Sam said, staring at the screen.

"And not that strong," I added.

Tate snarled. Swear to God, I was having an allergic reaction to him.

What did she even see in this bastard?

"What's the accuracy rate on this shit, anyway?" Enzo flipped his knife shut, dismounting his feet from the desk and leaning to peer at the screen behind Sam's shoulder.

"About eighty-seven percent, in the correct environment," Sam grumbled.

"What constitutes a correct environment?"

"No chatty assholes bickering around me, messing with my interviewee," Sam replied.

Luca and Enzo quieted down. I was glad Achilles was on Crimson Key. I didn't need a full audience for what was about to unfold. Lila's privacy mattered to me.

Sam rechecked that all the sensors were correctly applied on Tate and sat back. "Ready?"

Tate gave him another murderous glare. "Take a guess."

"Is this about Tiernan hijacking your private plane and changing its course mid-flight to New York?" Enzo tapered his eyes. "Because I think we can all agree you'd have done the same for Gia."

"Doubtful, since I'd had the fucking foresight to assign her security after I married her," he bit out.

"Much good it did you." I smirked.

A little over a year ago, I kidnapped his wife while she was under Camorra protection. But this wasn't what interested me about the conversation. Tate was under the assumption Lila was raped *after* we got married. Alternatively, he was setting up the starting point for his elaborate lie.

Tate shook his head, staring at the ceiling. "How did you even find your way to my private plane?"

Easily. Almost everyone in every private airport around New York was in my pocket.

"If I tell you, I'd have to kill you," I said wryly. "And I need some answers before I do that. Shall we?"

Sam began by asking him simple enough questions—his full name, address, childhood pet names, and so on. It turned out that Tate had an unholy number of pets growing up. None of them made it to maturity, though. Sick little fuck. Sam proceeded by asking him if he attended Luca's wedding (yes), who he came with (his wife), and where he stayed (at the La Casa Delle Rose, the Ferrantes' six-star resort).

From there, he moved on to yes or no questions.

"Did you see Raffaella Ferrante at the wedding?" Sam watched the screen intently.

"Yes," Tate answered.

"Did you speak to her?"

"No."

"Did you interact with her in a nonverbal way?"

"No."

"Did you follow her out of the ballroom at approximately ten thirty at night?"

"No."

"Did you touch her during the entire duration of the night?"

"*No.*"

Tate's tone was clipped, his posture and expression bored. I caught Sam's gaze.

"Well?" I asked.

"He's not bluffing." Sam tilted the screen so I could see it. "The needle didn't budge."

"Psychopaths lie and pass polygraphs all the time," I countered. "They will themselves to believe whatever comes out of their mouths."

I wanted Tate to be the rapist. Angelo was a can of worms I wasn't sure I wanted to open. And killing Luca's brother-in-law was essentially starting a war with the Outfit.

"That's generally true if the heart and respiratory rate are already jerky and inconsistent. Tate's as calm as a cucumber. There are no discrepancies." Sam shrugged. "I think he is telling the truth."

I dragged my teeth along my lower lip, mulling this over. Lila said she forgot the face of her attacker—but did it really make sense that she'd draw Tate and his features wouldn't bring back the memory if it were him?

Plus, as much as I hated him, he didn't give me rapist vibes. Now, Angelo, on the other hand, was the kind of prick to take what's not been offered. A Mafia brat who had the entire world handed to him.

I jerked my head in a nod, and Sam stood up, unhooking Tate from the lie detector. Tate remained completely still, his eyes flicking among the three of us.

"So, it happened during Luca's wedding?" He crossed one leg over the other, grabbing Enzo's soft cigarette pack from the table and helping himself to one.

"Yeah." Luca reached to light his cigarette.

"How is she?" He blew a stream of smoke.

"She's…" *Brave. Smart. Resourceful. Talented. Witty. So nauseatingly beautiful I cannot wrench my goddamn eye from her face whenever we're together.* "None of your fucking concern," I finished dryly.

Tate shrugged. Luca stood up to pour him a drink. Forever the diplomat. If Vello wanted half a chance to save his sinking empire, appointing Luca as the don was a no-brainer. Enzo was too nice, and Achilles too evil.

"So where were you between 10:33 and 11:04 that night, Tate?" I rotated my head toward the billionaire. "Because it sure as fuck wasn't in the ballroom."

"Gia didn't feel well. She was nauseous and needed some

medicine. I went to the nearest convenience store and got her ginger candy, a Sprite Zero, and an herbal inhaler."

"They didn't have Sprite Zero at the party?"

Tate returned my glare bluntly. "I can probably pull up the receipt through my online banking account, if you'd be so kind as to fucking give me my phone back."

Luca shot me a look. I nodded.

Luca pulled Tate's phone out of his pocket and handed it over. Tate's thumb flew over his screen while I traced my inner cheek with my tongue. I could still taste my wife in my mouth. She seemed to be resilient and tough as nails. Most girls in her position would shy away from men, spiral farther down the dark hole they'd been sucked into, but not her.

Sure, she slept like shit, but she still got out of bed every morning. Made coffee for us and Imma. Tidied up our room. Cooked with Tierney. Hung out with Imma. Sketched. Filled my apartment with random shit as she caught up on eighteen years' worth of online shopping.

"Here." Tate stopped scrolling, placing his phone on the table and sliding it toward me. I caught it. The transaction showed Luca's wedding date, at exactly ten forty-five at night.

Sam ran the distance between the manor to the convenience store and back on his laptop. "How did you get there?"

"I walked," Tate said.

Sam turned to me. "Everything checks, Callaghan. Do with it what you will."

I sat back in my chair, blowing air. A part of me was glad it wasn't Blackthorn. Killing someone so high-profile came with a shit ton of paperwork. Plus, a demented, completely fucked-up part of me didn't want Lila to be betrayed by one of the few men she actually *liked*, even if the fact she liked him in the first place made me want to feed him his own fucking cock.

This meant my suspect list had shrunk to the measly count of one person. Angelo Bandini.

We let Tate go, but not before he spent ten minutes showering us with a scathing rant about how we couldn't hijack planes like we were in a B-grade video game. He then finished it off by saying, "You know, Callaghan, I still can't fucking stand your ass, but at least you've proven to be a better husband than you are a human."

He offered me his hand.

I stared at it.

"Aww," Enzo cooed. "Mommy and Daddy aren't breaking up, after all. Hug it out, bitches. I love feel-good moments."

"You're so fucking camp," Sam grumbled.

Enzo's cheeks flushed. "Oh, yeah? And you're such a fucking homophobe."

Sam tilted his head. "Is that an admission, pretty boy?"

Luca ribbed Sam. "Enough. Congrats on the baby, Tate. Boy or girl?"

"Boy," he said, hand still outstretched to me.

"He has a name?" I asked.

"Astile."

Of course, he and his wife were too fucking special to sire a Jake or a Peter.

With a sigh, I took Blackthorn's hand and shook it.

Tate Blackthorn would never be my friend, but I guess he was no longer an enemy.

CHAPTER THIRTY
TIERNAN

After the polygraph, I stopped at Fermanagh's to drink a pint of Guinness with Fintan to take the edge off. I didn't want to face Lila before I sorted myself out. A lot of shit ran through my head.

Relief. Fury. Unfathomable bloodthirst.

Tate not being the rapist was both good and bad. I needed to finish that prick, whoever he was. But if it was Angelo, shit just got a whole lot more complicated.

Finally, I dragged my ass upstairs and opened the door. Lila sat with Imma on the couch. They were both holding and stroking Lila's belly. It was still mostly flat, but her tits certainly got the memo. They were heavier and more swollen than before. Tender to the briefest touch.

"Hi!" Lila squeaked when I walked inside, hurrying to greet me at the door. She pressed her sweet lips to mine, throwing her arms over my shoulders. I kissed her back, annoyed with how fucking natural it felt.

"*Good news!*" she signed. "*We felt the baby today for the first time. It is doing a fluttery thing. It's like tiny fish are swimming in my belly. You have to feel it.*"

She grabbed my hand and pressed it against her bare stomach below her pink crop top.

Anger seared through my veins.

I didn't want anything to do with this bleeding baby.

At first, I was indifferent toward it.

But that was before.

Before Lila became more than just business.

Before I found out the baby was probably pure Outfit and Camorra bloodline.

It was possible—likely, even—that Lila was pregnant with Angelo's child. And if that were the case, and Angelo's identity was exposed, I doubted he would end up with a bullet in his face.

More likely than not, Vello would seize the opportunity to marry her off to him.

Not that I cared. It was what it was. There were no real alliances in our world. But I needed the Camorra for my plans with the Rasputins. That was all. Nothing more. Nothing less.

Fine. *Fine.* I did care. It was going to hurt.

Not a fatal wound by any means, but…

Let's just say I wasn't *eager* to get rid of her anymore.

And there was Lila, delighted and bursting at the seams because she could feel the eejit's baby inside her. Fucking fantastic.

"I feel nothing." I wrenched my hand away, snarling in her face. Lila's mouth hung open, those cerulean eyes sparkling with hurt and sadness.

I sidestepped her, making my way to the kitchen. "What's for dinner?"

I knew she couldn't answer me with my back to her. I was being a cunt, and there was nothing she could do about it. I held all the power.

Then why did I feel so…*restless?*

If the baby belonged to Angelo, I had a huge fucking problem to solve in order to keep this woman.

And I promised her family I'd find her attacker and bring him to justice.

Lila's heels clacked across the floor behind me, and for the first time in days, she didn't prepare me a plate of whatever Imma had made but folded her arms and gave me a pointed look.

Ignoring her, I uncovered the saucepan on the stovetop, grabbed a fork, and ate the pasta inside while standing.

She signed something. I kept my gaze on the pasta.

She stepped into my line of vision, snatching the fork from my hand.

"*What's your problem?*"

I had a bevy of them, and the shit she stirred in me was at the top of the list.

"No problem," I said dryly. "I'm fine with playing house, Lila, but make no mistake—I don't care about the bastard in your stomach. You decided to keep it. I didn't stop you. But don't expect me to pretend it's anything more than an inconvenience to me."

My words made her flinch, and the only thing stopping me from pulling my gun out and putting a bullet in my own head was my ironclad resolution to kill Angelo before I left this earth.

It was the first time I truly hurt Lila—not scared or intimidated her—*hurt* her.

And it didn't sit right with me.

Luckily, I was trained to push through any pain or discomfort.

"*I see.*" Her chin wobbled, and her nose pinked, but she didn't let the tears fall. She pressed a hand to her stomach protectively. "*I guess this means you don't want to know the sex of the baby. I got my NIPT results back today.*"

I stared at her coldly, leaning against the kitchen counter.

I wanted to say yes. Not because I cared. Fuck knows I truly didn't. But because *she* did and because making her feel better was worth making myself feel like shit. Normally, anyway. But this wasn't about feelings. It was about drawing a line in the sand.

I couldn't afford to care.

She could be gone tomorrow, if they found out it was Angelo's baby. And I'd have no one to blame but myself for being an eejit.

Because beautiful Italian Mafia princesses of respectable pedigree weren't meant to breed with poor Irish scum who made their buck running whorehouses.

Empty. I felt so fucking empty I was surprised I was still up on my feet.

"*I'll take that as a no.*" She tilted her chin up regally.

I watched her turn around and walk away. Spine straight and head held up high.

And for the first time in my life, I felt the kind of pain I didn't like.

———

That night, I dissolved into the person I was before she stitched me up.

I removed the eye patch before I went to bed. I used to do it all the time before she moved into my bedroom. The patch was a bitch to sleep with, needed constant readjustment, and besides, it felt good not to have the string digging into my skull.

I refrained from removing it thus far, committed to not scaring my delicate bride. Now, it didn't matter anymore. She wasn't staying. Angelo was the father. That was why he told Chiara he'd agree to marry her.

Flicking the bathroom light off, I moseyed into the lit bedroom. Lila was standing by her side of the bed, wearing a pale pink babydoll dress that showed off her magnificent tits. Her hair was loosely French braided, falling over one shoulder.

She turned to look at me, her throat bobbing at the sight of my ghastly eye. Or lack thereof. There was a milky white ball where the eye should be.

Lila gasped, the back of her knees hitting the bed frame.

I sauntered into the room. "What's the matter, darlin'? See something you don't like?"

She pressed her lips together. I wanted this. To destroy what we had. Snuff that hope out of my system.

Another step toward her. She didn't cower. Didn't move.

"Do I disgust you? *Repulse* you?" I stopped when I was toe-to-toe with her, snatching her chin, tilting her head up to make her look at her brother's handiwork.

"Do you regret letting me kiss those lips?" I dipped my head down to brush my mouth against hers. "Suck this neck?" My lips fluttered along the side of her throat, and I gave her a nice, visible hickey. "Bite this flesh?" I sank my teeth to her collarbone.

She stood there, completely still, letting me take out my anger at Achilles, and Vello, and Tate, and Angelo, and the fucking *world*, on her.

For a moment, I thought we'd both finally snap. Rip each other's clothes off and find out what this sex thing was all about. That in the heat of this anger, confusion, and revulsion, I would finally suck those beautiful tits. Taste that cunt that smelled like the most delicious of meals.

But then Lila pushed me off her, a storm dancing in her pretty blues.

"*If you're trying to make me hate you, don't bother,*" she signed. "*This high school bully stuff doesn't impress me. I know who you are. How you've taken care of me. I don't know what happened to you today, but I'm going to take some space from you and hope you return to your senses tomorrow.*"

I wanted to smash the walls down, because Lila was more mature, more levelheaded than my own grown ass. Because she refused to give up on us, when I knew the only way to keep her was to kill her entire family.

"*I'm going to sleep in the recliner tonight. If Imma sees me on the couch, she'll ask questions.*" She shook her head. "*Oh, and by the way. It's a boy. We, dear husband, are having a boy.*"

CHAPTER THIRTY-ONE
LILA

"A boy? Bummer. I'd been hoping for a girl." Tierney pouted. "Less chance Tiernan would gift her a Kalashnikov for her second birthday. Mafia men are super chauvinistic."

My cheeks still stung from Tiernan's rejection yesterday. I'd spent the entire night curled on the recliner across from our bed, refusing to share a bed with him. He slept through the entire thing, his chest rising and falling evenly in the dark.

"*He doesn't care,*" I signed to my sister-in-law, flipping through racks laden with pastel blue baby onesies in a Manhattan children's boutique.

"Doesn't surprise me." Tierney seized five hangers with expensive baby clothes, tossing them into an embellished straw shopping bag. The store was all white and pastel colors, floating hangers and white rustic furniture.

It was adorable, and still, I couldn't muster any kind of excitement.

"Tiernan is truly fucked up in the head. Calling him damaged wouldn't even scratch the surface." She picked up a fluffy white bunny, adding it to her basket.

I pulled a face. "*I thought we were in a better place.*"

"The only good place a man could be in is the doghouse." She patted my shoulder. "All men are disappointments, Lila. But Mafia men are especially rotten. Hold your head high and don't let him have power over you."

I gnawed at my lower lip, wondering how much of our conversations she shared with him.

"You're out of it today, aren't you?" She looped her arm in mine, strutting toward the cashier. "Don't worry. This is just fun-shopping. I prepared a full list of baby essentials on my phone. I'll send it over to you. It includes links, so just follow them and order everything."

I put my head on her shoulder. Tierney had been good to me. Better than Mama. The latter still hadn't spoken to me, since I "came out." And if I were being honest, I didn't exactly miss her companionship anymore. She seemed unhappy to see me thrive. Whereas Tiernan's answer to me shooting him was giving me classes so that next time I could do it better.

Ugh. Tiernan.

"You'll be okay." Tierney squeezed my shoulder.

"Thank you," I mumbled.

Tierney ran up the bill and I handed the cashier my husband's black Centurion. The two Irish soldiers and Camorra chaperone assigned to Tierney grabbed the bags and carried them back to my sister-in-law's Range Rover. We drove back to Hunts Point and decided to stop at the Italian deli for a snack.

The sun hung high above the buildings, and though it wasn't particularly warm, it was no longer arctic, so we settled at a round table outside. I ordered a latte and a plum tart, and Tierney made do with unsweetened black coffee. She looked like a supermodel, wafer-thin and feline in features. Even in black leather pants, a nondescript jacket, and oversized sunglasses, she turned every head on the street.

The nice guy who usually manned the register was our waiter. He came over to set up our utensils, his eyes on me the entire time. Tierney watched the scene in amusement as I flushed pink. He wasn't necessarily my type—I didn't even *have* a type—but I'd never had an admirer. And, yes—the fact that his existence pissed Tiernan off wasn't exactly unwelcome right now.

"This is good, thank you," Tierney told him after he finished setting up our table. When he left, she shook her head with a smile. "He's got it bad for you, sis."

"*He's just being nice.*"

"Sure. And Tiernan is just being supportive of the U.S. Arms Sales and Defense Trade." She snorted. "A true patriot."

"*I'm going to the restroom,*" I announced, standing up.

"All right. Holler if you need anything."

I walked into the shop and took the narrow aisle toward the restroom, slipping inside and doing my business. After washing and drying my hands, I cracked open the door and stepped outside. Nice Guy was standing on the other end, in a small, darkened corridor that led to the shop's stockroom.

I smiled politely, trying to sidestep him. He blocked my way, shoving his body between me and the path.

"I can't stop thinking about you," he admitted, putting a hand on his chest.

I stared up at him. Unease prickled the back of my neck, and I became short of breath. I shook my head, pointing at my ring finger, and tried to sneak away from him again.

He moved quicker, this time placing his big hands on my shoulders. Panic flared inside me.

"Come on, now. I see the way you look at me. The attraction is definitely two-sided." He winked. "And that prick can't satisfy you, I can tell."

I had no idea what he was talking about. I only had eyes for my husband. Even if I did look at him before, which I didn't, I now clearly wanted to run for the hills and beyond.

I stared at him angrily, my fists clenching next to my body.

"Word on the street is you can't speak." He grinned, putting his hand on my cheek, crowding me so my back slammed against the restroom's door. "That's why he married you. Because you can't fight back. Well, how about we make this our little secret?" He leaned down, grabbing a handful of my ass.

My gun. My gun was in my bag outside. I cursed myself for not taking it with me. I pushed at him with a roar, but before I could put my hands on his chest, he was yanked back with force.

Tierney was holding him by the hair, the edges of his scalp burning pink, murder in her eyes. She looked so much like her twin brother in that moment, I whimpered.

"What the hell is wrong with you?" Tierney barked. "Assaulting a pregnant woman."

She slapped him hard.

He snarled, rubbing at his cheek. "She was asking for it, walking around with her tiny little pink babydoll dresses three times a week. Prancing around without buying shit."

"Oh, God." Tierney shook her head, looking aghast. "You're insane."

"I didn't even touch her!"

"*He touched my ass,*" I tattled.

Tierney screwed her fingers into her eye sockets. "Shit. Tiernan is going to have a field day. Enjoy your last few hours on earth, scumbag." She shooed the guy, who scrambled, ran to the register, grabbed his messenger bag, and fled.

"Jesus Christ." She put a hand on my shoulder. "You all right?"

I nodded, even though I had no idea if that was true.

Tiernan was right—I was never to move around without my gun again. Next time, I was taking my bag with me.

"Let me take you back outside. I'm so sorry." Tierney ushered me back to our table. "Do you want to talk about it?"

"*No,*" I said honestly. "*This guy is going to get fired, and I'm never going to see him again. Besides, he barely touched me.*"

When we sat down, the baby fluttered in my lower stomach again. I instinctively pressed a hand to let him know that I noticed, and that I was here, waiting for him.

"This is starting to feel real, isn't it?" Tierney smiled.

I nodded.

"How do you feel about it?"

"*Frightened,*" I admitted. "*Excited. Worried. Oddly enough, I'm not mad anymore. I am mad at my rapist, of course. I want him to die a painful death. But not the baby. Once I decided to keep him, I promised to love him without prejudice.*"

Easiest decision I'd ever made. My papa never loved me because of who he thought I was, even though none of it was my fault.

"I'll love him for you, too." Tierney leaned in to put her hand on my stomach, her expression sobering all at once. "I could never have a baby, you know."

"*Of course you will.*" My eyes softened. "*I will speak to Achilles myself. He will—*"

She pulled away, shaking her head. "Save your breath. It has nothing to do with your brother. When I was twelve, I had a hysterectomy."

I blinked, unsure what she meant.

"They removed my uterus, Lila." She licked her lips, staring at her hands in her lap. "Well, they didn't plan on it. But… Something bad happened to me, and there were complications." She pursed her lips. "We experienced a lot of dark shit, me and my brother. I'm not asking you to forgive Tiernan for his bad behavior, but maybe you can find a way to understand him."

My heart felt like it was melting into mush. I wanted to hug him. Hug *her*. But I knew Tierney would misread it as a sign of pity and wouldn't appreciate it.

"*I am so sorry.*"

Tierney shrugged, throwing me a casual smile. "It's fine."

"*Who are they? The people who did this to you.*"

She shook her head. "It's not just my story to tell."

"*You are your own person, Tierney,*" I signed stubbornly. "*Independent from your brother. You are smart, beautiful, kind, and worthy. Remember that.*"

"And you?" She directed those verdant eyes, a shade lighter

than my husband's, at me. "Do you remember how strong you are? How resilient? How kindhearted? I never thought anyone could penetrate the walls my brother erected between him and humanity. They were—still are—impassable. Even I can't get through them sometimes. But you did, somehow. You're doing his head in, Lila." She smiled. "Don't be mad at him when he gets angry that those walls are tumbling down. The debris must be a bitch."

CHAPTER THIRTY-TWO
LILA

When I got back home, there was a gift box waiting on the kitchen table.

It was wrapped in lush pink satin.

I shrugged off my jacket, hanging it by the door. Imma wasn't in. Her son was visiting from Italy, so she took a few days off. Was it from her?

I made my way to the present, examining it without opening it.

When I turned around, Tiernan was standing before me, hands stuffed into his front pockets. Through the fog of exhaustion, I noticed the dark circle under his eye.

"You haven't slept well?"

I took his silence as confirmation. He ambled toward me, bracketing my face in his rough palms, sorrow gleaming from his eye. I exhaled in relief when I saw his eye patch was back. It hadn't disgusted me, seeing his eye socket the other night. But it did remind me of the pain my own kin subjected him to, and I felt shame and anger.

"It looked like you slept fine last night."

"I look like a lot of fucking things I'm not."

"Oh."

"Yes. *Oh.*"

"Like…what?"

"*Gealach.*" He brushed his nose against mine, breathing me in, fingers curling around my waist. "I'm sorry I was a cunt."

I palmed his face and pulled him away so I could read his lips better.

"*I'm not your punching bag, Tiernan.*"

"I know."

I waited for him to acknowledge the gender of our baby, to pick up the conversation from last night, but when he finally spoke again, he gestured to the gift on the table. "Got you a present."

Swiveling to reach for it, he caught my waist, anchoring me back in his arms. "You can't open it, though."

I frowned. "*What is it?*"

"Deli boy's cock."

My eyes flared in horror, and I pushed him away.

"*Oh my God! Why would you do that?*"

His face bricked over. "Tierney told me what happened. No one's allowed to touch you without permission. That includes me."

"*You could've simply gotten him fired!*"

"He disrespected you. Disrespected *me*. After I warned him."

"*You can't sever a man's genitals just because he tried to touch me.*"

"Why not?"

I stared at him, dumbfounded. "*The punishment doesn't fit the crime.*"

"I know." He bowed his head humbly. "But chopping off his hands seemed like overkill. I couldn't fit all the organs into the one small box."

I clutched my head, probably to stop it from exploding. What could I say to that?

I clutched my head, probably to stop it from exploding. What could I say to that?

My family was far from the realm of normal, but my brothers had never done something so violent because of me. So far, my conscience was clean as a whistle. Until now.

"*This is not romantic. It's deranged.*"

"Let's settle for both."

Folding my arms, I shook my head.

"No? Fine. I'll ask next time before I chop off people's parts for you."

"*Is he alive?*"

"Depends on your definition of the word." He toyed with the edges of his phone. "I stopped the bleeding, so he didn't die. But he won't be able to fuck or piss normally. And, of course, it's not ideal that he lost his job, now that the medical bills are gonna pile up."

"*This is sick.*"

"We do terrible things for family."

"*You consider me family?*" A warm tremor passed through my chest.

He jerked his head in a nod. "Now, what do you consider romantic?"

I was out of ideas. I never had a boyfriend, and the little curated romance my mother allowed me to consume, in the form of books and old films, was set either in a fantasy world or a war.

"*I don't know. What do you usually do to woo a woman?*"

"Tip her handsomely."

Good point. I rubbed the space between my eyebrows.

"We can go on a date." He dropped his gaze to his wingtips.

"*No, thank you.*"

He lifted an eyebrow questioningly.

"*You acted like a jackass yesterday and then gifted me a human penis.*"

"Make you a deal. If you go out with me, I'll buy you whatever you want."

"*What kind of woman would exchange her favors for money?*" I stared at him, scandalized.

"Most of them."

"*That's very misogynistic.*"

"I happen to share the same sentiment about men. Humans are easily corruptible. It's how I stay in business. So. Date?"

"*No.*"

"If you come, I'll answer any of your questions, nothing off limits. You'll get an hour."

This did the trick. I was thirsty for his words, for his story. He watched my face intently, knowing his offer was too good to pass up.

"*Bastard.*"

He grinned. "Get your jacket."

We went downstairs to Fermanagh's.

The place was hot, humid, and stank of sweat, stale alcohol, and fried food.

As soon as the patrons spotted us, they stood from their seats, clapping and whistling, like we were some kind of royalty. Tiernan slung his arm over my shoulder, yanking me to his side. A mixture of pride and embarrassment fizzed in my stomach. I'd spent my entire life trying to avoid attention just to land in the center of it now.

My husband's eye landed on a table at the far corner of the pub, and the two men occupying it immediately grabbed their pints and shuffled to the bar. Tiernan pulled out a chair for me, but I chose to slide into the long, red vinyl couch opposite his seat.

Before we managed to settle, Fintan materialized with two sticky menus and a broad smile. "Hello there, brother, sister-in-law." He bowed exaggeratedly. "What can I get ya?"

"I'll have a pint and vinegar crisps."

"All right. Lila?" Fintan turned to me.

"*Lemonade with some ice, please.*" I smiled.

"Lemonade with ice," Tiernan repeated verbally. "And crisps for her as well."

Fintan not speaking ASL made sense. It seemed whatever the twins went through, Fintan wasn't with them during that time.

"You still haven't spoken to your ma?" Tiernan asked.

I shook my head, about to elaborate, when I noticed something from the corner of my eye.

A vase with red roses sat on the pub's bar. My blood curdled into ice.

They reminded me of the tarnished rose tiara.

Pull yourself together. It's just flowers.

But I couldn't look away. They were uncanny.

Tiernan waved a hand in front of my face, frowning.

"Have you seen a ghost?"

"*I saw much worse.*" I gulped hard. "*Flowers.*"

There was no point in lying to him. Not that I was at risk of receiving flowers from my husband at any point in our marriage.

"Flowers," he repeated dryly, turning his head to follow my vision, before whipping his head back. "I concur. Hate them. Puppies, too." He was being sarcastic.

"*They remind me of that night.*" I squirmed. "*I had a white rose tiara. But it became red after the attack. I still remember it, half-buried in the sand.*"

He was quiet for a moment. Suddenly, he stood up, ambled to the bar, and knocked the vase inward. Everyone's heads whipped and the chatter stopped to see what caused the clash. Tiernan returned back to our table and assumed his seat like nothing happened. "Where were we?"

Fintan reappeared with our drinks before I could produce an answer.

"Did you just knock down the vase?" He frowned.

"I did."

"Uh, *why?*"

"No more flowers in or around this establishment."

Fintan's eyebrows jumped to his hairline. "Because…?"

"I said so." Tiernan took the first sip of his Guinness, darting his tongue to lick the residue foam from his upper lip. "Now go deal with the flowerpots hanging from the windows."

Fintan left.

I shook my head. "*Thank you. But I can't avoid roses forever.*"

"Challenge accepted."

"*I'll need to get over it at some point.*"

"That point won't be tonight. Probably not tomorrow, either."

I took a sip of my lemonade. It was very sweet and made the baby cartwheel in my belly. Which reminded me of another, elephant-sized hurdle between us.

"Ask your questions," Tiernan said.

"*Can you stop calling me wiseass now that we're friends?*"

"Wiseass?" He tilted his head.

I typed on my phone, turning the screen so he could see it. **Gealach.**

"First of all, I'm not your friend. Second, *Gealach* means moon in Irish." A joyless smirk found his lips.

"*Moon?*"

"Mm. The first time I saw you, you were drowning in the night. I was in pain and in a terrible fucking mood. And you glowed. You shone so bright, I couldn't look away." His chest expanded with an inhale, and he frowned to himself. "You were my first dream, I think."

My heart shattered, scattering into tiny shards in the pit of my stomach.

Gealach didn't mean wiseass?

All this time, he was calling me his moon? Even at the fountain, when I was nothing more than his enemies' sister?

"*You were wide awake.*"

"Technically, yes. But when I stopped and tipped my head up, I asked the moon for a reason to live. We have a history of bargaining, me and him." He paused. "I think it gave me you."

The words settled beneath my skin. I felt the same. Existing was no longer enough. I wanted to live. And I wanted to live by his side.

"*Why did you tell me it means wiseass?*"

"Because you're a wiseass."

"*That's rude.*"

"You still like me."

"*What makes you say that?*"

"The way you look at me." He shook his head. "Like I hung the *gealach* in the sky to light the way for you."

It was true. Because in a way, he did. He gave me freedom. Agency. Normalcy. And his last name.

"*I also have a confession to make.*"

I swallowed, looking down at the sticky wooden table between us.

"*I kept it.*"

"Kept what?"

"*Your eye. I came back for it. I don't know why.*"

His mouth broke into a devious smirk. I forgot how much he liked those dark parts of me.

"Where?"

"*A jar. Full of isopropyl. Imma helped me.*" I pressed my lips together. "*I buried it in our garden. You can have it back, if you want.*"

"It's yours." He kicked back, eyeing me humorously. "You can have all my organs."

Not all of them. I can't have your heart, I thought.

"*Why did you call your pub Fermanagh's?*" I signed. "*Your last name is Callaghan.*"

"Mam was from Fermanagh County." He took a pull of his drink. "I spent my entire childhood frightened I'd forget her existence. Fermanagh's was my first business. I bought the nicest building on the block, an old church, and converted it."

"*When did she die?*"

"Before I was born."

"How is that possible?"

"Tierney and I were carved out of her body while she was still alive when she was thirty-eight weeks pregnant. They kidnapped us and left her to bleed out. They left Fintan behind, too."

My stomach lurched and rolled, twisting around my lunch, threatening to purge it.

"Who were they? Why did they do that?"

"The Bratva. Igor, more specifically. My father's business rival back in the day. They competed over large swaths of Europe's ports. Spain. Greece. Croatia. Da thought he was being ambushed at a port one day. Drew his pistol and aimed straight to the head. He thought it was a Bratva soldier. Turned out to be Igor's late wife, Luba. She came to speak to him personally, try to reason with him to strike a deal with her husband. She died. So Igor decided to take the most precious thing to him—his unborn children—killing my mam in the process."

"Why didn't he take Fintan?"

"Fin hid in the closet and didn't come out until he was sure the house was empty. Afterward, he sat there, in her blood, waiting for my father to show up. It fucked him up. They flew Tierney and me to Siberia, where we grew up until we managed to escape when we were fourteen."

Now it all made sense. The twins grew up in a work camp. They learned ASL because their supervisors wouldn't let them speak freely—and because they didn't want to be understood.

They'd been tortured. Sexually abused. Shaped into killing machines.

Funny, how I always thought I held the deepest, darkest secret. That my journey was the toughest, longest, most twisted. My childhood, in comparison to Tiernan's, was a walk in the park.

Tears rimmed my eyes. I didn't let them loose.

"How did you run away?"

"I formed a close relationship with Igor's son, Alex. We were about the same age." He smiled morbidly. "Igor raised his children in the camp to toughen them up, so we did everything together—trained, ate from the same plate, went through the same physical and psychological terror. I'd gained Alex's trust, and little by little, found out everything I needed to escape. The codes to the gates. Where they kept the keys to the doors. Maps of the area. Escape routes. It took us years to collect all this data and form it into a plan."

"*So how did you end up in North Africa?*" I remembered Tierney's mention of it.

"We had to erase our footprints and travel in a convoluted way. Besides, we weren't sure where Da and Fintan were. We were told they never bothered looking for us. That wasn't true. My father fought tooth and nail trying to get us back. Igor told him we never made it past infancy. But we found him, anyway."

"*Does this mean you were raised Russian?*" I blinked in confusion. "*You speak the language? Know the customs?*"

"Yes, and yes. Russian is my first language. English is my second." He used his index finger to sweep the stout's foam from the pint, popping it into his mouth. "Once we found our way to Da and Fin, we caught up on everything Irish. There was a language barrier at first. We decided to move to New York after a few weeks. Fresh start. By the time I set foot in Hunts Point, everyone mistook me for a born-and-bred Irishman."

"*It took you a few weeks to learn English and sound like an Irishman?*"

"I'm a fast learner."

"*More like a genius.*"

"Your words, not mine."

I could hardly breathe I was so choked up on my emotions. Now it all made sense. Why he killed Igor. Why he kept his skull, hollowed out on his office desk, serving as a pen holder. Why Alex was next on his list. The Bratva—the *Rasputins*—robbed him of his mother, his childhood, his future, his *happiness*.

"Our names were the only thing Igor allowed us to keep,"

Tiernan said. "It was Christmastime when he came for us, and Ma hung ornaments with our names on the tree. Igor kept the ornaments to taunt us with them."

I reached across the table, clutching his hand. I was so sick to my stomach I was afraid I'd vomit my own heart.

"Don't feel sorry for me, Lila." He pulled away, his words an order, not a request. "I'm not that boy anymore. I shed my former self like a snake's skin, leaving it in the dust of my own tragedy. It's Tierney I worry about." He worked his jaw back and forth. "A part of her stayed in Siberia."

"*How do you mean?*"

"She self-destructs."

"*And you don't?*"

"I will, eventually." A morbid smirk touched the corners of his mouth. "My self-control is far superior, though."

What did he mean by that?

I lifted my hands to ask, but he shook his head and tilted his wrist to show me his watch. "Your hour's up, Cinderella."

I peered at the time on my phone. He was right. Seventy-five minutes had passed.

"Now that I fulfilled my end of the bargain, would you be so kind as to let me take you out for grub?" Though I couldn't hear his tone, I knew he delivered everything he said acerbically. With enough venom to kill a snake.

Our ankles tangled under the table. It was the briefest touch, and yet it held so much meaning for me. I stared at the man across the table and realized that I was falling in love with him. As with every fall, once you lost your balance, crashing was a matter of when, not if.

"*Yes.*"

CHAPTER THIRTY-THREE
TIERNAN

I always thought a bullet would finish me off.

But in the end, it was my wife that turned out to be my demise. She didn't even do anything special. Nibbled on a slice of pizza while sitting in my lap, dangling her feet in the air, reminding me of our diabolical height difference.

The pizza place was packed with late-night clubbers. All my blood was concentrated in my cock. And all my cock wanted was to be buried inside my wife's pussy.

Not her ass. Not her mouth. *Pussy.*

I wanted my old life back. Where sex was something I approached on my terms. Recreationally. Sparsely. And as a form of punishment to others as well as myself.

All this Jane Austen yearning, frayed desperation bullshit made my skin crawl.

"*I need to pee.*" My wife hopped off my lap on the stool I was occupying. I stood up and followed as she wove through the crowd. No way was I letting her out of my sight.

It was jarring to care about a stranger.

I spent the majority of my adult life either killing people or screwing escorts. No part of me found humans a sacred species. Something worth preserving, let alone protecting.

But somewhere along the way I stopped seeing Lila as a human.

She was just *Lila*.

And the thought of some dipshite's filthy hands touching those dozen shades of golden hair—sunlight, sand, flax, and daffodil—made me...

What, arsehole? You gonna try being a good husband now? Write her poems? Fuck her next to candles and roses?

Of course not.

I wouldn't let roses anywhere near her. She hated them. What was this, amateur hour?

Lila stumbled over her own feet walking the straight line from our seat to the jacks. The sleep deprivation was taking its toll.

"*Are you going to stand on guard?*" Lila gave me an incredulous look.

"I'm coming in with you."

Lila rose on her toes, putting her hand on my cheek. "*Thank you for taking care of me.*" She reached up and kissed my eye patch, and I hoped what I was feeling was a fatal heart attack and not fucking flutters. "*From now on, I promise to take care of you, as well.*"

She walked inside, locking the door behind her.

I fished my phone out and texted Tierney.

> Tiernan: Do you still have those sleeping pills? I need to crush them into Lila's drink.
>
> Tierney: Aw, are we getting rid of her? I kinda got attached. ☹
>
> Tiernan: I'm not offing her, you eejit. She needs to sleep.
>
> Tierney: SHE'S PREGNANT, Tiernan. You can't just give her shit.
>
> Tiernan: She'll drop dead at this rate.
>
> Tierney: Is this concern I read between the lines, brother?
>
> Tiernan: She is my Camorra warranty.

> Tierney: Admit that you like her, and I'll give you a solution to her sleeping problem.
> Tiernan: I don't negotiate with terrorists.
> Tierney: To negotiate I'd have to budge from my demands. I'll do no such thing.

I heard the toilet flush on the other side of the door. I didn't have time.

> Tiernan: Fine. I don't want her dead. Happy?
> Tierney: Elated. <GIF of Jonah Hill screaming excitedly>

The faucet was running. Tierney was typing.

> Tierney: Whenever sleep escapes me, I find a willing victim and orgasm. HARD. A good orgasm always knocks me out.
> Tiernan: THIS is your advice?
> Tierney: Yup. It's a good one, brosky.
> Tiernan: Hate you, sis.
> Tierney: <3 <3 <3

———

When we got home, I filled Lila a warm bath and threw a pink bath bomb into it. The entire bleeding bathroom reeked of essential oils and strawberries. I made a note to torch down the apartment to get rid of the smell.

Not that it needed to be set on fire. The temperature was already at a record fucking high.

Lila must've been a lizard in a previous life, because she liked the thermostat on seventy-six.

I preferred it at forty-nine. We settled for seventy-six. Whoever said marriage was all about compromise had never wedded an Italian princess.

"Don't fall asleep in the bath," I barked out the order.

She nodded sleepily, shutting the door in my face.

While Lila took a bath, I took my sister's demented advice. It was shit terrible, but I had zero alternatives. Apparently, giving Lila pills could fuck up the baby. And while that sounded like a win-win situation to me, she seemed fond of the devil's spawn.

Ambling to the kitchen, I grabbed a whiskey bottle and poured three fingers into a tumbler, tossing it back and wiping my mouth. I fished out my phone and texted Rhyland Coltridge.

Coltridge was a newly minted tech billionaire. He was also a former escort who used to screw half of New York's socialites for a living. I had it on good authority he knew what he was doing in the sack. I needed expert advice. Someone who wouldn't run their mouth. For all his faults—and fuck knew I could write a dissertation about them—he was discreet.

I knew, because my sister had hired him to overcome her own hang-ups back in the day.

> Tiernan: I need advice.
> Rhyland: Is this Tiernan Callaghan?
> Tiernan: ...
> Rhyland: Don't reproduce.
> Tiernan: Sex advice, you low-grade gigolo.
> Rhyland: First of all? Very endearing. Second? I'm retired.
> Tiernan: 20K an hour.
> Rhyland: Sorry, should've specified: I'm retired AND a billionaire.
> Tiernan: I'll sell you my shares of App-date.

My having shares in his wholesome fake dating app had been a thorn in his side. Anyone associated with me was as good as dead in polite society.

> Rhyland: JK. Giving back is my passion.
> Rhyland: Talk to me, buddy.
> Tiernan: Virgin. Skittish. Needs to come hard. No full-blown sex.
> Rhyland: IDK if I'd call you skittish.
> Tiernan: Not me, you eejit. HER.
> Rhyland: Oh. Well, only one in five women orgasm from vaginal intercourse, so I wasn't going to suggest penetration, anyway. Your best bet is eating her out. The clit has over 10,000 nerve fibers. Not much room for error, unless your tongue is made out of sandpaper.

Groaning, I refilled my glass. A headache formed behind my eyelids.

> Tiernan: I've never engaged in such activity.
> Rhyland: Eating pussy? My condolences. Highly recommend. 12/10.
> Rhyland: I'll send a video with a demonstration on an adult doll.
> Tiernan: And you have that kind of thing handy because...?
> Rhyland: I taught a Harvard course last year. You know, as a world-renowned expert in pussy.
> Rhyland: We all leave our footprint on this planet. You fight overpopulation. I promote great orgasms.
> Tiernan: Let's promote bringing this conversation to an end.
> Rhyland: Forwarding you the reel. Make sure you sell your stock first thing tomorrow morning.

Tiernan: One thing, Coltridge.

Rhyland: Yes?

Tiernan: This conversation never happened.

Five minutes later, I was watching Rhyland pleasuring a plastic doll with far too much enthusiasm. Ten minutes later, I entered our bedroom. Lila was already in bed, running a towel over her damp hair.

I stopped at the foot of the bed.

"*What's wrong?*" Her bloodshot eyes clouded. Christ, how long had it been since she had a decent night of sleep?

"I'm going to help you fall asleep." I rolled the tip of my tongue over my teeth, tasting the residue alcohol. "If you let me."

I never asked for permission.

What I wanted, I took.

I did ask for permission now.

She sat up straighter, expression wary. "*How will you do that?*"

"I can touch you in a way that would make you very happy. Very sleepy, too."

She bit down on her lower lip, considering my proposal. I stood there, like a schoolboy, waiting for her words. Waiting to hear if she'd let me serve her. Kneel at her altar and eat her out.

Pathetic.

"*What if you hurt me by accident?*" She rubbed her button nose. "*That monster did. I can still feel it, sometimes. Between my legs. His rough fingers. His thing inside me.*"

I closed my eye, drawing in a breath. My bloodthirst for this faceless tool was infinite. I wanted his life more than I did Alex's.

"I would never hurt you like that." I found my voice, opening my eye. "Even if I wanted to. Even if you *begged* me to. Even if you cheated on me. Even if you killed me." And then, because it felt too raw, too real, I added, "Protecting you is a compulsion at this point. I'd stop the night from falling if darkness scares you, Lila."

Where the fuck did this come from? I had no idea, but it wasn't a lie.

I felt exposed in that moment. Like she had a loaded gun and a clear shot to finish me off. I hated it, and her, and *this*. But the thing about compulsion was, you didn't have a choice.

Lila nodded. "*I trust you. My body is yours.*"

She leaned back, popping the two first buttons of her silky white nightgown. Her breasts spilled out, full and round and perfect. Her pale nipples were diamond-like studs.

She didn't ask what I planned on doing to her.

If I were going to fuck her, eat her out, toss her on her belly and ride her arse.

Lila gave me full autonomy.

Joke's on her, because I hadn't the freshest clue what to do with it.

"If it ever gets too much, tug my hair," I said. "And I'll stop immediately."

She smiled in gratitude.

Now what? There was no buildup. No foreplay. I couldn't just rip her panties off and start feasting. I obviously didn't plan this sufficiently. Christ, the look on her face. The hope gleaming from her eyes. It was too late to back out now.

I'd been postponing this moment since our first kiss, not wanting to fuck this up. And now I was standing here and she was sitting there and we were both still, breathing heavily, and very, *very* quiet.

"*Can I see your penis?*" Lila licked her lips, breaking the tension.

I nodded solemnly.

I used one hand to undo my belt and pop my slack's button, then rolled down my zipper. I pushed my Armani briefs down. My cock sprang out, purple and fully erect. An angry vein rippled across it, root to crown.

She fell forward on her palms, crawling across the mattress to get a better look. A spike of arousal and horror shot through me.

Her face was now inches from my cock, and I'd never been this turned on in my entire bleeding existence. God, look at her. Something was very wrong with society, that it was legal for this scene to happen.

Her. Virginal, innocent, sweet to the point of toothache.

Me. Murderer. Psychopath. Pervert.

Lila tilted her head, studying my cock like it was a medieval painting.

"*Are they all the same size?*" Her head snapped up, her pale blues meeting my eye.

"No." I was glad she couldn't hear the strain in my voice. "Size, length, and width vary."

She frowned, tapping her lips pensively. "*Makes sense.*"

"Why?"

"*Because if…he…had one like yours, I don't think I'd have survived.*"

Something primal kicked me into high gear at her words.

I ducked down and caught her lips in mine to shut her up. She gasped into my mouth but opened up for more. Our tongues found one another. I sank to the mattress, laying her down. I braced my arms on either side of her head without mounting her. I didn't want her to think about that arsehole.

Our kiss deepened, and Lila reached for my cock between us. At the touch of her silky hand, it spasmed and pulsed, leaking into her palm. She moaned into my mouth and patted it like it was a dog's head. I didn't even care. It was perfect. She was perfect.

She was playful and confident and fearless. I no longer set the pace of what was happening. The conqueror became the conquered. And I knew, with amusing, dark finality, that I was completely, tragically, wretchedly hers.

She used her free hand to hold the side of my face, stroking her fingers along my cheekbone. Her mouth moved over mine, looking for different angles to deepen our kiss. Meanwhile, the hand that worked my cock discovered that if she stroked it up and down, it instinctively thrust into her. She did that while I went through Rhyland's idiotic video in my head, trying to remember all the right moves, and coming up blank.

Lila let go of my cock to tug her nightgown down all the way. She fumbled with the material. I pushed myself backward on my knees, watching her.

You bleeding idiot. You should be doing that to her.

"Should I..." I cleared my throat. "I mean, should I?"

Did you just mumble, motherfucker?

She bit her lower lip, nodding.

I unbuttoned her gown, searching her face intently for signs of discomfort.

My wife looked alarmed and a little overwhelmed, but not like she wanted to stab and shoot me simultaneously, like our so-called honeymoon.

"*I want you to put your penis in my mouth. See why you like it so much.*"

"No," I growled, a little too quickly, a little too harshly. "This is not about me. It's about you."

"*Shouldn't it be about both of us?*"

She reached for my face again and slowly removed my eye patch. I held my breath, forcing myself not to look away and hide.

"I think you are beautiful," she voiced out loud, to bring the point home. "*And if I had to choose a husband all over again, I'd still choose you.*"

I leaned down, taking her right nipple in my mouth, giving it a good suck. It was sweet and warm and smelled of her coconut body lotion. Lila arched, asking for more, and I used my left hand to tease her other nipple, tracing it with my finger, gently stroking and tugging, testing different pressures to see what made her toes curl.

Her tits were... Ah, fuck, was there even a word for this? I couldn't get enough. My tongue lapped against every inch of her right breast, then moved to the left. All the while, she was squirming, thrusting her pelvis upward, begging for something she didn't understand, and I didn't know how to give.

I kissed my way down her torso, not because I remembered Rhyland did that in the video—I couldn't recall my own bleeding name, let alone the tutorial—but because I wanted to know what every corner of her body tasted like. I ran my tongue along the curve of her waist, hands gripping her ass as she squirmed breathlessly—ticklish, duly noted—kissed her hip bones, nuzzled my nose into her pussy through her panties, inhaling deeply. I realized her scent was an aphrodisiac; it made my cock leak precum all over the sheets.

I wanted to rip her panties to shreds and gorge on her pussy without even knowing what it tasted like. But I had to be careful with her.

No, *wanted* to be careful with her. I'd won the most precious thing she had to give—her trust—and I wasn't going to fuck it up.

I moved my hands across her legs, massaging them, working my way up; I sat back on my knees, snatching her right leg by the ankle, pulling her panties off.

Her pussy was a work of art, and I'd visited most museums in the Western world.

An achingly tiny triangle, protected by golden curls a shade darker than her hair.

No one taught her to wax, trim, shave, seduce. And yet she was the sexiest thing I'd ever seen.

I kissed each of her toes, maintaining eye contact. She purred and stretched across the mattress like a lazy cat. I kissed the inside of her ankle, moving south, to the back of her knee, kissing and lapping at her inner thigh, slowly, slowly, giving her the chance to stop me, to change her mind.

She didn't.

My mouth watered the closer I got to her pussy. My cock twitched uncontrollably.

I stopped at her center, giving her a slow, earnest lick from arse crack to clit.

She moaned so hard I thought she was going to wake people in Nebraska.

Stroking her inner thighs, I started licking, using my free hand to feel for her elusive little clit. I wasn't completely hopeless. I knew its general whereabouts. When I found it, I started massaging it.

My wife tasted incredible. Of clean skin and sugar water and an addiction I never thought I'd pick. My tongue dug deeper, penetrating her, my thumbs spreading her wider. She arched tautly, like a drawn bow.

"Tiernan," she choked out my name, speaking it in her sweet, soft voice. "What are you doing?"

"Playing with my food," I murmured into her core, knowing she couldn't read my lips.

She reached for my hair. Gave it a good, earnest tug. I froze, lifting my head up to watch her.

"Shit. Was that too much?" I felt myself honest-to-god bleeding blushing. The fuck was wrong with me?

Lila snapped her head up from the pillow, face pink, eyes unfocused. She wrenched her fingers from my hair, yanking out a good portion of it.

"*Why did you stop?*" It was amusing, how I could hear her tone based on her sharp movements.

"You pulled my hair. That was our safe word."

Her eyebrows slammed together. "*I was close.*"

"You were?"

"*Yes. And I wanted to see what it feels like. Go back to it.*" She pushed my head between her legs hurriedly, and I laughed.

I went back to work, picking up the pace. Every time I thrust my tongue into her, her muscles squeezed, trying to trap it inside. And every time my finger pad flicked just below the clit, she writhed and whimpered.

She was close again.

So was I.

Without realizing it, I was rubbing my cock against the mattress, seeking friction. Lila yanked at my hair again. This time I glanced upward before stopping. She thrashed and moaned with abandon. I continued.

Her hips jerked, trying to escape my tongue, my lips, my fingers, and I clamped a hand around her waist, pinning her to the bed.

She came hard against my tongue with a rush of liquid heat. I knew, because I could barely pry it out of her cunt. A cunt that was now dripping.

My desire for her was violent.

I slurped it, rubbing myself faster against the bed. She whined in pleasure, stretching her leg.

My orgasm hit different this time. It built, like a castle, brick upon brick, curling skyward, looming over everything else, until there was nothing but pleasure, and her scent, and her flesh.

I came inside my hand so hard my vision blurred. Every muscle in my body was rigid. Every inch of it slicked with sweat. I buried my face in the crook of her knee, breathing her in.

"Oh, *fuck*." I kissed her kneecap, chuckling, my lips skimming along her smooth bronze flesh. "Jesus Christ. That was…perfect."

I wasn't an empath, but I did feel pity for the rest of the male population for living their wretched lives without knowing what my wife felt like. I stood up and proceeded to the bathroom to wash my hands. Returning two minutes later, I found my wife asleep, her head resting on the silk pillow, mouth slightly agape.

I pulled the duvet over her, kissed her forehead, and turned off the light. I paused in front of the bathroom again, only for a nanosecond, before deciding there was no way I was washing that woman off my skin.

Instead, I took her "pissed off" spot in the recliner in the corner of the room and sat back, watching her sleep.

All eight hours of the night.

CHAPTER THIRTY-FOUR

FOURTEEN YEARS AGO

They were ready.

The past twelve months, the twins diligently planned their escape, communicating via ASL in the dead of night so no one could see or hear them.

They had maps. The spare keys to Olga's car. A stash of food they kept under their portion of the wooden plank. Clean bottled water.

They had their father and brother's full names. An address in Ireland they stole from Igor's desk.

Most importantly—they had a plan.

That plan was missing one thing—the code to the main gate standing between them and freedom.

They were fourteen now, and old beyond their years.

Old enough to know what their escape would do to Alex.

There had been arguments about the latter. Tierney said they should confide in Lyosha. Tiernan maintained no one could be trusted, including God himself.

Now, Tiernan stared at his own reflection through a puddle of scarlet blood outside of Igor's office, smoothing his hair back with his fingers.

Igor was in America, which meant Alex had access to his office. Tiernan pushed the door open without knocking.

Alex was sitting on his father's throne-like chair, a sixteen-year-old prisoner girl in his lap. They were kissing ardently.

Anger singed Tiernan's blood. He'd never kissed a girl before. He fucked many in the ass. Boys, too. Whatever Igor told him to do for his own depraved, twisted entertainment.

He had to watch his sister being stripped by other prisoners. Being used by them.

He had to watch her bleed and bleed and bleed until Olga had no choice but to call a local vet to remove her uterus.

Alex wasn't subjected to all those horrors. He was allowed to grow at his own pace.

"Don't just stand there," Alex murmured into the pretty girl's lips. "Sit down, watch, and take notes."

Tiernan didn't budge. "Whose blood outside?"

"This chick's boyfriend wasn't happy about our hookup." Alex laughed.

"We need to talk."

That got Alex's attention.

"Leave." He pushed the girl off him. She fell on her ass comically, pouting before strutting her way out of the office.

"Well?" Alex wiped his lips with the back of his hand, looking very much like a fourteen-year-old kid. He fished a cigarette out of his father's pack, then struck a match. "What's up?"

It amazed Tiernan that Alex did not see anything amiss about their friendship. That he was able to buy into this unlikely bond, considering his father killed Tiernan's mother and snatched him from his home.

Then again, Tyrone did the same to Alex's mother when he was but a newborn.

"I need the code to the entrance gate," Tiernan said dryly.

Alex brought the match to the cigarette's tip, lighting it before shaking out the flame. "Do you, now?"

"Yes."

"You guys are leaving me?" He took a drag, releasing the smoke out of the corner of his mouth.

"We want to take dips in the water."

"When?"

"Whenever we want. Tierney's depressed." Not a lie. "She needs an outlet after what happened with her surgery."

Alex considered this.

"Can I come?"

"Sure."

"Then what do you need the code for?"

"We want to come and go as we please. Not depend on you. Besides, you're not always here."

Lyosha mulled this over.

"And you promise you won't leave me here?"

"I promise," Tiernan lied.

It wasn't the first or the last lie he would tell, but it was by far the most justifiable.

"I won't forgive you if you betray me." Alex snuffed out the cigarette in an ashtray. His hands shook.

"I wouldn't, either."

"I love you," Alex said dejectedly. His eyes met Tiernan's. "Like a brother. More than a brother, maybe. Because you are a choice. Slava and Jeremie aren't."

"I won't leave you, Lyosha," Tiernan said softly. "Not ever. You can trust me."

Alex gave him the code.

The next morning, the twins were gone.

———————

Four days later, they were in Yakutsk.

The journey was a blur of frostbite and darkness.

He and Tierney took turns driving Olga's old Lada Niva. Tierney spiked a fever the night they escaped but deliriously kept on going, unwilling to stop for more than getting gas. They peed into empty bottles of water. Ate and slept in turns.

When they rolled into the city, they sold the car to the first salesman *they found. They held the rubles in their hands with shaky, uncertain fingers. They'd never seen money before.*

It was nine in the morning, and too soon to wait for Dima, so they entered an eatery. There, they ordered eggs and ham and roasted tomatoes and mushrooms and kasha and butterbrots. Coffee and tea and sugared cranberries, too. After paying, they rushed outside to vomit everything they'd eaten. Their stomachs were too small for a hearty breakfast.

They walked to Lenin Square and arrived at eleven. Sat under the statue and checked their surroundings, anxious not to get caught.

Dima arrived at six past noon, just when they had started talking about their plan B. He was the only person in the square other than them.

Tiernan pushed to his feet. "Michael sent me," he said. "He asked you to get us out of here."

They had no passports. No birth certificates. Only the names their mother put on those Christmas ornaments fourteen years ago and the clothes on their backs.

"Mongolia," Dima said with conviction. "We'll travel there first, then move west. Maybe North Africa. We'll track your father as we move. For now, let's get on the train."

The train was marvelous. Tierney cried tears of joy when they entered the coach. Dima—who was in his mid-fifties, a graying fox of a man—talked very little.

Dinner was piroshki from the concession kiosk. One hour ate away the next until it was nighttime, and Dima and Tierney fell asleep.

Tiernan slipped into the back of the cart, wedged open a window, and stuck his head out.

Then, and only then, he let himself believe he truly escaped the claws of Igor Rasputin.

He tipped his head up and looked at the moon.

The moon stared back.

They smiled at one another, sharing a secret.

Finally, he was free.

CHAPTER THIRTY-FIVE
TIERNAN

Gealach: I have something for you.

I looked up from the text message on my phone, turning my attention to the woman lying in bed beside me.

She still looked impossibly tiny, and I wondered how she was planning on birthing an entire bleeding human. Seemed ambitious, even for a stubborn girl like her.

I elevated an eyebrow. "Yes?"

"*Tierney told me you two never celebrate your birthday.*"

"Tierney talks too much."

"*She said neither of you find anything worthy in celebrating the day your mother was murdered.*"

Since this wasn't a question, I didn't offer an answer.

"*We should change that.*" Lila wore a determined expression. "*I won't make you celebrate in December, but now is a good time. There's a few months' buffer from the actual date.*"

I put my phone down beside me, waiting for her to spell it out.

"*I got you a birthday gift.*"

"I wasn't born in July."

"*Yes, but you were born, and that's worthy of celebration. I got Tierney something, too.*"

I understood why my sister liked her. Lila made people around her feel seen. Probably because she'd been overlooked her entire life.

She turned to her nightstand and produced a small jewelry box from the drawer, handing it to me. I popped it open, staring at its content dispassionately.

It was a cross pendant. The type her flashy brothers would wear with their fucking ten-thousand-dollar dress shirts and diamond earrings. I closed it, handing it back to her.

"I'm an atheist."

"*I'm not.*" Her brows creased. "*And I want you to wear it and remember there is someone in this world who prays for you.*"

I didn't wear jewelry and didn't consider myself Catholic any more than a bleeding coffee cup. However, I didn't know the etiquette to refusing a birthday present, since I'd never been offered one before.

"I'm not gonna wear it."

"*Never say never.*"

"I'm saying it right now."

"*So grumpy.*" She pouted.

"So pushy."

She tried to produce an airy smile, but I could tell she was disappointed. "*Fine. Don't wear it. But keep it.*"

I shoved it into my nightstand drawer and stood up, getting ready for the day.

CHAPTER THIRTY-SIX
LILA

For a few short weeks, life was almost blissful.

Imma and I did some nesting, went to doctor's appointments, and cooked. Tierney visited me twice a week with tea. Both herbal blends from exotic places, and Mafia gossip about key players in the underworld. Mama still hadn't answered my message from weeks ago, but I no longer sat and stared at it like a kicked puppy.

Sleep and I finally got reacquainted. All thanks to my husband.

He spent every night worshipping my body, sucking my nipples, kissing and licking between my legs, sometimes putting his fingers there, too, and bringing me to soul-destroying orgasms after which I slept like a baby. Something about the way he exhausted my body awarded me with a peaceful slumber no brisk walk or a workout ever managed.

Tiernan still showed no interest in the baby, in his kicking, ultrasound pictures, or well-being. The pregnancy was a black cloud hanging over our heads. It seemed to serve as the thickest, most indestructible wall between us. But it always boiled down to the same thing—if Tiernan truly cared about me, he'd accept my child, too.

Because me? I'd welcome everything and anyone he brought with him.

My brothers visited me often enough. I took lunches with Enzo and Luca, who practiced their ASL with me. Even Achilles dropped by whenever he checked in on his so-called *investment* next door. Every time he popped up at Tierney's apartment to look for signs of a lover, he made sure to bring me something from the deli. Calzone or gelato. His visits surprised me the most. Because I knew Achilles didn't try to impress anyone, myself included, so if he chose to spend any amount of time with me, it was because he truly wanted to get to know me.

As for Mama, she sent things with Enzo. Books she thought I'd like, cookies she'd baked, and maternity clothes she'd bought for me.

"*What is she trying to achieve by not speaking to me? My secret's already out,*" I vented to Enzo one day, when we were both watching *Parks and Recreation* on my couch.

"You were the only thing she could control." Enzo shrugged, looking fifty shades of the golden boy that he was. The prettiest of the brothers. The kindest. *The most secretive.* "You know she loves you. She just doesn't know what to do with herself, now that you have a life of your own."

"*Is this because I didn't want to marry Angelo?*"

"Doubt it," Enzo admitted. "She dropped the subject like a hot potato after her talk with Tiernan."

"*How's the search for my attacker going?*"

I knew Tiernan was working on it, but I didn't ask about it. I didn't want to poke my own raw wound. But I also wanted to know when they found him. I needed that closure.

"There're a few roadblocks in Tiernan's way," Enzo said vaguely, rubbing the back of his neck. "But he's working on it. He needs some hard evidence before he calls in more people for interrogation. Anyway, back to Mama." He changed the subject. "Just remember she loves you to death, yeah?"

"*She should be happy for me.*"

"She thinks it'll blow up in your face. Tiernan doesn't have the best reputation."

"And what do you think?"

Enzo ran his knuckles along his jawline. "I think if anyone could melt the iceberg also known as Tiernan Callaghan's heart, it's you, sis."

———————

My blissful lucky streak came to an abrupt end one morning when Tiernan was pouring me a cup of coffee and Imma was huffing and puffing, scrubbing the same spot on the already pristine kitchen island with a frown.

"You have to visit your mama today," she declared in Neapolitan, her stern glower warning me off arguing. "It's her birthday, and she misses you dearly."

I grabbed my phone and texted Imma since she didn't know ASL. If she misses me so, she is welcome to visit me. Write a letter. Maybe even an email. I have an address now.

Imma read the text, her scowl deepening, and shook her head. She blew away the silver flyaways framing her tanned face.

"She is a prideful woman, and she spent her entire life protecting you. You're being a brat."

She took away my chance to go to school. To gain an education. To have friends.

"She did what she thought was right at the time."

Tiernan slid my coffee across the island, leveling me with a questioning look.

"There's a formal dinner at the house. Tonight at seven," Imma said. "You should go."

With that, she turned around and left the kitchen, leaving her phone behind so I wouldn't be able to answer her. I watched her back disappear behind a door. She was completely unreasonable. Mama was the one who cut *me* off for wanting to live a normal life. I felt like I was living in an upside world.

Tiernan slid onto the stool next to me. His smirk was as menacing as nightshade.

"*What's funny?*" I scowled at him.

"Your attitude." He grabbed an apple from the fruit bowl, taking a juicy bite. Even the way his white teeth sank into the flesh of the apple made my insides clench with desire. "You act like a rebellious teenager. You sass back. You're growing the fuck up."

I didn't like his patronizing words, though I privately admitted he was much older than me. Beyond the ten years that stood between us. He was forged in a work camp, grew up orphaned and haunted. He built businesses, destroyed lives, orchestrated entire operations.

Meanwhile, I was still figuring out how to get a high school diploma so I could pursue a higher education.

I took a sip of my coffee, shrugging off his comments.

"What's going on?"

I put my cup down. "*Imma is making me go to Mama's birthday dinner today.*"

"Is she now?" He gave me a wry once-over. "Maybe you should stop taking orders from the help."

"*I think we should go.*"

"I'm going either way," he surprised me by saying. He didn't ask me how I felt about it or invite me to come. And it was yet again a reminder that he may worship my body, but he didn't care one iota about the rest of me.

"*That's news to me.*"

"Brennan's gonna be there. We have some Bratva shit to discuss. Tierney is also bringing the Keatons."

He intended to go without me. That infuriated me. It was *my* family. And he knew how I felt about my mother.

"*How dare you make plans with my own family behind my back?*"

"Careful now, Lila." He put his coffee cup down. "That was never a part of our agreement."

"*I don't recall ever agreeing to anything other than sitting on your face.*" Anger tainted my cheeks pink. "*Everything beyond this scope is open for negotiation.*"

He ran his tongue over his teeth to suppress a smile.

"*That includes being your wife, by the way. We make the rules as we go. One of them is you share your social calendar with me. Always.*"

He sat back, looking almost like a proud father. "Excellent spine, *Gealach*. I suggest you use it on your mother tonight. I, however, don't take orders from anyone. Least of all a teenybopper."

"*So you won't do it?*"

"No."

His answer scorched a hole in my chest.

"*Guess you'll have to see my next move, then.*" I forced out a smile. "*We should take her a gift.*"

I couldn't shake off the sting of his rejection, though. I loathed when he made plans without me. Even more worrying was that there was Bratva news. Did that mean Alex was back on American soil? That soon a Mafia war would follow?

"I'll handle it." Tiernan stood up swiftly, grabbed his coffee, knocked it back like it was a shot, and shrugged into his light jacket.

He stopped briefly on his way out, assessing me with that precious gem eye of his. He tipped his head down, fusing his mouth with mine. I immediately groaned and surrendered to the kiss, feeling his hand cupping my bare knee under my summer dress, climbing up, brushing the seam of my opening ever so softly through my panties. Another yelp escaped me.

I opened my thighs for him automatically, craving more. His mouth disconnected from mine, trailing down the side of my throat, nibbling and biting as he tugged my underwear sideways, his rough fingers teasing and stroking my entrance. I shuddered all over, knowing Imma was in the other room, and that she could walk in on us any minute now. See me with my legs spread for him, fully dressed, letting him toy with me like I was his own personal plaything.

His middle finger grazed my slit, penetrating me halfway, while he pushed his thumb against my clit. I loved how he touched me. How he read me. How he took my cues and followed through. He was an assassin in every fiber of his body. Attentive to the shallowest breath of his target. I arched my back, offering him my strained, taut nipples through the dress.

Tiernan used his free hand to tug at the top half of my dress. My breasts bounced out, so heavy and full I barely recognized them as my own. My nipples were also two shades darker.

My husband leaned down to pluck one of my nipples, sucking it into his mouth, trailing the tip of his tongue over the outline of it, picking up speed between my legs, shoving two fingers in and out of me. I moaned harder, louder, squirming, knowing I was being shameless and improper, and that Imma could no doubt hear us.

And I didn't care.

I could excuse myself by arguing he was my husband. But the truth was, even if he were nothing but an acquaintance, I would still let him have his way with me.

The first tingles of an orgasm spread like wildfire through my body, heating it to a dangerous temperature.

"I'm close," I panted, placing my hands on his face, moving his mouth to my other nipple that felt exposed and bare and cold.

A thick, tight knot of pleasure uncurled beneath my bellybutton, threatening to tear my body apart. My orgasms were always so... *violent*.

"Yes." I tugged at his hair roughly. "Yes, yes, yes."

I was now riding his two fingers. He was knuckles-deep in me, and I knew I was ready for more. I *wanted* his entire cock. And I knew he wanted that, too. He always stared at my center a little too hungrily, even after he went down on me. Like he was leaving a place that was dear to his heart.

Suddenly, Tiernan ripped his mouth and fingers away all at once. A squeal of protest tore from the back of my throat.

"Never threaten me again, darlin'." He dipped his head down to my mouth. The kiss he gave me was dirty, hard, and punishing. Tongueless. He smeared my wetness on his fingers over the side of my cheek with a mocking smirk. "I'll pick you up at five thirty."

CHAPTER THIRTY-SEVEN
TIERNAN

My wife was fucking with me.

She wore a sheer lavender minidress to her mother's birthday. It hugged her breasts and waist snugly, flaring just above the navel to cover her growing tummy. Her supermodel-worthy legs were on full display, endless despite her short stature, shimmering with whatever cream she put on after her three-hour baths.

Lila looked both divine and royally pissed off.

She didn't speak one word to me the entire length of the drive to Long Island. Didn't greet me like she usually did, either. In our bedroom, with her legs spread, waiting for the first of at least three orgasms I awarded her each day.

Was it healthy for me to spend a few hours each night dedicated to the sole purpose of making my wife scream with pleasure? Doubt it. But it was fun. And fun was a concept foreign to me before Lila brought her sweet little cunt into my life.

"You gonna sulk much longer?" I momentarily tore my eyes from the road so she could read my lips. Her gaze was fixed on her window, and I knew she saw me in her periphery and decided to give me the silent treatment.

Was it nice that I denied her an orgasm this morning? No.

Was it the end of the fucking world? Also no.

Lila started making demands I never agreed to fulfill. Like

giving her a full report of where I was, when, and for how long. Not only was it not in my nature to accommodate this kind of fuckery, but it wasn't safe for her to know the details most of the time.

Granted, there were nicer ways to get my point across than leaving her high and dry.

Too bad I wasn't feeling very nice at all. Especially when I was reminded of the baby in her belly.

Her pregnant stomach stood between us at all times, reminding me someone else touched what was mine, spilled his seed inside her.

We drove through mundane traffic and arrived at the Ferrantes' gated community. By the heavy patrols and snipers, I gathered the Keatons were already here.

I parked at the fountain, surrounded by bulletproof vehicles the size of a house. I rounded the vehicle to open the door for my wife, who ignored my outstretched hand and strutted out on three-inch pink bottomed heels. Her bum was magnificent, her hair so soft I wanted to be buried inside it, and I resisted biting my fist as I followed her, swelling inside my slacks.

Servants opened the doors for us, and we were led to the candlelit drawing room, where champagne glasses were clanking. Antique furniture bathed in soft golden hues. Classical music floated from the surround system. Yet another luxury Lila couldn't enjoy.

I detected President Keaton sitting with Vello and Luca in the far corner of the room, engaged in conversation. Francesca, his wife, was draped across his lap. It was a tacky look for a president and a first lady. And yet it was clear the Keatons didn't spare one bleeding fuck what the world thought about them.

Chiara stood with Enzo. Achilles, Tierney, Sam, and Sofia were on the opposite side of the room.

I assessed Aisling Brennan. She had long black hair and sharp, elfin features. She was by no means a great beauty, but I suppose with her being a doctor and one of the richest heiresses in the States, Sam could swallow the disappointment.

If he felt such disappointment at all. He stared at her as though she was the most beautiful woman in the room.

Which, of course, couldn't be true, because my wife walked in a few moments ago.

Speaking of, *where* was my little silvery moon?

I turned my head to watch her make her way to her mother with confidence I knew she didn't possess. That never stopped Lila from facing her problems, though.

She signed to her mother, "*Happy birthday*," and handed her the gift I'd purchased earlier in the day: a hand-painted majolica ewer dating back to 1870 Naples. It was beautiful and rare and obscenely expensive, just like my wife. Much like her, it was obtained in a less-than-kosher way.

I could've gotten my mother-in-law a piece of expensive tacky jewelry. But if her relationship with my wife was salvageable, I wanted to try fixing it.

Chiara thanked her coolly and turned back to Enzo. Luckily, the latter had the good sense to gather his sister in a warm hug.

I watched as his hand rested on the small of her back, a burning sensation slithering up my spine.

I knew he was her brother.

I didn't care.

I did not like people touching my things. And I especially didn't like it when said thing was my wife.

I contemplated saving Lila from the awkward conversation with her mother—or at least redirect any hostile fire my way—but then remembered I had my own pressing matters to tend to and sauntered over to Brennan instead, plucking champagne from a server with a silver tray on my way there.

"Callaghan."

"Brennan."

"Meet my wife, Aisling."

"Pleasure," I lied. I didn't shake her hand. I was fond of my wrist and had an inkling Sam, like me, wasn't a fan of others touching his woman.

"Your wife is stunning," Aisling gasped in disbelief, ping-ponging her gaze between us. Yes, I wasn't much to look at these days, thanks to Achilles, but Lila never seemed bothered by that.

She always made sure I removed my eye patch when I came to bed, rubbing a soothing thumb along the indents it left on my skin.

"You're very lucky," Aisling added.

"Luck has nothing to do with it." I took a swig of my drink. "I'd have claimed her as mine if I had to burn down the whole country." I frowned, considering my ridiculous statement. "Canada, too."

Eventually, I'd have seen her in broad daylight. Noticed her.

Once I had, I'd have made her mine.

Even if I had to slaughter every single Ferrante in my way with my bare hands.

Even if she had to watch it.

She was an obsession. A compulsion. Martyrs had died for lesser causes.

I didn't love her. But there was no denying we changed each other in ways that benefited both of us. I needed some of her tenderness. And she, in return, received a blank check to be who she truly was—a little fucked up, a tad violent, entirely a sexual woman who deserved to be satisfied often, and hard. With me, she could be a teenager. Messy. Emotional. Confused.

She could make small mistakes without worrying about the consequences.

"Are you going to stop staring at your wife at some point?" Sam shot me a concerned look.

"Logic dictates that, yes." I tucked a hand into my front pocket. "But I wouldn't put money on it, Brennan."

We fell into boring small talk for a few minutes, most of it carried by Sam, who insisted on being civilized in front of his wife, before Achilles announced, "Enough of this bullshit. Let's talk shop."

"That's my cue to leave you to it." Aisling smiled, kissing her husband's lips and moving toward the Keatons. Sam watched her go, his eyes dimming like he just said goodbye to his last ever sunset.

I turned to him. "Well?"

"Alex's back." He cut straight to the chase, switching to an entirely new persona. "Landed in Vegas eleven hours ago. With reinforcements."

"What's the head count?" I asked.

"Five, at least. Couldn't confirm their identities, though."

Probably from his gulag. Fresh warriors he had trained, then planned to unleash here in the States.

"Is he making a move east?"

Sam shook his head. "That's the good news. I think we have four, maybe five weeks before he'll attempt retaliation. He needs to recoup. Get his ducks in a row. He just had an entire drug shipment stolen from the dock, so he'll deal with that first. Next, he has a few turncoats he needs to off in his own ranks. He'll probably strike after he's checked those boxes, though. He'd want your head on a platter when he assumes his place as pakhan. It'd be a nice touch if he has your skull when he makes the announcement."

"No doubt." I casually knocked down a vase full of roses on the fireplace mantel. A harem of maids hurried in its direction, sweeping the flowers and chucking them into the bin along with the broken glass.

I wasn't in any hurry to die anymore. Especially not before I sank my cock into my beautiful wife's cunt, which I planned on doing very soon.

"This means we have a couple weeks to start moving soldiers into his territory discreetly. Weapons, too," I mused.

"And we know his life better than he does," Achilles pointed out. "The blueprints to his estates and warehouses. The names and addresses to all of his first-rank soldiers. We can take them out simultaneously while we go after Alex and his brothers."

"Are you killing the baby sister, too?" Sam asked. Katya was eighteen, maybe nineteen, and apparently harmless.

I nodded. "No Rasputin left behind."

"Tiernan, how many soldiers do you think we're gonna need?" Achilles turned to me.

"Twenty, excluding you and me."

We were going to lose some Camorristi. He knew it. So did I. It was the sacrifice Vello agreed to make when I married his daughter.

"It's not just going to be us," Achilles said. "My father said either Enzo or Luca is coming. I'm leaning toward Enzo. He hasn't participated in many combats yet. This'll be a good exercise for him."

I flicked one look at the youngest Ferrante brother. He was talking to Lila, using sign language. He was as illiterate at ASL as he was in English. But he was the only brother who seriously attempted it in the first place. And she seemed to be the fondest of him.

"No." I turned to look at Achilles. "We'll take Luca."

"Luca's wife's pregnant."

"So is mine," I deadpanned. "Enzo stays here."

I trusted him the most to take care of Lila if something happened to me. Luca was reliable, but too caught up in his own affairs. "And I thought Luca and Sofia were having troubles."

"Not in bed, apparently." Achilles lit himself a cigarette. "We'll take the private plane. I have some weapons I've been meaning to try out."

It was a shame Achilles wasn't born in another century. He'd make such a prolific tyrant.

"They have a good amount of weapons, too," Sam warned. "But we have the element of surprise. Alex is under the impression his enemies think he's still in Russia. He flew in an intricate route, first to Germany, then to Peru, before landing in Vegas. He'll only deal with you after he sorts out the failed shipment and find out which one of his men messed it up."

Running a hand over my jawline, I asked, "How much does he know about Lila?"

"He knows you have a new wife, that she is pregnant, and that you spend all your nights in your apartment, meaning you aren't visiting your whores anymore. I'm sure he deduced you're fond of her," Sam said flatly. "He's evil, not dumb."

Achilles shot me a dirty look. "Are you fucking my sister, Callaghan?"

"She's my *wife*, you moron."

"That's not a good enough excuse," he volleyed back. "I'm paying you not to touch her."

"Been wiring you the sum back for two whole months now."

His sister's pussy was priceless. He couldn't pry me out of it using an entire Navy SEALs unit.

"Now I have no choice but to do the same to you." He cast an evil eye my way.

"Your only way of fucking me is if I'm a corpse," Tierney deadpanned, swaggering past us in perfect timing, hips swinging, holding a glass of pink champagne. "Because there's no way in hell I'm letting you screw me while I still have breath in me."

"I never said you needed to be alive for the occasion, Cumcake," Achilles said mildly. "You'd probably be tighter dead, with the number of assholes who went through you."

Tierney laughed, knowing she had the upper hand when Achilles's ears turned red.

Then a crew of servants appeared at the door and announced dinner was ready.

Chiara Ferrante sat to the right of her husband, wearing a necklace that cost over two million dollars and a dissatisfied frown.

The frown was directed at her daughter.

Said daughter happened to take a seat in my lap, ignoring the chair next to me, digging her sweet little ass into my already painful erection to make a point. The point she was making? Never leave her dissatisfied and start something I had no intention of finishing.

The chitchat had ceased as soon as Lila assumed her position in my lap. All heads turned to us. All but President Keaton's.

"The caprese is divine," he announced, spearing a tomato with his fork. "Who made it?"

"We hire chef Ambrose Casablancas for special events," Vello boasted. The diminished man resembled an ugly baby bird. Pink and plucked, with plumes of white hair sticking randomly from his bald head.

Keaton raised an eyebrow. "I tried hiring him for an event at the White House. He said he doesn't associate himself with politicians. I see he doesn't extend the same disdain to criminals."

"He says criminals at least have the decency to own up to their sins," Vello explained. "I don't disagree."

"He's a cook, not the fucking pope," President Keaton grumbled.

"Call him a cook to his face." Enzo grinned into his drink. "See how that works out for you."

Meanwhile, Lila pretended to readjust herself directly on my cock, leaning forward to reach for her glass of water and spreading her thighs just enough to nestle the length of me between them, then squeezed hard.

I suppressed a groan, my jaw tightening.

A second round of appetizers was ushered to the table. Tierney and Achilles were locked in some kind of who-blinks-first game. The air was thick with violent tension. I thrust my hips forward, teasing Lila's opening through our clothes as I reached for a piece of calamari and popped it into my mouth.

"*It's unbecoming for a woman to sit in a man's lap at the dinner table,*" Chiara finally signed to her daughter.

Lila flashed her a slow provocative smile. "*He's not just any man, Mama. He is my husband. I'm sure everyone at the table already knows he fucks me senseless every night.*"

"What a terrible day to have eyes." Enzo gagged on a piece of bread, coughing it into his fist. "Why did I go straight to the naughty parts when I started learning ASL?"

"Because you're a pervert?" Luca offered indifferently.

"Because you're mentally eleven," Achilles guessed in unison.

"Wait, what did she sign?" Luca frowned.

Enzo rolled his eyes. "Put more time and effort into your ASL studies and find out, *stronzi.*"

Vello looked like he was about to expire on his lasagna.

"*How dare you speak to me that way, and under my own roof?*" Chiara's dark eyes singed like two burning coals.

"*Did I do you a disservice?*" Lila cocked her head, blinking innocently. "*Doesn't feel very nice, does it? Imagine what the last eighteen years have been like for me.*"

"Burn." Enzo coughed into his fist.

"Sign slower. I'm trying to translate all of this into English." Luca scrolled on his phone, glowering.

"Maybe it's best if we switch to another topic," Francesca Keaton suggested cordially.

"Agreed." Enzo shoveled food down his throat, turning to the president. "Dude, isn't your wife, like, fifteen years your junior?"

Jesus. The Ferrantes were a right mess. And here I thought my family was fucked up.

Keaton pinned Enzo with a look that could decimate armies. "Didn't your big brother fuck your ex-girlfriend?" he retorted.

Achilles grinned behind his glass of wine. "She called him mid-act to dump him, I dicked her so good."

"You did have an unfair advantage, Achilles." Tierney raised her champagne in a toast. "Dick is your entire personality."

At this point, Vello decided the best course of action was to start a new conversation. One in a language everybody spoke, and not about his children's sex lives.

"President Keaton. It appears we have an...*insect* problem in this house." The don cleared his throat emphatically. His way of informing him that the place was bugged.

"That's quite unfortunate." Keaton sat back, one arm flung over the back of his wife's chair.

Francesca Rossi was a mother of three. Charitable, beautiful, and the most popular First Lady in the last twenty years. She was also the subject of many hit pieces in the media. Partly because she married her husband when she was a teen and he was in his thirties. But mostly because she was a Mafia princess.

The Keatons never denied their affiliation with the Chicago Outfit. Oftentimes, Keaton would strike deals with less-than-reputable fellas to get his way. We had one together, in which I cleaned Hunts Point's streets of sex workers, instead opening off-the-grid brothels where employees were tested for drugs and STIs and got steady, fair pay under the table.

Overall, the American people were happy. The economy was strong, crime rate was relatively low, and the world wasn't on fucking fire.

"What can be done about that?" Vello asked, while Lila artfully dropped her own fork. She bent to get it, grinding her pussy along my dick through our clothes.

My pulse drummed across the side of my neck.

I was very close to losing our little game.

Too bad I never lost, and an eighteen-year-old girl—no matter how pretty, how enticing, how good with a needle, a pistol, a *cock*—couldn't change that.

"Not much." Wolfe sat back, not an ounce of apology in his voice. He was playing with a lock of his wife's brunette hair, and it sickened me, how other men pretended other women were attractive when my wife was in the room. "Have you tried pest control?"

He meant, of course, people like Brennan. Former fixers, sometimes dirty feds, whose sole job now was working for the likes of Vello and myself to ensure our places weren't bugged.

"I did. They're all useless." Vello picked up his wine glass, staring into the crimson liquid. "I rather hoped you could…"

Wolfe tilted an eyebrow.

"*Exterminate* the type of insect plaguing my house."

Wolfe's mouth pinched in barely contained amusement.

"While history rewards high-risk presidents, I'm not dumb enough to test that theory by telling the head of the FBI how to conduct his business," Keaton said outright.

Luca gave the president a flat stare. "Throw us a bone here."

"You're asking for an entire damn skeleton," Wolfe's lilt sharpened like a knife's edge.

His wife put her hand on his. His expression softened immediately.

"I *will*, however, suggest you look into a different couch in the drawing room," Wolfe's voice dropped an octave. "The current one doesn't complement the curtains. And maybe freshen up all those chess pieces in your office."

A satisfied smile pulled at the don's lips. "What excellent suggestions. Our place could use a little facelift."

"You'd need to burn the entire motherfucking house, and it'd still be distasteful," I muttered into my drink.

Brennan choked on a bite of his rare steak. Wolfe caught my eye, smirking.

"And you, Tiernan?" The president splayed his fingers over the pristine white tablecloth. "How's married life treating you?"

"I've had worse ventures."

"What a glowing endorsement." Keaton grinned. "You know, it's not all bad once one yields to their emotions."

Lila had her back to me when I smiled, moving a hand over her magnificent hair. "Oh, I'm not one for pesky feelings. My wife is, at the best of times, a harmless hobby."

Chiara's fork clanked across her plate noisily.

Her chair scraped across the floor.

Vello reached for her shoulder, signaling her to stay put. She sat back, sending him a death glare.

I wondered when she'd pull the trigger and finally poison him.

I hoped it was tonight. The birthday dinner could use some entertainment.

More food rushed to the dining table. Everyone was in a festive mood. Not me, though. I was laser-focused on Lila, who was still dry-humping me to oblivion. Determined not to let her have the last laugh, I pretended not to care, eating, drinking, and carrying on a dull conversation with Sam, Achilles, and Keaton.

The issue started when Lila found a rhythm that teased my length and crown just enough to mimic fucking to put me on the fast lane to a climax.

It was the way she rubbed her hips together over my cock that made it impossible not to come in my pants. My jaw flexed as I painfully bit down on a groan.

Precum gathered at my tip, and heat shot through my cock. *Fuck.*

"Excuse me." I lifted my wife gently, placing her in my seat.

I strolled to the bathroom, the image of an unruffled prick. I bypassed the cabana near the dining room, choosing the bathroom on the other end of the first floor. I was about to slam the door behind me and tear my mickey off into the toilet when a small hand flattened against it.

My *wife.*

She smiled cheerfully. *"Enjoying dinner?"*

I yanked her inside and locked the door behind us, then descended upon her mouth like it was water in a desert. She pulled away, looking me square in the eye.

"I'm afraid I can't allow that until you promise me two things."

I would promise her the president's balls for dessert to get a kiss at this point.

Still, I didn't blink. Didn't flinch. Only stepped back serenely, showing her that I could—and indeed would—resist her. "It's cute when you do that."

"*Do what?*"

"Act like you have power in this marriage."

Any other woman would hurl sharp objects at me at this point. Not Lila. She learned the game. And, although she was dealt a modest hand, she still made the most out of it.

"*Don't let your ego stand in the way of a good orgasm, Tiernan.*"

I was going to indulge this nonsense, because *she* was the one who gave me shit.

"What are your terms?"

"*One—never use sex as a weapon against me,*" she signed. "*You don't have to always touch me, but if you do, don't leave me hanging intentionally. It's disgusting and immature.*"

I was getting schooled by an eighteen-year-old. One who handed me my own ass tonight and taught me a lesson.

Worst part was, I wanted to be my teacher's pet.

"Acceptable," I said laconically. "What's your other demand?"

"*Always tell me your plans. Where you're going. Who you're with.*"

This posed more of an issue, since I sometimes visited high-risk places. I didn't want her anywhere near them.

But I wasn't ready for this thing between us to end.

Whatever it was.

"Fine," I rasped.

She nodded, satisfied, and then, like a rabid badger, flung herself on me, planting wild kisses all over my face until she realized I was perfectly still. I waited. She stepped back. Glared at me with the prideful hurt only a gorgeous woman experiencing her first rejection could feel. Poor Lila.

"*What's wrong?*"

"I've some demands of my own."

"*Okay.*"

People probably speculated what we were doing away from the table, and it wasn't playing chess with Vello's bugged pieces.

"Never blue ball me again."

She nodded.

"And never, *ever* go anywhere I'm at unless it's a place you know is safe for you—Fermanagh's, your parents', your brothers', etcetera."

"*So you could cheat on me?*" She frowned at me furiously.

I almost laughed. Unfortunately, I had no spare energy to muster since all my blood was in my cock right now.

I ate the distance between us in half a step, lifting her face up to mine. "Tell me you're jealous, and I promise I'll never touch another woman again. It would be the first time I keep my word, but for you, I'll do it." My gaze dropped to her pouty, pink lips.

I hadn't touched anyone. Not since that night with Becky. But I needed her to admit I wasn't the only one going crazy here.

She tipped her chin up, examining me through hooded eyes.

"*You make me jealous.*" Her throat worked around a swallow. "*You make me so sick with jealousy I can barely even stand it when you speak to other people. I'm jealous of the clothes you wear. Of the soap you use. Of the air you breathe. I hate so much that I like you. But the truth is…I do.*"

True to herself, there was nothing cautious and measured about the way she said things.

She was intrepid and direct and much, *much* braver than I was. At least in that regard.

And I was done fucking talking, anyway.

My mouth came down hard against hers, my fist instinctively tightening around her hair from behind. Her arms locked around my neck. The kiss was carnal and desperate. Greedy and wet and sloppy, and my heart picked up, and my entire bleeding existence enhanced.

I'd been reduced to nothing but desire because of this woman, and now I was sneaking in other people's toilets for stolen kisses like a teenage fool.

I grabbed her ass and hoisted her up, wrapping her legs around me. She weighed next to nothing, even pregnant, and again the thought of her assault drifted into my mind.

It was always there, in the back of my head.

An obsession I couldn't get rid of. A hunger that replaced my need to kill Alex and his siblings.

And yet, I'd been stalling getting that hard evidence against Angelo, instead jerking around exploring other less-likely options. Because Angelo could take her from me.

More accurately, he could try.

And then I'd have to go to war with the Outfit, the Camorra, *and* the Bratva to keep her.

It wasn't an ideal scenario, but one I was 100 percent prepared for.

She was mine. No replacements. No refunds.

"I want to have sex with you." She spoke out the words into my mouth, our ragged, rough breaths meeting in the middle. "Now."

God, I loved her voice. It felt like sunrays dancing on water. It fucking *sparkled*.

I couldn't deny her. Much less wanted to.

But I wasn't going to allow both of our first times to be in the bathroom where the help took their shits.

"Your bedroom upstairs. Now." I bit down on her lower lip.

I released her momentarily. She grabbed my hand, unlocked the door, and pulled me up the stairs and to her room. My first time in her childhood shrine.

Uncoincidentally, it was a replica of what her mother had prepared in my apartment.

Childish. Unassuming. Infantile.

Flamingo-feathered lamps, a mountain of throws, and a ceiling glittered with stars.

And everything was so goddamn *pink*.

The setting was irrelevant, though. I locked the door behind us, seized the back of her head, and kissed her, slow and tender this time, walking her back to her bed while she clawed at my clothes, yanking my dress shirt from my slacks, unbuckling my belt, sinking her fingernails into my skin.

I broke the kiss and tilted her jawline with my thumbs so she would look at me. "We need to keep it quiet."

"*Why?*"

Why, indeed? Was there better revenge for her brothers' taking my eye out than having the entire Ferrante household, guests and servants included, listening as I defiled their precious baby girl? But somewhere down the line, tormenting the Ferrante men became marginally less satisfying than...well, Lila herself.

And, fine, maybe I respected her. Enough to protect her privacy.

"Because you're mine. Your moans. Your pleasure. Your words. No one else is allowed to hear them."

Lila nodded eagerly, fusing our lips together again, falling to the bed and taking me down with her. Her legs opened for me. She didn't wear any leggings.

Slipping a hand under her dress, I found a tiny pair of underwear, completely soaked.

"Lace," I growled into her mouth approvingly. "I don't remember you owning fine lingerie."

"*Your sister took me shopping. I told her I wanted to seduce you.*"

Like she needed to seduce me. She could roll in pig shit and I'd lick her clean from head to toe.

Reaching between her legs, I used the tip of my pinky to drag her dress up, sensually slow. Lila's breathing ceased and we both watched as a tiny, lacy white thong appeared, covering a pale triangle. The part that covered her pussy lips was cotton, and it was drenched with her juices. I slowly removed her underwear to reveal a trimmed little cunt.

I looked up. Blush crept onto my wife's cheeks. "*She told me to groom down there, too.*"

I made a mental note to treat Tierney to her favorite funnel cake. And maybe an entire Miu Miu shop.

"Sure you want this?" I asked, glad she couldn't hear my voice cracking midsentence.

"*I'm sure.*"

She trusted me with her body.

With her secrets.

With her heart.

The first person who ever did. I wanted to earn it. To deserve it.

I removed her dress but kept her heels on, struggling to maintain a detached air. Once I was done, I took off all of my clothes. Even the goddamn socks. I wanted this to be...*right.* Then I stood before her and gave her a few seconds to take it all in. Her icy blues roamed my body, and she gulped. Then she pushed forward onto her knees and crawled across the bed, fisting my cock and giving it a stroke. The first time she had touched it since the first night I ate her out.

I hissed in pain and looked away.

Still, I let her explore it.

She touched the tip first, her lower lip trapped under her teeth, then ran her slender fingers over the length of it, cupping my balls. I closed my eye and sighed. I had my dick hoovered by countless women whose damn job was to suck cock, and never was it this erotic, this satisfying, this...*thrilling.*

Lila kissed the tip of my cock, and I couldn't take it anymore. I gently shoved her down and nestled between her legs. Hot. Wet. Welcoming. And I wasn't even in yet.

I drank her in, wishing for the first time I had two eyes again so I could see more of her. There wasn't enough. Not nearly enough of this woman. I ducked down to kiss her, and she met me halfway, sighing into my mouth, her fingers caressing my shoulders, my rib cage, my back. Soothingly, like she knew this was new and terrifying to me as much as it was for her.

I covered her entire body with mine, introducing her to the full weight of me before I was inside her. Giving her another chance to change her mind. My cock latched hotly against her hard, round stomach, and I quickly averted my mind from the baby inside it.

I didn't want to fuck this up.

Do.

Not.

Fuck.

This.

Up.

Tiernan.

I froze, remembering my first time back in the gulag. Knowing I was only capable of taking a woman punishingly, like a gun was pinned to my temple. My breath hitched, and I slammed my teeth together, loathing myself for not being able to do this.

The most natural thing in human nature.

"Look at me." She took my face in her hands, anchoring me to this moment. I was glad she couldn't hear the thumping of both our hearts beating out of whack. And I was glad she chose to use her voice. It…soothed me. "You can do this. You escaped hell. You're here now. And I will never let you go through it again."

Before I could overthink it, Lila took matters into her own hands, rolled her hips, and scooped my cock into her, sliding it inside in one slick motion.

A grunt escaped me.

She felt heavenly, blissfully tight. Hot and wet and *right*.

We both stared at each other in surprise, getting used to the sensation.

The more I let myself feel it, the more divine it felt.

But I wasn't all the way inside her, and she already looked uncomfortable.

Very carefully, I pressed deeper. One inch, and then another. Her throat worked around a swallow. I leaned down to kiss it. "Shhh, sweetheart. Almost there. Take it all in for me, okay?"

She nodded, eyes glistening.

Another inch.

Finally, I was buried inside her to the hilt, my balls flush against her tight rectum.

Heaven.

I started moving inside her. It felt like coming home. I watched her alertly, looking for signs of pain or distress. But all I found was a flushed, deliriously happy water nymph in an erotic vortex of passion.

One who couldn't hear herself and moaned with abandon.

"Sorry, darlin', I have to." I grabbed a pink teddy bear from between her satin pillows and pressed it against her mouth to stifle her moans. She bit hard on it, her eyes rolling inside their sockets.

I picked up my pace, my balls tightening, my forehead slicked with sweat. She was close. So was I. Each time I plunged into her, the entire bed shook, the headboard banging against the wall.

She clenched around me, milking the orgasm out of me, and I lost the remainder of my self-control, of whatever chivalry I managed to scrape from the bottom of my godforsaken soul, and went wild.

I all but nailed her into the mattress, sinking into her again and again. Deeper, faster, harder. Our gazes locked, the stupid teddy bear between us. I tossed it aside. Kissed her ardently. I felt the walls of her cunt shuddering around my cock like an earthquake. Pulled my face back to watch her. She was moaning loudly again. I pressed my palm to her lips, keeping her quiet.

She grinned, licking my salty flesh.

Fuuuuuuuuuuck.

I grinned back. Feeling...*feeling*. Shy, almost. Boyish. All those emotions I never got to feel when I was actually at the correct age to explore them.

We stared at each other, grinning like two fools who just conquered the world.

Because we both managed to do something we didn't think would ever be possible.

Fuck the fear and trauma out of one another.

We won. Not the rapists, and the abusers, and Igor, and that faceless asshole who took her that night.

We. Won.

We stayed like this—thrusting, bucking, arching, licking, laughing, until Lila turned serious. Her smile fell. She threw her head back and gave one sharp moan. She spasmed in my arms, her muscles clenching, ripples of goose bumps cascading down her perfect silken skin.

It was my cue to finally let go.

"I'm coming, sweetheart."

She nodded, caressing my temples with a loving smile.

I came inside her, the satisfaction of doing so *brutal*.

I rolled over beside her as soon as I was finished, tossing an arm over my face.

We were quiet for a few minutes. Just panting and staring at the horrid, pink, starred ceiling.

She was the first to turn to me. "*When can we do it again?*"

I suppressed a laugh. "As soon as we get back home, I'm canceling my shit for the next forty-eight hours so we can practice."

Her face lit up. "*Good. It was fun.*"

I wanted to agree but was too fucking stunned to do so.

She licked her lips, suddenly unsure. "*You liked it, right?*"

Oh, God, *Gealach*, if only you knew.

"That I did," was all I could manage.

I put my hand over my mouth so she couldn't see it but spoke the words audibly.

"You eejit bastard. You're so fucking screwed."

When we returned to the table, the chatter quieted down and all eyes swung to us. I had smoothed out my hair and suit to stoic perfection before we left her room, but Lila looked exactly like a woman who just got railed hard and fast while biting her childhood teddy bear's bum to stifle the moans. Her hair was in complete disarray, her dress unevenly flung over her legs, lips swollen, and makeup smeared.

We sat down in undignified silence in our seats and grabbed our cutlery. The food was cold, curling at the edges as it began to lose its freshness.

"Well, this is…" Enzo blew out a breath, chuckling good-naturedly. "Definitely putting the nickname *Deathless* to the test. The fuck you doing, Callaghan?"

"Your sister," I drawled, taking a sip of my wine. "Thought we were clear on that."

Chiara looked ready to faint. Good. One less person to gawk at my wife.

"Ugh." Enzo downed his wine like a shot. "I miss the person I was twenty minutes ago."

"This really couldn't have waited a couple hours till you got home?" Luca scowled.

Lila twirled spaghetti around her fork and slurped it, ignoring the chatter by setting her attention on her plate.

"What my wife wants, my wife gets."

"Even if that thing is a dead husband at the dinner table?" Achilles mused.

I pinned him with a look. "I don't remember stuttering."

Lila giggled, reaching for her glass of sparkling water, and my chest filled with stupid, disgusting pride. Because I made her laugh. I made her orgasm *and* laugh. She better fucking like me, or else.

"Mother Mary, I truly lost her." Chiara clutched her giant diamond necklace. "Nothing in this…this *hussy* in front of me resembles the sweet child I put in this man's hands only a few months ago."

"Call my wife a hussy one more time," I challenged, continuing to eat my meal calmly, "and her pretty little pink dress will turn red."

"Chiara, zip it," Vello barked. "Callaghan—no more disappearing acts while you're on my property, you understand?"

"Loud and clear." I flashed him a soulless smirk. "Next time, I'll stay here and do it right in front of you."

CHAPTER THIRTY-EIGHT

THIRTEEN YEARS AGO

Three months after their great escape, the twins reunited with their family in London.

Tyrone was tall and regal and broken. Older than they'd imagined. He was handsome, but haggard in a way a man who had lost everything was. And Tiernan knew, on first sight, that his father had never gotten over his mother and never would.

It was on his scrawny fourteen-year-old shoulders to steer what was left of the family from troubled waters. To put it back together and take over the family's business.

One of Tiernan's many disappointments in his father was that he looked nothing like them. He had dark hair and hazel eyes.

It was also why he took an immediate liking to Fintan. His older brother looked like a slightly older, fuller version of him, with the same crimson hair and green hooded eyes.

They flew straight to America, where Tyrone's secondary school friend helped him set up a business in Hunts Point.

The twins spoke ASL to each other—hoping to leave Russia and the memories it held behind. They didn't know much English, and Fintan was the one to patiently teach it to them.

Fintan talked relentlessly, making sure they heard his voice, accent, pronunciation, and slang. He taught them how to pour Guinness correctly, with the pint slanted just so, and how to curse in Irish and "Amhrán na bhFiann." He read them books. Ulysses *and* The Picture of Dorian Gray *and* Gulliver's Travels. *Made them watch, then recite, every* Father Ted *episode.*

He taught them how to play cards, how to cheat, and how to win. How to cook, do the laundry, whistle, and even how to have fun. How to steal a car. How to smile disarmingly at police officers when caught. He taught Tiernan how to flirt and how to steal a heart and how to break it.

In lieu of a fully functioning father, Tiernan leaned into his relationship with his brother. Adopted his Irishness and carved himself into something so eerily similar, no one could have guessed the brothers grew up in different countries.

He loved Fintan something fierce. A love that was different than the one he had for Tierney. With Tierney, it was all laced with worry, and anxiety, and a cloying desperation to protect her. His love for Fintan was more free. He took, not just gave.

Unlike Tiernan, his twin sister couldn't find it in herself to forgive her surviving relatives for what happened.

She reinvented herself as a New York siren. Her accent was American, all nasal vowels and laid-back intonation. Her clothes were Italian and French. She was cordial with Fintan and Tyrone, but kept her loyalty to Tiernan only. She blossomed like a rare flower tangled in ferns. A completely different breed from the men in her family. Flirtatious, careless, and extravagant. Disarming in a way only a woman who tasted the wrath of a lethal weapon could be.

They all worried about her, but decided not to poke the wounds she concealed so expertly with makeup and designer clothes.

They let her pretend everything was okay, hoping one day she, herself, would believe it.

Over the next three years, Tiernan had slowly discovered the extent of his own trauma. It was like unmooring a festering, infectious wound after a long journey. Getting the first good look at the pus and the clotted blood, the gore and the slithering maggots.

He didn't like girls. No, scratch that. He detested the entire human race. Could only enjoy women the way Igor had taught him to—from behind, in the arse, when they were hurting. He had no interest in what wasn't offered for a wad of cash. And he never formed any relationships deep enough to allow intimate questions.

He was an excellent soldier, sniper, negotiator, and executor; everything Fintan lacked in discipline and character, he made up for in spades. But he was cold, and growing colder by the day.

And he couldn't, for the life of him, find a good reason to stay alive.

The only thing he felt was pain. It was everywhere, reminding him he was still breathing.

Breathing was becoming a chore, and he had quite enough of those already.

He was an eighteen-year-old who never smiled, never laughed, never took joy in alcohol, music, food, a passionate fuck.

He kept waiting for happiness and relief that never came, until one day, he stopped waiting.

The decision to take his own life was a pragmatic one, devoid of depression or big, morbid feelings.

Tiernan didn't like pointless things, and he found his own life lacking in meaning. Save for Tierney, no one truly wanted or needed him. And recently, Tierney didn't look like she needed anyone much.

As with everything else, he considered the different forms of suicide and landed on a bullet to the head. Drowning was unnecessarily cruel, and flinging oneself off a cliff was too unreliable. He wasn't in the mood to drool in a hospital for the next fifty years in a vegetative state. He just wanted an out.

He chose a .45 caliber and drove to Fermanagh's, considerate enough not to make a mess at Da's new mansion. Went up to the steep rooftop of the converted church with a bottle of whiskey. Drank himself into a deeper state of numbness.

It was dark, raining, and sufficiently miserable. A good night to take your own life.

Wrenching the gun from his holster, he pressed it to his temple.

His index began to push the trigger when he heard a familiar voice.

"Don't you fucking dare, lad."

Fintan.

His older brother staggered across the steep roof, looking fifty shades of ossified. Fintan yanked the gun from Tiernan's temple, slapping it away. It skidded across the roof, tumbling into the gutter.

"What do you think you're doing?"

"Relieving myself of my oxygen duty, until you came along."

Fintan tugged him up by the collar of his shirt. He wasn't much of a fighter, or a mobster, but he was built like a Callaghan. Tall, broad, muscular, inherently strong. Tiernan whirled around to glare at him.

"You really that unhappy?" Fintan's face crinkled softly.

"I'm really that unbothered," Tiernan corrected on a snarl. "Nothing means anything."

"Bullshit."

Fintan snatched the back of his baby brother's neck, plastering their foreheads together. He was panting hard. So was Tiernan, he now realized.

"You have everything to live for, brother."

"Yeah? Like what?"

"Revenge, for one thing. You cannot let Igor win."

Oh, but he'd already won. He shaped Tiernan into the monster he, himself, couldn't stand.

Tiernan said nothing. Fintan clasped his cheeks, growling into his face. "You can't die before you kill him, because it's your duty not only to avenge your own pain, but Tierney's and Mam's, too. Da's honor. You're the only one who can take him."

Fintan was right.

A vendetta was a good enough reason to live as any.

And Igor did deserve to die.

"If you still feel like you want to die, you can do it after you kill Igor," Fintan bargained. *"Your death isn't going anywhere, so to speak."*

Tiernan gave him a rueful smile.

"And who knows? Maybe by the time you kill him, you'll find something else to live for." Fintan shrugged.

Unlikely, *Tiernan thought. Nothing could reignite his lust for life. If, indeed, he was ever born with it.*

And still, Tiernan decided to take Fintan's advice and change his plan.

Kill Igor first. Die after.

After that pep talk, Fintan didn't leave his brother alone for a few good months.

Tiernan was lucky if he could take a piss in peace.

His brother was overbearing, but his plan worked.

Tiernan waded through the trenches, coming out of them in one piece.

Fintan stopped following him like a puppy when Tiernan killed his first Bratva soldier.

The twinkle in his eye said it all.

He had found something to live for.

And that something was Igor's death.

Tiernan made a deal with himself.

He'd kill Igor first and then give himself one year exactly to find something worth living for.

Three hundred and sixty-five days to wait for something spectacular to come along.

And on the last day, he'd kill himself.

He knew nothing quite so lovely could ever be found, though.

No magic was strong enough to save him.

CHAPTER THIRTY-NINE
LILA

Two weeks later, Tiernan and I went to check on one of his gambling joints on our way to a restaurant. He took me on a date three times a week, explaining that I needed to feel like a teenager and let loose. As soon as we walked inside, he led me downstairs to his office.

"Wait here." He kissed my lips and headed upstairs to the cardroom.

I shook the rain off my coat and hair, watching the miserable weather through the window. The clouds were gray, dense, and pouring rain.

I settled into his plush recliner and rummaged in my coat's pockets, realizing to my annoyance that I forgot my phone in the car. Pregnancy brain was a real thing. I was beginning to forget all kinds of stuff.

With a sigh, I took the stairs up to the cardroom in search of my husband. I found him leaning over a blackjack table, monitoring a heated game of cards. To his right were a few Irish soldiers, filling him in on something. And to his left was none other than… *Becky*.

My heart exploded at the sight of her, heat spreading across my body, down my arms, making my fists curl. It was the first hit of real, potent, red-hot jealousy I'd ever experienced, and I was so consumed with it, it robbed me of my breath.

She rubbed her fake tits against his arm, whispering into the shell of his ear.

I watched their lips hawkishly.

"Was it something I did?" I could practically *see* her whining. She wore a black leather miniskirt and a red strapless heart-shaped corset. Tall boots and puffy hair with so much spray I hoped she'd die of gas emission.

"Becky, you're a prostitute. Were you expecting a ring and a honeymoon in Paris?" Tiernan's eye never wavered from the green fuzzy table.

"I thought I was your favorite."

"This is why you're paid to fuck, not think."

"You never come here anymore." Her bottom lip rolled sulkily.

"Fintan's running the place just fine."

"The girls don't like him. For one thing, he never uses their services. And his nosy girlfriend loiters around, always in everyone's shit to make sure he doesn't drink or gamble."

"I'm off the market." Tiernan parked his elbows on the table.

"Till when?" she pressed.

"Death and beyond."

His words didn't pacify me. The fact that he was talking to her at all made me want to bash his head against that table.

I took a step forward and cleared my throat.

Tiernan's eye snapped to me in a flash. His pupil dilated as he took notice of me.

"Darlin'."

Darlin', my ass. His exchange with Becky reminded me of her existence, and the fact that he brought her to *our* home, had put her in *my* dress, and screwed her in *my* kitchen.

I turned around and briskly made my way to the exit. He was beside me immediately, his stride quicker than mine. He was talking to me, but I didn't look to see what he was saying. The door was manned by two Irish soldiers, and when they saw us approaching, their boss at my heel, they blocked my way outside. One of them put his hand on my shoulder to push me back into the club. Tiernan responded by twisting his wrist and breaking it in one smooth, frighteningly practiced move.

"Fatal mistake," I saw his lips move. "Nobody touches my wife."

Rolling my eyes, I pushed through the door and headed to the car. A puddle lay at my feet between the Mercedes's passenger door and the curb. I took one look at it, then at my velvet Jimmy Choos, and sighed.

"*I hate you, but not enough to ruin these perfectly good shoes.*" It wasn't anyone's fault the weather decided to act up this week. Not even Becky's.

Tiernan shouldered off his peacoat and splayed it on the ground beneath me, so I didn't tarnish my pink pumps.

Finally, I speared him a pissed-off glare, stepping onto his jacket. "*The wool of your stupid coat got stuck in my heel.*"

My husband's cold, flat mask melted momentarily. He somehow understood exactly what I was doing and why I was doing it. We had an audience.

Becky. His soldiers. His clientele.

He needed to sacrifice his pride to restore mine.

"My bad, sweetheart." He slung my arm over his shoulder and took a knee, literally on his knees for me, as he lifted my leg. He rested my knee on his muscular thigh, rubbing the fuzzy wool from my heel with his thumb.

"Next time I'll wear cashmere."

"*You make sure you do that.*"

I could feel the stares of the entire club burning a hole in the backs of our heads as they watched on in bewilderment.

"*Why did you speak to her?*"

"She's an employee."

"*She wanted to fuck you.*"

"So? People want shit they can't have all the time."

"*You fucked her in our home.*"

"I'm sorry." He looked sincere.

"*In my dress.*"

"I wanted her to be you. I knew I couldn't touch you, but the thought of having anyone else was rather…unexciting."

"*And then there was that stupid receptionist.*" I narrowed my eyes.

"She was just bait. I never touched her."

"*You're a horrible person.*"

"Yes, but I'll make a damn good husband if you let me."

"*I don't know if I could ever forgive someone who's been this cruel to me.*"

"That's fine, I'm not that person anymore." He shrugged. "You turned me into someone else completely."

Beyond his shoulder, I spotted Becky, puzzled at the sight of me standing on my husband's designer peacoat, giving him shit.

"Do you want me to fire her?" he asked, his eye searching mine. "Say the word, and I will. I'll fire all of them. Every single woman under my employment. There's no one else, Lila," he said. "There never really was."

Pacified, I licked my lips. "*No. I'll never take away someone's job for no good reason. And my ego is not a good enough reason.*"

"I'll make sure Fintan deals with this club," he promised. "I won't ever see her again."

"*Just promise me you and Fintan treat these girls well.*"

He looked surprised and a little annoyed. "Of course. They get paid in cash. Crazy tips."

"*And the clientele?*"

"Adhere to the club's rules."

I studied him with a pout, watching as the wait turned him inside out.

"*You can take me to the restaurant now.*"

When we drove off and I saw Becky loitering at the entrance, shooting me a furious scowl, I made sure to flip her the bird.

CHAPTER FORTY
LILA

Summer slinked away, giving room to chilly fall days. The leaves turned yellow, then orange, then, finally, brown.

My belly swelled and stretched, the baby kicking and somersaulting playfully inside it. We had our own games now. I poked him; he punched or kicked back. I sang; he stirred. He was my companion when I ate, slept, sketched, and read.

I loved him extra hard, to make up for the fact his father didn't.

Tiernan took me to the shooting range twice a week now.

I didn't know whether it was because he was determined to help me protect myself or that I was so absolutely terrible at it. Maybe both.

One day, when Tiernan drove us to our biweekly practice, he veered out of the city and onto the highway.

"*Where are we going?*"

"Outdoor range. You've graduated to moving targets. In real life, the person you need dead isn't going to sit around and wait for you to pull the trigger. You need to be prepared."

Was this his silent way of telling me he was worried I was a target? I wasn't stupid. I knew his showdown with the Bratva was fast approaching.

The journey consisted of long, winding roads curling up hills and mountains, into woodlands just beyond Scarborough. At some point, the houses, streets, and electricity poles gave way to wilderness. Until, beyond the clear, cloudless sky and hills, I finally spotted a lone house.

Once we arrived, I realized the place was a cabin of sorts. It didn't seem like a formal shooting range. More like someone's home. I flashed my husband a curious glance as our boots chomped gravel on our way toward empty stables on acres of foliage.

"Safe house," Tiernan explained, taking my hand in his and lacing our fingers together. My heart exploded into a trillion fluttering butterflies.

He'd been inside me, kissed me, licked me everywhere, and yet, this—*this*—had me blushing down to my toes. This simple touch that didn't scream lust, but whispered intimacy.

"What for?" I asked verbally, unprepared to let go of his hand to sign.

"Sometimes we need to lay low. Other times, we smuggle people in and out of the country. Always good to have a place off the grid. Even better to have one away from cellular connection, so you can't be tracked."

I gnawed on my lower lip, taking this in.

"If ever things get fucked—and I mean your parents are dead, your brothers, Tierney, Fintan, me—you come here. There's a loose brick at the back of the house, smeared in tar. There's a phone number on a note under it. You call it three times and hang up. They'll take you out of the country. Understand?"

Why was he telling me this now? What was he preparing for? And why did I have a feeling today wasn't just about the shooting range, but also about familiarizing me with this place in case things went south?

"Tell me you understand, Lila." He squeezed my hand after a moment.

"Yes," I said thickly.

We stopped at the backyard of the house, which was outlined by a split-rail fence.

Tiernan stalked into a nearby shed and took out a clay-shooting machine. We got to work.

Unsurprisingly, I was just as bad at hitting moving targets as I was still ones. Worse, actually.

When we were done practicing for the day, he put his hand on my shoulder, peering into my eyes.

"We'll practice some more, but in the meantime, I want you to remember a very important rule, *Gealach*. When the target is moving, you wait for a clear shot. Promise me you won't lose your only chance at survival by panic-shooting."

"*I won't panic-shoot. I promise.*"

"That's my girl." He ducked his head down to kiss me, his hand on my waist, the other cradling the back of my neck. "Now let's christen this field. It's been four hours since I've been inside you."

His fingers were in my hair, and my mouth was on his, and my nails sank into his skin, and his touch was everywhere, all at once— everywhere but my belly, of course. Never my belly.

We went tumbling down the damp overgrown weeds.

Angrily, I bit down on his lower lip, drawing blood, sucking it, and groaning my frustration into his mouth. All he did was laugh, kissing me harder.

"My little demoness," he murmured, licking his own blood from the outline of my lips.

As he unbuttoned my clothes quickly, quickly, quickly, like the world was ending, I realized he unleashed something carnal in me.

Something nothing, and no one, could ever cage and lock back up.

And even though I was in an arranged marriage, I felt...

Free.

———————

When Tiernan stopped in front of Fermanagh's, he didn't park the car.

"I'm meeting your brothers and Sam in Harlem." He kept his shades on.

"*Is this about the Russians?*"

The answer was in his silence.

My heart sank. I didn't want him to go to Vegas. I didn't want him to risk his life for this stupid...*nothing.*

"*Why? Igor did terrible things to you, but Alex was nothing but a true friend,*" I pointed out.

"Alex must retaliate. He's the new pakhan. Plus, I betrayed him. I'd rather kill him than die."

"*When will you go to Vegas?*"

"This week."

"*This week?*" My heart dropped to the pit of my stomach. "*When were you going to tell me?*"

"As soon as I had a concrete date." He turned his attention to his phone in the central console. Flipped it screen-up to check his messages.

"I don't want you to die," I blurted out.

I was afraid. It was okay to be afraid. It was not okay to be a coward.

And a coward wouldn't have admitted her feelings.

This seemed to grab my husband's attention. He put his phone down and placed his thumb on my jaw, his fingers wrapped around the nape of my neck.

"They call me Deathless for a reason."

"*Koshchei, right?*" I remembered. Of course I remembered. I remembered everything about him. "*That's the name Igor gave you.*"

"Yes."

"*I read the tale,*" I signed dejectedly. "*The God of Death gets impaled through the chest in the end.*" Tears clung to my lower lashes. "*He dies an agonizing, violent death. And he dies a villain.*"

"I *am* a villain," Tiernan said, not an ounce of regret in him. "I am selfish. Soulless. Perverse. A few soft kisses and hard fucks did not change that. Nothing can, sweetheart."

The words were a bucket of ice thrown over the past few weeks. How foolish I'd been to think he developed feelings for me just because I developed feelings for him. Mama was right. I opened my legs and lost my mind to this man. Just like she'd expected.

I swallowed hard. *"I can't change your mind, can I?"*

He shook his head gravely.

"Well, then." I opened the door, hopping out. *"Have fun planning your own funeral, Tiernan."*

CHAPTER FORTY-ONE
LILA

I couldn't see straight as I walked the distance from the car to our building, Irish soldiers engulfing me from all sides.

I wasn't ready to face Imma in the apartment, so I slipped into Fermanagh's instead. The place was packed as always. Drunken old men and sex workers aplenty. It could be argued that a man of Tiernan's means who truly cared about his pregnant wife wouldn't want her to live in a place like this. Now that he had ripped the rose-colored glasses from my eyes, I could finally admit this to myself.

Weaving into the back of the bar, I grabbed curry chips and a Coke and dragged my way up the stairs, contemplating knocking on Tierney's door.

I loved Imma, but she'd never relate to me. In her view, Tiernan was a splendid husband. He gave me a credit card and no blue marks on my body. The rest, to her, was just white noise.

Mafia wars?

Seedy neighborhood?

Unspoken feelings?

All pesky female delicacies I shouldn't worry myself with as long as he kept me lavishly clothed and safe.

My phone vibrated in my pocket with a message. I pulled it out.

> Tiernan: Found a great audiologist. He specializes in cochlear implants. We are seeing him Tuesday.

Tuesday was three days from now.

It was his way of pacifying me, and it didn't work at all. I had a belly full of baby he refused to acknowledge and a husband who was going to fly off to Vegas in a few days to engage in semiautomatic weapon carnage. Not to mention he was taking two of my *brothers*, my own flesh and blood, with him. My lack of hearing was the least of my problems right now.

Tangled in a web of my own thoughts, I pushed the door open, my boots landing on something smooth and slippery. I raised my foot and frowned down at it.

An envelope.

An envelope addressed to *me*.

To: Raffaella Ferrante

My name was handwritten in cursive. My pulse quickened, and I bent down to retrieve it, my swollen belly making it almost impossible to do so.

I put the curry chips on the table, examining the simple white letter between my fingers.

I'd never received any mail here. All my medical and occupational therapy correspondence arrived at my parents' house. And I never received *personal* mail, period. This didn't look like a bill.

And there was another thing that made the back of my throat burn with bile.

Ferrante.

I wasn't a Ferrante anymore. I was a Callaghan. It seemed deliberate and wicked. A way to remind me my marriage was one of convenience, not love.

I broke the seal, retrieving the letter inside it.

Raffaella,

I know your dirty secret. The one you and your husband are trying to hide from the world.

  I know about your bastard child.

  If you want your marriage to survive and your secret to remain this way, meet me at a place of my choosing next week.

  Bring 150K in cash.

  Come alone.

  Wait for further instructions for location, and DON'T tell your husband.

  If you don't do as I say, you and the baby will die.

My back hit the wall, and I sucked in a breath, my lungs burning with panic.

Whoever wrote this had intimate knowledge of our lives.

Very few people knew about what happened to me the night of Luca's wedding. And up until a second ago, I thought all of them were allies.

Who could know this? Who could be privy to this kind of information?

Tiernan had spies monitoring his enemies' every move. What made me think his rivals didn't do the same?

There was no address from the sender. Which seemed to confirm it was slipped under the door, not sent via post. This made me even more nervous. Who could have access to this place? It was swarming with Irish soldiers twenty-four seven.

Whoever wrote this had skills and technique, access to the depths of the Irish and Italian operation.

And they were right. If word got out that the baby in my stomach wasn't Tiernan's, he *would* leave me. He'd have to.

But…why risk death and deliver this letter? More importantly, why now?

Why not when we first got married?

The pregnancy would soon come to fruition. The baby was almost here. And it was clear Tiernan and I had become more than just an arrangement. We both had something to lose now—each other.

I pressed my hand to my belly. The baby kicked hard, rioting against the quick thrashing of my heart, the panic coursing through my system.

Tiernan wasn't going to like this letter.

Understatement of the year. He was going to tear the entire world apart.

It would likely distract him from his operation with the Russians, which demanded all of his attention.

And yet, I couldn't handle this on my own.

…or could I?

It seemed straightforward. Bribery happened all the time in the underworld.

And 150K wasn't even an unattainable amount of money. Enzo would give it to me in cash, no questions asked. All I needed was to pay the money and make the person shut up.

Would they, though?

My head began to spin. I sank down to the floor, burying my face in my hands.

I needed a plan.

And then I needed a plan B.

But I wasn't going to lose them.

Not the baby, and not my husband.

I was going to fight with everything I had to keep them.

CHAPTER FORTY-TWO
LILA

Three days later, we visited the hearing specialist.

Dr. Castile was a man in his sixties, with Santa Claus's white beard and eyebrows to match, rosy cheeks, and a sturdy figure. He took great care while checking my ears and going over my blood work and test results.

Tiernan sat manspread, looking every bit the scary mobster that he was, shooting questions like a firing squad, demanding to know when he could take me to the opera.

This should have been one of the most monumental and happiest moments of my life, but my mind was a million miles away.

With the letter I received, which was burning a hole in my bag.

With the prospect of losing him. Of failing to navigate this situation.

In Vegas, where danger awaited my husband, my protector, my...well, *love*.

I was in love with him.

In love with his words and his thoughts and his warped sense of humor. With his violence and darkness that he wore like an impenetrable armor. An armor only I got to peek under.

I was in love with his veiny hands, broad back, neck kisses, Latin tattoos, hugs from behind, and that one green eye with the golden flecks that missed nothing and rarely blinked.

And I'd never been closer to losing him.

To the Bratva.

To our secret.

To this baby in my womb.

My lack of hearing didn't make me incomplete—I was still a whole, round, three-dimensional human. With talents and weaknesses and likes and dislikes.

But the possibility of losing Tiernan? That would finish me.

"Well, Mrs. Callaghan, I am pleased to inform you that you're an excellent candidate for a cochlear implant," the doctor concluded, gathering papers on his desk. "You have sensorineural hearing loss and an excellent grasp of speech understanding. Your MRI also suggests your ear anatomy is compatible with cochlear implantation."

"Does this mean she'll be able to hear?" Tiernan spun his pinky ring.

"There is no guarantee to anything in this life, but all the signs are extremely positive," the doctor reiterated.

"Just like that?" I asked verbally.

Dr. Castile offered a kind smile. "Just like that, I suppose."

All this time I could've had a hearing aid and my mother didn't even present me with the option. Shockingly, I was too exhausted to muster fresh rage. What more could be said about a woman who cut ties with her daughter the minute I decided to show the world who I truly was?

"Of course, this will have to wait until after the arrival of your baby," the doctor said.

"Of course." Tiernan's mouth twisted in a crooked, dark grin devoid of joy. "The baby comes first."

Nothing had changed. He still didn't want this baby.

I had no guarantee his disdain for him wouldn't outweigh his fondness of me once the baby was born.

I was going to get what I thought I wanted.

To hear music. Bask in laughter. Bathe in all the sounds I always wondered about. Birds singing. Church bells ringing. Waves crashing on the shore.

But I might lose the one thing I didn't even know I needed.

Still, I was going to tell him about the letter. After Vegas. When his mind was clear.

Even if it meant losing him, I couldn't lie to him. He deserved more.

When we exited the clinic, my husband put his hand on the small of my back. He opened the door for me.

"I thought you'd be happy." He wore an odd expression. "This is your dream, Lila. To dance to music."

My dream had changed. The current one was to live happily ever after with my husband and son.

Bonus points if they tolerated each other.

"*When are you leaving?*" I changed the subject.

He ran his tongue over his teeth. "Plane takes off tomorrow evening."

I closed my eyes and gulped in a breath that didn't reach the bottom of my lungs.

"You're going to waltz, Lila," he reiterated. "Often. And well. You'll be the belle of every ball. I'll make sure of it."

I smiled a sad smile.

"*What good would waltzing do me if I have no husband to dance with?*"

CHAPTER FORTY-THREE
TIERNAN

132 DAYS TO SELF-DESTRUCTION

The morning I flew to Vegas with Achilles and Luca, I stopped at my sister's apartment to ask her to take care of Lila. I issued similar requests to Da and Fintan. Not that my father was capable of taking care of a goldfish, but hey, at least he'd feel included.

Camorra and Irish soldiers were already in Vegas, preparing ammo and transportation.

I didn't want to go.

But I didn't have a choice, either.

Alex had every reason to kill me. Which was ironic, because for the first time, I actually found a reason to live.

My little expiration project proved to be successful. Fintan was right. I found a reason to live. I just hoped I didn't die doing something stupid.

I showed myself into Tierney's apartment, as always.

I heard the shower running and waited in the living room until my sister was done. Her place was too frou-frou for my taste. Compensation for the time we spent sleeping in piss-soaked cots, I suppose. I gave myself a leisurely tour, checking out the new art she purchased.

Something on the credenza under a genuine Emilia Spencer

painting made me stop. A piece of mangled paper peeking from under a vase. It had a phone number and a name.

Tom Rothwell.

My nostrils flared.

That eejit.

That goddamn fool.

"Hey." Tierney materialized from the corridor, draped in a silk black bathrobe. She used a towel to dry the red strings of her hair. "What's up?"

Whirling toward her, I held the piece of paper between my index and middle finger. "You tell me."

Her pink cheeks paled, her lips pressing into a hard line.

"Wow, a piece of paper." She rolled her eyes with a laugh, recovering. "Call the press."

"Tom Rothwell is a federal agent."

I made it a point to know everything that happened at 26 Federal Plaza. I had surveillance of everyone coming and going into the building around the clock.

There were two governmental agencies any prolific criminal worked hard to avoid—the FBI and the IRS. Tierney willingly keeping a fed's number could only mean one thing.

"There's more than one Tom Rothwell in the world." She folded her arms defensively. "Maybe even in New York."

"Cut the shit, Tierney." I pinched the bridge of my nose. "What the fuck are you doing, talking to the feds? Are you really that far gone?"

We were both screwed up, but I always held myself together. It worried me that I was putting my trust in this woman to protect my wife while I was gone when she did a shit job protecting her own ass.

"Fine." Tierney shrugged. "So what if I'm talking to him? It's got nothing to do with our work."

"*Everything's* to do with our work."

"He doesn't care about the Irish. We're small fry. It's the Camorra he is after," she insisted. "If I could help him—"

"You couldn't," I snarled. "The Ferrantes will find out before you make a move. If they haven't already."

Vello had dirty feds working for him. He knew the FBI better than they knew themselves.

I massaged my temples, using every ounce of my self-control not to strangle her. She was going to rat out the people I was going to board a plane with tonight to take down the Bratva. My sister was batshit.

"Relax, we only had a coffee. *Once.* He knows nothing, and I don't intend on giving him anything until you settle things in Vegas."

Now that I thought about it, she'd been sulking a whole fucking lot recently. My sister could never be accused of being happy. But recently, she was downright miserable. I was too drunk on my wife's cunt to pay attention.

"What's your angle?" I growled.

Her cheeks were ablaze. "You wouldn't understand."

"Try me."

"I'm tired of this life, Tiernan. Tired of capitalizing on people's weaknesses and addictions. Tired of the parties and pretending to be something I'm not. A social butterfly. An it girl. I want to retire somewhere nice. Coastal. European. I want dirty martinis and a clean conscience. Good books and maybe a gently reared husband to cook for every evening. It's not much…" She stared hard at her toes, painted in shiny black. "But it's enough for me."

"You can have all those things without throwing everyone you know under the bus," I whispered.

"No, I can't." She looked like the little girl in Siberia. Flustered, scared, and unsure. "You don't have Achilles breathing down your neck, holding your future in his palm, dangling it in front of you."

"What are you talking about?" I stared at her in disbelief. "I married the don's *daughter.*"

"Come on, Tiernan." She shook off my hand, which I hadn't realized was clutching her wrist. She glided toward the kitchen. "You wanted Lila from the get-go. Fell for her before you even put a ring on it. *You spared her life*," she whispered the last part. "You've never shied away from killing someone."

"I'm not in love with her," I corrected wryly. "We learned to get along, as you will with whoever Achilles chooses for you."

"That you'd let him choose *anyone* for me shows how little you care about me. The power the Ferrantes have given you has corrupted you." She wrenched an open wine bottle from her fridge, taking a swig from it.

"There was nothing left to corrupt." I parked my elbows on the breakfast nook between us.

"Besides, the Ferrantes rule the East Coast. Refusing Achilles meant war. I needed to bide my time. See how shit unfolded."

This was a bold-ass lie. I never tried to free her of the arrangement. I didn't think it was necessarily a bad thing for Tierney to settle down with someone who wasn't scared of her antics. If Achilles chose well—which he'd promised me he would—my sister could finally be at peace.

Tierney put the wine on the counter and splayed her fingers, staring at her burgundy nails. "I'm going to ruin this bastard, Tiernan, if it's the last thing I do in this life. I promise you, none of the heat is going to circle back to us. We'll get immunity."

"Jesus fucking Christ." I ran a hand over my hair. "Listen to yourself. If the Ferrantes catch you, I won't be able to help you. Nor will any of your fancy artist and politician friends. And if this somehow touches Lila…" I raised a finger between us in warning, struggling to control my anger. "It's not just the Ferrantes you will have to worry about. I will personally put a bullet in your head."

"Why?" Her eyes zinged victoriously. "Thought you said you didn't love her."

"I don't," I countered. "But I vowed to protect her. She's my wife."

"If you really want to protect her, strike an immunity deal wit—"

"Don't finish that sentence."

My sister huffed, realizing she wasn't gonna win this one. "Anyway, what'd you come here for?"

"My wife, actually." I turned my back to her, pretending to examine a painting on her wall to avoid her shit-eating smirk. I stuffed my hands into my pockets. "I need you to keep an eye on her while I'm in Vegas."

"Of course," she said diligently. "Unlike you, *I* don't mind admitting I love Lila."

"She's going to have around-the-clock security," I ignored her dig. "Plus, I hired Ransom Lockwood's company to do patrols around the neighborhood, so all I need is for you to keep her company and take her to her OB-GYN appointment."

"Gotcha."

"I'll see what I can do about Achilles."

I turned around, scanning her face. She looked exhausted, but also tough as nails.

"Okay," she said quietly.

"But I mean it, Tierney. Don't fuck with the feds. If you do, I won't be able to save you. Not this time."

A sad smile touched her lips. "I know."

———————

My next stop was a sex shop.

I was only going to be gone for a couple days, but Lila needed to sleep, and she couldn't do that without at least two orgasms.

I'd put her to bed every night for the past few months after pleasuring her with my tongue and cock. She was dependent on it. It was a habit we'd need to break at some point. But that point was going to come *after* I killed the Rasputins and found her rapist.

Besides, I'd met worse chores.

At the store, I purchased a suction vibrator and a wand massager. I steered clear of mammoth-sized dildos. The mere thought of something else inside her made my eye twitch. I could barely come to terms with the fact the baby was going to come out of her cunt.

The *baby*.

Now that we were a few weeks shy of his arrival, all sorts of thoughts crept into my head.

We did not think this arrangement through.

What if he were another race? Half Asian? Black? Pacific Islander? A dead giveaway I wasn't the father? My entire suspect list was Caucasian, but there was a vast different between Italian Caucasian and Irish Caucasian.

What if she'd pour all her love and attention on the baby and forget about me?

Yes, I was jealous of an unborn baby.

No, I wasn't above such notions.

I all but stomped my way back home, clutching the discreet sex shop bag in a chokehold. When I walked in, I spotted Imma in the kitchen, making pasta and singing out of tune in Italian.

"Imma," I barked. "Take the evening off."

She looked up from the boiling tomato sauce, startled. "Where would I go?"

"Do I look like a fucking tour guide?" I gestured to my face. "Have my driver take you to the movies. Or drive you up and down the street in circles. I don't care."

She gave me a disgruntled glare, but didn't argue.

I found Lila in our bedroom, drawing. She looked up from her sketchbook when I entered. Set her pencil down and flipped the sketchbook over on her nightstand.

"*When are you leaving?*"

I could hear her disapproving tone through her hand gestures alone. The only other person I knew so thoroughly, so completely, was Tierney.

"About an hour. Plane's engine is already running."

I was keeping her brothers waiting, but I didn't care. I found myself increasingly caring less and less about what happened outside my bed, and the woman inside it.

Pushing off the wall, I advanced toward her.

"What's in the bag?"

"Something to hold you over until I come back." I took a seat on the edge of the bed, seizing her chin and tilting her face up. "And I *will* come back, Lila. That's a promise."

She tore her gaze from mine, seized the bag, and rummaged through it. Lila wrenched the vibrator out, frowning and examining the box from all angles, like it contained ancient ruins.

"I won't be here to help you fall asleep." What the fuck was stuck in my throat, and why couldn't I swallow it? "So I bought this to keep you company."

By my wife's expression, she was ready to hurl the vibrator at my head. I waited for her shock to subside, then asked, "Do you want me to show you how to use it?"

She didn't say anything for a long while. Then, finally, she signed, *"I'm an eighteen-year-old girl with access to the internet, Tiernan. I know how to use a vibrator. I've probably watched more porn than a millennial watched* Friends *in their lifetime."*

I gave her a blank stare. Then, incredibly, I started laughing.

And I mean *really* laughing. The kind of laughter that bubbled from the pit of your stomach and utilized every muscle in your body.

I never laughed. Barely even smiled before Lila came along.

She watched me with a proud grin, taking pleasure in her conquest.

"Besides, all these times, I didn't fall asleep because of the orgasms." She shook her head. *"I fell asleep because I was in your arms and finally felt safe."*

Her words struck a place I didn't know existed inside me, so I decided to change the subject.

"Does this mean your online shopping includes sex toys, and I bought this in vain?" I gestured to the vibrator between us.

She shook her head. "*I don't have any toys. You're always available when I…*" She stopped, considering how to put it. "*Want to go to sleep.*"

"Feel free to use me for power naps, too."

"*I'll let you know how your gift measures up in comparison to you.*"

"Then I better remind you how good I am."

My mouth came crashing down on hers, my tongue plunging between her lips, and I could taste her misery, the sadness born from my leaving, maybe for good.

It only made me more fucking feral for her. I tugged at the front of her pink frock, unbuttoning the silvery buttons until the dress spilled and pooled around her waist like a puddle, without breaking our kiss.

After unclasping her bra, I let it fall across her arms, cupping her tits. I reached down to taste one of her nipples. It dampened with warm milk. A shock of primal pleasure made every single hair on my body stand on end.

I pressed my hand to her spine—her back slim, every vertebra pronounced—bringing her closer, twisting my tongue around her nipple, using my teeth to tug at it teasingly. She tipped her head back and moaned, fisting my hair.

Her breathing quickened. I trailed my tongue along the blue veins of her tits. Sucked the other nipple. Another burst of sweet, warm milk on my tongue. My hand snaked down her waist, moving between her legs, brushing her panties to one side. I found her core, spread her arousal along her lips and her clit, and rubbed it in a circular motion, using two fingers to spread it open.

Lila's mouth latched to my throat, sucking hungrily, leaving a mark. She sank her teeth into it, then moved her lips along my pulse soundlessly, thinking I wouldn't understand what she was saying.

You're destroying me, and I'm too far gone to care.

I pulled her in and kissed her cheek to keep myself in check. She tasted like my sweet ruin, my absolute downfall, and still, I gulped her up, manically, aching for more. I was on the brink of doing something I couldn't fucking afford.

Staying. I wanted to stay.

I'd never veered off target. Starting now was a dangerous precedent.

I playfully stuck my tongue in her ear and gave it a lick, before nipping on the lobe of her ear. She giggled and squirmed.

"Tiernan…"

I pushed two fingers into her, curling them to tickle that spot that always made her go wild. I pressed my thumb to her clit, kissing my way down her body. Collarbone. Breasts. Rib cage. Waist. I pushed her legs open, holding her by the back of her knees, and got to work, flattening my tongue against her pussy with her panties still yanked to one side, my fingers still inside her.

"God…"

"Nah. Even he doesn't get to touch my wife."

I licked and teased and sucked until she had her first orgasm, before pushing up and kissing her, using one hand to jerk my cock free.

"Hold on to me, sweetheart," I murmured into her mouth, sliding inch by inch into her. She arched and moaned, her sweet breath skating over my face. Her muscles clenched around me, the familiar rush of heat coating my cock. I couldn't even tell if I was enjoying myself or not, I was so laser-focused on making her come a second time.

She needed to sleep well tonight.

That's all that mattered.

I pounded into her the way she loved being taken—with long, controlled, deep strokes at first. Then, when I felt her trembling, gasping for air again, I picked up the pace.

It was only after she fell apart inside my arms that I quickened my pumps, fusing our mouths in a dirty, tongue-filled kiss, hitting the magical spot deep inside her that was already making her quake again. My balls tightened and an explosion of heat sizzled down my spine. I came so hard I saw stars. I collapsed next to her on the mattress. Lila was still breathless, blinking at me with that sweet innocent expression of hers.

This thing between us had no business being this fucking good. It was ruining my focus, priorities, and fucking life.

"What are you thinking?" She spoke, rather than signed. She only did that when she felt extremely comfortable and placated.

I reached between her legs, curling my index into her drenched pussy, and with our mixed cum wrote one word on her upper thigh—*mine*.

I popped my finger into my mouth, rubbing the residual nectar of her cunt on my gums like it was high-end coke. I'd never sampled the shit I sold—hard drugs were a red line—but there was no point in denying it. I was a junkie. Addicted to my wife. There wasn't a low too low for me to stoop to in order to get my next hit.

We both stared at the possessive word for a long moment before she spoke again.

"*If I weren't pregnant, I'd tattoo over your handwriting to keep it there forever.*"

"If I wasn't made too jealous by the prospect of a tattoo artist laying their hands on you, I'd let you."

I considered hopping into the shower for exactly one second before remembering that (a) smelling like the Ferrantes' baby sister's cunt was exactly the kind of punishment her brothers deserved, and (b) I, myself, took strange comfort in smelling Lila on my skin.

"I have to head out in the next ten minutes. Just texted my driver to round up the car." I strode over to my walk-in closet, tugged a fresh shirt from a hanger, and buttoned it on my way back to the bedroom. Lila covered herself up with her dress and sat on the bed, staring at me through tear-coated eyes.

I'd rarely seen her cry.

She was braver than all of my soldiers combined.

I didn't miss my other eye often. But when I did, it was because it took me twice as long to watch every atom of my wife's existence every night. To count each of her thirty-three beauty spots—yes, including the one behind her ear. Her fourteen freckles, all of them peppered across her celestial nose. All the twenty shades of yellow and silver in her hair.

"There is something I want to give you before you go."

She reached for her nightstand and took her sketchbook, tearing a page and handing it to me. I tugged it from between her fingers and flipped it.

It was me.

A portrait of me, to be exact.

Much like the one she drew of Tate, but somehow…better. Sharper. I looked more alive in the drawing than I did in real life.

It looked like I was forged through marble and flames.

And it was the first time I stared back at myself and liked what I saw.

I swallowed hard, loathing how vulnerable this made me feel.

I leveled my gaze at her. "Cheers."

God, did my voice just break? Good thing she couldn't hear it. Only I didn't mind her knowing.

She shrugged, downplaying it. *"You were so touchy about the Tate portrait; I couldn't send you off without letting you know how I feel."*

Dangerous, now. There was a difference between playing house and fucking one's delectable wife and actually falling for her.

"And how do you feel?" I asked anyway. I wasn't normally a reckless cunt. She brought that side out of me.

"I…I think I love you," she blurted out.

Our gazes clashed.

There were two instances when I never believed someone's words—when they had a gun pressed to their head or when they just had an orgasm. Lila just had three.

She stared at me wildly, searching my face, her eyes so big, so blue, so heavily lashed, my heart skipped a beat. How easily this unassuming creature had undone me.

"Please don't go," she added with a choke.

I said nothing.

"No. I won't let you leave," she tried another method, punching the bed.

I was going because I wanted to return.

And I wanted to return because I wanted to be with her.

The only way out was through. I could never live with myself if I let her stay by my side without settling the score with the Rasputins. The code of honor cemented that women and children were beyond the scope of retaliation, but my entire existence attested otherwise.

I'd broken the code myself several times. I wasn't putting my trust in anyone else when it came to her.

Rolling my nightstand drawer open, I produced the cross pendant Lila had gifted me, securing it around my neck. She stared at me through tear-curtained eyes, and it hurt so fucking much I actually contemplated closing my eye so I wouldn't have to see it.

I leaned down, cupped her cheeks, kissed her forehead, and stared into her eyes.

"Don't follow me."

———

The drive to the private airport was silent. The journey from the car to the airplane on the tarmac a haze. The sketch burned a hole in my front pocket, and all I wanted was to stare at it until my eye bled, because *she* drew it.

I was met with stoic Luca and pissed-off Achilles on the plane. The rest of the soldiers were already in Vegas.

Luca plucked a red grape from a charcuterie platter, going over the blueprints of the warehouse we were going to raid. Achilles sprawled across from him in a recliner, thumbing through his phone with a frown.

Luca was the first to look up and acknowledge me. "Jesus fuck, were you mauled by a pack of wolves on your way here?"

He referred to the scratches, love bites, and sex hair.

I plopped on the seat opposite him and lit myself a joint. I didn't usually smoke. I did now. I needed to take the edge off.

"Who tried to kill you?" Achilles asked. He looked somber. Probably pissed that the assassination attempt failed.

"Your sister." Smoke skulked out of my mouth, crawling in the air, invading his space. "Fucks like a champ. Thanks for making me spell it out for you."

Their smug smiles melted away.

The rest of the journey was blissfully quiet.

Time to paint Las Vegas red.

CHAPTER FORTY-FOUR
TIERNAN

And there he was.

The motherfucker.

The spawn of the man who'd taken my childhood, my innocence, my memories.

Alex Rasputin was a red dot slowly moving on my screen.

Each of the Bratva's four Mercedes vans that drove from Vegas to Indian Springs had a tracker installed. Achilles and I huddled in front of the screen in our own van, watching the red dots moving toward us.

"Do we know which van Alex is in?" I asked Sam through our radio. He was back in Switzerland, playing house with his wife. Sam did legwork and hacking, but he no longer engaged in actual combat or exposed himself to heat. "*Too many fucking children to take care of. And I'm not selfless enough to allow my wife to remarry if I kick the bucket,*" he once explained.

"Third one," he provided from the other end of the line. "And they're heading your way. Should be there in the next ten minutes or so."

It was a one-lane road in the middle of the Nevada desert with nothing but golden dunes on either side of it. Our vans were parked behind a large knoll concealing a curve in the road.

On top of that knoll, Luca and three other snipers were laying low with M16s angled at the road.

Alex and his crew were headed to their weapon warehouse. Little did they know, we were going to tag along and do some shopping ourselves.

"Do you have everything you need?" Sam asked through the static humming of the encrypted radio.

Achilles peered around the mountains of semiautomatic firearms and grenades we were sitting in. "Got enough ammo to blow up the entire Strip." He turned to me, wrinkling his nose. "Ever heard of taking a shower, Callaghan?"

"Sure have." I pulled my balaclava down my face, shoving a loaded magazine into my AK-74. I favored it over the M16, because it was the rifle I was taught to use in the camp.

"And?"

"And I'm not washing your sister's juices off me till I'm back in New York where she can rub them right back."

"My sister's…" Achilles tapered his eyes, snarling. "Now you're just begging for me to stick a grenade launcher up your ass."

"Since when do you care?" I double tapped the mic connected to my Bluetooth to cut the sound off for Sam. "Last I checked, you were eager to hand her off to your unfriendly neighborhood psychopath when you tracked me down."

Achilles scratched at the tattooed side of his neck pensively. "I knew."

"Knew what?"

"That she was deaf, not mentally challenged."

"*What?*"

He shrugged. "Found out when I caught her reading *War and Peace* when she was twelve. I came to see her and my mother in Ischia. Wanted to surprise them. When I caught her reading, I turned back and walked away."

"Why?"

"Figured if she wanted me to know she could read, she'd have told me herself."

I couldn't fault the logic, but I could fault the asshole for doing jack shit about it.

I stared at him, dumbfounded. "Why the fuck didn't you help her escape your mother's claws?"

"I did." He cracked his knuckles. "I supported your marriage. It was the perfect way out for her. She and my mother aren't good together. Chiara projects all her trauma on Lila."

It was the most profound shit he'd ever said to me, yet I wanted to punch all his teeth out of his mouth. He sat around and waited for Lila to suffer in order to help her. What kind of brother was he?

"Besides." He flipped his firearm cloth open, revealing his own rifle. "Once I heard you didn't kill her on that fountain the night I scooped your eye out, I knew she had you in her pocket. That sealed the deal for me. She's your exception."

"My exception?"

He nodded. "Your Achilles' heel. Everyone has one."

I'd ask him what his was, but I suffered from an acute case of not giving a fuck.

"Speaking of sisters." I struck the bottom of the magazine to ensure it was locked in, giving it a tug. "Mine wants you to get off her back."

"And I want James Dean's face. We all want the unattainable." He grabbed his M16, making sure that it was cocked, before pulling his balaclava down his face. "What else is new under the sun?"

"Cut the crap, Ferrante. I'll give up Harlem if you let her go," I said, knowing damn well I was willing to forfeit a lot more than that for my sister's happiness. "She wants out of the game. To go away. Start fresh."

"The underworld is not a McJob. You can't hand in your two-week notice." Achilles zipped his protective vest up to his neck. "Tierney knows too much about the Camorra for us to let her walk away."

"I'll give assur—"

"This conversation is over. She's nonnegotiable where I'm concerned. If it makes you feel any better, I'll make sure she's happy. Happier than anyone else could make her."

The conversation was far from over. If push came to shove, I'd slit Achilles's throat myself. However, now was decidedly not the time to deal with it.

The red dots on the screen shone brighter, nearer. I tapped the side of my Bluetooth to connect Sam back into the line.

"Well, boys. It's showtime," Sam announced into our earpieces. "Knock 'em dead, and don't forget to bring me a souvenir."

On cue, two bulletproof vans jam-packed with Camorra soldiers revved up their engines, flooring it from behind the dune and onto the road, blocking the path for Alex's truck.

Our van followed last, parking behind the two trucks, as another layer of barricade the Russians couldn't plow through.

I slid the door open, watching as four Bratva soldiers poured out of the first van, firing a round of bullets at our vehicles. Camorra snipers on the dune took them down like soda cans.

Pop, pop, pop, pop.

They jerked comically as the bullets hit them, falling to the ground.

Another set of soldiers hopped out of the Bratva's vans. The last van on the line backed quickly, wheels screeching, but Luca put two bullets in each of its front wheels, making it sag onto the concrete road with a thump.

Springing out of the van with my firearm cocked, I jerked my head toward the third van. Achilles followed me.

Chaos erupted, with swaths of Bratva soldiers pouring out of their vans, shooting indiscriminately. They emptied most of their clips within two, maybe three minutes. I watched as two Camorra soldiers fell from the dune like a mouton in a guillotine. I thought I saw Luca duck away before they got him, but I had no time to check.

The third van stood still and stayed locked. Nobody came in. Nobody went out.

Jackpot.

We both headed toward Alex's van.

Achilles fired a round with his M16, spraying the Russian soldiers and taking a bullet that landed in his body armor.

"*Vafammoc.*" He spat on the ground.

"You hurt?"

"Nah, I took a bet with Enzo they wouldn't even touch me." He flicked gunpowder off his shoulder nonchalantly.

I put bullets in two Bratva soldiers' heads on my way to the van when they tried to jump me from behind. The third soldier was too close for a decent aim, so I hit him with the back of my rifle, caving his skull.

When I reached the desired vehicle, I produced a prick punch from my pocket and set it between the gap of the sliding door. There was no point trying to shoot my way into the truck. It was bullet-proof, windows included.

"Cover for me," I ordered Achilles, since I had my back to the commotion. He pressed his back to mine, shooting at everything that moved toward us while I pried the sliding door open. It clicked, gliding just enough for me to take a grenade out of my pocket, pull the pin, toss it inside, and slam the door. I grabbed Achilles by the collar and dragged him behind a dune on the side of the road to avoid the shrapnel. Halfway through, he roared, "duck!" and before I had the time to process the word, grabbed the back of my head and shoved me to my stomach.

A bullet flew a millimeter from my head.

A second later, Achilles rose from beneath the dune, aimed at a Bratva sniper who had assumed his place on a dune, and shot him clean between the eyes.

"Fuck," I groaned. "That was close."

"Spared ya."

"Surprisingly."

"Nah. You make my sister happy." He yawned. "*Too* happy sometimes, unfortunately."

The grenade exploded, shaking the van behind us. Black smoke curled from the gaps in the doors and windows. The unmistakable scent of burned flesh wafted through the air.

It was weird to think of Alex as dead.

Weirder still to think that I killed him myself.

For a few moments, I just stood there, staring at the van.

The hubbub around us died, along with two dozen Bratva soldiers who were splayed on the road. A few Irish and Camorra soldiers also lay lifeless at our feet.

"Okay, lover boy. Let's see our handiwork." Achilles advanced toward Alex's van. He slid the door open and popped his head inside. Ripped the balaclava from his face to inspect the massacre.

"Hmm," he said, tone flat. I studied his back, oddly uneager to step forward and see for myself. "Interesting," he mused.

"Don't fuck with me," I growled. "What's the damage?"

He turned around, casually waltzing over to a mostly dead Bratva soldier on the road. The wounded mobster was still groaning into the asphalt, desperately trying to stop the blood spritzing through a gush in his neck. Achilles lit himself a cigarette, unzipping his combat pants. He took a piss on the Russian's face. "Why don't you take a look while I go make sure my brother isn't bleeding out all over the side of the road?" Achilles asked around his cigarette, the Bratva soldier gagging and choking on his urine.

I stuck my upper body into the van. Tore the balaclava from my face, propping it against my sweaty forehead.

Carnage.

Blood everywhere.

Body parts scattered—the driver and the guy next to him took the biggest hit, with their limbs tossed about like doll parts.

Flesh melting into metal. Charred, unrecognized faces.

Blood. Internal organs. Piss. Shit.

And then there was Alex. Lying under a pile of bodies to shield him. His gun cocked and pointed at me.

Alive, well, and royally pissed.

He didn't come out of it completely unscathed.

His brow was busted, he had some cuts on his cheeks, and his left arm was at a weird angle, suggesting he might've broken it.

We stared at each other, motionless, for a few moments.

He didn't shoot.

Neither did I.

Finally, I hopped inside, pressing the sole of my boot against his windpipe.

"Well, well, well." I smirked. "Fancy seeing you here, Lyosha."

———————

Alex was the only one who came out of the ordeal alive from the Bratva's side. After shoving him into one of our vans, we did a body count to assess the damage on our side. Six Camorra soldiers, two Irish. We loaded them into a different van, leaving the Bratva corpses to bake in the Nevadan heat.

"How long till we get to the warehouse?" Luca plopped down on the seat next to Alex, bandaging his arm with precision.

Alex was zip-tied, mouth taped, and staring daggers at me.

"Twenty more minutes according to Waze," I said, ignored his ogling.

"And we're sure we won't find any surprises there?" Luca squinted.

"Sam said Slava and Jeremie are there, waiting for Alex." Achilles downed an entire bottle of water. "Maybe a few soldiers manning up the entrance point, but that should be it."

"Do we kill his brothers when we find them?" Luca turned to face me.

Alex didn't flinch, but I knew better than to interpret that as indifference.

"Not before I say so."

"And the sister?"

"Stayed home. I'll deal with her tomorrow." I had no issue killing women. Especially a Rasputin woman.

I took out Lila's sketch when no one was watching. Well, no one but Alex. But I could withstand that embarrassment, seeing as he had about another hour before I put a bullet in his head.

The portrait was splattered in blood—probably Bratva's—and wrinkled as shit. I still pressed it to my nose and breathed it in, relishing the fact she held it not too long ago, thinking of me as she drew me.

The rest of the journey was quiet. Luca was busy treating his broken limb, Achilles was staring out the window pensively, and I was messing with my phone, trying hard to look like my skin wasn't crawling with Alex's unrelenting gaze.

Something was amiss.

This felt easy.

Too easy.

The Russians were more capable than that. I knew, because I trained with them for fourteen years.

"How's Sofia doing?" I penetrated the silence. Luca's head snapped up. He looked dazed.

"Huh?"

"Your wife. She's pregnant," I reminded him. "How's she doing?"

"Okay, I guess."

The fuck was wrong with him? I'd detected more emotions from a cum stain.

"You guess, or you know?" I pressed.

Luca shot me a cold glare. "Get off your high horse, bastard. A few months ago, I had to pay you not to rape my sister. You're no authority when it comes to marriage."

"That miserable, huh?"

Luca worked his jaw back and forth. "You've no idea, man."

Our vans arrived at the warehouse twenty minutes later. We went through the first and second lines of guards fairly quickly, seeing as I dragged a half-butchered Alex out of the vehicle, pointing a loaded gun to his head and threatening to blow it off if they didn't let us through.

Once inside, Camorra and Irish soldiers started unpacking and sifting through Bratva weapons to see what we could take. They raided every corner of the two floors, top to bottom, peeling the floors and stripping the walls to ensure everything was inspected.

"Find the brothers and bring them to me," I ordered Luca and Achilles, pushing Alex up the metal stairway. "*Alive.*"

They went to hunt for Jeremie and Slava while I led Alex to his second-story office. He cooperated, cool and composed even as his broken arm began swelling and the gash in his forehead reopened.

I sat him in a chair, tied him to it, and ripped the tape from his mouth.

"Happy to see me?" I used the tip of my gun to tilt his chin up so our gazes locked.

He smiled a genuine smile, teeth bloodied, face busted.

"Always, *Koshchei.*"

CHAPTER FORTY-FIVE
LILA

"*Thanks for coming to my OB-GYN appointment.*" I reached to clasp Tierney's hand in the back seat of the Mercedes. We were driven by my driver, with an Irish soldier in the passenger seat.

Tierney squeezed my hand back. "Of course. We're family now, and I love you. Besides, Tiernan's not here. I figured you could use the support."

"*Actually, he's only been to my first appointment,*" I confessed, feeling the tips of my ears pinking. "*His emblematic middle finger to me, since he didn't want me to keep the baby.*"

"What an asshole." Tierney frowned, surprised. "Wait, so who did you go with up until now? I know you're not on speaking terms with your mom."

"*I went by myself, mostly.*" Enzo managed to come twice, and Luca once. "*Well, with my harem of bodyguards. It's fine, though. I had my Kindle. When you have your books, you're never really alone.*"

But I *felt* alone since he'd left. Not to mention, I couldn't sleep at all. I didn't even try his stupid vibrator. What made me fall asleep weren't the orgasms—it was him holding me after sex. Knowing he was in the apartment with me. That he'd keep me safe even if it cost him his own life.

"You look worried," she said.

"*I am worried,*" I admitted.

"Spill it, little moon," Tierney knew Tiernan called me *Gealach*. For some reason, that filled my chest with warm pride. "I know you want to ask me something."

"*Do you think he'll be okay?*"

"I grew up with Alex and Tiernan, and all I can say is that they're both unkillable. I also can't envision either of them pulling the trigger on the other. I mean, accidents happen, but…" She sighed. "I don't know. I think Tiernan will get out of it."

We stopped at an intersection merging with a highway.

"*Do you think he'll ever warm up to the idea of the baby?*" I asked. "*You know him better than I do. Is there hope for us?*"

Tierney's eyes softened, and a small smile tugged at her mouth. The light turned green and our vehicle slid into the intersection.

"I think—"

Our car jerked sideways suddenly, careening in circles and crashing into another vehicle. My body slammed against Tierney.

Hot metal seared the side of my torso, and I arched, hugging my belly with a pained scream.

We were hit. Another car sped into the intersection on a full red light, crashing into us.

The airbags were activated, and I spotted my bodyguard sitting in the passenger seat unbuckling himself and crawling toward the back seat. Tierney was covered in blood—warm, thick, coppery liquid all over her beautiful face—but she didn't even care. She was trying to unbuckle me first.

My heart beat so fast and so hard I could actually hear it between my ears. It was the first sound I ever heard, and one I already wanted to forget.

I looked down and saw my abdomen crushed between my knees, squeezed in an unnatural angle.

Everything was painted scarlet.

Everything.

My dress. My arms. My legs. My heart.

The once-white roses. The tiara of flowers.

It was my attacker who did this. I knew it.

I trembled, realizing I was losing blood, but I wasn't sure where I was bleeding *from*. Everything was numb, and I became lightheaded. My eyes rolled inside their sockets.

Tierney grabbed my shoulders and shook me, her lips moving.

She was screaming.

I didn't hear a thing.

Finally, Tierney stopped screaming and sagged beside me.

My eyes fluttered shut. Behind them, I saw the red and blue swirls of police and ambulances approaching.

The baby...

The baby...

My baby...

CHAPTER FORTY-SIX
TIERNAN

"If you're here to kill me, do it now, *Koshchei*. Long speeches have never been our style."

Alex spoke coldly, and in Russian. I hadn't heard Russian in so long I almost convinced myself I forgot it.

I set my gun down on his desk, pulling out a dull knife from my pocket, running the pad of my finger over the blade. "You wound me, Lyosha. Thought you'd want to catch up."

He licked the corner of his bleeding lip, staring at me with those arctic eyes that watched me being raped and tortured. Starved to near death and dipped into ice water.

"I kept tabs on you over the years. I know everything there is to know," Alex said matter-of-factly. "I've no use to catch up with you. I know your life better than you do."

One corner of my mouth tilted. "Is that so?"

"It is." He sprawled in his seat regally. "I know, for instance, that you recently got married. That you married her for territory, alliance, and to drag the Camorra into our war." His pack-a-day voice was toneless. "I know you weren't planning to fall in love, but that it happened, anyway. She was already in your system that first night, when she put a bullet in your shoulder."

My smirk didn't waver, but alarm bells began blaring in my ears.

How the fuck did he know *that*? It was a very specific piece of information. One I hadn't shared with another soul.

Alex continued, cracking his neck. "I know your father is barely functioning. He never forgave himself for what happened to you and your sister. He is letting you lead the operation, but you wish you had an equal, an adviser, someone to strategize with. Fintan is still struggling with alcohol and gambling. He's a decent guy, but useless. I know Tierney is chummy with SSA Tom Rothwell. You should take care of that. Once he sinks his teeth into something, it's impossible to shake him off."

My pulse drummed against the side of my neck. Lyosha knew things that could ruin us completely, and he just…sat on this shit? Impossible.

How did he get access to all of this information? There was a mole inside us. I needed to find it. If it wasn't too late.

"I have friends in every snake pit, Tiernan." He studied my face with amusement. "Yours included. Hungry dogs are never loyal."

"My soldiers are well rewarded."

"Monetarily, perhaps." He arched a golden, thick brow. "But there is darkness, depravation only betrayal can feed. This is what I tap into when I find my spies. People who want to see the world burn."

Instead of confirming or denying his words, I drawled, "Seems like you've been busy writing my biography. I love meeting fans."

"It's not admiration if you know the person intimately. I loved you like a brother, Tiernan."

"Yeah? Well, you treated me like the family pet." I spat on the floor.

"No, my father did. Igor was never good at letting go of grudges. May I remind you, Tyrone killed my own mother when I was a few weeks old."

"I was reminded of that every day for fourteen years."

Alex stared at me indifferently, as though I was a petulant child.

"Don't pretend to be so calm." I stepped toward him, aiming the blade of my knife at the center of his neck. "I killed your father.

Your pakhan. I kept his skull as a souvenir. Neither of us is here to reminisce about the good old days."

"I'm aware you killed my father. I was the one to direct him straight into your path. He wasn't supposed to be at the gentlemen's club you caught him in."

I stopped rolling the tip of the blade over his skin, scowling. "Liar."

My phone vibrated in my pocket. I pulled it out. Fintan's name flashed across the screen. I sent him to voicemail.

Alex shook his head. "Got a hot tip you were going to wait for him in the back alley of the club, where you knew he'd exit to avoid heat."

But his version of things seemed as logical as any. Igor wasn't supposed to be in New York that weekend. He had the feds crawling up his ass, breathing down his neck. I remembered my surprise when I realized I could off him that night, instead of next year, like I'd planned.

I arched an eyebrow. "And you just let it happen?"

Alex shrugged. "Igor was my father, not my dad."

"And?"

"On top of that, he was also a shit pakhan. Lethal combination," he finished. "It was time I took his place. The Bratva was falling apart. I spent the last few months trying to undo decades of damage in Moscow. The gulag in Siberia is gone now. Dismantled. I freed all the prisoners." Pause. "Other than Olga. I killed that bitch myself. Never liked her."

A stone rolled off my heart at his words. I'd dreamed of going back there one day and doing it myself.

"Igor betted on all the wrong people. Formed alliances with toothless old dogs. He made us weak and vulnerable. And he didn't play nice with the feds, which landed us in a world of pain," Alex groused.

That wasn't news to me. I just didn't think Alex was that much of a sick bastard to actually lead his father to slaughter.

"You brought reinforcements from Russia," I pointed out.

"I did," Alex confirmed. "But not to take you out. I needed them to train my new soldiers. I wasn't gonna come for you, Tiernan," he said, voice as even and calm as though we were discussing the weather. "Not to kill you, anyway. I wanted to clear things up and go our separate ways."

Fintan was calling. Again.

I killed the call. *Again.*

Beyond the door, I heard Camorra and Irish soldiers discussing finding a stash of M16s and depth charges.

Why would the Russians need depth charges?

"Eliminate cargo ships carrying drugs for competitors," Alex read my mind.

I almost smiled. We used to read each other's minds all the time.

"You wanna tell me you knew all this shit about my life, yet you had no idea I was coming for your ass today?" I tucked the knife into my pocket. I wasn't going to draw out his death. He didn't do anything to me. It was his dad I had beef with.

"Oh, I knew. I just didn't think you'd be such a cunt that you'd throw a grenade into my van. Especially after the betrayal at the gulag." He almost pouted. "I'm a little hurt. All puns intended." He jerked his chin to his broken arm.

"You're telling me my slaughtering dozens of your men was your plan all along?" One corner of my mouth kicked upward in amusement.

"You killed low-ranking men. New recruits. Nobodies. Haven't you noticed they didn't give you much of a fight?" He tilted his head. "By the way, Jeremie and Slava have been waiting in the concealed underground bunker with some of our infantry fellas. They should be greeting your soldiers in…" He tried flicking his gaze to his Rolex, before remembering he was handcuffed. "*Now.*"

A forceful blow sounded from downstairs. Shouts in Russian and Italian erupted. We got lit up by heavy machine guns by the sound of it. I heard the thuds of men falling to the floor. Achilles cursed in Italian. A hand grenade exploded.

Alex chuckled. "Never gets old."

I shook my head. I always admired Alex's shrewdness. In another life, we'd still be friends.

He could've killed me. He had every opportunity to do it today. He had the upper hand. Knew he was being ambushed.

"You let me kill twenty of your soldiers?" I shook my head.

Alex jerked his healthy shoulder. "You needed to get it out of your system. And I knew I could take out you and those Italian fuckers, if need be. Besides." A sly grin marred his face wickedly. "I needed to get rid of Igor, and a Julius Caesar–style assassination would've made taking over incredibly difficult, as you can imagine."

Mother. Fucking. Fucker.

That was a level of sly I could only aspire to.

Finally, I let myself grin, shaking my head. "You're a bastard."

Alex shrugged. "Eh, well, better than being a traitor."

"I didn't want to be," I offered honestly. "It was either that or death."

"I would've died for you back then," he said seriously. "You were the family I chose. I'd have done anything for you, if you just *asked*."

I clutched my jaw in my fist to stop myself from apologizing, because I knew he was telling the truth, and still, no part of me—past or present—was willing to run the risk of telling him my real plans. It was what it was. All rebirths required a death. My sacrifice was my friendship with the person I considered my brother.

Still, I couldn't see myself taking Alex's life, in the same way I couldn't see myself doing it to Tierney or Fintan. No matter how much time had passed, he was still my brother.

"Well, unzip me so we can sort this shit out," Alex grumbled. "My arm's killing me."

I pulled my knife out and rounded his chair, slicing the zip tie between his wrists. He stood up and staggered to his desk, where I grabbed his arm and helped relocate it. Alex tore his dress shirt off his chest, wrapping it around his shoulder to create a makeshift sling around his arm. He had an identical tattoo, the same as mine, on his shoulder.

Oderint Dum Metuant.

We got it together with Tierney when we were fourteen. The night before she and I ran away.

My phone buzzed. Fintan again.

I looked up at Alex. "We need to wrap it up quickly."

He was busy tending to his arm. "You blew up my vans, killed my soldiers, stole my ammo, and slaughtered my pakhan. Give me your best offer and I'll see if it's good enough to keep you alive. I have my own reputation to uphold."

"My best offer is not to put a bullet in your head," I said generously. "Your father stole our childhood, our innocence, our family, our *mother*. I'm not budging an inch. It's a matter of principle."

Downstairs, there was a pause between shooting, the *clinks* and *clanks* of magazines changing echoing through the hanger.

Alex looked up. "I *am* sorry, you know."

"Wasn't your fault."

"Doesn't make me any less sorry."

We stepped outside and took the metal stairway down to the ground floor, where the Camorra and Irish barricaded themselves behind flipped tables while the Bratva advanced toward them in full field gear.

I spotted Jeremie and Slava, each of them hulking at six three with corded muscles. They must've taken after Igor's second wife, because their hair was black, not blond, and the blue in their eyes several shades darker than Lyosha's.

"What the fuck is Alex doing on his feet?" Achilles raged behind a table, firing a round of ammo despite his broken arm.

"Fixing this shit," Alex barked in English. "Cease fire. Now."

Both sides put their weapons down. Luca and Achilles slid from behind the tables, foreheads creased in confusion.

"We've reached an agreement," I announced.

"That's not for you to determine." Luca pulled out the magazine from his rifle, checking how many bullets he had left as he wiped his brow. "You dragged us into a war that's already in motion. You're done calling the shots."

"We have no natural border with the Bratva," I reasoned. "And they're willing to give concessions. For one thing, we're taking all the ammo we found here today, even though they one-upped and ambushed us."

"That's right." Alex's stare swung between the two Ferrante brothers in disdain. "Let's all pretend what separates them from being great warriors is not enough bullets."

The Camorra and Bratva were natural rivals. Their mutual hate spanned centuries down each bloodline.

"Dead people make great enemies. Live ones, not so much." Achilles spat on the floor, his gaze never wavering from Alex. "He's a loose end, Callaghan. I don't like those."

"We'll set some ground rules regarding New York. It's a better deal than offing these fuckers and waiting for someone to take over and avenge them," I replied tersely, turning to Alex. "I trust your word."

"Well, I don't," Achilles said. "I'm taking something— *someone*—as a guarantee." He looked between Jeremie and Slava. His eyes settled on Jeremie. He was busted up and bleeding, but looked proud as hell. A good soldier. One you wanted on your side in a war. "This one. I always wanted a tank."

"*Te pokhozh na litso so shramom,*" Jeremie said with a smile.

"The fuck did he say?" Achilles narrowed his eyes.

"He said it'd be his pleasure," I translated.

Actually, what he said was *You look like Scarface.* But I'd had enough bloodbaths for one day.

"Take him, and do what with him, exactly?" Alex asked through a clenched jaw.

"Why, find him a nice Italian girl to marry. This is how alliances are made." Achilles patted the side of his tactical black pants, fishing out a cigarette.

Alex gave him a flat stare. "An Italian girl won't do."

"And why the shit is that?"

"He's prone to headaches and has a limit on his credit card."

Every Bratva soldier in the room laughed.

Achilles grinned serenely. His smile promised pain.

"Sounds like a real pussy. Don't worry. We'll make a man out of him."

My phone rang again. Jesus fuck, Fintan needed to familiarize himself with the concept of working hours. I pulled it out.

Only this time I saw a different name on the screen.

Lila.

My wife never called me for obvious reasons. She texted.

I slid a finger over the screen and then pressed the phone to my ear. Didn't speak. The meaning of it slammed into me all at once.

If someone kidnapped her...

"Tiernan." I heard Fintan on the other end of the line. He sounded choked up, panting like he ran from New York to Vegas. "It's Lila and Tierney. There's...there's been an accident." He wheezed. "Lila's in a bad way."

All the blood drained from my face. I squeezed my phone to the point where it almost burst into fucking pieces.

"Where is she?"

"In the hospital now. Tierney, too—"

"Which hospital?" I swiveled to signal Luca to call for the airplane.

Luca turned around and made the call. Achilles curved a questioning brow. I'd always been a cold-blooded creature, but right now, I felt like ripping every inch of my flesh, I was burning so hot. The only reason I wasn't on my knees, a bleeding fucking mess, was because I needed to fix whatever happened to her, make sure that she was okay, before I could let myself fall apart.

"Saint Andrews on Fifth. Someone T-boned them. They say the baby's in danger." Fintan's voice was thick and scratchy with panic. "The bleeding…"

"Is she conscious?"

"No."

I closed my eyes. The room spun, anyway. A black hole sucking me into darkness. I couldn't fucking breathe. Worse still, I didn't see the point in doing so.

Lila.

Lila.

Lila.

I forgot what to do. What to ask. How to function.

"Are you there now?" I strangled out.

"Yeah."

"Put her doctor on the phone."

I heard shuffling, and awkward explaining, and the back and forth between Fintan and a male doctor.

"Dr. Delgado here. Are you Mrs. Callaghan's husband?"

"I am."

"I understand that you're out of town? Vegas?"

"I'll be there in two hours."

"How do you—"

"Just fucking come out with it. Tell me what's happening." I was already rushing toward the door, leaving an active warfare between two Mafia organizations behind.

It all seemed so tedious all of a sudden.

The Rasputins. The Bratva. Honor. My own boo-hoo childhood trauma.

More money, more territory, more weapons, more drugs. More, more, more, when none of it mattered. None of it made me happier. Only she ever did.

"Mrs. Callaghan's spleen was ruptured during the car accident. The vehicle slammed into her side of the car. We are now managing her blood loss. She also suffers from multiple lacerations and a concussion."

"Will she be okay?"

The Ferrante brothers tried catching up with my pace as I made my way to our van.

"She suffered some blood loss, and we're monitoring the concussion closely. But we have every reason to think she'll pull through."

"And the baby?"

Silence stretched on the other side of the line. It was only then that I realized I didn't want this baby to die. Or rather, not to live. Lila was attached to it. She glowed when she caressed her belly. And if she could love something that symbolized the fucked-up shit that happened to her, then by God, so could my sorry arse.

Dr. Delgado cleared his throat.

"Your wife's survival was our first priority, Mr. Callaghan. Now that we managed to stabilize her and stop the internal bleeding, we're going to run some tests. A world-renowned obstetrician is seeing her as we speak."

"I'm heading there now. Keep me posted." I killed the call.

When I turned around, Luca and Achilles stared back at me, faces etched with worry. Jeremie was held by the collar of his blood-soaked shirt by Achilles.

"Fill us in," Luca demanded.

"Lila and Tierney were in a car accident. It was bad. They're in the hospital."

"Are they okay?" Luca rubbed his knuckles over his chest.

"Lila's stable. They don't know about the baby yet."

"Plane's ready." Luca jerked his chin at the van. "Let's hit the road."

We clamored into the van, leaving our driver and about a dozen soldiers behind to fend for themselves. Luca insisted he'd drive.

"And Tierney?" Achilles asked after a long stretch of silence, as Luca floored his way out of the warehouse and onto the open road on his way to the private airport. Golden clouds of sand swirled behind us.

I turned toward him, dazed. "What?"

"*Tierney*," he repeated, nostrils flaring. "Your fucking sister, Tiernan. You didn't even ask about her, did you?"

Fuck. What was wrong with me?

I pulled my phone out and texted Fintan. He answered after less than one second.

"Stable, conscious, in the room next to Lila."

"The fuck is wrong with you?" Achilles twisted his mouth, snarling at me from across the back seat. "She's your sister."

My phone lit up with a text.

> Fintan: I'm not going to leave their side until you get here. Don't worry, lad.
> Tiernan: Make sure there are two soldiers outside Lila's room at all times. You stay inside until I get there. No one comes in or out other than medical staff.
> Fintan: Understood.

I thumped my head against the seat back.

What the fuck was happening to me?

From infancy, I'd been carved to control myself. Trained to recognize a seed of emotion and promptly poison it before it could grow. I spent three decades perfecting the art of knowing my own limits, both mental and physical, and testing, stretching them, moving the goalpost to become as deadly as a weapon of mass destruction.

I never *felt*. Feelings were foreign to me. I *sensed*.

Sensed when it was time to strike.

To hit.

To run.

And yet the thought of my wife being in danger brought me to my knees.

What hit me the hardest was the regret.

The guilt of never acknowledging her pregnancy while it was still there.

How could I hate something she loved so much? I couldn't. That was the truth of it.

If she loved this child, then I would learn to love him, too.

He wasn't only the rapist's. He was also hers.

Fifty percent of him was pure gold.

She wanted me to be the father.

And I failed her.

If she lost the baby, I'd never forgive myself.

Alex was right. I was *Koshchei*. The *Deathless*. Just like the Russian folklore villain, I, too, hid my death inside something to protect it.

That something was Lila.

She was tangled into my being, her messy, coarse vines gripping every fiber of my soul.

She had the power to destroy me.

And I would let her.

I'd gladly burn for this woman just so she could feel the warmth of my flame.

The more I tried to unlove her, the deeper she burrowed into my skin.

I was done fighting. She was now a part of the fabric of my godforsaken soul.

And it was time she knew that.

CHAPTER FORTY-SEVEN
TIERNAN

"The fuck you think you're doing?"

Luca's voice impaled my rage-fueled brain from behind my back.

I didn't bother turning to face him. "What does it look like I'm doing?"

"Buying yourself a one-way ticket to prison. Five to seven years, I believe," Luca said flatly.

"Pointing a gun to the pilot's head and telling him to 'go faster' like it's a roundabout ride at a zoo," Achilles sighed. "Cunt move, even by your standards."

I looked down to see the pilot trembling, his forehead slick with sweat. His crotch had a dark piss stain. Fucking amateur. I tucked my gun into my holster and kicked the pilot off his seat with the tip of my boot, taking his place.

Achilles popped his head into the cockpit. "What in the shit are you doing now?"

"He's too slow. We're not constrained by operational logistics of commercial airplanes. I don't care if I burn through the fuel. We're going at 700 mph."

"The limit is 600 mph," Luca pointed out.

"If the fucking sky police fines us, I'll foot the bill."

My hand flew to the overhead switch panel, increased the power, and gradually lowered the pitch attitude to maintain the altitude.

"Tell me you know what you're doing." Luca scrubbed his face tiredly.

"I know what I'm doing."

"Do you mean it?"

"No."

I took an aviation course, but never put in the flight time. My memory was a bit rusty on the ins and outs of it. But hey, we were still in the air, weren't we?

"Are you going to kill all of us?" Achilles inquired indifferently. "If so, I'll go ream the flight attendant's ass, so at least I can die doing something I love."

"Here." I stood up and grabbed the pilot by the collar, dumping him back into his seat. "That's better. Now that we're at maximum speed, how about I'll dig my gun into your temple to make sure you don't decrease it, and you won't bitch and moan to me about health and safety?"

He nodded, gulping.

When we arrived at the private airport, I rushed into the Ferrantes' Escalade and leaped out as soon as we hit the Manhattan traffic. I stalked my way between the vehicles waiting at a red light to the front of the line and yanked a biker off his Ducati. I wasn't gonna wank around sitting at a standstill while Lila's life was hanging by a thread.

I floored it to the hospital. As I pulled into a double park, a GMC truck zipped past, grazing my left side and slamming me against a lamppost. My right knee smashed into the concrete. I limped my way into the hospital, dragging the leg as I did, ignoring horrified looks and Good Samaritans wanting to help.

I pushed a few nurses out of the lobby elevator to make room, both for myself and my psychotic meltdown. By the time the elevator pinged open, my knee was the size of a fucking basketball. I crawled the length of the corridor the rest of the way, bypassing Enzo and his little minions. He was standing outside her door, yelling in Italian into his phone and ignoring his slithering, bleeding brother-in-law.

Was it my best look? No.

Did I give a shit? Also no.

Two of my soldiers were waiting by her door. I swung myself upright and stumbled inside.

Beep.

Beep.

Beep.

And there was Lila. *My* Lila.

So beautiful. So pale. So angelic I sometimes second-guessed she belonged to this ugly world.

Her eyes were closed. Her face was bruised. Her stomach was… intact?

I knew jack shit about pregnancies. The baby still seemed to be in there. But that didn't mean he had a heartbeat or that he survived.

The sound of a toilet flushing came from an adjacent toilet, and Fintan got out, zipping his trousers. "Brother."

We collapsed into a hug. It took everything inside me not to sob like a little bitch. Fintan was the first to disconnect.

"I'll go call the doctor, yeah? He said he's got some news."

I nodded, advancing to Lila's bed and taking her hand in mine. Cold. Frail. Hooked to so many tubes and strings.

I needed to find out who did this to her. Who drove the truck that hit them. I was going to kill that person in a way so painful it had yet to be invented.

"Darlin'." I crouched down, pressing her hand to my lips. "This is the last time I'm leaving you for more than ten minutes. Whose stupid idea was that?"

The door swung open again. Fintan lumbered in with Dr.

Delgwhatever. An overweight, bald man with the grace and poise of an elderly water buffalo.

"Mr. Callaghan. How do you do?"

"Take a wild fucking guess, Einstein." I held my wife's hand in mine like it was a grenade I didn't want popping. "You've got news for me?"

"She came to earlier. She's asleep now. We ran some cognitive tests and she seems alert and coherent. The operation, as you know, was successful."

"And the baby?"

He cleared his throat, taking a step back just to be on the safe side. "He's well. Strong heartbeat. We're monitoring both of them."

There wasn't a word in the English dictionary for how I felt in that moment.

Relief. Joy. Unimaginable peace.

Escaping Igor's hell was just another Tuesday in comparison to this.

"That's good," I said. "We want everyone in this room to make it out of this ordeal alive."

Fintan shot me an alarmed glare. Yes, I did, in fact, just threaten a doctor in uniform.

"O-of course," the doctor mumbled. "Please let me know if you have any further questions."

"Will she be up soon?"

"She fell asleep an hour ago, so I think you have some time," the doctor said.

"I'll go see my sister, then."

"She's awake in the next room," Fin said, his smile a little wobbly.

"Your priorities have changed," Tierney croaked.

She looked like shit.

Face swollen, lip busted, every inch of her flesh painted purple and blue.

I sat next to her bed, holding her hand. I didn't deny it.

I came to Lila first.

And I would do it all over again if I had to.

She smiled sadly at my silent admission. "I heard the baby will be fine."

"Physically, yes," I drawled. "I'm going to be his father, so not too much hope for him in the other departments."

"Will you?" she asked sleepily, her eyelids fluttering like keeping them open took a Herculean effort. "Be his father, I mean. The plan was to…what were your exact words? *Unhand* her as soon as she gave birth."

"Plans change."

Apparently, so do fucking I.

Tierney nodded silently, a tear escaping her black eye.

"What is it?" I leaned forward, thumbing the tear away. "You need more morphine? Food? Something to drink?"

She shook her head, her lower lip trembling. "Lila is your number one now, not me."

I didn't say anything, because her assessment was correct. She waited for the denial, and when one didn't come, she continued. "As she should be. But I need someone to put me first."

"I'm sure you'll find—"

"That someone is myself."

For the longest time, I protected Tierney like she was my own daughter. Now, I had a wife to think of. A son on the way. And if Tierney went to the feds, if she put Lila at risk and made me choose between them, I knew where I'd land. So did she.

"Tier." I pressed her hand to the steady thrum of my heart. "It's not too late to turn this ship around. Stop fighting. Settle down. Marry a powerful man. Let him take care of you, darlin'. You've fought your whole life. Isn't it time you let go?"

I would let Achilles marry her. I could count on one hand the number of men who were able to handle this banshee, and he was one of them. He'd take good care of her. Keep her safe. And, in time, she might even show him all the broken pieces in her. They could put them back together. Like a fucking 5,000-piece puzzle.

She shook her head.

"I'm tired of un-accidental car crashes. Of the smell of gunpowder and the taste of blood. Of striking alliances based on who can help me survive, not who I truly care for. Let me fight my way out of this world the way *I* see fit. I'm a big girl. I can take care of myself."

Survive. I detested the word. It implied luck and a degree of victimhood.

"You survived nothing, sweetheart; everything you faced, you fought and overcame. You'll brave this storm, too."

"I can't." Tears streamed down her face, fast and steady now. "I have no more fight in me. I'm exhausted."

"Tierney..."

"*Please,*" she breathed out. "Trust that I'll keep you, Lila, and my nephew safe. Because I always will. I love you all to death. Let me sacrifice the Ferrantes to save myself. That's all I ask."

I squeezed her hand in mine.

A silent yes.

Then I let her go.

CHAPTER FORTY-EIGHT
TIERNAN

~~130 DAYS TO SELF-DESTRUCTION~~.

I wanted to live.

I found my purpose.

The spectacular thing worth living with my past and nightmares.

Her.

CHAPTER FORTY-NINE
LILA

The first thing I saw when I woke up again was my husband, sitting next to me, his head hung between his massive shoulders.

He was staring at his folded fingers, looking comically giant on the flimsy plastic chair.

A rush of warmth spread across my chest.

He was here.

He survived.

… and so did I.

I reached to touch his hand to alert him that I was awake. His head snapped up. His eye was a pool of misery and concern. The sadness in it tore me to shreds worse than the accident did.

"How are you doing?" he asked.

I mustered a weak smile. "*It was just a scratch. Me and the baby are okay.*" Not that he wanted to hear about the baby. "*Tell me you didn't kill Alex, Tiernan.*"

"Who cares—"

I put my palm up to stop him. "*I do. I don't want you to dwell on what happened to me, at least not yet. Distract me. Tell me what happened in Vegas.*"

My husband never took orders from anyone. Let alone a hundred-and-six-pound teenager. Still, he humored me.

His jaw flexed, and he ran his tongue along his straight upper teeth. "He's alive. We struck a deal with the Bratva. Achilles took a souvenir in the form of his brother, Jeremie. It's all settled."

I smiled, even though it hurt my face. "*Good.*"

"Are you in pain?"

"*No,*" I lied. The doctors prescribed me with the minimum dose of morphine, but I opted out of it, for the sake of the baby. Every breath made me feel dizzy with pain.

"*Did you get hurt?*"

"No."

"*Do you know who slammed into us?*" I knew better than to believe it was an accident. Especially when the other vehicle managed to escape.

"Working on it."

"*Is Tierney okay?*"

"She's fine." When he realized how snappy he sounded, he added, "Awake and pissed off, which means she's back to normal."

We stared at each other, the silence in my ears louder than ever before.

"*What's with you?*" I cocked my head, frowning.

Did he want the baby to die? Was he disappointed that he pulled through?

"I have something to say."

Oh, no. That didn't sound good. I waited. When he said nothing, I nervously joked, "*Are we waiting for each other's permission to speak now? Because you know I'm defiant.*"

Tiernan didn't smile. He was very still, as usual. Sculpture-like. Ice ran in his veins. I looked down, following his line of vision.

His hands were trembling.

And then the man who never blinked, did, in fact, blink. A rare moment of letting himself go. Of forgetting his indestructible self-possession at the door.

"I love you."

And for the first time in my life, I was crushed that I couldn't hear. Because his words—*these* words—I wanted them in my ears, in my heart, in my veins.

"I love you with a force that could destroy planets and universes, Lila." His face twisted in self-loathing. My expression must've given my glee away, because he sighed. "You shouldn't bask in it, *Gealach*. You should be very, very afraid. I have no red lines when it comes to you. No logic. I will love this baby as my own, because anything born of you is bound to be perfection. He *will* be mine. And I would kill for him. Die for him." The words rushed over my skin, heating it with pleasure even my orgasms couldn't give me. Nourishing me back to life.

"But make no mistake," Tiernan continued. "I will always love you more. Than him. Than me. Than this world. My love for you is not pretty, or flowery, or romantic. But it's real, and it's everlasting."

My eyes filled with tears. I pressed my fist to my mouth, trying to control the sob that wrestled out of it.

"*So you don't want to send me away?*"

"Darlin', I barely even let you go to the restroom by yourself before we had sex." He shook his head incredulously, leaning forward in his seat. "I want you next to me forever."

"*And my baby—*"

He looped his fingers around my wrists, stopping me. "*Our* baby."

"*Our baby…how do you know you'll love him?*"

"Because he is a part of you, and I love all the parts that make you."

"*Surely, not all of me.*" I pouted, knowing he would indulge me.

He always met me where I was. And he never made me feel less than because of my disability.

"All." He took my hand, peppering kisses all over my palm so as not to touch the needle-poked side of it. "Even at your worst, you're the best thing that's ever happened to me."

A single tear slipped from his eye. He touched his cheek, startled, then squinted up at the ceiling, checking for leaks.

"*I'm afraid you just cried your first tear, hubby.*"

"Impossible." He scowled. "My cum is probably leaking from other holes in my body, seeing as I haven't been in you for over thirty-five hours."

I barked out a delighted laugh, which I immediately regretted, seeing as my collarbone was shattered.

Yes, someone tried to kill me a few hours ago, and yes, my rapist was somewhere out there, still threatening me. Maybe the two things were connected. But we had each other, for real now, and that felt more powerful than any obstacle thrown in our way.

"*Gealach.*" Tiernan brought me back to reality. "Your mam is outside. She wants to speak to you. I told her to sod off in five different languages, but she is still there. With cannoli."

"*Really, five?*" I elevated an eyebrow, impressed.

"English, Irish, Russian, Italian, Neapolitan," he counted them. "I can add ASL into the mix, though." He frowned, absentmindedly dropping more kisses over my palm. "Drive the point home."

I grinned. "*It's fine. Let her in.*"

"You sure?" He didn't look too enthusiastic. "Stress is not good for you and the baby."

The fact that he now cared about the baby made me feel like I was walking on clouds.

"*I'm sure. You need to take care of that knee.*"

I gestured toward his leg. His knee was the size of a football, and he was bleeding through his slacks.

"I can stay in the room."

"*I can handle her. This conversation is long overdue. Send her in.*"

He placed my hand next to my body gently and stood up, but didn't immediately leave.

"*What?*" I blinked up at him.

"Nothing."

"*Tiernan.*"

"You didn't tell me you love me back."

I pressed my lips together, on the verge of giggling. I hadn't felt this light and happy since the day I was born. I was positively drunk on it.

"*I already told you I loved you.*"

"After I gave you three orgasms. That doesn't count."

"*I'm waiting for the perfect moment. Don't rush me.*"

He offered me one of his villainous expressions—cold, dead, unimpressed—but a hint of pink gathered at the top of his cheekbones. He was blushing. And if I wasn't in so much pain, I'd kick my feet.

"Fine. I'm leaving. But I reserve the right to barge in here and give your mam a piece of my mind—and fist—if she misbehaves."

"*Wow. You got it bad for me.*"

"Thought I made that clear three times a night for the past few months."

Grinning, I signed, "*Go. Don't worry. We'll figure everything out when I get discharged.*"

"It's you and me against the world." He leaned to brush his lips over my forehead. "But I like our odds, darlin'."

A few moments later, the door to my hospital room slid open and Mama poked her head inside.

"Can I come in?"

I nodded, watching as she sashayed in, tossing the door shut with the back of her designer heel as she balanced a silver tray full of cannoli. She wasn't wearing one of her prim dresses, and her hair wasn't done for once.

She looked…worn out. Humbled. And twenty years older.

She slid the tray on the stand next to my hospital bed and took a seat next to me. Ran her palms up and down her thighs to get rid of the sweat.

She didn't make eye contact with me when her lips moved. "Tiernan told me that you and the baby are okay."

"*Yes.*" I wasn't going to make it easy for her.

"I'm so glad, *bambina mia.*"

I simply stared.

"Thank you for agreeing to give me the time of day. God knows I don't deserve it."

I didn't have it in me to be compassionate to her. I shrugged.

"I've been a horrible mother to you, haven't I? Not just through the length of your pregnancy. Since you were born."

I licked my lips. I had nothing to say to that, since I wholeheartedly agreed. In retrospect, she robbed me of so much. And these past few months…

"You're not Vello's," she blurted out.

I slammed my brows together, staring at her. A sense of déjà vu washed over me. I couldn't say I was surprised, exactly. I had to be a perfect idiot not to see how different I looked from the rest of my family. But growing up, my mother always insisted nothing was amiss. That I took after a mysterious French great-grandmother who was very fair.

"I never wanted to marry your father." She shook her head. "Actually, that's putting it mildly. Back in Secondigliano, my mother was married to the don. They had no boys, just me, so it was up to me to marry someone to take over the business. My father made me break up with my boyfriend to marry Vello. His right-hand man."

She tore her gaze from me, staring at the floor.

"*And your mama said nothing about it?*" I asked.

My mother laughed humorlessly, eyes sparkling with tears. "It was hard for her to fight him, seeing as she was dead." There was a pause. "My mother killed herself. Slashed her own wrists in her bed after years of my father's abuse. He hit her a lot. And when he didn't hit her, he cheated on her. She was still stupid enough to love him, anyway. He broke her heart every single day. I was the one who found her."

I could see where this was going. My mother had never seen a Mafia marriage maturing into something other than a complete disaster, so she didn't think the option existed.

"I'll get to who your father is in a second." She plucked a tissue from her purse, dabbing her sunken eyes. "Anyway, my father made me marry Vello. I did not like him at all. Wasn't attracted to him, either. He was twelve years older and very rude. Neither he nor my papa cared one bit about what I wanted. On the night we got married, Luca was conceived." Her mouth pressed into a grim line. "He raped me, and when I tried to fight him, he slapped me. The first four years of his life, every single time I looked at Luca, all I saw was that night I wished to forget."

Something cracked inside my chest and a flood of sympathy rushed forth. I grabbed her hand, squeezing it. That didn't take away all the mistakes she made with me, but I was starting to see that in her warped, twisted logic, living a life of social deprivation was better than marrying a man like Papa.

"Achilles's conception was the same story. There was pain and there was blood. Vello had spared me for a while after Luca. He didn't like my body after the pregnancy, anyway. So he took a mistress."

"*He raped you every time you had a child?*"

Bile slithered up my throat. Even at our worst times—and God knew we started on the wrong foot—Tiernan never took me against my will. I couldn't fathom the thought of sharing a roof, a table, a *bedroom* with the beast that raped me the night of Luca's wedding.

"No, not all of them. Enzo was…a spontaneous event. We were both drunk and merry for a change, one summer in Ischia. And believe it or not, but sometimes I think this is why Enzo ended up the way he is—so warm and loving. Nothing like his brothers, who are rough around the edges."

"*Vello cheated on you throughout your marriage?*" I didn't know at what point in the conversation I stopped thinking of him as Papa and started thinking of him as Vello, but I knew once I crossed that mental barrier, there was no going back.

Mama burst into a bitter fit of laughter, blowing her nose. "Of course. He had a string of mistresses. Soon after I birthed Luca, he had a baby with one of them, too. He still sees his son often. I never met him. Don't want to, either. Apparently, he truly loved the mother, though."

I never felt so much disdain for Vello. I was actually relieved he wasn't my father.

"After Enzo, I slipped into depression. I didn't eat or sleep. Finally, a friend signed me up to an art class at our country club. Nude model painting. It was thrilling. I loved everything about it. The smell of paint, the blank canvases, the artists, the models…" She trailed off, biting her lower lip. "The teacher."

Mama had an affair? I wanted to throw up and fist-pump the air simultaneously. Though I had a feeling I wasn't going to love where this was going.

"Hugo was a Swedish painter. He didn't have a dime to his name. But he was everything I looked for in a man. Quiet, kind, loving. I knew conducting an affair could get us both killed. But, please understand, Lila, I'd never done anything selfish in my life at this point. Always lived for other people. So when Hugo and I found out we were pregnant with you five months into our affair, I wanted to up and leave. Take Luca, Achilles, Enzo, and you and save you all from the awful life in the Camorra. Of course, once your father found out, he had other plans."

Oh, I bet he gave her hell.

"Reasoning with him was out of the question. He'd never let me take his three healthy, strong boys. They were his future, his legacy. Instead, I planned to escape. I was going to smuggle your brothers out of the country. But one of his soldiers found out. Sent word to him. One night, when I snuck out to meet Hugo at his apartment, I found him stabbed to death in his own bed."

She drew a shaky breath. "Vello didn't even close his eyes after he killed him."

My father was dead.

My *real* father was good and kind and caring and artistic, and Vello killed him.

I was reeling with so many emotions, I didn't know what to do with myself.

"Vello let me keep you, but he never took to you. It didn't matter, because I did. I clung to you like you were my last hope in this life. A proof that once upon a time, I was happy, even if for a short time. God was good to me in that sense. He sculpted you to be the spitting image of Hugo. You look so much like him, Lila. Same fair hair. Same blue eyes. These past eighteen years, the only thing keeping me from falling apart was you. I realize now how unfair it was to you, but you were my fondest memory of my lover. Truly a gift." She burst into tears. "You were the perfect baby. Happy and low maintenance. And when we found out you were deaf, I almost thought it was kismet. My way to keep you close and next to me."

"Mama, you disowned me because I chose to show the world who I really am," I reminded her.

But my expression was soft. I couldn't muster any rage against a woman who suffered so thoroughly.

"I was so terrified for you." She buried her face into the crinkled tissue, coming up for air only so I could read her lips. "Tiernan Callaghan's name is synonymous with death and chaos. I didn't want you to end up like me and my mother. Raped, abused, cheated on. It took almost losing you in a car crash for me to tell you all that's been weighing on my chest for the past thirty years."

"You could've told me all of this earlier."

"You weren't ready. I kept you younger than your years on purpose. It was only during my birthday dinner that I realized you weren't my sweet, obedient girl anymore. That you somehow bloomed into a woman in a few months, and I wasn't even there to witness it."

She sniffled, patting her nose with the crumpled tissue. "Does he make you happy?"

"*Yes, Mama. Very.*"

"Has he ever forced himself on you?"

I shook my head. "*Even on our wedding night, he didn't touch me.*"

"That's because your brothers bribed him not to," she balked.

I considered her words. "*Tiernan is not strapped for cash. If he wanted to rape me, money wouldn't stand in his way.*"

She stared at me in wonder. "Does he cheat on you?"

My mind immediately swerved to Becky. But could I really call it cheating? It was before we were together. Before we kissed. Before I revealed to him that I was who I was.

"*No.*"

She visibly sagged with relief.

"*But my feelings for him scare me. I would die for him, and that doesn't feel right. This man has a lot of blood on his hands, and I look past all that. When does a monster stop being a monster, Mama?*"

"Oh, *bambina*, when you love it."

I smiled miserably. Falling in love with my husband was a terrible inconvenience.

"I'm happy for you, Lila. I am. I was a terrible mother for the longest time. I thought if I got the point across that I don't support your marriage, you'd come back to me. That we could raise this baby together, maybe in Italy, and leave this place. I am sorry for trying to take yet another decision out of your hands. I now see you chose right. And I respect that." She looked uncertain all of a sudden, almost shy. "If ever you find it in your heart to forgive me, I promise to make it up to you."

"*I forgive you. I'm not moving past everything that happened right now, because that is a lot to ask, but I definitely want to try to restore our relationship.*" I lowered my hands, mulling it over. "*And I want to hear more about my late father. See some of your paintings, and his. I always thought it was odd I was the only one in our family who loved drawing."*

"I will tell you all about him. I will make it up to you," she promised. "And I'm going to start right now."

CHAPTER FIFTY
LILA

Three days later, I was discharged from the hospital.

Tiernan was insufferable. Whatever precautious measures he took to keep me safe before the accident were nothing in comparison to what I had to endure now.

"Hunts Point's on lockdown. No one comes in, no one comes out," he announced to his soldiers before I'd been discharged. When we pulled up at Fermanagh's, the neighborhood was barricaded. When the media started asking questions, Tiernan's friends at the NYPD called it a drug raid.

I was always with Tiernan, and *we* were always surrounded with enough soldiers. Worse still, we now had to drive with a four-vehicle entourage. He was resigned to wrap me in a bubble until we found whoever caused the accident.

"It's all connected," Sam announced the day I returned from the hospital.

We were all in the tiny living room of our apartment. Achilles, Luca, and Fintan included. "Whoever is responsible for the car accident is likely the person who sent Lila that letter."

The first thing I did when Tiernan and I came back from the hospital was show him the letter I'd received. Hence why we were having this meetup. I'd never been one of the boys, so to speak.

Had never been included in an important meeting.

Now, I was sitting in my husband's lap, privy to everything that was said.

"You think it's the guy who attacked her?" Achilles folded his arms over his chest.

"Yeah, and I think he's freaking the fuck out," Sam provided. "That letter? Reeks of sloppiness."

It was weird, having the men discuss something so traumatic that happened to me so openly. Then again, they were all trying to help. And Tiernan had his arms around me, which made me feel invincible.

"Why now?" Luca frowned.

"Baby's almost here." Fintan took a pull of his pint. "Now's the time to try to blackmail you for money."

"He tried to kill her." Tiernan bared his teeth.

"*Or* he tried to warn her," Fintan volleyed back.

"That list…" Sam tapped his chin. "We sure managed to cross a hell of a lot of names from it. Anyone outside it isn't possible—it was a private event, on a private island. People can't just sneak inside. We narrowed it down to just a few potential attackers. And Blackthorn's off the list. So."

He hung his expectant gaze on Tiernan.

"Don't look at me. I told you from the get-go I think it's Angelo. He had a motive—Chiara was nasty to him. He was seen asking Lila to dance earlier that night. She made him feel like he was not good enough for her daughter. And at our wedding, he was acting suspicious. Disappearing for big chunks of time from the room and coming back looking like he fought a bear."

Luca and Achilles exchanged glances. Something unspoken passed between them. Luca nodded.

"Weren't you supposed to come back with some proof about Angelo?" Luca asked.

"Couldn't find any," Tiernan said.

"So you just dropped it?" Achilles cocked his head, frowning. "Doesn't sound like you."

"Unless you didn't really want to find the fucker," Luca mused. "Why'd you stop looking?"

"I didn't," Tiernan hissed through gritted teeth. "I checked all the other fuckers on the list. But, now that you mentioned it, the fact your mother wanted to marry my wife off to Angelo if he *raped* her wasn't a great incentive."

Was this why there were no new developments regarding the identity of my attacker for months?

Because all this time, Tiernan wanted to keep me?

"Yeah, well, no one's trying to take her away from you anymore," Luca assured him.

"I'm well aware no one's stupid enough to try." Tiernan's arms tightened around me.

"Riddle me this, though." Achilles turned to Tiernan. "Why would Angelo, who is rich and successful, poke around in this swarming beehive and send Lila a letter? He doesn't need the money."

"He has a point." Sam shrugged. "If Angelo did it, he'd try to put as much distance between you and him as possible."

"Unless we have the angle all wrong." Fintan cocked an eyebrow.

"Meaning?" Tiernan asked.

"Maybe the two incidents aren't connected, and he has nothing to do with the car crash. Maybe he wants to meet Lila to straighten things out. Make sure she doesn't talk. I mean, *we* know she doesn't remember his face. He doesn't. He wants to get her alone so he can scare her into silence. He has too much to lose."

"And the accident?" Achilles asked.

Fintan shrugged. "Could be any of our enemies, and there are too many to choose from. Maybe they thought it was Tiernan in the car, saw the two women inside, freaked out, and fled."

"Either way." Sam twisted his wedding band. "All roads lead to Angelo Bandini."

Luca sucked his teeth. "Fintan's math is mathing."

Achilles shrugged. "Fuck it. We have no other leads."

"Whoever it is, he wants her to come alone, judging by the letter. I say either you beat Angelo to it and kill him," Fintan said. "Or trust the process, let her go, and see what he wants."

"That's a no," Tiernan drawled, and though I couldn't hear him, even I knew his tone was deadly. "She's not going anywhere unprotected."

Sam's gaze skated between my husband and my brothers. "Didn't know you had such a hard-on for Tiernan to get Harlem."

"It's not about Harlem anymore." Tiernan tightened his hold on me. "This entire city can burn to the ground and I wouldn't even blink. It's about my wife, and about justice, and about making sure she is safe. I'd tear the world to shreds for her, and they know it."

Luca snapped his fingers. "Bring in my brother-in-law. We have a bone to pick with him."

Tiernan was restless for the rest of the evening.

He fawned over me like I was about to shatter into minuscule pieces at any minute.

"More iced tea?" He stomped into our bedroom with a pitcher and some cookies. Imma was sent to my parents' house. He became so unbearably paranoid he didn't want anyone around me. He even closed down the pub.

"*No, thank you.*" I stared at the pitcher, horrified. "*The baby is pressing against my bladder. I want to pee just looking at it.*"

"What about the cookies?"

"*Heartburn.*"

"Italian soup? There's leftovers from Imma's—"

"*For the love of God, sit down.*" I rolled my eyes. "*I'm pregnant, not dying. And I don't want to eat or drink. I just want to spend some time with you.*"

I patted the space next to me on the mattress to make a point.

He still looked unconvinced. Rolling my eyes, I fell forward on my palms and crawled across the bed until my face was flush with his groin. I touched his stomach through his black dress shirt. His sinewy abs immediately contracted beneath my fingertips.

He said something. I didn't bother reading his lips.

Suddenly, all I wanted was his cock in my mouth. It was unfathomable to me that it hadn't happened before. I loved his body. Every inch of it.

I felt his groan as I tugged on the zipper of his slacks. I looked up, and his face seemed almost…pained. His lips slightly parted. I knew it was on the tip of his tongue to tell me I didn't have to do it.

I also knew he wasn't chivalrous enough to speak those words.

Even in love, my husband wasn't a hero in anyone's story. He was a villain. And I wouldn't want him any other way.

Freeing him from his pants and boxers, his shaft sprang free, slapping his stomach, leaving a tear of precum on his prominent abs.

My breath skated across the crown of his cock. A ragged sigh escaped him, his breath quickening. I wrapped my hand around the base, surprised with how hot and velvety it felt. I dipped my head, giving the tip an experimental lick, screwing the tip of my tongue to the place where another pearl of liquid awaited. It was salty, earthy, and delicious.

Palming the underside of his cock, I let its weight sit on my tongue. As soon as I fastened my mouth around it, the last shreds of his self-control evaporated, along with all that fake gentleness that grated on my nerves. He fisted the back of my hair—tight enough to hurt, but not to make me flinch—and pushed my face farther down his length, making me take two more inches. A muscle in the back of my throat jumped, triggering my gag reflex. He guided my face up, not letting me pull away from his penis as our gaze struck.

His lips moved very slowly. "I'm going to fuck your pretty mouth now, darlin', hard and fast. If it gets too much, tap the side of my thigh, yeah?"

I nodded, and he let go completely. His hips snapped and he thrust all the way into me. Nausea bubbled up my mouth, but I managed to swallow it down. His tip touched the back of my throat, and I loved the rush of excitement it gave me, having my mouth so full of him.

I was on all fours, sucking him off while he controlled the pace and rhythm by holding the back of my head, sliding in and out of my mouth. Each time he pressed home, I took a deep, greedy suck, trying to keep him there, flicking my tongue over the bottom of his cock, breathing through my nose. He reached to cup one of my veiny breasts, tugging at the nipple roughly.

Wetness pooled between my thighs, and I knew I was drenched. Desperate for his cock to fill me. I ground against the bed, using one hand to work his cock and the other to massage his thigh as he plowed deeper and jerkier into me.

I wondered if he was going to come inside my mouth when he pulled out of me all of a sudden, guiding me down the bed gently, so as not to touch my collarbone. I gasped, catching his hungry gaze as his thick cock bounced between us, pushing my knees apart and stroking the wet part of my panties, driving me even wilder.

Moaning, I arched my back in offering. He tugged my panties down my legs impatiently, stuffing it in the pocket of the slacks bunched at his knees.

Ripples of pleasure crashed inside me, cluing me in on an orgasm before he even touched me.

"Time to fuck you nice and good, *wifey*."

My round belly stood between us, so all I could see was his face and shoulders. Recently, it had gotten harder to have sex unless I was on top of him.

He pushed two fingers into me, sinking into my wetness, and pulled them out, sucking them clean. "Ready."

He hitched me up by the waist and turned me over so I was on all fours facing the headboard. His knees sank to the mattress behind me. Tiernan slammed into me all at once, and I cried out, throwing my head back with a moan.

He'd never taken me like this before, always watching out for my delicate soul and trauma. I wished he hadn't. There was something so exhilarating about this position. About the fact I couldn't see his face, read his lips, sign to him. I was completely at his mercy as he drove into me, riding me from behind.

Picking up the pace, he leaned over, his six-pack colliding with my back, and tilted my head sideways, awarding me with a filthy, bruising kiss. With each slam of his hips, I groaned into his mouth, our juices dripping down my inner thighs.

A mouthwatering rush of heat found itself in my core. Every muscle in my body burned and tensed. I was a marionette on tight strings. When I arched my back and felt my climax taking over me, the invisible strings cut off. I collapsed on the bed limply. My husband caught my waist from behind, both to protect my pregnant belly and to steady me. He pumped into me a few more times before I felt the heat of his cum spreading inside me, then pulled out.

When I turned around, he already looked perfectly composed, tucking his shirt back into his slacks and zipping himself up. Not a hair on his head was out of place.

Tiernan picked his phone up from the nightstand. Checked his messages. Arched a brow.

"Angelo's en route to your family's basement. Turns out he was in the area." He leaned to kiss the top of my head. Every inch of my skin still hummed with postorgasmic shivers. "Get dressed. You're leaving."

My eyebrows pinched together. "*I'm coming?*"

"You just did. But, yes, you're coming with me to your parents'."

"*It's nine thirty.*"

"Yeah."

"*And there are about forty Irish soldiers roaming this building.*"

"Yeah."

"*Most likely, the only person who wants to hurt me, Angelo, will be in the same basement with you.*"

Chagrined amusement touched his frown. "Is there a point somewhere in your little speech, *Gealach*?"

I shook my head, more confused than ever. "*Why do you need me there?*"

"Because I love you." He stared at me incredulously. "Isn't that enough?"

A little earthquake in my chest, its ripples making my entire body tremble.

"*I don't want to see him.*"

"You won't," he assured me. "You'll be upstairs with your mam and Imma. He'll be downstairs, playing catch with his internal organs."

I slipped out of my dress and wobbled into the walk-in closet to pick out a fresh one and a pair of new panties. When I opened my underwear drawer, a strong, manly hand reached from behind my shoulder to close it back shut.

"No." His lips moved on the shell of my ear. "I want you to walk around leaking my cum."

His hands slid down from my shoulders to my breasts, cupping them, thumbs caressing my tight, dark nipples. I tilted my head against his chest, moaning. His hands traveled lower, to my stomach. I froze.

For the first time since we got married, Tiernan touched my stomach.

Tears gathered behind my eyes and nose. Grateful, happy tears, and a rush of joy coursed through me.

Splaying his fingers over the round, hard belly, he moved his lips along the crook of my shoulder.

"Sorry about the mess, little guy."

I snorted, feeling more cum dripping out of me as my abdominals contracted. I turned to him, draping my arms on his shoulders.

"Tiernan," I spoke.

"Wifey." He encircled my waist, drawing me close.

"I have something to say."

"I'm all ears."

"I love you."

This wiped the cocky smile off his face.

"Is it your orgasm speaking again, or is it you?"

"Both…?" I scrunched my nose.

"Wrong answer, rascal." He tapped my nose.

I laughed. "Just me."

"Say that again." His eye darkened, his starvation for affection gleaming from it.

"I love you."

He closed his eye. Inhaling the words into his body. "Now sign it."

Dropping my arms from his shoulders, I signed, "*I love you.*"

"Now *kiss* it."

Reaching on my tiptoes, I sealed his mouth with mine, telling him with my body how I felt, and the ferocity with which I felt it. It was tender and slow and romantic, devoid of our usual carnal hunger.

His forehead dropped to mine. We were both breathing hard.

And for the first time in my life, an elusive, power-drunk feeling washed over me.

I was untouchable.

CHAPTER FIFTY-ONE
TIERNAN

Enzo hauled Angelo by the hair, yanking him up from the bucket of water his face was pushed into. "Hi. Me again." My brother-in-law flashed a lazy smile. "Sorry the polygraph wasn't working and we had to resort to good ol' fucking your face up."

Angelo's frostbitten blue face glared at him. His dark blond hair dripped ice water.

"Apology not accepted," he hissed. "You broke the machine right in front of me when we got here."

"It was an honest mistake," Enzo grinned.

"You *shot* the fucking thing."

Enzo shrugged. "I have bad aim. Ask anyone."

"He's shit," Achilles confirmed. "And so are you."

"I already told you, I didn't do it," Angelo spat out the words.

"I'll ask again." Achilles strolled around the chair Angelo was bound to. He was tied in front of a desk with a bucket of water. "Where were you between 10:33 and 11:04 on that night, Bandini?"

To make it less awkward, Luca had extracted himself from the situation. It was bad manners to slaughter your brother-in-law when your wife was expecting your baby. Even if you felt more strongly about turtlenecks than about said wife.

"Not with her," Angelo hissed out in pain.

Enzo rolled his eyes exasperatedly, shoving Angelo's head back into the bucket. Gurgles and bubbles resurfaced on the water. I glanced at my watch, leaning against the wall, cross-legged. By the time this was over, it was going to be closer to two in the morning. Lila could sleep in until the late afternoon if she wished to, but I still didn't like the idea of my wife having to stay late because of this gobshite.

Enzo pulled Angelo's face from the water again. Forty minutes in, and we still got a whole lot of nothing from him. No surprises there. Outfit members didn't break easily.

"So? 10:33 to 11:04?" Enzo swirled the ring on his pinky.

"I was at the mansion," Angelo maintained.

"I vote we start cutting off his body parts." I uncrossed my arms and pushed off the wall, losing patience. "Begin with the fingers and work our way up. He obviously needs to be...*incentivized.*"

"Trust me when I tell you my motivation is sky-fucking-high," Angelo snarled. "I told you the truth. I was inside the mansion. I don't know what else you want me to say."

"How about the truth?" Achilles suggested. "We checked the CCTV footage. You slipped out of the ballroom during that timeframe."

"Y-yes." Angelo's teeth chattered, framed by blue, numb lips. "I said I was inside the mansion, not in the *ballroom.*"

"Where were you *inside* the mansion?" Achilles asked, producing his phone out of his pocket.

"We have footage access to all of the grand rooms."

Angelo pressed his lips, tipping his head back with a heavy sigh. He looked about ready to shoot his own head and be done with it.

"You won't find the footage." His voice cracked.

"Oh?" Achilles feigned surprise. "And why's that?"

"Because I slipped into one of the bedrooms."

"Partied so hard you needed to take a nap?" Enzo made a mock-sad face.

"Something like that," Angelo sneered, cutting his gaze to me.

"Look, man, I'm sincerely sorry for whatever happened to warrant this kind of interrogation of me. Whatever happened to your woman—"

"To my wife," I corrected crisply.

"To your *wife*, must be pretty bad. But I'm telling you, you're barking up the wrong tree here."

Achilles and I exchanged looks. I nodded once. Achilles pulled his gun out and shot Angelo's splayed fingers on the table, blowing up his pinky.

"*Fuck!*" Angelo kicked back, squirming in the seat he had his legs tied to, howling in pain.

"Anyway." Achilles said nonchalantly, holstering his gun. "You were saying, you were in a bedroom?"

Angelo panted hard, nodding violently. "Yes, yes."

"What were you doing there?"

"I was there with…someone."

"Lucky you." Achilles's mouth twisted with a smirk. "Care to tell us who it was? Just so we could give them a call and confirm your alibi."

"I can't tell you." Angelo spat blood to the floor.

"Why not?"

"Because it'd ruin her life," he groaned. "And it'd ruin mine, too."

Enzo beamed, the picture of sunshine and teddy bears. "She married?"

"No."

"Betrothed?"

Angelo stopped to think about it, then shook his head.

"Then it's not that big of a deal if you tell us her name," Achilles concluded. "I mean, there's the humiliation of having to admit to fucking you, but we'll keep her secret."

"So." I pressed my knuckles to the desk on the other side of Angelo, studying him from above. "Who's the lucky lady?"

He closed his eyes. Looked away. Shook his head.

Achilles sighed, pulled out his gun again, and shot his ring finger. Angelo kicked the desk and fell backward to the floor, screaming. "Goddammit!"

"Stop protecting her." I rolled my sleeves up my elbows, ready to get this shit over with. "Your only chance of coming out of this basement in less than sixty pieces and reunite with lover girl is if you cooperate. And since you're the only viable name on our list of suspects, it's on *you* to convince us you were accounted for within this timeframe."

I rounded the desk, stopped in front of him, and pressed the sole of my army boot to his groin. "Now, before I destroy the crown jewels…"

"It's your sister!" The confession ripped from his mouth.

Behind me, I heard Achilles's gun drop to the floor. I glanced back. Asshole looked like a kid who just witnessed the Tooth Fairy being gang raped by Santa Claus and the Easter Bunny. His expression was demonic.

"What?" I asked.

"You heard me," Angelo groaned as I pulled him back into a sitting position. "I was with Tierney. That's why I didn't want to tell you. Because you're her brother. And because…" He trailed off, his gaze skating to Achilles.

I followed his line of vision, just in time to catch Achilles pouncing on Angelo, dropping him back on the floor with a roar. He straddled him, grabbing his head and bashing it against the cobbled ground. Enzo and I jumped on him, each of us seizing one of his arms and dragging him off Angelo before he killed Luca's brother-in-law.

My sister was single, an adult, and could shag whoever she fancied.

"Move before I kill both your sorry asses as collateral damage," Achilles growled.

He fought us, trying to break free. He almost managed to escape twice, before we heaved him up the stairs and hauled his ass outside. We locked the dungeon, then returned to Angelo and straightened him up.

Enzo lit a cigarette and massaged his temples. I poured myself a whiskey.

"You said you were with Tierney," I drawled, my back to him.

"Yeah," Angelo coughed, gurgling on his blood before spitting it.

I didn't actually care who my sister was screwing. It was her prerogative to carry on an affair with Angelo Bandini. What did bother me was that if Angelo was telling the truth—and he had no reason to lie, seeing as I was going to ask her in exactly two minutes—that meant that the rapist's identity was still a mystery.

"You were with her the whole time?"

"Yeah." Angelo was now openly weeping. He was a pretty boy, but I couldn't see what made him so fuckable. "The entire time. You can ask her."

I remembered Tierney split from us sometime during the night. In fact, I had spent most of it in Vello's cardroom, cleaning everyone's wallets out in a game of craps.

I picked up my phone and called my sister. She answered on the first ring.

"Were you fucking Angelo the night of Luca's wedding?"

"Good evening to you, too, brother," she greeted sarcastically. "I'm doing well, and yourself?"

"Answer the fucking question, sis," I warned.

A pulse of hesitation. She didn't want to get him in trouble with Achilles. This was why she tried to stir us from the idea of him being the attacker whenever we discussed the list together.

"What is *he* saying?" she asked cautiously.

"He is claiming he was with you during the time Lila went missing."

Another pause. "If I answer truthfully, you can't let Achilles kill him."

"I won't."

"Then, yes. I can confirm his alibi. He was with me the entire night."

I killed the call. Set my phone down.

Enzo wiped a hand over his mouth. "Fuck me, but *'o chiattillo* is telling the truth. Which means…"

Which meant we were back to square one.

Only without any promising leads.

Angelo wasn't the rapist.

I couldn't let this go. Not because of my pride, or even Lila's. But because whoever it was, he was coming after her and our baby. My only consolation was that, now that the issue with the Bratva was solved, I could throw myself into finding this bastard.

I was going to kill this cunt if I had to personally assassinate every single person on that guest list.

"Untie the motherfucker," I told Enzo, turning my back on Angelo and going up the stairs.

Back to the drawing board we go.

———

After I tucked Lila into bed and informed her that Angelo wasn't the attacker, I met Tierney and Fintan downstairs for a pint.

"We were going at it like rabbits in Achilles's room." Tierney played with the stem of her chilled white wine, sitting cross-legged across from me. "He is surprisingly agile and feral, you know, for a pretty boy."

"Christ. Like I didn't need intense therapy as it is," I mumbled into my Guinness.

"Is it still going on between you two?" Fintan asked her.

"No. He broke it off when he realized how serious Achilles is about protecting my nonexistent virtue." She pouted. "Speaking of, I do hope Achilles was there when Angelo spilled the beans."

"He was," I confirmed, letting her bask in his misery. "And he lost his ever-loving shit."

"Really, now?" Her eyes sparkled excitedly.

I nodded. "Enzo and I almost tore his arms off trying to unpeel him from the poor bastard."

"He's got it hard for you, sis." Fintan lifted his pint in a cheers motion.

"I know." Tierney swirled her wine, a faraway look on her face. Her bruises were meticulously covered in makeup. "I cannot wait to destroy his life."

"He took two of Angelo's fingers," I goaded.

She winced, before remembering she was a cold bitch who wasn't supposed to care.

"Shame." She slouched against the vinyl bench. "He has talented fingers. I shall always remember them fondly."

"Oi." I tossed a crisp at her. She caught it in her mouth and wiggled her brows, chewing.

"Add that to your list of things to talk about with your nonexistent therapist." She laughed.

We fell silent, each of the siblings sipping their respective drink.

I was running several options of who the attacker might be in my head.

"How's Da doing?" Tierney broke the quiet.

"Grand, yeah." Fintan stroked his chin. "His depression seems to be under control. The new meds are working wonders."

It was the best-kept secret of the underworld that my father was down for the count his entire career, battling depression. I took over his work when I was fifteen and never looked back. It was as though he'd waited for Tierney and me to come along so he could finally collapse into the breakdown he had when Mam was murdered. I remembered not understanding him one bit. His despair, and inability to move on, push forward, rejoin society.

Now it was crystal clear to me, though.

I, too, couldn't think of myself without Lila.

That he made it so far without killing himself was a heroic act in itself.

"So what're you going to do?" Fintan turned to face me. "Now that Angelo provided a sufficient alibi."

For the first time in my life, I wasn't forthcoming with my siblings. I didn't tell them the truth. I just told him what I wanted the world to think. I couldn't trust anybody anymore. "I'm going to send her off to meet him, if he ever contacts her again. And then I'm going to give him what he wants and make sure he pisses off. If it's money he wants, he is welcome to it."

Fintan nodded. "Can't say I blame ya."

Tierney stared at me in disbelief. "What if he harms her?"

"Why would he?" I asked. "He had eight months to do it. He got as far as our apartment. Could've finished her off while she was under him, if he wanted."

They both gave me disturbed looks.

I rapped my knuckles on the table. "Another round?"

CHAPTER FIFTY-TWO
TIERNAN

Three days later, Lila's attacker came forth.

I had a feeling he was biding his time, watching us, trying to see how the Angelo Bandini angle was going to unfold. Now that Angelo was out and about, walking on his two useless feet—albeit missing a couple fingers—it was obvious we crossed him off the list of suspects.

And even though the other, unchecked candidates were extremely unlikely, I wasn't going to rule any of them out.

"*This time he sent me a message straight to my phone.*" Lila handed me said phone. "*I wonder why?*"

The message read:

> If you want to stay alive, meet me tonight at 11pm at Fort Market port. Come alone. Shake off your husband/security detail. Bring 150K in cash.

The reason as to the why was simple. He could no longer risk slipping mail into the building without going unnoticed. The place was more secured than the White House now.

I grabbed the phone number and sent it for Sam to analyze, even though I knew the fucker 100 percent used a burner.

"Confirm you'll be there." I handed her back the phone. "I'll go see him myself."

Her head shot up and she glared at me. "*I'm coming, too.*"

"You're not."

"*Tiernan, I want to confront the man who did this to me.*"

"Why?" I asked coldly. "Are you expecting any insightful input as to why he brutally raped you? Because you won't find a plausible excuse."

"*I want him to hurt—*"

"He *will* hurt," I promised. "I will make it slow, and gory, and unbearable. He will regret the day he was born."

"*I need this for closure.*" She glared at me.

"You're not coming, and that's that." I slipped into my peacoat. I had 150K to liquidate in a few hours. Hardly a fucking problem for me, but a big hurdle for a sheltered teenager like Lila. This whole operation felt botched. Amateur. This wasn't necessarily a good thing. Stupid people made the most dangerous enemies. They couldn't tell a terrible idea if it hit them in the face with a shovel.

"*Think about it.*" Lila jumped to her feet, chasing me across the too-small apartment. I hated that she didn't have a sprawling mansion, a proper nursery, and a walk-in closet she could get lost in.

Not that she'd ever complained about it despite her plush upbringing.

"*He threatened he'd tell the world our secret. Reveal that you are not the real father if I don't come there on my own.*"

"First of all, he wouldn't be alive to do that." I slipped into my smart shoes. "Second, even if he did tell, it wouldn't change a thing. I'd still be married to you, and the baby would still be mine."

That seemed to placate her as she stopped by the door, placing her hands on my shoulders.

"*Promise?*"

I stared at her, aghast. "Just fucking try to get rid of me, Lila."

That earned me a precious smile from my favorite girl.

"Thank you," she said.

"I love you."

"*Good for you.*"

She was still mad. I yanked her close, kissing the tip of her nose. "Hey. Say it back."

"*Fine, I love you, too. That being said, I want to be there, please.*"

I leaned down, catching her lips in mine in a sweet kiss. She'd be pissed when she found out I directed all of her incoming messages and calls to my phone. "Never fucking happening. Have a good day, *Gealach.*"

CHAPTER FIFTY-THREE
LILA

The clock struck ten thirty when I put my sketchbook down and rose from the couch.

I couldn't sit around twiddling my thumbs while my husband was having a showdown with my rapist.

Fury and exasperation swirled in my gut. I knew Tiernan wanted to keep me safe, and I appreciated his protectiveness, but I was my own person, and I wanted to confront my attacker. I deserved to give him a piece of my mind. I even fantasized about telling him everything verbally. Watching his shock as he realized I could speak.

Tiernan made me promise I'd never follow him, never put myself in harm's way, but we'd never discussed this rule in the case that *I* knew his life was in danger. He was underestimating the man who raped me. Sure, his actions so far were a little chaotic, but ultimately, he had managed to sneak under everyone's radar undetected this many months into the pregnancy.

Obviously, he was doing something right.

I was going to break my promise to my husband. Just this one time.

I grabbed my pink gun and tucked it in the satin ribbon holding together my pink maternity dress. It was easily concealed between the rich fabrics of my frock. I slid my phone into my purse and took the stairs down to the pub. Fintan and Tierney weren't there, and it was still closed to the public. An ocean of scary-looking Irish soldiers looked up from their pints and game of cards. I shot them a glare and punched my phone's keyboards, using a text-to-speech app.

"I want to go to 7-Eleven to get some chocolate."

They looked between them, hesitant. I wasn't one for rash decisions and didn't have a sweet tooth. And I never asked my bodyguards to take me anywhere. In fact, I usually pretended they didn't exist.

A bulky guy named Flynn stood up. "Give us a list, will you? I'll go grab whatever ya fancy."

Shaking my head, I typed on my phone, transferring my text into words.

"I don't know what I want. I need to go there and see."

"It's late," he argued.

I tossed a shoulder up.

"And cold," someone else said.

I rolled my eyes.

"Tiernan said not to let you out of our sight," a third soldier chimed, his throat bobbing with a swallow. I couldn't believe the man put fifty soldiers in charge of protecting one tiny woman who never left the house. This was overkill, even for my husband.

"Good thing you are coming with me, then," my phone sing-songed my words.

Heaving out a sigh, the largest soldier pushed off his seat, draining the last of his Guinness. "Be back in a few."

"I'll come with." A second soldier stood up. Then a third, and, to my horror, a fourth.

God, I couldn't take them all down.

"I'm not getting into the car with all of you," my phone declared robotically.

"Boss says four soldiers is the minimum for your security," mammoth soldier replied.

"I don't feel comfortable being in a confined space with a bunch of big men. Do you know what happens to men who make me feel uncomfortable?" I arched an eyebrow.

Another round of frustrated scowls ping-ponged in the room.

"Ah, shite." The mammoth soldier, who was also the highest ranking one, tore his jacket from the back of his booth and stomped to the door. "Make it quick."

I followed him, waiting while he pulled the car from the garage and rounded it to the front of the pub. I slid into the back, right behind the driver's seat.

He started driving down the street, taking a turn right into an intersection.

Heart thrumming, I pulled my gun out of my waistband and pressed it to the back of his closely shaved head. He froze. I cocked the gun.

Pushing my phone screen into his face with my other hand from behind, I pointed at the address the attacker had sent me earlier in the day. "Floor it," I said vocally.

He gulped, nodding once.

Ten minutes that felt like two hours later, I hopped out of the car before he even made a full stop, still aiming the pistol at him. There wasn't much he could do to chase me. He was armed to his teeth, but he knew moving a hair on my head would land him in all of Dante's circles of hell.

I moved quietly in the night. The port was an abandoned cluster of warehouses sitting in a deserted harbor. The stench of stale weed, piss, and human decay hung in the air. Whoever had invited me here knew Hunts Point well enough to choose this strategic location. The buildings were all flat-roofed, two-storied, arranged in a U-shape. If you stood at the center of that U, you were a plain target.

My husband knew that, which was why I spotted him almost immediately, moving sleekly close to the walls of the buildings, disappearing into crooks, checking his surroundings calmly. It was possible my attacker was not going to show himself to Tiernan, but it was extremely unlikely said attacker was going to slip under Tiernan's radar this time.

I scanned my surroundings for a hideout the way my husband had taught me and settled behind a broken-down car that slumped on the side of the port. It was rusty and loaded with old shopping bags inside. I had a good view of Tiernan, though. And that was what mattered.

My husband stopped in an alcove, pulled out his phone to check it.

Smart boy.

I needed him alive.

The baby kicked inside me, demonstrating his disapproval at my quick heart rate. I wasn't stupid. I figured Tiernan forwarded my messages to himself to communicate with the attacker. They were likely texting now.

I noticed the duffel with the money my attacker asked for sitting in the center of the U.

A shadow danced across the roof above Tiernan's head. My eyes snapped to it. A person. Dressed all in black, wearing a balaclava. He was army-crawling across the roof, a rifle in his hands. Because he wasn't standing up, Tiernan couldn't see him.

But I could.

The person aimed their firearm at Tiernan, but he had a terrible angle. My husband knew better than to make himself vulnerable. Still, if this was a seasoned sniper, it was game over.

If it were Tiernan on the roof, he'd take the shot and kill him in a heartbeat.

This is your attacker, Lila. The man who took the most precious thing you owned. Your innocence.

The person on the roof scratched at their balaclava, frustrated, scooting forward, trying to get a better angle on my husband.

I choked on my breath, jerking my own pistol and aiming it at the person on the roof. He was closer to me than he was to Tiernan, but it was still going to be a hard shot. In the pitch dark. With a moving target lying flat a few dozen feet above me.

But one shot was all I had.

Especially if this guy knew what he was doing.

My heart pounded so hard I was nauseous.

I ran through all of Tiernan's instructions in my head.

Steady hands.

Wide stance.

Use your dominant eye.

Squeeze when you exhale. Your money shot is when your lungs are empty.

Study the wind.

Shoot dirty.

I took a deep breath.

The person on the roof scooted forward, cocking his rifle.

Tiernan's head shot up at the sound.

I exhaled all the oxygen from my lungs.

Then I took my shot.

The pink gun fired, the bullet spinning in the air for a nanosecond before landing clean in the attacker's head. He fell from the roof, landing on the ground.

Tiernan whipped his head in my direction. I raised my hands in truce. He stepped from the shadows, brows creased in confusion, gun aimed toward me.

He looked *pissed.*

That's when I realized he didn't recognize me.

Had no idea who I was.

My attacker didn't come out of this alive.

But neither would I.

CHAPTER FIFTY-FOUR
TIERNAN

I pulled the trigger a fraction of a second before I spotted the flash of a pink dress.

Everything turned black.

Jerking my pistol sideways, every fiber of my body hoped it was enough to skew the bullet far enough from my aim.

I never missed.

But I needed to miss *now*.

The tiny figure ducked behind the broken window of the piece of junk car, the sound of my shot ricocheting through the air, the scent of sulfur in my nose, on my tongue.

The entire world hung, suspended on a string, and I knew I wouldn't give myself time to mourn the loss of my wife if I killed her. I'd kill myself on impact.

I shot so fast in her direction I nearly outran the bullet, my heart in my fucking throat.

Lila.

Lila.

Lila.

My wife sidestepped the rusty car, and I saw she was unscathed. All the air left my lungs. My knees buckled. I fell down on all fours, fucking heaving from terror.

She could've died.

I could've *killed* her.

A few seconds later, I felt her dainty fingers on my shoulders. She kneeled down in front of me, gathering me into her arms. I pushed her away, standing up swiftly, livid.

"What in the ever-loving *fuck*?" My roar reverberated through the air. Snatching her shoulders, I shook her roughly. "What are you doing here? How did you get here?"

I was losing my shit, mind, and control. The thought that someone could've hurt her, that *I* could've been that someone…

Her big blue eyes clung to my face wildly. My grip on her tightened, becoming more punishing.

"I'm going to disembowel every gobshite who's been assigned to watch you."

"*I threatened one of your soldiers at gunpoint.*"

Of course she did.

Falling in love with a normal girl was too big an ask.

I had to go for the deranged Camorra principessa who looked like an angel and recreationally licked blood and shot people.

"I told you to never go anywhere where you're unsafe."

She pushed up to her feet, patting down her dusty knees.

"*You could've died!*"

"It was a chance I was willing to take. You dying wasn't."

"*Well, as it happens, you dying is a chance I wasn't willing to take.*" Her expression was thunderous. "*By the way, this is a very weird way to say thank you for saving your life.*"

What Lila didn't understand was that I'd choose to be mutilated to death and resurrected twice a day until the planet exploded before seeing her endure a minor paper cut. Did she save my life? No. I saw the dipshit on the roof and had my gun aimed at him. I'd been hoping to extract information from him before killing him.

That wasn't the point, though.

The point was that she cared.

Cared enough to risk her life.

Cared enough to go to the trouble.

I'd been the responsible adult in every relationship I'd ever had. With my father, brother, sister, Alex, the entire Irish operation. I made the calls and decided who lived and who died.

And though I still wanted to strangle her for giving me a heart attack, I couldn't pretend it didn't affect me that she risked her own life just to save my ass.

"Are you hurt?" I asked. I was sulking. Another side effect of being in love. Jesus Christ, it was like being plagued with an incurable disease.

She arched an eyebrow, folding her arms over her chest. "*Are you done with your tantrum?*"

"Almost." I grabbed her cheeks in my palms. "Need to do this first."

I leaned down and kissed the living shite out of her. A kiss that put to shame every other kiss in the history of kisses. With tongue and teeth and moans and groans. With adrenaline-soaked urgency only being reminded of what your own mortality could cause.

I took a step back, putting on a ruefully unbothered face. "That's your official thank-you. Having said that, *never* do it again."

We both turned and walked toward the lifeless figure that laid beneath the warehouse roof. It was splayed on the concrete, a river of dark blood oozing from the balaclava. A clear shot to the head. My chest nearly burst with pride. She was a good student.

I kneeled down in front of him, turning to her when I spoke.

"You want to see his face?"

She nodded. "*I'm glad I was the one to kill him. He killed a part of me all those months ago. He deserved it.*"

I ripped the balaclava from his face and squinted at the sight in front of me.

It was…

A fucking *nobody*.

Not anyone I recognized, and certainly no one from the Irish, Camorra, or Outfit.

I was confused to say the least.

Lila tugged on my sleeve from behind, and I turned to look at her.

"*I know him.*" She breathed out, eyes wide. "*Roger. He worked on Crimson Key for at least a decade. At my parents' country club and sometimes in the mansion, when there were big events. I bet he was a member of the staff during Luca's wedding.*"

I said nothing.

"*I'm happy it's done.*" She fell into my arms while I was still crouching. "*I'm tired, Tiernan. Tired of poking this wound that keeps opening, gushing out. Tired of the violence and misery finding this bastard brought with it. I want to forget he ever existed and move on.*"

Stroking her back absentmindedly, I sent her to wait in the car for me while I cleaned any potential evidence from the crime scene. I followed her alertly with my gaze until she climbed in and locked herself inside the Mercedes.

After she was gone, I yanked his wallet from his pants—which I knew I'd find because whoever sent this asshole here wanted me to find it—and called Sam. I wasn't convinced by what I was seeing.

"Brennan," he answered.

"Roger Carsodo. Run his name on your system," I clipped out. I held his driver's license using the tips of my fingernails. I never left evidence behind, and I wasn't going to start now only because this case was personal to me.

"*Pfft.* Forget about it," Sam confirmed my suspicion. "Family man. Veteran. Kids, wife, pets, a steady job. Landed on Crimson Key because his daughter has a rare lung disease and the humidity is good for her. I'm sending you his full bio."

I killed the call and skimmed over the file Sam popped in my unencrypted chat app.

Roger Carsodo didn't fit the profile.

He was well into his fifties, slim and relatively short.

More importantly, he had a wife and four children at home.

Frail enough not to attack a girl so viciously and violently, old enough not to be hard and ready in the seconds it took him to push her skirt up and violate her.

Yeah, he was a waiter at the wedding, but he had worked on Crimson Key for years. He was known as a devout Catholic and a family man.

It seemed the real attacker greased Cardoso's palm. Paid him to take the fall. Kill or get killed. Roger took it, likely because the overdue medical bills kept piling up. He sacrificed himself for the greater good of his family.

But even poor people like Roger didn't do this kind of shit for a few bucks. He needed to make sure his family was taken care of, which meant whoever attacked Lila had money.

Fucking loads of it.

Lila was terrified and exhausted from this ordeal. I wasn't going to share all of this with her. As far as she was concerned, this shit was over. Done. She killed her rapist and was happy about it.

This was her truth, though. Not mine.

I was going to find that sneaky asshole.

Even if it was the last thing I did.

CHAPTER FIFTY-FIVE
LILA

"*What will you do with Harlem, now that it's yours?*" I asked as we drove to my baby shower at my parents' house.

It was a last-minute gathering, but Mama insisted we should make up for some lost time.

She'd been the picture of a perfect mother since our talk at the hospital, dropping by with food and clothes, sometimes accompanying Tiernan and me to our weekly checkups at the doctor's office.

I was excited to spend time with Tierney and Sofia. Really, I was excited to see everyone other than Vello.

I was relieved to find out he wasn't my biological father, and unlike with Mama, I saw no reason to try to patch things up with him. It wasn't my fault I wasn't his, and it certainly wasn't my job to make him love me. If he wanted us to be strangers, that was exactly what we'd be.

"Nothing," Tiernan clipped out, his gaze unwavering from the road.

"*You mean, you're going to keep things as is?*"

"I mean, I'm not getting Harlem."

Rearing my head back, I frowned. "*Vello refused to fulfill his side of the bargain?*"

It wouldn't surprise me. The man was a menace.

"He tried giving it to me. I declined it."

"*Why?*" I asked incredulously.

"Because finding that asshole had stopped being about territory and prestige a long time ago."

His veiny, big hand tap-tap-tapped the wheel impatiently. "And I don't want you to ever doubt why I'm here. Besides, I've no interest in Harlem anymore. Alex and I have bigger plans. The Midwest is wide open, waiting to be claimed. Fewer feds' eyes on it, too."

"*You should've taken what's yours.*" But even as I said this, I couldn't deny the pleasure it gave me to know he gave up Harlem to show me his devotion. "*I already know that you love me.*"

"I have claimed what's mine." He ran his palm over my stomach, up my torso, thumbing my chin. "She's sitting next to me, and I'm never letting her go."

———————

Thirty minutes later, we parked in front of my parents' house. The front lawn was decorated with arches of balloons in blue, white, and gold. The cobbled pathway leading to the doors was lined up with little stork signs that exclaimed: *It's a boy!*

My heart pitter-pattered. Not only did Tiernan accept the baby, but Mama did, too. The two most important people in my life.

Tiernan rounded the car and opened the passenger door for me. He offered me a hand, keeping my palm in his as we made our way inside.

We were greeted by my family. Tierney was there, too, looking especially beautiful in a risqué black Balmain dress that clung to her killer body, black lacy gloves, and a pearl choker.

She was never going to get Achilles off her back if she continued baiting him, looking like she did.

A part of me suspected she didn't *want* him to stop.

"You look so beautiful, *bambina mia.*" Mama kissed my cheeks with glittering eyes. "Glowing."

"Thank you." I held her wrists, kissing her back.

"And you're wearing pink." Tierney's grin was conspiratorial. "To a blue-themed party. That's so...*you.*"

Luca, Achilles, and Enzo hugged me, too. Sofia and I rubbed each other's bumps, giggling. It was the first time I saw a genuine smile on her face. I knew better than to think that smile was because Luca and she were doing better. She still lived in Chicago, and he still lived in New York.

Vello wasn't in attendance. Mama said he was feeling unwell, and I didn't push. Frankly, I felt more relaxed without him being around.

There was food, cupcakes, virgin cocktails, laughter, and a game of trivia. Mama brought out the big guns at some point. Thick, dusty photo albums of me as a baby. I held my breath the entire time Tiernan and Tierney examined them, knowing their infancy did not include baby pictures, smash cakes, colorful bikes, and Barbie-themed Band-Aids.

At some point, I had to excuse myself to go to the bathroom. Peeing every ten minutes was the unfortunate by-product of having a six-pound human using your bladder as a pillow. I slipped into the restroom, did my business, and washed my hands. When I got out, I saw Achilles and Tierney huddled in a darkened corner of the hallway. I froze. She was pressed against the wall, him crowding her, his arms on either side of her shoulders. It was the first time he paid her attention all evening. He'd refused to look her way the entire evening. I suspected it had something to do with the revelation she'd been sleeping with Angelo. It was hard to think of Achilles as heart-broken. Then again, his behavior had always been so weird around her.

Stepping back behind the door, I studied them, waiting to see if Tierney needed any help.

I loved my brother, but I was fully prepared to jump to my sister-in-law's defense and protect her.

"Did you touch my mistress?" Achilles's face gave away nothing.

"Hmm." Tierney yawned in his face provocatively. "Which one?"

"Don't fuck with me, Tierney."

"Honey, don't you worry your ugly head about that. I'll never fuck you."

I pressed my lips to suppress a giggle.

"I only have one. Tessa." The corded muscles in his tanned arms flexed. He looked like he was trying his best not to touch her and losing his control rapidly. Every hair on my body stood on end. I really didn't want to smash something on his head but could see it happening if things went south. "She says her legs were broken with a baseball bat."

"You mean, she can't open them for you anymore?" Tierney clutched her choker in mock horror. She laughed, patting his shoulder good-naturedly. "Oh, come, Achilles. I'm harmless enough. The only thing I've ever killed is a sourdough starter."

Achilles obviously wasn't buying it.

"Did you do it yourself or send someone else?" he asked.

"I'm a hardworking gal." She flipped her hair to one shoulder. "If I want to get something done, I always do it myself."

"Thought you said you'd never hurt another woman."

"*That* woman has a rap sheet a mile long," Tierney quipped. "Have you read it?"

"No."

"She's not exactly a symbol of feminism. Child abandonment, child neglect, solicitation, statutory rape of a seventeen-year-old boy…" She listed the colorful past of my brother's mistress. "Honestly? She's lucky I stopped at her legs. That neck was sooo squeezable."

Achilles's mask slipped, and a flash of surprise crossed his face. A rarity in itself. "Didn't know all that."

"Even if you did, it wouldn't have made any difference to you." She shrugged.

He didn't deny it. "This was your payback for Angelo."

"If I can't get some, Ferrante, then neither can you."

"Listen carefully now, *piccola fiamma*." He snatched her jaw, making her meet his eyes. "You're making one fatal mistake after another. Don't push my limits. That self-destruction button of yours will get you killed one day, sweetheart. And I just might do the honor."

Unable to stomach any more of this, I stepped out of the bathroom and cleared my throat, making myself known. Both their gazes fluttered to me. Achilles stepped back, sneering at Tierney like she was garbage.

"Your little friend saved the day." He rearranged the choker around her neck gently, without touching her skin. "I'm watching you, Tierney."

"Keep looking, asshole." She smiled serenely. "Because that's all you'll do when it comes to me."

"You okay?" I asked verbally, putting a hand on her shoulder.

She nodded, putting on a brave smile, but the light in her eyes was gone.

"Me? Oh, grand. Don't worry about me at all. What about you? Having fun?"

I nodded.

"Great. That's all I needed to know."

———

When we got to the gift portion of the event, worry began nibbling at the corners of my gut.

Imma gifted me the most beautiful changing table, powder blue and carved lavishly, but it was ginormous and would never fit into our bedroom, unless we removed a few pieces of furniture.

Mama bought the baby a SNOO.

Luca and Sofia gifted us a bougie designer stroller, a baby tub, and a car seat.

Achilles and Enzo contributed a bunch of toys and the rocker I'd put on my registry.

Tierney, an entire wardrobe of designer onesies and extravagant Burberry and Gucci baby blankets.

While I appreciated everything, we simply didn't have space for all these things. I already knew I'd have to send Imma back to live with my parents, since there weren't enough bedrooms in the apartment.

I suppose I didn't really need my vanity…or my walk-in closet. My clothes could fit into some drawers, and I could convert the closet into a space for the baby's changing table and clothes.

An hour later, Tiernan and I got into the car and made our way to the apartment. I continued trying to shift things around in my head to accommodate our growing family. Maybe we could keep the stroller in the communal hallway? I was sure Tierney wouldn't mind.

But the truth was, squeezing things into our apartment was the least of my worries. We lived above a crowded pub. Surely, the constant hustle and bustle would wake the baby. And how was I to take him for strolls when we needed fresh air? We lived in an unsafe neighborhood.

"I'm sorry I didn't give you anything for your baby shower." Tiernan snatched me out of my own thoughts.

"*Please don't be.*" I shook my head. "*We've both had so much on our minds lately.*"

"I did get you something small." He reached across the central console, took my hand, and pressed my knuckles to his lips. "I hope you like it," he murmured into my skin.

"*I'm sure I will.*"

"Mind if we make a pit stop to see it? It's just around the corner."

"*Not at all. I'm all yours.*"

In every single way possible.

We drove from Massapequa to Huntington in silence. I drummed my fingers on my thigh, feeling the baby readjusting inside my tummy. It had become unbearably uncomfortable for both of us lately.

Tiernan killed the engine in front of a stunning gray-stoned colonial with black shutters and floor-to-ceiling doors and windows. It was a jaw-dropping mansion with two white columns on either way of the entrance, a grand balcony above it, four chimneys, and two wings spurting from each side of it. There must be at least nine bedrooms in this place, I thought, as I took in the manicured bright green bushes bracketing the serpentine pathway to the house.

Tiernan stared at the manor. Grimly, he turned to me, rummaging in his pocket and depositing a small set of keys in my hand. "Here's the something small I got you."

"*You got me a key?*" I blinked, confused.

"Not just any key." He gestured at the mansion. "One that opens the door to this house."

I stared at him, processing the meaning of his words.

"Is this big enough for us?" He searched my face, something urgent flicking behind his eye.

"*I'm sorry?*" My pulse hammered against the side of my neck, my heart expanding like a sponge.

"Is the house big enough?" he repeated. "For you, me, Imma, the baby, and the other two or three you'll want in the future, since, unlike me, you don't detest people."

Stunned, I stared at him, looking for the right words.

He…bought this? For me? For *us*?

"It's a little shy of twelve thousand square feet. Ten bedrooms. Way too many baths. A pool. A tennis court. I think I'll convert it to a stable, though. I know you like horses." He scratched his jaw absentmindedly. "The kitchen is huge. There are two of them, actually. Imma will be happy. And the nurseries are good-sized."

I seized his jawline, making him stop talking. I shook my head. He looked…dejected. Like he lost, somehow. And I knew why.

"*Thank you. I appreciate it. But if you're doing this just to appease me, please don't. We'll find a way to fit everything in our apartment. I don't even need half the things we were gifted. I'll happily donate them. And Imma can stay with my parents. I'll be okay. All I care about is being with you.*"

"I'm not letting you and the baby live in Hunts Point." He stared at me like I was insane. "Living above a pub…it's no place for a new mother and a child."

"*But you love Hunts Point.*"

"There are things I love more. One of them happens to sit right in front of me."

"*You don't have to choose.*"

"I do, and I am. I'll be in New York daily, for work. You'll be close to your parents and have all the assistance you need."

I was going to argue, but it seemed his mind was set. I started signing something, but he ignored me, slipping out of the driver's seat and opening the door for me.

Hesitantly, I stepped out and allowed myself a good look at the house.

It wasn't as grand and flashy as my parents', but ten times prettier. It looked like something out of the historical books I read about England, where soirees took place and people fell in love.

I got a little choked up as the soles of our shoes slapped the bricked trail toward the dramatic black door.

"Don't you dare cry, *Gealach.*" Tiernan squeezed my hand in his, his expression stone-cold and oddly focused, like he was in the middle of an important mission. "We haven't even reached the best part yet."

The best part?

What could be better than gifting me an entire freaking house for my baby shower?

We walked into the foyer, and the scent hit me immediately. Fresh paint. This must've been in the works for a while now. A small tremor danced behind my sternum. Dark hardwood floors and crown moldings greeted us. The hallway was vast and newly remodeled. The house was empty, but still felt somehow full. Of promise and character and memories just waiting to be created between these walls.

My husband tugged me toward the kitchen.

The island and woodwork were painted navy, the backsplash a crème, veiny marble accented in blue. The parquet flooring still emitted the pleasant scent of freshly sawed wood.

Tiernan turned to spear me with a look. "I can already see Imma standing here, yelling at me not to leave crumbs in her kitchen."

A giddy giggle escaped me.

We went up the wide-set stairway and onto the second floor. First, we checked the residential wing of the house. The master was luxuriously sparse, with separate bathrooms for both of us and a walk-in closet I could easily get lost in. The nursery was painted baby blue, one wall already wallpapered with teddy bears hanging from balloons. It was big enough to fit everything we were gifted, and more.

"Tiernan…" I choked out, breathless.

"Shh. There are two more surprises." He yanked me to the other wing of the house. This feeling, of unrestrained happiness, was foreign to me. I felt like I could burst any minute with all the glee brimming inside me.

Tiernan stopped in front of a closed door, only a few feet away from a set of double doors down the hallway.

He opened the door.

It was an art room.

With huge windows to let the place air, a heavy wooden easel, a desktop, and portable drawers with supplies. There were canvases and brushes and pencils and paints. Inspiration boards and palettes and different shade lamps.

Tiernan knew nothing about art, and yet he took the time and the effort.

He did this for me.

He did all of this for me.

I cupped my mouth, overcome with emotions.

"*This is perfect. Is it okay to cry now?*" I signed. "*Because I'm danger-ously close.*"

"Almost." He put his finger in the air, motioning for me to hold. "Give me about…" He scowled at his watch. "Eight more minutes."

I couldn't imagine anything better than what he'd already shown me. But I nodded my agreement, letting him lead me back into the hallway, and in front of the double doors.

He stopped, turning to me fully. He shoved his hand into his front pocket, producing something small in his hand.

"*What's this?*"

"I know that Tate Blackthorn gave you your first dance. I can't take that away from him. Truth be told, I'm not sure I want to. It's your fondest memory, and as much as I hate him, I love that you have something that pleased you so much."

My heart accelerated. My breath hitched. Tiernan's fierce gaze bore into me, scorching through all of my protective layers.

He was wrong. It wasn't my fondest memory at all. Every single moment with him was better than my first dance. Even the bad times, when we fought and drove each other to the brink of madness. Because we still did it together.

"But I wanted you to know that next to me, you'll dance every night until your feet hurt. You will hear music and enjoy it."

He raised his hands, unveiling a small hearing aid in his palm. It was a clear small tube attached to something that looked like a USB.

"Your doctor told me you won't be able to hear the nuance of the music, but you can follow the soundwaves."

And then I knew what it felt like to have your heart burst, because mine did, and warmth poured into my chest.

Tiernan reached for my ears and put the small device in each of them. He flicked the back of one of the devices. A static screech filled my ears, making my head hurt. I stumbled back, wincing.

He reached to grab my hands and steady me. I stared at him, shocked. Was I going to hear now?

"I love you."

My heart skipped a beat.

I heard him.

His voice was rough. Husky. *Beautiful.*

"I wanted it to be the first thing you'll ever hear," he explained. "So I'll say it again—I. Love. You."

I wanted to fall down on my knees and scream in triumph. Listen to my own voice. Bask in my laughter.

But before I could do any of that, Tiernan pushed the doors open and in front of me stood a lush, huge ballroom.

A live orchestra sat on a stage, musicians poised and swathed in formalwear.

Violinists, cellists, clarinet and flute players, trombones and trumpets. Bass and snare drums.

"May I humbly ask for the pleasure of a dance with you, Lila?" He bowed his head, and I realized I heard him because he spoke, not because I could read his lips.

That *voice*. This *man*. God help me.

Tiernan offered me his open palm.

I took it.

We stepped inside.

The band began to play on cue.

The music filled my ears.

The harmony, the sound, the emotions it stirred in me…

I couldn't breathe; I was so overwhelmed. It was pleasant and happy, but I got choked up on my own emotions.

I started shaking in his arms as he swept me elegantly across the dance floor in a waltz. Tears leaked from my eyes, and this time I let them fall. I didn't feel weak. On the contrary, I'd never felt more powerful in my life.

"You waltz?" I heard my voice. It sounded slurred in comparison to my husband's. But it was pretty. I liked it. It was...*kind.*

"For you, I do," he confirmed. "We're not talking about the dance classes I took last week, though."

I listened to the edge of his voice.

To the playful lilt of his sarcasm.

To that low, soothing, manly baritone that I always fantasized about.

Whoa.

"What are they playing?" I asked.

I doubted whatever version of this song entered my ears was the complete product, but it was enough.

"'The Blue Danube' waltz by Johann Strauss." He smiled down at me, happy because I was. "We're going to go through all of the classics, darlin'. And then we are going to attend every ball in greater New York and flaunt your moves," he continued, just as I stomped on his foot, my huge belly poking between us. "Well, we have a few months to practice."

I tried to laugh, but the thrill of it all finally took its toll on my body. I fell to my knees in the middle of the ballroom and started sobbing uncontrollably.

Music.

Sound.

Love.

This man had given me so many things. And we almost never happened. It took a terrorizing tragedy to put us in each other's paths.

Tiernan sank down to the floor, wrapping his arms around me. His fingers disappeared in my hair. He kissed my tears while I hiccuped, clutching him desperately, never wanting to let go.

Was it terrible that I was glad I had been raped and brutalized? I marveled at the stunning realization that my rape—the lowest point of my life, of my existence—carved my path to this beautiful life I had today.

If it hadn't, I wouldn't have ended up here. With this man. Who had given me all I'd ever wanted, and things I didn't even know I could dream of having. I'd always dreamed about a dashing prince. Heavily lashed, with pouty lips and big, beautiful eyes.

As it turned out, I fell in love with the complete opposite of it. With a Nephilim, a fallen giant, hands scarred from murder.

No, he wasn't just my lover.

He was my god.

It was only when the music died, when the final note was struck by the orchestra, that I took in the room I was standing in fully. Beforehand, I was too overwhelmed to examine it.

It was filled with roses.

In every color and shape.

Every corner. Every crook. The heavy scent of them in my nose, sweet and pleasant.

White. Yellow. Lavender. Peach. Green. Orange. *Red.*

He made me face my fear of roses.

In a safe space. Erasing my last memory of the flower and replacing it with something I never wanted to forget.

Tiernan cupped my cheeks, staring down at me. "Hey, Moon."

"Hey, Sun." I put my hands on his, keeping them on my face. I leaned into his palm.

"Thank you for this dance."

I closed my eyes, breathing him in. "Thank you for this life."

CHAPTER FIFTY-SIX
TIERNAN

68 DAYS UNTIL (CANCELED)
SELF-DESTRUCTION PROJECT

Lila went into labor at our new house surrounded by enough medical staff to open a field hospital.

There were four nurses, one doula, two OB-GYNs, one pediatrician, and an ambulance on standby.

Some would have called it deranged. I called it adequately cautious.

"Is she giving birth or being exorcised?" Enzo followed the trail of personnel when the staff filed inside. Imma and Chiara were with Lila in the next room, yelling hysterically at her to take deep, calming breaths.

"A lot of shit can go sideways during birth." I led us into my office. Not that I needed to explain myself to him. His biggest responsibility was not shitting his pants.

Enzo gave me a whatever-you-say-little-princess look, lighting a cigarette and flicking the match out my office window with a knowing smirk.

"Now you can't go anywhere near her for the next month." I pointed at the cigarette.

"Fuck off. She's my sister."

"That's unfortunate. I'm sure our kid will still be bright."

"No thanks to you, Carrot Top."

I tsked. "Is that all you've got?"

"You're right." He rubbed his chin absentmindedly. "I need to work on my material, now that you're about to become the most insufferable, overprotective dad that has ever disgraced this universe."

"You mean graced."

He smiled breezily. "I don't remember stuttering."

I heard the crunch of gravel beneath my office window, signaling that a car was approaching. I glanced out the window. A catering truck parked across the street, so as not to block the way to the other vehicles.

"What's that?" Enzo stuck his head next to mine, looking down.

"She missed prosciutto during the pregnancy."

"Let me guess, so you bought an entire drove of pigs?"

I wondered how mad she'd be if I relieved her brother of a few of his organs.

"No." I glowered at the idiot. "But I did order seventeen different types from Parma to make sure she has variety."

"Man, you're so whipped all you need is a cherry on your head."

"Keep running your mouth and the room *will* turn red," I warned.

Enzo snorted. "Stop seducing me, bro. I'm into chicks."

The lies people told themselves were too much sometimes. Not that I gave enough shit to put a mirror in his face.

"Tiernan." My mother-in-law pushed the door open without knocking, out of breath. "She's asking for you." Her gaze flicked to her son. "*Sfacciato!* Put that cigarette down before I burn a hole through your forehead."

"What cigarette, Mama?" he asked with smoke skulking out of his mouth, tossing the thing out the window and smiling angelically.

I sauntered to the next room, finding Lila sulking on a big bed in a very small babydoll dress and no underwear. She was covered in sweat head to toe and looked exhausted. Her water broke almost two hours ago. The first hour, she was her sweet, perky self. The last thirty minutes, though, I had to clear all the sharp objects from our bedroom.

"*Gealach*," I greeted. "Did you change your mind about me being here?"

She had asked me to evacuate her bedside until the baby was out. Not because she felt uncomfortable with me witnessing the birth. Apparently, threatening the medical staff and trying to black-mail the baby while still in the womb to make his exit quickly and painlessly was considered "unbecoming," or, as Imma put it, *screan-zato. Unhinged.*

"*No*," Lila signed. "*I still don't think you have the stomach for it.*"

Ridiculous. I had killed hundreds of people with my bare hands.

"What's the issue, then?"

"*I need you to get rid of Mama and Imma.*"

I stared at her like she asked me to carve Wyoming out of the map and drag it into the Black Sea.

"Are they bothering you?"

"*My mother already panic-vomited twice, and Imma bursts into tears every time I have a contraction. The woman is a nurse. They've both completely lost it.*"

"You are loved, darlin'." I leaned down to kiss her forehead.

"*Love is overrated.*" She swatted me away. "*Get rid of them.*"

"I'll have them go down to the living room until this is over."

"*No.*" Lila shook her head adamantly. "*I don't want them in this zip code, Tiernan.*"

I shot her a flat stare. "I'm a murderer, not a magician. I only know one way to extract people by force."

A contraction shuddered Lila's entire body, making her arch and spit out a string of words in Italian I was sure wasn't a love poem. In the hall beyond the closed door, I heard Imma breaking down in a sob. Chiara moaned like she was delivering the child.

"*FIND A WAY,*" my wife signed.

I scurried my ass out before she made herself a widower and kicked the two women out.

Four hours later, my son ripped into the world like a lion. With a victorious roar, fists curled in anger, legs kicking and thrashing, protesting the invasion of his perfect bubble.

Earlier, Lila allowed me to stay with her if I promised to be on my best behavior.

I held my wife's hand and watched as he appeared between her legs in all of his purple-white flesh glory. New and wrinkly, unfocused, his ribs tightening each time he took a greedy breath to resume his screaming.

There was nothing particularly noteworthy about his scrunched, long-suffering face. It was full of white stuff.

It was his head that confirmed the suspicion I'd had for the past few weeks, since Lila killed the wrong guy.

More specifically, the shocking thick mane of hair covering his entire skull.

The unmistakable, rare, and familiar shade of dark red. Burgundy. Of the *Callaghans.*

Red. All I saw was red. Rage took over my entire fucking being. *Fintan.*

Fintan was the rapist.

It all made sense.

His name was on Sam Brennan's list. In plain sight all along.

It had never occurred to me to look into him as a suspect before the warehouse incident because…

Because you're a fucking gobshite who spent your entire life assuming the best about him.

I'd ignored his name because he disappeared often to get drunk or make illegal bets. Him not being by my side on that night was nothing special.

He had a girlfriend, but that meant very little to men of our trade; he had substance abuse issues, so it was likely he wasn't on his best behavior that night. And while Fintan was a scaredy-cat not accustomed to violence, he certainly possessed a mean streak.

He'd taken one look at Raffaella, concluded she wasn't going to fight back, rat him out, or complicate his life—and decided to destroy hers.

The writing was on the wall. How he protested the marriage from the get-go. How angry he was when it went ahead. And how concerned he'd been when he first heard Lila was sentient.

The last nine months rushed into the forefront of my mind.

He'd sent her a letter, had likely slipped it under the door himself. Why?

The answer was simple—he wanted her alone so he could kill her and get rid of both her and the baby. Bury his secret with them.

He tried twice—once when he crashed into her and Tierney in that intersection, after which he panicked and tried to pin it on Angelo—and a second time when he arranged a time to meet her at the dock, but I showed up instead.

He was the one who sent that Roger prick to the port and ordered him to kill whoever showed up, Lila or me. Because once I was gone, there'd be no one to retaliate.

He thought he could get away with it.

Until the very last moment.

The red flowers at Fermanagh's…

My jaw locked. They were unevenly red. *Old.*

He kept her blood-soaked tiara of roses.

Made her live under the same roof with it.

My heart thrashed so hard it nearly cracked my fucking ribs.

I couldn't make a stink about it. Not here, not now. With Lila writhing and aching as the doctor stitched up the sore place between her legs. A nurse dabbed her temples with a cloth, and my wife's arms stretched open, waiting to be filled with the baby she just birthed.

My baby.

He was fucking mine.

I would raise him as my own, and he'd look exactly like me.

No one would question his origin.

"*Gealach*, he is beautiful," I praised, pressing my lips to her sweat-coated forehead. She shuddered under my lips. I pulled back and caressed the damp hair away from her face.

One of the nurses placed a much drier, slightly less sullen version of our newborn in her arms.

His hair.

I couldn't stop staring.

Did Lila know?

I couldn't stomach what it must do to her.

She sniffled, looking up at me through glittering eyes, waiting for my words. She couldn't offer me any of her own, seeing as her hands were busy cradling our baby to her chest.

"You did so good. I'm proud of you." I kissed her mouth, then leaned down to kiss the crown of my son's head. I looked back at her so she could read my lips, speaking as slowly as I could.

"I love you, sweetheart. You fractured my soul and dug so deep into it, you are now ingrained in all that I am, and all that I ever will be. As for our son." I placed a hand on his tiny shoulder, smiling down at him. "I already love him more than I do anyone else in the world."

But you.

She would always come first.

Before our son. Before myself.

I stayed for twenty more minutes, fussing and cooing over them, feeding her prosciutto and watching as she nursed the baby for the first time.

Finally, when the baby was napping, she turned and told me,

"You haven't had a second for yourself. Why don't you go take a shower and a nap?"

"It's fine," I said, even though every fiber of my body itched to go to Fintan. "I'm happy to stay."

He was probably halfway across the continent by now. Not that it'd help him.

She shook her head, smiling.

"Mama and Imma should be here any minute in case I need anything. And now that he is napping, it's smart if I do the same. Please. Go rest. For me."

"Does *he* have a name?" I rubbed my thumb across her flushed cheek.

She looked down at the pink scowling thing sleeping in the bassinet next to her. "Gennaro, I think." A tender smile touched her pink lips. "He looks like a Gennaro, right?"

He looked mostly like a Fintan to me.

He also looked entirely too Irish to carry such a distinctively Italian name.

"Yes," I said, nevertheless. "Gennaro. *Nero.* Perfect."

I loved her just a little more than anyone ought to be loved. For taking her tragic circumstances, accepting them, and shaping them into a triumph.

"Nero, stop hanging from the chandelier," I tested the name humorlessly. "Nero, put that gun down. No firearms before you're six. Yeah. Got a nice ring to it."

She grinned at me, aglow. "He'll be Nero to the world, but Enni to me. I'll protect him in all the ways my parents never protected me."

I believed her. She was going to be the mother she'd deserved.

"Go now." She reached to caress my jaw. I leaned into her touch instinctively.

"You sure?"

"Certain," she verbalized.

Nodding, I kissed her again and closed the door behind me.

"Sir." One of my errand boys appeared as soon as I stepped out into the hallway, catching my step.

"Do you need your drivers? Soldiers? Should I fetch anyone?"

I shook my head. "Get the car running. I'm leaving alone."

I wasn't going to take a shower, a nap, or a piss.

On my way out, I bumped into Imma, Chiara, and Tierney making their way to Lila. They were carrying food platters, plush teddy bears, and handknitted blankets.

"How's the bundle of joy?" Tierney cried out with joy.

"See for yourself," I answered cryptically, not stopping to greet them as I advanced toward the door.

Five minutes later, I was in my car, driving toward my father's place. Fintan's phone was still there. I knew, because I had a tracker on it, as with everyone in my family.

How did the saying go? If you love someone, let them go. Just make sure you know exactly where their ass is twenty-four seven, because you have deep-rooted trust issues.

You put him in charge of her.

Forced her to spend time with him on a weekly basis.

He was her keeper. After our wedding. At the hospital. The only man who was allowed to stay with her alone.

I veered off the convoluted country path to the shoulder of the road, pushed the driver's door open, and vomited the entire contents of my stomach onto my shoe.

Wiping my mouth with the back of my sleeve, I took a few deep breaths, forcing myself to calm down. I'd never been this disoriented in my entire life.

Repositioning myself in the car seat, I flicked the engine back to life and resumed my driving.

Fifteen minutes into my drive, my Bluetooth rang with an incoming call.

Fintan, the screen said.

So. Tierney met her new nephew.

Figures. My sister's favorite cardio was running her mouth.

I hit the green button. Why the fuck not?

"This is not what it looks like," my older brother said in a high-pitched voice.

I allowed a beat of silence, just to screw with his nerves, before replying dully, "If you want to prolong your death by making me do a paternity test before killing you, I'm not opposed to that. As long as you're aware I'd be twice as pissed if I find out you lied on top of raping my wife. And let's just say I'm already not in a generous mood."

I was never angry. It was a pointless emotion, and I was notoriously stingy with those. But right now, I was sick with rage. Poisoned with the cloying, unfamiliar feeling of helplessness.

He hurt her.

My own kin.

She was going to look at our son's eyes, and face, and *hair* each day for the rest of her life, knowing it was a Callaghan who ripped her innocence from her.

"I didn't s-say…I mean, what I was gonna…" He stumbled over his own words. "I did it. I'm not d-denying it." Fintan broke into a sob, and I heard glass shattering on the other side of the line. "B-but listen to me. J-just *listen.*"

He was slurring. He was drunk. *Again.* Usually, that'd make me concerned. Now, my only worry was that his liver wouldn't fail on his miserable arse before I had the chance to finish him off myself.

I deserved the fucking honor.

I heard a duffel bag being unzipped. Clothes stuffed into it in a hurry. He didn't even have the foresight to make an escape plan. How did we share DNA?

"I'm not okay in the head, Tiernan. I'm not. I need help. Think about it. I watched Mam being carved open like a bleeding animal when Igor pulled you and Tierney out. I was just three. A small boy. I was sitting in a pool of her blood when Da found me."

"Your sob story didn't give you the right to rape my wife." I choked back a roar, keeping my voice flat and even. "We're all fucked up in the head. You're nothing special."

A text message popped on the screen.

> Tierney: I gave him a thirty minute head start. Where's the joy of the hunt if the prey just sits there, waiting for slaughter?
>
> Tierney: Cute baby, btw. <3 <3 <3

"I—I didn't know she'd turn out to be your wife!" Fintan whined. "Not t-to mention that you'd catch feelings for her. I thought it would be the f-first and last time I'd ever see her. And you know what they said about her!" he spluttered. "That she was severely mentally d-delayed. Too dumb to know what's ha-happening around her." He hiccuped.

Keys jangled. Dropped to the floor. Being picked up again.

I said nothing.

"Please, *please* believe me when I say I never meant for anything to happen this way."

"You had seven months to come clean to me. Why didn't you?"

Silence. I was nearing Da and Fintan's mansion.

"I thought I could take care of it in another way."

"But you didn't. You should be halfway across the ocean by now. Why did you stay?"

"I—I kind of figured it could…that I would…I mean, if the baby wouldn't have come out with red hair…" He swallowed audibly. "He could've come out blond. Or, with brown hair. Or, I don't know…" Another pause. "It doesn't have to change anything between us. This all happened before you got together. I haven't touched her since and never, *ever* will. And she doesn't even *remember*." He choked out that last word, breaking into a fresh bout of sobs. "I swear, Tiernan, I didn't mean to hurt anyone. It was just harmless fun. And I was plastered. I mean, completely drunk. Had I known you were going to wed her…fall in love with her… *Christ*, I'd *never*." He sounded on the brink of vomiting. "You're my brother. I love you. You've always been my number one. Please. There's no need for anyone to know this. I certainly won't tell. And…and…Lila!" he exclaimed. "Think about her and the baby, how crushed they'd be if they found out. We're getting along so nicely. She trusts me."

That, she did.

I thought about all the times I left her with him again.

I'd punch my own face if I wasn't driving.

"And I'll do whatever you want me to. Go to rehab. Move away if need be." A wet snort escaped him. I couldn't believe I carried the same DNA as this pile of shite. "We can pretend it never happened. As far as the entire world knows—it never did. Only me, Tierney, and you know."

"The accident in which she almost lost the baby…" I said, leaving the rest of it hanging in the air.

Fintan understood what I meant. "I…I sent people to do it. But I told them not to kill her, just the baby," he lamented. "I swear it."

"Who?" I demanded. They were as good as dead now.

"The loan sharks I used to owe money to." Pause. "I told them if they managed to kill the baby, I'd pay them five million."

I stopped in front of the Tudor-style, white-bricked mansion and killed the engine. Closed my eyes.

He is your brother.

He picked up your pieces when you found your way home.

Taught you English.

Saved you from offing yourself when you didn't think life was worth living.

Taught you how to find joy in the life you have left.

If it wasn't for him, you'd have killed yourself after killing Igor. You wouldn't have Lila. Or Nero. This life.

"Please." I heard him again. I opened my eyes and looked out the window to the second floor, immediately finding him peering from behind the curtain of his bedroom.

"Tiernan, forgive me. I would've never touched a girlfriend of yours. Let alone your wife. Anyone who's important to you. I'd never done anything like it before. Not ever. I was feeling wild that night. And drunk. So fucking drunk. I was livid with the Camorra for taking out your eye and having the audacity to invite us as guests. I knew the Ferrantes only issued the invitation to show off what they'd done to you. Like you were a circus monkey or something."

This was likely true. I'd shown up anyway, not too proud to give up on the chance to squash my beef with Tate Blackthorn. He'd been meddling in my legal business for months before that.

"It was my *fuck you* to them for what they did to my little brother. A one-off. An *only*-off. You have to believe me."

I didn't utter one damn word.

"You forgave Alex Rasputin for what his father's done. You spared his life. I'm sure you have it in your heart to forgive another brother. I'll get better. I'll get *sober*. I'll repent this sin. I swear to you. I will. And I'll be the best damn uncle in the entire world."

"I believe you," I said, finally. "I'm going to come inside now. You will greet me unarmed. You will have a duffel bag ready with your bare necessities. I'm going to drive you to a rehab center in Connecticut. And I'm not going to discharge your arse until you're as sober as a nun for one whole bleeding year. After which you're moving to Ireland, and I'm never seeing you again. Am I clear?"

"Y-yes," he spluttered, breaking into a sob. "Thank you, brother. Thank you so much. I won't let you dow—"

I killed the call and got out of my car before waltzing toward the front door. Fintan's sports car was the only one parked in front. Shame he wouldn't have time to say goodbye to Da or Maggie.

I unlocked the front door and stepped inside. A few minutes later, Fintan took the stairs down, holding a duffel in his hand. He stopped when he reached the last step.

We stood in front of each other, somber and subdued.

He looked like hell. Face splotchy and swollen, eyes bloodshot, hair a tangled mess.

I forced myself to push aside the thought of him touching my wife, prying her sweet, delicate thighs open, pushing into her virginal cunt, snatching her virtue, spilling his seed inside her, hitting her, splitting her lip, her temples, her cheeks...

My nostrils flared.

You're alive because of him.

Remember that.

I opened my arms, palms up, my expression tranquil, my posture casual.

"You are absolved. Come and get your forgiveness, brother."

His breath picked up, the tension between us brewing like a cyclone that started in the very foyer we stood at. "Just like that?"

"You saved me when I wanted to kill myself," I said. "I'll spare your life this one time. There won't be a second."

His entire posture deflated. His resolve broke, and he hurried into my embrace, throwing his arms around me, weeping into my neck. "Oh, God. Tiernan. God. Keeping this secret to myself all these months...it ate me alive. I couldn't bear it."

His duffel fell to the floor. I held him for a moment, breathing in his familiar scent, of alcohol and leather and his favorite cologne.

Placed a soothing palm on the back of his head with my left hand.

Pressed my lips to his ear.

Used my right hand to draw my gun.

"You've always been a stupid cunt, Fin. But for you to think I'd let you get away with what you did to my wife, you've really outdone yourself."

I put a bullet in his spine. He dropped to his knees before me. I stepped back, watching him tremble and convulse, holding his back with shaky fingers as he stared in horror at the scarlet liquid pouring out of him.

The surprise and disappointment in his face were exactly why I'd lied to him. Why I gave him futile, foolish hope.

"B-brother…" he stammered weakly.

"You're not my brother. Alex is. Always was. Not you." I rounded his limp figure on the floor. "Now I'll ask questions, and you'll answer them. I'll kill you anyway. If you say the truth, I'll take minutes. If you lie—hours. Am I understood?"

He nodded quickly. Hysterically.

"Why did you do it? Remember. The truth."

"I swear I did it because of what they did to you," he groaned, losing blood. I was lying. He was going to die in the next fifteen minutes or so. I would still make it painful, though.

"But also…she was so fucking beautiful, Tiernan. It was almost painful to watch."

"Did you plan this all along?"

He shook his head.

"*Words*, fucker." I stopped my pacing to grab his ear and rip it from his head.

He arched, howling in pain. "N-no," he cried out, heaving. "Th-there wasn't a plan. She was just there. Gorgeous. All alone. Nobody paid attention to her. Nobody but me."

"You followed her into the woods?" I prompted.

He gave me a hesitant look, probably knowing I was going to rip something else from him soon. He wasn't wrong about that.

"Answer me," I said.

"Y-yes," he chattered. "She went outside, and I followed her. At first, I thought I'd corner her in one of the rooms, cop a feel, n-nothing more. But then she surprised me by leaving the property through the cellar and heading to the shore."

"Was she upset?" I kneeled down and undid his trousers. Touching my own brother's knob was not on my to-do list in this lifetime. Poetic justice required it, though.

Fintan winced, knowing where it was going.

"Sh-she…was beside herself."

"Did she fight you?" I took my dull knife out of my pocket. He stared at it in horror.

"*Did she?*" I roared.

"Yes," he admitted. "She fought tooth and nail. Managed to get in a few blows. Cracked my rib."

I grabbed his limp knob in my fist and slashed his balls off. Blood sprayed everywhere.

His scream put another hole in the ozone layer. Fucking weakling.

"I tried to finish her off in the hospital room when you were in Vegas," Fintan spat out blood, staring at me with wild hatred in his eyes. "But your asshole brother-in-law, Enzo, had the foresight to loiter there. He wouldn't fucking leave. Even when he wasn't in the room, he was just beyond the door."

In the end, I did the right thing by keeping Enzo in New York. He saved my Lila.

"You're about to die in the next three minutes," I informed him flatly. The color slowly drained from his face. "Blood loss. There's no saving you now. One last question."

He stared at me, pure hatred radiating from his eyes.

"Go ahead." He sounded surprisingly calm, having come to terms with his own demise. "One last answer before my forsaken soul ensures you join me in hell, lad."

I chuckled wryly. "Don't need your letter of recommendation. I have a saved spot there. My question is…" I stalled, bracing myself for the answer. "Did she bleed?"

"Huh?"

"Did she bleed when you raped her?"

"Oh, yes." A serene, psychotic smile spread across his lips. "She did. From her face, from all the beatings. From her cunt, from plowing into her while she was dry and virginal. It was a thing of beauty. For one moment in time, she was an ugly, terrible mess—"

I kissed the cross pendant on my neck—for Lila, not for me.

Apologized to Mam in heaven.

And shot my own brother in the face.

Rolling him over with the tip of my loafer, I spat into the blood-gushing hole at the center of his forehead. I punched in a number and glued my phone to my ear, not removing my gaze from the corpse. The line picked up before the connection sound started.

"Lyosha, I need you to take the fall for something."

His silence told me he immediately understood.

I'd long suspected Fintan was Lyosha's mole. Everything made sense. Fintan needed the money to keep gambling without getting into more debt—and Alex paid that money in exchange for information to keep his finger on my pulse.

Fintan never gave up on alcohol and gambling. He simply sold all of my secrets and plans to the Bratva and used the money to pay for his addiction. This was how Alex knew about the most intimate details of my life—including when Lila shot me on our wedding night. How she stitched me back together. That I was falling for her.

This also meant Fintan gave Alex the heads-up before I came to Vegas to claim his life. If things were different, I'd be dead.

But me being dead was Fintan's ideal outcome. He'd seize full control of the Irish operation, all the money and prestige, and there'd be no one to avenge Lila's rape.

Fintan betrayed me in every single way possible.

"When and where?" Alex asked.

"I'm texting you the address now. It needs some tidying up."

"I'll bring my...*cleaners*, *Koshchei*." I heard the curve of a smile on his mouth.

In the end, he was more of a brother to me than Fintan ever was.

EPILOGUE
TIERNAN

**22 DAYS POST FAILED
SELF-DESTRUCTION PROJECT**

Fintan's body resurfaced in Lake Mead, Nevada, three months later.

It was in pristine condition due to being kept in a Bratva freezer for the duration of his mysterious disappearance. Minus, of course, the organs I chopped off him.

The Bratva assumed responsibility for the death among the underground circles, claiming retaliation for Igor's death.

"Killing Tyrone would've been redundant. He already died the day my father slaughtered his wife," Alex had explained to his soldiers while they didn't know I was on the other line. "Now, Fintan, who Tiernan actually loved. I got him where it hurt. We're now even and ready to start doing business together."

Now, I waited for my beautiful wife in my car outside of the community college she was attending. She breezed out of the doors, Nero strapped to her chest in a BabyBjörn. Her flawless face broke into a grin when she spotted me.

She quickly kissed her two friends goodbye, tossed her backpack across her shoulder, and speed-walked toward the Mercedes. A line of cars formed behind me, honking in protest of my double-parking.

They could wait. Weather forecast said there could be a drizzle, and I wasn't going to let my wife and son get wet.

I got out of the car and helped her take Nero out of the BabyBjörn, strapping him into his car seat. He was fast asleep, his red, thick hair dancing in the wind.

I gave Lila a long, sweet kiss on the month. "How was class?"

"*Great. My teacher wants to display your portrait in a gallery. He thinks the blood is acrylic paint and praised me on how realistic it looked.*" Lila looked amused.

"Always happy to be of help." I opened the passenger door, helping her climb in.

I slipped behind the wheel, kicking the car into drive.

"*Did you hear about Fintan?*"

It didn't feel great not telling her Fintan was her attacker, but she was on such a high after Gennaro was born, it felt cruel to poke in that wound one more time. As far as she was concerned, the matter was dealt with. And it was.

I nodded. "I did."

"*Why do you think Alex killed him? It sounded like you and he already buried the hatchet.*"

I allowed myself one lie to her. One, white, tiny lie in the entire length of our marriage. And only to protect her and Gennaro.

"He needed to save face after what happened in Vegas, and Igor. He had my blessing."

"*Are you sad about it?*"

"It is what it is," I said vaguely. "Comes with the job."

When we got home, Lila put Nero in his crib and took the baby monitor with her before we left his room. Imma was in the kitchen, preparing enough food for an army. Lila's mother and brothers were coming over for dinner, but we still had an hour to burn, and I knew exactly what we'd do with it.

We walked silently side by side to the ballroom. Opened the doors and reached the center of the room. There was no need for music. I kept my promise to her from the day of her baby shower, and we danced every evening.

We started moving to a soundless tune, our only music our heartbeats thudding against one another.

"Six weeks," I said. She was going to get surgery for a cochlear implant. Everything was booked and ready to go. "Are you excited?"

She nodded. "It'll be practical to hear, but I don't feel like I need it anymore."

"It was your dream to listen to music," I pointed out.

Lila often wore her hearing aids, but not always. She attended speech therapy twice a week and joined the National Association of the Deaf, where she volunteered and helped with donations.

We swayed together, her arms tightening around my shoulders, her body pressing against mine, letting me know what she needed.

"I think…" She licked her lips, her eyes heavy-lidded.

"That's always a good start," I drawled. "What are you thinking, *Gealach*?"

"That I would like another dance."

"Yeah?" I smirked.

"A horizontal one."

"I see."

"Without any clothes on." She bit down on her lower lip, grinning. "It'll help me find my muse for this next painting I'm working on."

"Well." I pretended to weigh her request seriously. "You're the artist. Who am I to question your process?"

And I dove in, kissing her hard, drowning in her perfection, never coming up for air.

LILA

SEVEN WEEKS LATER

My rose-gold ball gown swished along the staircase of our mansion. I stepped over the hem, almost tripping forward. A rush of giggles bubbled out of my throat, and this time, I heard it.

I plastered my palm over my mouth, shaking with laughter.

"You're going to wake the dead," my husband muttered next to me, before sweeping me into his arms, carrying me honeymoon-style to the second floor.

His voice was magnificent. Low, gravelly, and deep. His accent also contributed to its sexiness. I could listen to him for hours.

"And you care because…?" I pouted.

"I'm responsible for many of their deaths, and they'll come after my ass."

I giggled, flinging my head backward so I could get a better look at him. I no longer needed to read his lips, but it was a force of habit. The cochlear implant meant I could hear, but it was still muffled and in very low decibels. I didn't regret going through with the operation. Not that there was anything wrong with being deaf. My decision wasn't a product of shame or prejudice. I simply thought it would be practical.

I didn't compose music anymore. My obsession and fascination with it diminished, now that I had a family and my art to focus on. But I still wrote my son one lullaby to remind him of the resilience of the human spirit and how obstacles were nothing but reminders you could overcome anything.

"How was your first ball with music?" Tiernan grinned down at me.

I circled my arms around his neck, knowing full well that

attending balls was far from the realm of his regular hobbies. People openly stared at his eye patch, and not everybody was happy to see the princess of the Camorra and king of the Irish Mafia at swanky New York parties, but I didn't care.

I loved dancing.

I loved dancing with my husband.

And life was too short to give a damn about what anyone who didn't truly love you thought about you.

Let them talk. About my age. About the wrongness of us. His mysterious past. My overbearing mother.

We were happy. And that's what mattered.

"It was wonderful," I purred.

"Good."

"And I want to do it all over again tomorrow." I kicked my feet while cradled in his arms, and he rolled his eye exasperatedly, an indulgent smirk tugging at his lips.

When we got to the second floor, Tiernan cautiously helped me back to my feet. I padded toward my son's room, peeking into his crib.

He was sleeping soundly, but began stirring as soon as I opened the door and traces of the corridor's light seeped in.

Yawning toothlessly, he tried stretching inside his swaddle, groaning when he realized his attempts were futile. My chest flooded with warmth.

"You coming?" Tiernan kissed the back of my shoulder from behind, his erection pressing into my backside.

Glancing up, I touched his cheek gently and pressed my lips to his. "I think I'll nurse him before we get into bed. Wait for me."

He grunted.

"Naked," I added.

His disgruntled expression wiped off his face. He kissed the back of my head. "If you need anything, let me know. Sleep tight, bud." He leaned to kiss Enni's head as I picked him up.

After Tiernan was gone, I took Gennaro to the rocking chair, settled in, and popped one shoulder of my dress off. Enni's mouth found my nipple without opening his eyes, the scent of my milk calling to him. He latched hungrily, sucking and grunting his approval.

We were going to baptize him in Naples next week, at the church where all of the Ferrante siblings had been baptized. This wasn't a gesture of goodwill from me to Vello—I couldn't care less what he wanted. But to Mama, who always searched for an excuse to return to Secondigliano. And while things were not perfect between us—probably never would be—I had assumed the big shoes of the nurturing adult in our relationship. Because I had managed to escape the prison that was the Ferrante family name, and all that it entailed, while she was still behind the gilded bars, watching as little by little her children slipped away from their father's abusive hold.

I ran my fingers over his hair and smiled.

Oh, *Tiernan*.

My brilliant husband, who taught me how to shoot, how to dance, how to overcome my trauma, knew exactly how intelligent I was. And yet he foolishly thought I hadn't figured out what Fintan's disappearance meant.

I knew Gennaro was Fintan's.

The hair gave it away, of course, but there were other telltales.

Those pale shamrock eyes.

The fair skin that promised to burn before tanning.

The slight cleft in his chin—another thing the siblings shared— that was impossible to miss.

I had noticed the impatience in Tiernan when he saw Enni for the first time. He'd wanted to go to Fintan. At the time, I had hoped he would do the right thing by me.

He did.

Fintan disappeared the same day I gave birth.

"Probably because of substance abuse," Maggie and Tierney

speculated. Tiernan said nothing. He made no effort to appear surprised or worried about his brother.

I was glad Alex took the blame for this. That Tiernan trusted him enough to ask him for it.

It was a secret I'd take to my grave. The fact I knew it was Fintan.

To protect Tiernan, Enni, myself, and our marriage.

In the meantime, I basked in my good luck. Gennaro was the spitting image of my husband.

As for Tiernan?

He'd never know that my memory returned to me sometime during the thirty-second week of my pregnancy.

I had been biding my time, waiting for him to find out about Fintan on his own.

And that if he hadn't finished him…

I'd have done it myself.

THE END

ACKNOWLEDGMENTS

This book could not have happened if it weren't for many beta readers. Due to the many different cultures I have implemented, I had the privilege of having a lot of eyes on it before release.

My gratitude to my hard of hearing expert, Meghan, for your time, attention to detail, and for educating me. To my Italian beta reader, Veronica, in charge of the Italian and Neapolitan representation, and Aisling for going over the Callaghans' Irishness. Also to Bryanna for reading and providing important feedback. Special thanks to Dr. Claire Reed for going over all the complex medical situations I put my poor characters in. Your contribution was priceless. And to my seasoned betas—Vanessa, Tijuana, and Liah. Thank you for always staying by my side.

Special thanks to Bryn Donovan for the flawless developmental edit, Amy Briggs for the line edit, Paige Maroney Smith for the "everything" edit, and my Bloom editors, including the absolute goddess Christa Désir, as well as the amazing Letty, Gretchen, Holly, Susie, and Kylie.

A huge thank-you to my author friends who keep me sane(ish): Parker, Ava, Leigh, Harloe, Shain, and Lilian. Love you big and so, so grateful for your insight and support.

A big thank-you to my agent, Kimberly Brower, my PA, Tijuana Turner, Bloom Books, my U.S.-based paperback publisher, and to

Hodder & Stoughton, my UK and Commonwealth publishers, for making my dreams come true.

A huge thank-you to Gisel at Neptune Designs for the stunning covers and Sara Camponeschi for the skull illustration.

Finally, I would like to thank you, the reader, for taking a chance on my work. It means the world to me and I couldn't be more grateful.

With love,
L.J. Shen xo

ABOUT THE AUTHOR

L.J. Shen is a *New York Times, Wall Street Journal, USA Today, Washington Post,* and #1 Amazon bestselling author of contemporary and NA romance. Best known for her angsty, dark books and barely redeemable alpha heroes, she writes fairy tales with teeth and claws.

She lives in a picturesque beach town with her family, pets and inner demons, and enjoys reading, traveling, cooking and spending time with her grumpy cat.

Website: authorljshen.com
Facebook: authorljshen
Instagram: @authorljshen
TikTok: @authorljshen
Pinterest: @authorljshen